TWISTED JUSTICE

Also by Patricia Gussin

Shadow of Death

TWISTED JUSTICE
A NOVEL

PATRICIA GUSSIN

Oceanview Publishing

IPSWICH, MASSACHUSETTS

2776736

Copyright © 2007 by Patricia Gussin

FIRST EDITION

ISBN 978-1-933515-08-3

Published in the United States by Oceanview Publishing,
Ipswich, Massachusetts
Visit our Web site at www.oceanviewpub.com

10 9 8 7 6 5 4 3 2 1

PRINTED IN THE UNITED STATES OF AMERICA

This book is dedicated to my wonderful kids

Ben

Wayne

Lynne

Joe

Lisa

Bill

Jeff

ACKNOWLEDGMENTS

I am so appreciative of my two editors, Stacey Donovan of Amagansett, New York, and Enid Perll of Sarasota, Florida. More than editors, they are valued friends. Also thanks to Mary Bole, Denise Janiak, and Connie Flasher, who so generously volunteered to read my manuscript in its formative stage. Susan Greger, Maryglenn McCombs, and Mary Adele Bogden of Oceanview Publishing, and Susan Hayes are simply the best, and I can never thank them enough. But most of all, I thank my fabulous husband, Bob Gussin, medical scientist, fellow author, and the one who reads my manuscripts first draft though last. And finally, I want to pay tribute to my mother, Gerry Plese, who was a wonderful, gentle lady, beloved by all.

CHAPTER ONE

Dr. Laura Nelson bolted through the swinging doors slowing for an instant to thrust outstretched arms into a green sterile gown. Twenty minutes earlier she'd flipped off her bedside reading light and slipped into a deep sleep, but now the familiar surge of adrenaline put all her senses on alert.

"Status?" An order, not a question as latex gloves snapped into place.

"Motor vehicle trauma. Ten-year-old kid." The quaver in the macho chief resident's voice did not bode well. "Truck rammed a car at high speed."

Laura pivoted toward the small patient centered under the glare of the operating room lights. What she saw made her heart quicken. Not waiting for the nurse to tie the back of her gown, Laura rushed to the central position at the surgical table.

"And?"

The ashen faces of her team told her that the child was in dire shape. Although not a pediatric surgeon per se, Laura was a thoracic specialist and she was the first surgeon called for all major chest emergencies.

"She was thrown from the car. Multiple injuries. Rest of the family —"

"Pressure's falling fast." The gray-haired anesthesiologist at the head of the table interrupted.

Until she'd arrived, the anesthesiologist had been in charge.

Surprised at the tremor in his voice, she noticed how frail he looked hunched behind the bank of machines.

In the harsh glare of overhead lights, Laura assessed the small form strapped onto the narrow table. She focused for only a minisecond on the exposed patch of mottled skin surrounded by green surgical drapes. At least the team had the child prepped and ready to go.

"No pressure. Can't keep up with the blood loss." The anesthesiologist spoke urgently from the head of the table. "We're transfusing, but —"

Then Roxanne, the scrub nurse, motioned toward the foot of the table. What Laura saw there made her gasp.

"The drainage bottle – full? That's way too much blood for a child this small. Holy shit, where is it coming from?"

"Two chest tubes in," the anesthesiologist reported. "Neck's immobilized, but the spinal cord's transected at C-6. I'm ventilating her. I'm ready."

"We're going in now."

Roxanne slapped the scalpel into her hand, and with no hesitation Laura excised the child's thin chest straight down the middle. Urgently the surgical team dissected tissue while swabbing the operative field with gauze patches as Laura quickly cut through the sternum with a scissors-like instrument, then pushed aside the tissues that separate the sternum from the heart.

The room was silent except for the rhythmic heaves of the ventilator and whooshing of gases from the canisters. Nobody's favorite music blared. There was no bantering. Just quiet until Laura spoke, "Bright red blood – got to be arterial – pulsatile, but not spurting." Her voice sounded steady, but her heart was pounding. Anger started to creep into her consciousness, but she shoved it back. She had to stay focused. "Have to isolate the source and patch it. I just hope there's time for this. Pressure?"

"None." The voice at the head of the table faltered as the anesthesiologist cleared his throat. "And the EKG's erratic."

"Did anybody detect evidence of a penetrating injury?" Laura asked. Hemostat in one hand and forceps in the other, Laura tried to find her way in the bloody surgical field. She had to find the source of this catastrophic bleeding. She could feel beads of perspiration forming on her forehead. Something unusual was happening here, and she couldn't find it in all this blood.

A young resident from the emergency room stood behind the surgical team, observing. Taking a slight step forward, he responded in a barely audible tone. "Dr. Nelson, when we examined the patient in the ER, she had multiple contusions and lacerations, but then her neck was broken. I mean, we got cervical spine X-rays and all. It wasn't until we got the chest X-ray that we did a thoracentesis. We found blood. We put in chest tubes, but —"

"Wrong priority." Laura snapped, shaking her head. "Thoracic trauma always takes precedence over neuro or orthopedic injuries. I'll bet there's something sharp in there, and deep."

"Laura, I can't keep up with the blood loss," the anesthesiologist announced. "If there's something to fix in there, now's the time."

Amid her crisp orders, the surgical team explored the pleural space that surrounds the lung tissue. Soon, Laura's hands were deep inside the chest, but there was so much blood she couldn't examine the major vessels of the heart. New blood was pooling as fast as the team could remove it, hampering her methodical search for the point of bleeding. When her hemostat struck something hard, she stiffened.

"More suction, please. There it is." She paused. "A shard of glass. Penetrating the intrapericardial portion of the ascending aorta."

"The aorta, Dr. Nelson?" a surgical resident questioned. "Wouldn't she have bled out by now?"

"Consider the tamponade. Pressure within the pericardial sac can plug the hole at least temporarily. But it's broken through. Roxanne, we need an aortic graft."

"Right here," the nurse had the package already in hand.

"We'll take our best shot. What's her name?" Laura asked softly.

"Wendy Ruiz."

Laura sighed. "Hang in there, Wendy."

"We're losing her, Laura. Flat line." The tone urgent now as the anesthesiologist peered over the partition into the operating field.

"But we're so close." Laura held up her hand for the Teflon patch that would be sewn over the hole when the glass was removed.

"Flat line," repeated the anesthesiologist. "I'm giving epinephrine, but —"

"Just give me the patch," ordered Laura, ignoring him. Without looking up, she jerked her head in the direction of the senior resident stationed across from her. "You pull out the piece of glass. I'll slap this on and secure it while you suture it into place."

"No response to the epi, Laura." The grim tone spoke defeat. "Total flat line."

"Sutures ready, Dr. Nelson," said Roxanne. Despite the fact that they were best friends, Roxanne Musing always addressed Laura as "doctor" during surgery.

"On the count of three," Laura said. The resident angled the hemostat while an intern retracted the child's ribs to give the team maximum working space within the small chest cavity.

Laura waited for the brief interlude between respirator heaves and started her count. She anticipated a gush of blood. There was none. Instead, a piece of glass the size of a roofing nail was extracted from the large blood vessel leading to the heart. A slow flow of blood mixed with soft clots began seeping out, which made Laura hesitate momentarily before applying the patch out of sheer desperation. But it was too late. The child had exsanguinated. How could that have happened in a major trauma hospital like City Hospital?

"It's over," she said. "We just lost a ten-year-old kid."

Laura looked at the stricken expression on the ER resident's chubby face.

"Why didn't the ER call me in sooner?" she asked, ripping off her gloves. "The accident happened two and a half hours ago for God's sake. I only live ten minutes from here. This child should not have died."

"The severed spinal cord —" he began. "We tried."

"We should've diagnosed pericardial tamponade, and we should've known by the blood from the chest tubes that there was massive intrathoracic bleeding." Laura tossed her gloves on the instrument table in disgust. "The ABC's of trauma," she continued, "dammit. 'C' means circulation."

The team stood motionless amid the mingled odors of blood and gases and sweat. Finally the anesthesiologist started writing in his clipboard. "Time of death: 1:45 a.m., June 3, 1978."

"That poor child." Laura blinked away a lone tear. "Shouldn't have happened."

Laura and Roxanne had waited for the orderly to remove the body. A meaningless act of humanity, but Laura felt they owed the child that much and that Roxanne would feel that way too.

"I know. Though she would've been paralyzed if she'd lived. Tough life for a kid."

Shedding their surgical gowns, the two women headed for the doctor's lounge.

"We have got to do a better job here at trauma management," Laura said, letting her shoulders slouch and averting her eyes to the ground. "When I was a med student in Detroit, we developed the fastest, most comprehensive trauma response in the country. Maybe the world —" Laura stopped speaking abruptly. What was this "we"? She'd been a mere student. No she hadn't played a role, not personally.

Roxanne put an arm around Laura's shoulder. "Hey, two thirty in the morning is no time to solve all the problems of the world."

"Wendy Ruiz was the same age as my twins. My God, the

Ruizes were coming back from Disney. I took the kids there just last week. I-4, same route. I mean, it could have been us."

Roxanne frowned. "It's late. Why don't you head on home?"

"One cup of tea to unwind," said Laura as they stepped into the empty lounge. "After I pop out my contacts — I've had them in way too long. And one of your mother's chocolate chip cookies would help right now."

Roxanne nodded, a complicit smile on her face.

At thirty-four, Laura Nelson was already a respected thoracic surgeon in the Tampa Bay area. In the operating room, she exuded self-confidence without the theatrical outbursts made prototypical by her male colleagues. Outside of it, her optimism and energy made her popular with administrators and patients alike. But despite admiring colleagues, Laura had no real friends. Roxanne was the only exception, but even with Roxanne she could not share confidences. Not that she didn't long for a confidante, but she had unspeakable secrets, dangerous secrets. Besides, Roxanne had never been married. How could she even begin to understand the complexities that underpinned her relationship with Steve.

"I'll make the tea," Roxanne offered. Placing the Ruiz chart on the coffee table, she picked up the kettle from the small stove in the doctor's lounge. "I've only been on since three this afternoon, so that makes me the fresher of the two of us walking zombies."

"Thanks, Roxie." Laura sank into one of the vinyl chairs. "I've got to speak to the family before I leave."

Frowning again, Roxanne sat in the chair across from her. "I hate to tell you this, but that child's mother and an eight-month-old baby girl were DOA. The father's still in the OR with major orthopedic and abdominal injuries. Two of the other kids are in surgery, and a five-year-old boy with only mild contusions is in the ER. He's ready for discharge if they could find a relative."

"So this man lost his wife, his baby, and little girl," Laura sighed deeply. "This part will never — it just gets harder."

Roxanne gestured to the chart. "Listen, why don't you just write the operative note? The bad news can wait a bit, you know?

Mr. Ruiz was still in surgery when we started the case, so at best he'll be groggy right now. I'm doing a double, so I'll check in with him and cover for you until you get in for rounds tomorrow."

"Thanks, Rox. You know the worst part —"

"You did everything you could."

Laura signed the necessary paperwork. Sipping her tea and munching her third cookie, she changed into white slacks and a pale yellow shirt, pulling her hair quickly into a ponytail. Checking her watch, it was now after three.

"Steve should be home by now. I called him at the station before I came in to let him know about the accident — that I wouldn't be home until morning."

Roxanne sighed. "Your life is a logistical nightmare."

"That it is," said Laura.

At Channel Eight News, Steve Nelson loosened his silk maroon tie beneath the hot studio lights as the crew closed down the set.

"'Stagflation' — Jimmy Carter sounds more boring every day. Slow night for national. Good thing we got the tip on the Ruiz crash. Local stuff is always good for ratings, right, George?"

George Granger, the burly director of *Nightly News at Eleven*, scowled at Steve. "Goddamn tragedy is what it is."

"Drunk driver wipes out a whole family in one split second," Kim Connor, Steve's coanchor, added from her corner of the set. Dabbing a sheen of sweat from her face, Kim fingered the bangs of her short black hair. At thirty-two, she was the younger, albeit senior, member of the studio anchor team. A Tampa Bay celebrity known for her Latin beauty and sharp wit, Kim's dark eyes sparkled off screen, yet when reporting the litany of human disasters that made up the news, those same eyes reflected a depth of sincerity that had endeared her to her audience. Recently, however, Kim had seemed disinterested, even apathetic, and both Steve and George were concerned.

"Yes, it's very sad," Steve went on, tugging off his navy blue blazer.

Steve's blonde wavy hair and deep blue eyes complemented his partner's more flamboyant looks. While Kim was popular with just about everyone – particularly the masculine gender — Steve was popular with the more senior Tampa Bay audience. Handsome in an all-American kind of way, he was conservative in his dress and demeanor, and less passionate, more predictable than Kim. George had moved Steve up from field reporter last year, gambling that the two would make a good team. Kim's dynamism and experience would carry Steve's adequate, ultimately mediocre, performance. As it turned out, Steve's ego had far overshadowed his talent.

"Speaking of ratings," George added, "I don't have to tell you two about the ratings. Still falling."

"We'll get 'em back." Steve stood at the mirror, smoothing his hair. "We were number one just a couple of months ago, remember?"

"Nobody remembers in this business. Management wants to know what's happening now," George persisted. He was a behind-the-scenes pro who had worked his way up from location producer to news room director. "They're on my ass. Is it the in-house coverage? The editors? The field coverage?" With his two index fingers, he pointed straight at Steve. "Is it the anchors?"

"C'mon, George." Steve glanced across the table to Kim, but she remained silent, sorting papers in her briefcase. "We've both got plenty of fans all over the Tampa Bay area."

George shrugged. "It's late. I'm headed to my place on Longboat Key for the weekend." He pointed at Steve once more. "We'll talk about it Monday, when we're fresh. Kimmie over there looks beat. Lemme tell you though, we don't get the ratings up, my ass is in a sling, which means —"

"Got it." Steve cut him off. "Maybe I can get the inside scoop on the Ruiz family from my wife. She's operating on one of them right now."

George waved a hand. "That'll be old news by tomorrow night. Have her give me a call at the condo if she has anything special, but don't bug her. And you," he turned toward Kim, "you get some rest. If I didn't know you better, I'd think you were someone else."

Kim responded with a thin smile as George slung his sports jacket over his shoulder and walked out of the studio.

"You know, Kimmie, the boss has a point." Steve hovered over Kim's desk, hands in his pockets. "You weren't at the top of your game tonight."

Kim finally looked up from her briefcase. "So the bad ratings are all on me? Up yours, Nelson." She slammed her case shut and gave him a universal gesture.

"Hey, I didn't mean that." Steve plunked down on the chair beside her and gave her hand a quick squeeze. The studio lights had dimmed as technicians covered the cameras and adjusted the set for the morning news, but Steve still noticed the bronze smudges on the tissue Kim had used. She always wore heavy makeup on the air, but tonight it seemed even thicker. He tried to look more closely at her face and thought he could make out a definite bruise across the left cheek. Her eyes looked okay, but she was also wearing more eye makeup than usual and, for the first time, he questioned the uncharacteristic cut of her clothing. Kim was known for her low, teasing necklines, intended to highlight her tanned shoulders and to expose just enough cleavage to invite those head-turning stares. Tonight she wore a red turtleneck cotton sweater over a black knit skirt.

"Kim, will you tell me what's going on?"

"I don't know what you're talking about."

"Look at you." He traced a finger over her cheek and Kim flinched, pulling away. "Come on, we've been working together for more than a year. Those are bruises, goddamn it."

"I don't want to talk about it."

"Kim, you're in some kind of trouble. Maybe it'll do us both good to talk about it."

She glanced around the empty studio. "Please, not here."

"Then let's go somewhere, get a drink."

"It's late. I don't want to be out in public."

"We can go over to my house."

"I can't."

"Why not? Laura left a message that she won't be back until morning with that big highway crash. Our housekeeper has an apartment over the garage and she'll head for it as soon as I get back. Come on, you can follow me home."

"What about your kids?"

"They'll be asleep. It's the middle of the night, remember?"

"Well, I do need to talk to you. I've been thinking about leaving Tampa altogether."

Steve felt his body jerk, but he attempted a smile. "When we get to my place, we'll talk about everything."

Steve headed up Davis Boulevard in his white Ford Fairlane. Kim followed in her yellow Firebird, top down in the sweltering South Florida night. It was early June and already the temperature was unbearable. Steve hated the heat, blaming his wife for dragging him down to South Florida so she could be closer to her family. But he did have to admit that Tampa had been good to him. Back in Michigan, he might still be a struggling social worker, not a big-deal celebrity. Where would he be if they had stayed in Detroit? Compared to that Tampa was a sultry paradise. But what had Kim meant about leaving Tampa? Deep down Steve knew that the clowns who ran the station considered Kim the stronger half of the night anchor team. Just the thought of losing Kim triggered a surge of acid reflux. Nearly retching, he reached into the glove compartment for a slug of Mylanta.

Grudgingly he considered his anchor status. There were rumors, totally unfounded, that he got this job because of his wife. Laura had operated on George's nine-year-old daughter over a year ago after the child had been thrown from a horse, sustaining near fatal chest injuries. Laura was just doing her job, but George treated her like some kind of a hero. Soon after that Steve was picked for the coveted nightspot. Yes, it was his dream job. Normally just the thought of being in so many Tampa Bay households every night made him puff out his chest. But now he was worried. Worried about Kim. Had someone beat her up? The word "abuse" stuck in his mind. But most of all he was worried that she may leave Channel 8 and where would that leave him?

"Let me get you a drink." Steve spoke softly as he ushered Kim through the vaulted foyer to the large family room in the far corner of his home. The room was cluttered with kids' stuff and Kim suddenly lurched forward, tripping on a fragment of a train track. Steve grabbed her arm to stop her fall and supported her as she bent to remove her spike heels. Why had he led her to this one room in the house where he and Laura allowed the kids to leave their toys strewn about helter-skelter? He knew the answer: because it was the farthest room from the upstairs bedrooms.

"I don't know why I'm whispering," he said, setting down a bottle of Scotch and two glasses on the square polished brass and glass coffee table. "It's almost two, the kids are sound asleep."

"Dios mio, this room is larger than my whole apartment in Temple Terrace," Kim said as Steve poured drinks.

"Ice?" he asked.

"Please."

As Steve returned to the kitchen, Kim picked up her glass and wandered back out into the foyer. With wide eyes she inspected the sparkling crystal chandelier, the gleaming hardwood floors, the intricate pattern of the Oriental rug in hues of gold.

"Quite the hacienda. Your wife has good taste," she said as he plunked a couple of ice cubes into her glass. Steve followed her into the formal living room with its marble fireplace and elegant furniture and exquisite window treatments.

"How can you have such expensive stuff with so many kids?" Still barefoot, her feet sank into the plush carpeting as she stepped inside the living room.

"They don't spend much time in here," Steve said, taking her elbow and silently leading her back to the family room.

"As you can see, they do hang out here." He gave a well-appointed dollhouse a nudge with his foot as he closed the door be-hind him.

"I don't know shit about kids," Kim mused as she glanced at the pictures lining the shelves on both sides of the fireplace that dominated the room. She walked over to pick one off the shelf.

"You know, we don't really know each other that well, even though we've worked together for a year. I didn't even know you skied," she added, suddenly shy as she examined the family of seven. In colorful ski apparel and with grins they posed at the bot-tom of a mountain. Stamped in the corner was the "Vail" logo with the date 1975.

"We try to get to Colorado once a year. Didn't make it this year or last because Laura was too busy." Steve took the photo out of her hands. "Enough about family. Come on, sit down." He gestured to-ward one of the two oversized beige and black sofas angled to face the big screen TV. "Let's get to know each other better now. Tell me what happened."

Kim fingered the bruise on her cheek as she settled on the leather sofa. Then she took a long sip of her drink and shrugged. "I shouldn't be telling you, it's personal shit."

"Come on, it's trouble if you let a guy do that to you." Steve had been heading to the opposite sofa when he turned back to sit next to her. Somehow he had to make her drop the idea of leaving Tampa, but now that she had an abusive boyfriend shouldn't he be more worried about her safety? "It's Frank. Am I right?"

Steve slung his arm casually around her shoulder and turned her face to him. "He did this to you?"

Kim turned slightly, but he could see tears welling in her dark eyes. Taking a folded handkerchief from his pocket, Steve handed it to Kim and waited as she dabbed at her eyes, the bronze makeup mingling with tears to stain the white cloth.

"Come on, Kimmie, tell me about it." Steve tried for the pa-ternal tone that he used for certain news stories.

"The truth is, I'm scared." Kim's voice trembled and Steve felt his tone must have worked because Kim began her confession.

"Frankie's told me enough stuff to know he's dangerous, Steve. And I . . . I don't know how to get away from him. At first it was so good — gifts, nightclubs, that kind of thing. Remember how much fun I was having?"

Steve nodded.

"Well, now he's just insanely jealous. At first I thought if I went along with what he wanted, he'd trust me. But he's just gotten worse. He's so paranoid he even sleeps with his gun."

"Shit — but if he's connected —"

"You're not supposed to know that. Me and my big mouth." Kim inched closer to Steve so close they were touching. "You know, what scares me the most is that he wants to get married. Last night he started talking about us having kids. When I told him I didn't want any, that my career was more important — that's when he hit me."

"Married?" On impulse Steve grabbed both her arms and pulled her face to face. "God, Kimmie, that's crazy. Marry somebody who beats you up? That's insane. What you gotta do is break it off." Taking a deep breath, Steve considered options before he continued. "But you can't let him chase you out of Tampa either. We're a team. We're great together."

"I know, Steve. But look, there's a job in Atlanta. I'm scared shitless. Look, I'm shaking."

Now holding both of her hands, Steve leaned forward. Not only was she shaking, she was shivering. "You're cold," he said. "Let me put my arms around you."

Without hesitation Kim nestled against him, closer and closer. Then reaching up, she turned his head to hers and pulled him to her so that their lips touched. Steve did not push back, but let his lips explore hers as he drew her more tightly into his arms. When she pressed her lips more insistently, Steve could feel the warmth of her breasts against his chest. Steve momentarily jerked back. What was happening? Was Kim coming on to him?

"Shit, I'm sorry." Kim pushed Steve back with both hands. "I shouldn't have done that."

"It's okay, it's okay," Steve murmured. He reached for her hands and pulled her firmly against him, urgently covering her mouth with his own.

CHAPTER TWO

The metallic blue station wagon was the only car on the road at three thirty in the morning as Laura pulled out of the "Doctors Only" lot and headed for home. Approaching the sole traffic light on her route, she glanced up as she habitually did. The brightly illuminated billboard above featured her husband and his sultry colleague, smiling down on Tampa from their news desk. The familiar caption: THE DYNAMIC KIM AND STEVE, CHANNEL EIGHT NEWS TEAM AT ELEVEN.

That her husband was a television personality, Laura still found incredible. She'd never envisioned that employment scenario fifteen years ago when she'd married the serious, reticent college student. But since they'd moved from Detroit to Tampa, Steve had changed dramatically. That had been seven years ago. No longer the dedicated inner city social worker, Steve had had morphed first into a field news reporter, and then hit the top — the coveted anchor spot.

Stopping at the flashing red traffic light, Laura took a last glance at the billboard. She managed a tired smile. Her husband certainly was attractive. And articulate. And becoming arrogant, even egotistical. Steve had changed so much, but hadn't she too?

A grimace replaced her faint smile as she thought of the pressure George Granger was putting on Steve. Channel 8's ratings were slipping. She realized that George wanted Steve to succeed as a gesture of gratitude to her. Laura was no expert when it came to communication, but she was worried that Steve came off too remote on camera. Too much like a robot reciting the news. She couldn't sense any passion or compassion, like he really didn't connect with the news he reported, most of it tragic. Maybe viewers felt this way too. If so, how long could George keep him as anchor? The thought of Steve losing his job make Laura shudder. Not so much for the money. They could live on her income, but it would shatter his ego.

As Laura pulled up to her two-story stucco home with its red tile roof and wrought iron balconies, she switched off the headlights and parked in the driveway instead of the three-car garage. This was her routine, not wanting to risk waking the housekeeper or the kids at night with the rumble of the garage door. She let herself in through the kitchen, dark except for the luminescence of the microwave clock. She intended to head directly upstairs, but as she rounded the corner into the foyer, she noticed light seeping beneath the family room door. Surprised that her frugal housekeeper had left it on, Laura turned the door handle. She opened the door and without entering reached in to hit the dimmer switch.

Laura heard shuffling inside before she saw them. She blinked and stifling a gasp, adjusted her glasses. Knowing she was at the brink of exhaustion, she squeezed her eyes shut. Steve and Kim on that billboard had thrown her. She had to get a grip. But when she opened her eyes, she groaned. "Oh, no," escaped before she clamped her mouth shut and started grinding her teeth. The real Steve cringed in front of her, hair tousled, blue eyes flashing with panic. And Kim was real too and half naked.

Laura's hand flew to cover her mouth. Too shocked to speak. Too paralyzed to even breathe, she remained locked in that position. As for Steve, he just stood there, his chest bare, her favorite afghan clutched around his hips. Kim was the first to move, turning away from Laura, bending down to pick up her bra and sweater. The bra she stuffed in her purse. The sweater she pulled over her head as she struggled to adjust the tight skirt she must have pulled on in haste.

Still Laura had not moved. Hands over her mouth, her eyes focused on Kim as she smoothed her short black hair. From where she stood, she blocked the doorway. No words had been spoken.

Steve was the first to break the silence as Kim shifted her gaze from husband to wife and back. "Laura, let Kim leave, okay?"

Laura dropped her hands and took a step backward. Tears had sprung to her eyes. Her voice sounded hoarse. "How could you?"

Kim grabbed her spike heels and carried them in her hands as she passed by Laura in the hall and sped toward the front door. The door clicked shut. The turn of a car engine penetrated complete silence.

"Honey, I don't know what to say," Steve began, stepping toward Laura. "Kim came by because —"

Laura held up her hands to stop him. "Not out here." Tears now streamed down her face so violently that she choked on her words. She pointed toward the family room, still strewn with Steve's clothes. The bottle of Scotch and the two glasses, one smeared with brilliant red lipstick, made her want to slap him.

How could he do this? To her? To the kids?

Laura let her body sink into the plush chair facing the sofa where Steve positioned himself; the sofa where he and Kim had obviously been together. Still wrapped in the pale blue afghan that he'd grabbed to conceal his naked chest, Steve reached sheepishly for his clothes which he folded clumsily and set on his lap.

He cleared his throat. "I can explain."

Laura blinked away nonstop tears. "You can?"

"It's not — Kim followed me home after the program. She needed to talk."

Laura got up, walked across the room and pulled out a wad of tissues. She blew her nose and dabbed vigorously at her eyes. "Is that right?" she said, returning to sit on the arm of a chair. She wished she could think of something more relevant to say, but her mind felt paralyzed.

"Yeah," Steve blurted. "The guy she's seeing beat her up pretty bad, and she needed a shoulder to cry on. We didn't mean to — it just happened." Steve's fair skin looked ghastly pale. He leaned forward in his seat, wringing his hands. "Laura, honey, it shouldn't have happened, but it did. I'm sorry. It never happened before and it will never again. I swear. You mean the world to me."

When Steve stood, his clothes dropped from his lap onto the carpet. He took a tentative step toward Laura, but she held her hand out to stop him. Tears had refilled her eyes and she wiped them away with her other hand. Slowly, she rose off the arm of the chair. Like a robot she headed toward the staircase. What else could she do right now? Check to make sure the kids were asleep? Go to her room — no longer "their" room? Lock the bedroom door? Yet as she passed by the front door, she did not round the corner toward the stairs. Instead she opened the front door and walked out of the house.

Laura couldn't think. She couldn't feel. Without premeditation, she started up the station wagon and drove to the hospital. This all must be a nightmare. Too much fatigue. A full surgical load. Five active kids. Maybe tonight hadn't really happened. She'd wake up. The Ruiz girl would be stabilized in the recovery room and she'd return home to find Steve snoring in their king-size bed.

Laura parked at the entrance to the emergency room. Talking to no one, she walked through the trauma bays. She rode the elevator to the fifth floor and headed directly to the tiny, drab on-call room the hospital kept reserved for her. Just enough room for a narrow cot, made up with white sheets and a cotton blanket and a sink, shower, and toilet. And, of course, a nightstand upon which sat the telephone. Nothing on the walls, not a speck of color or cheer in the room. Still, she felt the familiar sense of comfort that hospitals brought to her.

All night long, Laura lay between starched sheets, trying to accept the jarring reality that Steve had had sex with Kim Connor right there in their house. All of their children had been upstairs. Could he be in love with Kim? For some reason, she was unable to accept that he loved another woman. Wouldn't she have known?

And hadn't he said it was the first time? But could she believe him? Should she have suspected this? Did she deserve this betrayal?

The hospital's pulse had been imprinted on Laura from the early days of her medical training, and this morning she felt it take over as she lay in the small, dark room. It had taken all night but in the eerie silence of the morning lull, she began to come to grips with reality. Finding Steve and Kim had not been a dream. She would have to figure out how to deal with it. She forced herself to get beyond the hurt just long enough to focus on the past few years of her life with Steve.

Squeezing her eyes shut, she could see Steve as a young college sophomore. She'd met him at the bookstore at Michigan State. He'd been stocking shelves, and she'd been looking for the freshman English text. He'd introduced himself and offered to give her his copy from the previous year, so she'd gone with him to his dorm room. To this day she could still feel the thrill of his touch when he'd reached for her hand to guide her along the path. Once there, they'd listened to some music and discovered they were both Elvis fans. She'd offered to buy him coffee, and he'd smiled that dazzling smile of his. After that they'd been inseparable. Imagine, she, a girl who had never even dated in high school — except for proms and football games — having a college boyfriend before classes even began. They had a whirlwind of fun and as Laura looked back, maybe mistook infatuation for love.

Or maybe things had just gone too fast. Within four months Steve had proposed and, despite her parents' misgivings, they were married at the end of her freshman year. Living in Spartan Village — student housing for married couples — they'd made ends meet with her part-time library job and his in the bookstore. She had scholarships; his parents took care of his tuition. She was nineteen, he was twenty-one. Within fifteen months they'd had their first child, and three years later, their second. In those early years, they'd been happy and successful, Steve with a degree in social work and she with a biology degree. Then it was on to the University of Michigan in Ann Arbor for a Master's degree for Steve and to University Medical School in Detroit for her. With a surge of sorrow, Laura's thoughts drifted back to Detroit. Moving there was when things started to go wrong. Med school was so demanding and there'd been three more children. But when —

No. Suddenly Laura threw off the top sheet and climbed out of bed. Stop thinking about what happened in Detroit. Not after finding Steve with Kim last night. Things were so different in Detroit, and that was so long ago. Concentrate on now. Life with Steve — all aspects of it. Things hadn't been right between them for some time. And the children: what was right for them?

Trying to sleep was hopeless, so Laura showered and donned surgical scrubs. Each morning brings to any hospital an abrupt transition as nursing shifts change, X-ray techs and lab technicians juggling baskets of needles and blood tubes crowd the corridors, and trays of food arrive. Teams of doctors converge at nursing stations to write new orders that send the nursing staff scurrying. Laura, in tune with this rhythm and without a flicker of sleep, prepared to face her patients by making early rounds. Then she'd go home and face Steve. But what would she say to him? As she dried her hair, a knock on the call room door interrupted her struggle to figure out the rest of her life.

"Come in," she called, anticipating the cleaning staff.

"Hey, what are you doing here so early?" Roxanne asked. Her hair, tucked away all night in a surgical cap, now sprang out in every direction, giving her a wild look even though she had changed into a neatly pressed gray plaid shirtsleeve dress and black flats. "The desk said they saw you come back in."

"I couldn't sleep," said Laura, avoiding her friend's gaze as she went back into the tiny bathroom to hang up the damp towel.

"Sorry to hear that. Remember we said we'd speak to Mr. Ruiz together."

The words blurred. Wendy Ruiz. Only once last night did

Laura even think about that devastated family — she was too focused on her own. She felt selfish, guilty. Her problems were nothing compared to Mr. Ruiz's losses of his wife, baby, Wendy. What about the other kids? Had they survived surgery last night? And the father's injuries? How severe were they?

Laura finally faced Roxanne with red-rimmed eyes and a swollen face.

"Oh no, what's wrong? Here, sit down." Roxanne pointed to the cot. "Tell me, what is it?"

Laura's voice was husky. "I . . . I don't know what to do. I found Steve last night . . . with a woman."

"Last night? I thought you were going straight home?"

"Roxie, it was Kim Connor and yes, it was in my family room."

"No! Has he been seeing her?"

Laura choked back a sob. "I don't know. He said no, but you know things haven't been good between us. Not that we fight a lot. It's just that we hardly see each other. What with the kids, his late-night job, my crazy hours at the hospital. Maybe if I'd stayed home. No, that's ridiculous. I just don't know."

Roxanne nodded slowly. "So what are you going to do?"

"I don't know. I don't see how we can stay together after last night — and it's not just that."

"I know. Laura, I'm your friend. I could tell that you haven't been happy for some time."

"Even so, the kids. I have to think what's best for them. My God, he had sex right there, with five kids right upstairs. What if they'd seen it? What if he does it again?"

"Laura, is what you want a separation?" Roxanne pressed. "It's got to be about what you want. The kids will be okay either way. What's right for you will be right for them."

"Maybe. The truth is Steve and I have each gone our separate ways. He's become 'Mr. Newscaster Celebrity' and I've become a surgeon." Laura snuffled and reached for a handful of Kleenex. "I've been thinking about this all night and no matter what I do, I have to face him this morning — after I talk to Mr. Ruiz." Laura grabbed a wad of tissue and wiped off her glasses. Then she used it to blow her nose. "What's the update there?"

Roxanne sighed. "I've dropped by twice. First time he was still too groggy to talk, so I checked on the other kids. The eight-year-old had a splenectomy, and the six-year-old had a skull fracture with a subdural hematoma and multiple extremity fractures. Both boys. They'll be okay. The five-year-old, Jose, is still in the ER, if you can believe it. I stopped by and had hot chocolate with him. He's so adorable, such big black eyes. He's looks so pathetic in that skimpy hospital gown, I'm going to buy him something else to wear. He doesn't know about his mom yet," she said quietly. "Peds psychology will see him this morning."

Guilt stabbed inside Laura. Her problems were minor compared to this. "So sad," she murmured.

"I stopped by again, about an hour ago. Mr. Ruiz had been told about his wife and the baby, and he was, well, inconsolable."

"You didn't tell him about Wendy?"

"No, Laura, we agreed you'd tell him — it's expected that the doctor will, of course. But I had no idea what you'd been through at home."

"You did the right thing. It's something I have to do." Laura brushed her wet hair back and secured it with a plastic clasp. She grabbed a clean, starched lab coat and stuffed a handful of tissues in the pocket.

"Come on, let's go see him. Wait a sec, though. Let me call my housekeeper. I want her to take the kids to my mom's for the weekend. I need to hash things out with Steve, but not in front of them."

They found Louis Ruiz in a semiprivate room on the orthopedic floor. The door to the room was open and the other bed vacant. As Laura and Roxanne approached, the man lay silent, staring straight ahead, not even noticing them. His longish black hair had been combed neatly back, accentuating the pallor of his skin. Both legs were elevated and wrapped in pneumatic cuffs below the knee to minimize the chance of blood clots. Bulky dressings covered both hips and thighs, and a trapeze-like contraption hung over his chest.

"Mr. Ruiz," Roxanne began softly, "this is Dr. Nelson. Remember I told you she'd be in first thing this morning." Her voice broke as he turned his sad, intensely black eyes to her. "Laura, this is Wendy's father."

"Mr. Ruiz, I am so sorry." Laura faltered. "About your wife and your baby."

"Thank you," he said weakly. "But—?"

"Last night we operated on your daughter Wendy. She had serious injuries."

"How is she? Can I see her?" He struggled to sit up. "Her mother, the baby — I have to tell her."

Roxanne reached for his free hand, the one unencumbered by the intravenous needle. "Please don't try to move."

Laura held onto the bed railing and spoke quickly. "She . . . Wendy . . . had a fracture in her neck and a big piece of glass in her chest, piercing the big artery leaving the heart. Mr. Ruiz, she didn't make it. She died on the operating table. I'm so sorry."

Laura paused. Experience told her to expect any reaction from violent outcry to stony silence. She watched Ruiz's dark eyes search Roxanne's as if she could defy this report, yet only tears flowed as Roxanne grasped his hand.

"I want you to know that we did everything possible for Wendy, Mr. Ruiz. Her injuries were just too severe. Again, I'm so sorry." Laura looked to him for a response, but there was none. She chose not to tell him that even if Wendy had lived, she would have been a paraplegic.

After a few moments, Roxanne broke the silence. "You've got rounds, Dr. Nelson. I'll stay here for a while."

Laura left quietly and completed her patient rounds before heading home at nine o'clock to face her own life. As she approached the parking lot exit, she heard her name.

"Dr. Nelson!"

Laura turned, shifting her bag on her shoulder as a middle-aged man with thick wire-rimmed glasses trotted toward her. He was tall and lanky with tufts of gray hair sticking up behind a severely receding hairline. "May I have a word with you?"

She assumed he was a relative of one of her patients. "Do I know you?"

"I'd like to talk to you about the Ruiz family," he drawled, sounding distinctly native Floridian.

"Are you a reporter?" she asked, careful to remain civil. Though her husband was a newscaster and depended on these reporters in the field, Laura disliked them intensely.

"Ah, no," he said. "I saw you coming out of Ruiz's room and I know you operated on one of the kids and that the kid died on the table."

"Who are you?" He surely didn't look like a close relative.

"I'm a personal injury lawyer," he said. "Representing the interests of Mr. Ruiz. Wrongful death, that sort of thing."

"There's nothing I can do to help you."

"Here's my card," he said, holding it out. "Sam Sanders. Give me a call if you change your mind."

But Laura just turned away, leaving him with his hand outstretched.

CHAPTER THREE

Laura was nibbling a crumb cake at the round table in the sunny breakfast room when her husband came down at nine thirty. Warm sun pouring in the windows abated her shivers, but she wished it could warm her heart. This room had always been her haven, where she spent most of the time with the kids over breakfast and dinner, homework sessions, doing puzzles, playing board games. The décor was bright with yellow and white patterned wallpaper, light oak cupboards and floors, and stark white appliances. The room had never failed to cheer her, but as of today, she knew things would be different. While her coffee went cold, Laura waited for Steve. She'd pulled her hair into a hasty ponytail and wore dark prescription glasses over red-rimmed, puffy eyes.

Steve plodded down the stairs, tousled in his green corduroy robe and baggy gray sweatpants. His hair had been forgotten and he hadn't shaved. He yawned as he poured himself a cup of coffee. "Coffee, Laura? You okay?"

"Yes." She squeezed her eyes shut. "We need to talk, Steve."

"Okay. Where are the kids?" He glanced around the silent kitchen. "I barely slept last night."

"I asked Marcy to take them to Mom's," she answered. "I'll pick them up tomorrow."

"Mike has baseball practice," Steve said.

Laura almost screamed. Here was Steve sitting here like nothing had happened. Just a Saturday morning, sharing a casual cup of coffee. She wanted to lash out, to bite him, hit him, hurt him, but she had warned herself to keep it together. To say what she had to say, to forego yelling and screaming. Her problem: she didn't know what she was going to say. She didn't know which direction to take. Her life and the lives of her kids hung in the balance.

"This is more important than baseball practice. This is about what we're going to do with our lives." Try as she might she couldn't keep the rage out of her voice. "You should have worried about Little League before you totally screwed up all our lives."

"Whoa!" Bleary eyed, Steve slumped into the closest chair. "Honey, last night was a big mistake that will never happen again. I already told you. You're too important to me, you and the kids."

Laura burst into fresh tears and pounded her fists on the oak table. "I just can't believe it."

Steve jumped to his feet and began pacing. "Honey, I'm so sorry, beyond sorry. What else can I say?"

"I don't know what you can say," she cried, starting to sound hysterical. Then out of nowhere she felt a jolt from somewhere inside her so powerful that her body stiffened. She said, "All I know is that our marriage is over." Then Laura's hands flew to her mouth as she processed the finality of what she'd just blurted. Until the words issued from her mouth, she hadn't been sure of what she wanted.

"What? You can't be serious — we have five kids. Last night was just a stupid mistake."

Laura grimaced. Shaken, but strangely resolved, she shook her head. "Maybe, Steve, but what's done is done. We can't pretend it never happened."

"For God's sake, Laura, we've been married for fifteen years. I'm so sorry, I really am." He pulled out the chair next to hers, sat down, and reached for her hand, which she jerked away.

"The truth is," she sniffled, "we haven't been happy since I don't know when. We've both been working so hard and, you have to admit, we've both changed."

"So what? We're still the same underneath it. We still love each other."

"Really?" Laura's voice broke. "If that was true you wouldn't be with —"

"Laura, last night was the first —" he finally backed off as she continued to inch farther away from his touch — "and the last."

Laura blinked back more tears. "Don't deny it. Things between us haven't been good —"

"Nothing we can't work out, Laura. You work such crazy hours, and I've been under tremendous pressure at the station."

Laura shook her head and averted her eyes. "After last night, it doesn't matter what you say."

Steve raked his hands through his hair. "Hey, c'mon. You need me. You're so attached to your career, you couldn't handle the kids alone. Besides, I'm there for them, and they need me. Especially Patrick."

"Do they now? And don't use Patrick as a pawn. He's fine and you know it." Laura cupped her hands over her face, telling herself to ease up, to keep this horrible conversation as civil as possible.

Steve leaned closer and put his arm around her. "Please, let's not let one mistake ruin everything for us. Think of the kids. They need a mom, and I've been a great dad. Everyone knows that."

Laura hesitated before pushing him away. "No. Let's just talk about how we're going to do this. Now. Today. I want you to move out. Find a place. Stay in a motel. A separation." She paused, shivering again, not so much from anger as fear. This was her life she was discarding. And Steve was a good father. The kids would miss him terribly. Should she reconsider?

"Look," he said quietly, "if it'll make you happy, I'll stay somewhere else for a couple of days. I can understand why you're pissed. God, if I ever found you with someone, I don't know —" His voice trailed off. "You don't have to worry about Kim either, she's leaving Tampa."

Laura winced. "Stop. As long as you're not here, you can be with whomever you want."

Steve smiled ruefully. "Laura, c'mon. Just cut me a little slack. A mistake. I swear."

"No."

"Okay, okay. I'll give you some time. Just don't tell the kids? Say I'm on business. Will you do that?"

"I'm not going to tell them I caught you with Kim in their own house, that's all I know right now."

"I don't think leaving is a good idea. I know we can work things out."

Laura shook her head. "After what happened last night, we can do two things," she improvised as a renewed wave of hurt reinforced her resolve. "Choice one. I go to George Granger and tell him about you and Kim. You know how he feels about me. No way he'll keep you on at the station."

Steve's face swelled with anger. "You'd try to get me fired? You know he's already on me about the ratings."

"I'll call him today, right now. I don't want to, but —"

"You wouldn't do that!"

"Or, choice number two. You just leave. It's the sensible thing to do. We'll figure out the best way to tell the kids. The best way for them, not for you," she continued, sadness softening her voice.

"Laura, please. I'm asking for another chance. Kim doesn't mean anything to me. It'll never happen again. How many times do I have to tell you?"

"You're right," she said slowly, "it will never happen again — to me."

Kim Connor opened her eyes, glanced at the clock on her bedside table and groaned. Ten-fucking in the morning. She squeezed her eyes shut and yanked up the covers, but the doorbell chime did not stop.

"Fuck." She crawled out of bed, grabbing a paisley silk bathrobe on her way to the door. Peering through the peephole, she sighed in recognition and unhooked the chain.

"Carmen? You okay?" Kim reached for her friend's hand. "Come in, honey."

"I'm okay. Sorry I'm so early, but man, he did a number on you."

Kim reached up and touched her face. "Must look awful. I'm still half asleep."

"Hey, you're gorgeous no matter what. Go fix yourself up and I'll make coffee."

Carmen Williams was the only friend that Kim Connor had — girlfriend, that is. They'd met in a club in Ybor City, Tampa's historic Cuban enclave, ten years earlier. Both twenty-two. Both heavy into cocaine. No money, loaded with debt, they'd resorted to prostitution to support their pricey habit. Not really professional whores, just selling sex when desperate for a hit. Each was Hispanic on their mother's side, and a mix of European on their father's. Kim's Hispanic genetics dominated with her dark hair, olive complexion, and coal black eyes. She was small boned, hot-tempered, and provocatively sexy. Carmen's skin was lighter, her eyes a tawny hazel, her heavier build characteristic of her father's family. Her long, auburn hair was her best feature, and when she bothered with makeup, which was rarely, she could look genuinely glamorous. Unlike Kim, Carmen had never recovered from her addiction.

Soon after they met, the pair of friends was literally taken off the street by Father Sean Darby, a young priest assigned to Our Lady of Perpetual Help in Ybor City. He had campaigned hard with Catholic Social Services for a drug rehab program in his parish, documenting the rise of drug-related crimes in the neighborhood. One scorching summer night, Kim and Carmen, stoned on coke and liquor and looking for their next fix, stumbled into Father Darby and offered sex for cash. The priest, clad in street clothes, simply ushered them into his storefront rehab center. Kim began to recover, and the politically astute priest used his connections to get her a scholarship at the University of Florida, where she excelled in her communications major. Carmen, however, could never beat her cocaine habit and still lived from job to job out on the fringe.

Today, Carmen looked clear eyed and perky. She wore a halter top with matching slacks in bronze and black patterns and her hair was arranged in a trendy French braid secured with a black ribbon. As Kim splashed water on her face, tenderly fingering the deepening bruise around her eye and cheek, she wondered why her friend had come over so early. Impromptu visits like this usually meant Carmen needed something — money, usually — but Carmen also knew that Kim often slept until noon after her late TV gigs. Something was wrong, she knew it.

"Here, sweetie." Carmen handed Kim a mug of black coffee. "As usual, you don't have milk or cream, so I'm having mine, ugh, black too."

"Sorry. Can't risk the calories." Kim yawned as they settled at the table in her small alcove of a kitchen. "So, to what do I owe this pleasure?"

"Honey, we need to talk. Where were you last night?"

"What do you mean? I was on the news, in front of all of Tampa Bay."

"No, I mean after," Carmen persisted.

Kim frowned. "Why?"

"Frankie called looking for you."

"Shit, no." Coffee leapt from her cup as Kim lurched forward. "What time? What did you tell him?"

"I didn't know what to tell him. It was two thirty, and I'd just walked into my place. At first I thought maybe you came over, that you two'd had another fight after what he already did to you the night before. But what could I say? I said I didn't know where you were."

"Uh-oh," Kim exhaled.

"He was pissed. I mean freakin' uptight."

"He was supposed to be in Miami."

"Said he stopped off at the station to say good-bye first. How sorry he was, flowers and all. Some flunky kid at Channel Eight said he thought he saw you go off with Steve Nelson. God, Kimmie, tell me that's not true."

"He . . . he knew I was with Steve?"

"Damn," Carmen leaned forward, her eyes wide. "You were?"

"I didn't plan it. I mean, I had to tell him about maybe leaving Tampa for that Atlanta job. After the other night with Frankie though," she paused and touched her face, "I just lost it. Plus, you know how Steve always makes me feel safe — so buttoned up and all. The truth is I always did want to do him and last night it just happened. *Dios mio*, if Frankie finds that out —"

Carmen put down her coffee cup on the table. "All Frankie knows is that some kid *maybe* sees you going off with Steve, honey. He doesn't know the rest. God, I can't believe —"

"Neither can I," Kim cut in. "That's not even the worst of it. His wife walked in on us."

"You're fucking kidding."

"I wish. Talk about being pissed. She's harmless, but Frankie —"

"What's gonna happen? To Steve, I mean. He's got all those kids, right?"

"I don't know. I've got my own problems." Kim got up and started to pace back and forth in her small kitchen. "Shit, if Frankie went to the station first, he probably came here after. What am I going to do?"

Carmen tried to smile. "You're the only friend I've ever had, honey, and as much as I hate to say this, you'd better get out of Tampa. Take that Atlanta job. After the other night, Frankie's gonna keep beatin' the shit out of you whether he finds out about last night or not. What you told me about him wanting kids and you don't. That's a blow to his macho ego and that fucking guy's in love with you. You told him your career is more important to you than he is? He can't handle that."

Kim's eyes welled with tears. "You're right. I'm so scared. And his work stuff scares me too. The people in Miami he's dealing with — his plans for here."

Carmen nodded. "I've heard some stuff in the Ybor clubs about his boss. You know it's Carlos Tosca in Miami?"

Kim shook her head. "Whoever it is, I know he's dangerous.

Carmen, you better keep your mouth shut out there. These guys don't fool around."

"Like I don't know that. That's why I brought you this." Carmen proceeded to remove an object from her purse and laid it gingerly on the table.

"That's a gun." Kim's eyes were wide.

"Yeah, a pistol or a revolver? I don't know shit about guns. The guy I got it from did tell me it's got a hair trigger, so be careful."

Kim stood back, shaking her head, dilated eyes still focused on the weapon. "Carmen, are you crazy? I've never even shot a gun."

"Doesn't matter, there must be some kind of a safety. Right? Don't all guns have one?" Carmen gingerly rotated the gun in her hand, inspecting. Then she shrugged and set it down on an end table.

"Look, that's why I came over instead of calling. You tell Frankie you lost your house key. It happened to me once, a busted key chain, you know? So you got back here after work and then you went back to the station to look for it, but you couldn't find it, and you spent the night there. Totally deny anything that kid said about Nelson, okay? That's for starters. And this," she indicated the gun, "is for protection. Understand?"

"Okay," Kim said slowly. "Okay, honey, I'll try the key thing — and this. Thanks."

"Best you get somebody to show you how to use it."

"Uh-huh. Maybe I'll ask Steve. He knows about guns."

"Good." Carmen smiled. "Listen, I'm back in NA. Got a new sponsor. I'm really gonna make it this time."

"Oh, Carmen, I hope you do. I'll help you all I can."

"You already have, saved my life so many times. That's why I'm here." Carmen got up and hugged Kim, avoiding her friend's bruised cheek. "I'm sure gonna miss you, but you have to get out of here, Kimmie. You gotta get out from under Frankie's influence."

CHAPTER FOUR

Laura tossed her canvas bag on the kitchen counter, reached for a fresh-baked oatmeal cookie, and glanced up at the clock. Not bad, five thirty. All week she'd managed to get home at a decent hour by postponing all but emergency cases. For the first time in ages, she'd been home five nights in a row for dinner.

"Marcy?" She knew her housekeeper couldn't be far. Pots bubbled on the stove and the smell of roast beef made Laura realize she'd skipped lunch.

"Hey, home early again." Marcy Whitman clucked as she headed for the stove, grabbed a spoon and started stirring a pot. "You're cheating. I make the kids wait until after dinner before diving into the cookies."

Rotund, with her salt-and-pepper hair pulled into an old-fashioned bun, Marcy looked older than her fifty-six years. She'd worked for Laura and Steve ever since they'd moved to Tampa, when Laura began her internship seven years ago. Patrick had been only ten months old; the twins, three; Kevin, four; and Mike, seven. Thank God for Marcy, Laura repeated at least a dozen times each day.

As for Marcy, she claimed the children gave her the will to go on once she'd lost her husband to cancer. Fiercely dedicated to the Nelsons, she lived in a small apartment over their attached garage so she could be on call for those frequent occasions when both parents worked erratic hours.

"Friday, I never thought it'd come." Laura slumped into the nearest kitchen chair. "How're the kids?"

"They're all in the family room," Marcy said.

Laura started to get up.

"You had a few calls."

"Who?" Laura grabbed one more cookie and started stuffing it into her mouth.

"Your mother. She wants to know if you'd like her to stay with you over the weekend. You know she's worried about you. And a lawyer. Says you know him, a Mr. Sanders. And then Roxanne. She called about this Mr. Sanders. She wants you to call her before Monday morning."

"Oh? I'll call them later." Laura wiped the crumbs off her lips. "I'm going in to check out the kids."

Laura stepped across the hall and was about to call out, "I'm home," when she suddenly stopped. She sensed before she saw the serious expressions on her kids' faces. They were deep in discussion and did not notice her arrival at the verge of the door. Mike, her oldest son, sat stiffly on one end of the sofa. He looked so much like a younger version of his dad that she flinched. Broad shoulders, wavy blonde hair, but with Laura's green eyes. Like Steve, Mike was clean cut and smart, yet unlike Steve, he was modest, even oversensitive. Hard for Laura to accept, but Mike was fourteen now. Steve had been nineteen when she'd met him. So much had happened to both of them since then. They were now two entirely different people. Gone their rosy eyed optimism, gone their shared values.

"They're not telling me anything," Mike was saying. "But Dad was at my baseball game yesterday, and he said he was coming back." Laura grimaced at the new pitch in his voice. Puberty, a tough transition for any kid under the best of circumstances.

Next to him sat Kevin, age eleven, another blonde, but with fine, straight hair with shaggy bangs brushing his eyebrows. His freckles seemed apt to his role as family clown, but at the moment his blue eyes — the medium blue of his father's — clouded over with unfamiliar worry.

The younger three were sitting Indian style on the floor in front of their brothers, a half-finished puzzle before them. It was one of those rare occasions when the television was turned off. Natalie and Nicole, identical ten-year-old twins, flanked eight-year-old Patrick.

Laura felt her heart turn over in her chest. Should she walk in or lurk out here and listen?

"He's never coming home," Nicole announced with smug authority. "Mom won't let him live with us anymore."

"You shut up, Nicky," shouted Patrick, clenching his fists. "That's not true. Is it, Mike?"

"Daddy would never leave us by ourselves," said Natalie before Mike could respond.

"We're not by ourselves, silly," Kevin interjected. "We have Mom and Mrs. Whitman."

"Who cares anyway," said Nicole in a strangely cold tone.

"You're a mean jerk," Patrick yelled, reaching over to shove Nicole.

"You're just a stupid baby," Nicole shouted. "Get away from me. And don't touch my puzzle! I'm not kidding."

"But he's gotta come home," murmured Natalie.

"Who cares?" Nicole said again, shrugging. "Mom doesn't want him anymore. He did something mean to her."

Laura stood silent, listening.

"Oh, just forget it," Kevin slammed shut the book on his lap. "C'mon Mike, let's go outside and have a catch." Jumping up, he grabbed his catcher's mitt, and slammed the door on the way out to the backyard.

Laura slipped back into the kitchen as the kids filed out the door behind Kevin.

"What can I tell them that will make them understand?" Laura's shoulders slumped against the refrigerator.

"I'd start with Mike," Marcy said, nudging Laura aside so she could open the refrigerator. She pulled out a gallon of milk. "He needs to know what's going on. Adolescence is tricky. You have to face up to the facts."

"I know, but how do I explain about Steve, you know, what he did — what this is all about?"

Marcy shook her head sadly. "Now that you're sure you want a permanent separation, it's better to tell the kids."

"What if I'm not doing the right thing?"

Marcy left Laura alone as she left to pour the kids's milk in the dining room.

"Kevin seems fine, doesn't he?" Laura asked when Marcy returned.

"That's Kevin."

Laura always marveled at this child's ability to avoid anything unpleasant or controversial. "But Nicole sounded so — I don't know — tough — that worries me."

"I'd be lying if I didn't say me too, Laura. I don't know if that's better or worse than Natalie, who cries at the drop of a hat and refuses to even go out to play with her friends."

"Damn Steve anyway." Laura wrung her hands. "How am I going to deal with this?"

"I've cooked a great roast with mashed potatoes, fresh string beans, and peach cobbler for dessert. After that, at least tell them that you and Steve are separating, but that they'll still have a father."

"You're right, Marcy. What would I do without you?" Laura gave the older woman a hug.

"Oh, now. You all sit down to dinner and straighten things out."

"Come on, kids, let's eat while we talk about this," Laura began. "About me and Dad. First of all, you're always going to have a mom and a dad. You know that, don't you?"

Each child reacted differently as she struggled to find the right words to tell them that nothing would be exactly the same, but that everything would still be okay. Mike was studied and solemn and seemed especially protective of her. If he did not reject her outright, the others would follow. After the others went to bed, she'd need to spend time alone with him and try to make him understand.

Kevin said practically nothing, trying to blink away his tears. The twins reacted according to their distinctly polarized personalities, Nicole seeming actually pleased, and Natalie distraught and weepy. But it was Patrick that most worried Laura. So different from the others with his chestnut brown hair and hazel-flecked eyes. The baby of the family, born with a heart murmur, Patrick was used to getting his own way. Everybody said that he was Steve's favorite. And now he stubbornly refused to accept her explanation that Daddy would live somewhere else and see them on weekends.

"That's not true, Mom," he yelled, pushing his untouched food aside. "My dad is going to live right here with all of us! I mean it." There were no tears, but the animosity in the little boy's flushed face was blatant. He shoved his chair back and bolted for the door.

"Come on, honey," Laura rose to go after him, "Dad will be here tomorrow for you —"

Mike jumped up. "I'll go make sure he's okay."

"I'm goin' with Mike," snuffled Kevin.

Nicole came over and gave Laura a hug, "Everything will be okay, Mom. Thanks for explaining to us. I tried to tell them, but they just wouldn't believe me when I said I knew Dad wasn't going to live here."

"I love you, Mom." Natalie joined her sister and Laura and she put her arms around them both. "We get to see Dad, don't we?"

"Of course you do," Laura said softly.

"Even if I don't want to," challenged Nicole.

"Of course you want to," murmured Laura, trying to comprehend what was happening to her family.

The phone interrupted.

"Why don't you two go out and play. I'll clean up here. Then maybe we can all watch a movie," Laura suggested as she rose to answer the phone. She pushed the peach cobbler away, and steeling herself, assumed it would be Steve, calling about moving back in again as he had all week under the pretense of making arrangements for picking up the kids.

"Hello?"

"Dr. Nelson? I'm so glad I caught you at home," drawled a vaguely familiar male voice. "I've tried you at the hospital, but —"

"Who's calling, please?"

"Sam Sanders. We met briefly. I'm an attorney handling the Ruiz case."

Laura was silent. Roxanne had warned her that this man was going all over trying to get evidence against the hospital and the doctors. Apparently, the truck owner's insurance had lapsed, his license was invalid, he had a history of DWIs, and no financial resources. As a result, this Mr. Sanders was trying to sniff out some malpractice somewhere, looking for enough evidence to convince his potential client to sue any deep pockets.

"Look, Mr. Sanders, I'm really busy right now. Perhaps —"

"Won't take but a minute," he drawled. "I heard that you were mighty upset with the Tampa City emergency room performance that night."

"That's not something I can talk about right now."

"And why is that, if you don't mind my asking? Nobody at the hospital wants to talk to me either — except for one of the nurses, that Roxanne Musing you work with. That makes me wonder."

"That's not what I meant. I meant that I just don't have anything to say. And I don't appreciate your calling me at home —"

"I do apologize," he interrupted. "Maybe you did all you could, maybe not, but that little Ruiz girl was alive when she got to that hospital in that helicopter, and I'm making it my business to find out why she died. I'm sure you don't disagree that Mr. Ruiz deserves some compensation for all his losses. He's a carpenter and won't be working for some time. I intend to see that his family is compensated for any mistakes that were made."

"I am truly sorry about the Ruiz family, but there's nothing I can do. Now goodbye, Mr. Sanders."

Laura made a mental note to call Cliff Casey, Tampa City Hospital CEO, on Monday to pass along Sanders's threat of a liability suit in case he was not already aware of it. Maybe this weekend Roxanne would come over with the little boy. With a stab, however, Laura realized that none of her own children would be home. They'd be off visiting Steve in that dingy, cramped apartment he'd borrowed.

She sat down and ate half the peach cobbler while thinking about Roxanne. Was she developing a personal relationship with Louis Ruiz? On the day after the accident, his five-year-old, Jose, had been discharged from the hospital to the Hillsborough County Children's Home. When Roxanne found out, she pleaded with the county to let her take the child to her own home. It was the least she could do, she told Laura, for such an unfortunate man who'd just lost his wife and both daughters. The other two boys would recover, but only after extensive hospital stays and huge medical bills.

CHAPTER FIVE

The next Thursday, Steve sat crouched behind his cluttered desk in his office at the TV station. Posters of media spots filled the room's walls, a series of candid shots of Kim Connor and himself. Such an attractive pair, everyone said. So why had everything fallen apart?

Tomorrow would be exactly two weeks since Laura walked in on him and Kim. She was jealous and angry. But this was going on too long. Staying in that cramped downstairs apartment in Old Hyde Park, courtesy of a reporter friend on assignment, was getting old. When the kids were there, they had nothing to do since all their friends and toys were at home on Davis Island. Tomorrow he'd surprise Laura with a box of Godiva chocolates and convince her that enough was enough. Then he'd be back home in his own bed with his own big screen TV, stereo system, walk-in closet full of clothes and, hopefully soon, with his wife.

But if not, there may be another option. Truth be told for the first couple of days after Laura kicked him out, he'd fantasized about Kim. About how they'd fallen into each other's arms, how soft her breasts felt against his chest, the velvety touch of her skin, the fragrance of her hair, the fullness of her lips. He'd never imagined that passion could be so hot and intense. Then he'd wondered dreamily how long Kim had had such a strong sexual attraction to him. About how blind he'd been not to recognize it sooner. Would they become lovers and leave Tampa together so Kim could get away from that abusive guy? If so, how would he deal with Laura and the kids? Lots of guys were divorced and still got to see their kids. But deep down Steve knew he didn't want a divorce. And he couldn't give up his kids. He wanted to see them every day, not on some rotation schedule.

But Steve's fantasy and resultant dilemma dissipated the following Monday when Kim made it unmistakably clear that she had no intention of seeing him outside the studio. Her excuse: that night she'd been distraught, too upset to think. It had just happened, she told him, and it would not happen again. If her boyfriend, Frank Santiago, ever found out, they'd both be dead. Santiago was dangerous — the worst kind of dangerous — "in-the-mob" dangerous.

Steve had questioned whether Kim really knew what she wanted, but he could tell she was truly frightened by her gangster boyfriend. And what implication did that have for her threat to leave Tampa? He couldn't get a straight answer. She'd been avoiding him all week, and now she was due any minute. He needed to talk to her about why George had wanted to see him and refused to say why. Something was going on behind his back, he knew it.

Steve also knew he should be concentrating on his news stories: Menachem Begin's upcoming visit to the U.S., the imminent marriage of Princess Caroline of Monaco to Philippe Junot, what to do about swine flu vaccine. Inconsequential stories compared to his pressing personal problems. He'd begun to sweat despite the air conditioner running at full blast when Kim breezed through the open door of their shared suite.

"Hi there," she said, already reaching into her trim briefcase to pull out her briefing notes. Kim always showed up prepared.

As Steve looked up, she didn't even glance his way, but headed to her desk. As usual her desk was clear of any clutter or personal mementos. There was only a small clock encased in pink marble and an ornate box of multicolored woods for her pens. "Hey, yourself."

Steve rose from behind his matching desk of light oak, crowded with papers and strewn with office supplies fighting for space among the haphazardly placed pictures of his kids. He stepped across the room and closed the door behind her. "So what does George want to see me about?" He walked over and tried to place a hand on her shoulder. "And don't tell me you don't know."

"Whoa, back off." Kim shrugged him away. "What's your problem, anyway?"

"What's my problem? Maybe you can tell me."

"Come on," she said, "why don't you calm down so we can discuss this."

"George called last night to tell me he wants to see me first thing. Look at me, Kim, and tell me you don't know something."

"Shit. I wanted to tell you firsthand, from me, but I couldn't call you at home, obviously."

Steve shook his head. "Don't tell me you've gone back to that creep? After what he did to you?"

"That's what I'm trying to tell you. I'm getting out of it my own way. Frankie's a very dangerous man. I keep telling you that."

"So I get kicked out of my house, and you go back to that . . . that mobster. That's what's dangerous."

"I'm not going back to him. Last night I handed in my resignation because I took that job in Atlanta. Bigger market, more money. No Frankie."

"You're taking the job? But Kimmie, you can't just leave," Steve stammered. "We're a team. Professionally, I mean."

Steve followed Kim's gaze as she glanced out the window of their office, just in time to see George Granger approaching.

"Here he comes. I gotta get changed. I'm sorry, Steve, I really am."

As the door to the adjoining dressing room shut behind her, Steve steeled himself. The set look on George's face as he entered the office told him all he needed to know.

"Steve. So Kim's told you I see. I've been warning you about the ratings, and now with Kim leaving, we have no choice."

"What do you mean, no choice? What about me?"

"Listen, Steve, this is tough on me too. You know how much I

like you personally. I so admire your wife and I realize that you have
a family, but —"

"But what? Even if Kim leaves, I can still go on with another
anchor." Steve started to pace. This was his dream job. How could
he go back to the anonymity of a desk job? Or worse yet, back to life
as a social worker?

George coughed. "Listen, Steve. The decision went over my
head. We're bringing in new talent from Memphis."

"Please, George, you're not even going to give me a chance?
I'll be good — great — with someone else."

"There'll be a fair severance." George was not deterred. "But
they want you to clean out your desk tonight."

"You're kidding, just like that? I'm not going on the air
tonight? You're the goddamn producer and I'm just the scapegoat
so you can save your own ass on the ratings. I can't believe you're
doing this."

Redness crept up George's neck. "I really am sorry, Steve. Will
you need any help here?"

With a sweep of his arm, Steve sent the contents of his desk
onto the floor.

Steve spent an hour roaming the Tampa streets. It was hot and hu-
mid and he had nowhere to go. An hour ago, he was a "star" in the
Tampa area and now he was nothing. Had George found out about
Kim and him? That ratings crap was bullshit. Was it Kim? Or was it
Laura who told him? Could either of them be that vindictive? But
Kim would have been too scared that her boyfriend would find out.
So it must have been Laura.

Steve wandered into the Bayside Saloon and settled at the bar
next to a graying man in a faded blue suit. He ordered a Scotch,
neat. He knocked back the drink and indicated to the bartender to
bring another.

"Hey, can't be all that bad," the stranger said. "Let me buy
you another and I'll have one myself."

Steve grunted. The two men drank in brooding silence until Steve ordered his fourth Scotch.

His neighbor at the bar extended a look of condolence. "Female problem?"

"You can say that again," Steve said slowly. "And worse."

The man scrutinized him. "Hey, aren't you the TV news guy? You're the one on those billboards. Knew I recognized your voice."

"Yeah, that was me. Till I got canned."

The man nodded slowly. "Sucks, my friend, which I know 'cause it happened to me. Name's Roger Crossman, was a lawyer right here in Tampa. Know what it's like to get the boot."

"Maybe I'll sue the bastards."

"Might work," Roger commiserated. "Wrongful dismissal."

"It's really all her fault. Laura, my wife. Took my kids. It's her fault I lost my job."

"You still married to her, buddy?"

"Damn right. Temporary glitch is all. Not only was I stupid enough to bring another woman back to my house, I was stupid enough to get caught."

"Oh man, I've heard that before. So she hitting you up for child support?"

"Hell no. She makes the bucks. Big-shot surgeon."

"Lemme give you some advice. I had it all, the job, the wife, the kids. Fuckin' pressure of it all landed me in some a those pricey dry-out spots, more like clubs. Didn't do shit." He shook his head. "Wife married a local judge. Turned my kids against me. Haven't heard shit from them in five years."

"Sorry, pal," said Steve, feeling sorry for the poor drunk, but not in any way relating to him.

"So lemme tell you what's gonna happen, buddy. The wife, she'll divorce you. Forget her money, she'll go for custody and child support. You'll be paying plenty for a long time."

Steve slammed his drink on the bar. "I can see her doing that just to spite me."

"And she'll turn your own kids against you," Roger slurred.

"Wife's got the kids and soon they don't want no part of their old man. Trust me. Any on'a my kids gave a damn about me, I wouldn't be sittin' here now."

Steve was silent. He'd talk to Laura tomorrow. Tell her he was fired. For sure, he'd head back home. Concentrate on getting a new job. Forget this separation stuff. Whatever this guy was blabbering didn't apply to him. But as Steve finished his drink, he replayed Crossman's words over and over: "Got a joint bank account? Empty it. Got valuables? Take 'em. Don't end up like me."

On Saturday morning Steve was late picking up the kids. He'd spent most of Friday at the Bayside Saloon again, deep in conversation with Roger Crossman. Though he'd promised to take the kids to Busch Gardens, a raging headache and queasy stomach made him irritable and impatient. All day the kids pestered him to go on roller coasters and water slides, and when he refused, they sulked. Patrick had clung to him constantly, but Mike and Kevin tended to wander off like maybe they distrusted him. The girls bothered him more than they normally did. Nicole was her usual outspoken self while Natalie mostly whined.

By late afternoon Steve felt better. He wanted to stay at the amusement park for dinner, but the kids just wanted to go to home and watch TV. Steve couldn't help but dwell on Crossman's warning. Maybe it was happening already. When he took the kids home he'd have a talk with Laura. She'd seemed a little more sympathetic this morning when he told her about losing his job. Of course, she acted like it was none of her doing. But it had to have been her, and now that she'd assuaged her jealous pride, maybe she'd just get over this.

As soon as Steve pulled into the driveway on Davis Boulevard Saturday evening, he knew it was bad timing. "Shit," he mumbled as he carried the twins' duffel bag past the familiar car parked in front of him.

"What'd you say, Dad?" Kevin piped.

"Nothing."

"Grandma and Grandpa are here," called Natalie excitedly as she ran ahead.

"Laura, we have to talk," Steve said as soon as there was a moment of privacy. The kids had charged into the house amid hugs and kisses and now crowded around their grandparents.

"Not now. My parents will be leaving soon, and then I need to spend time with the kids before they go to bed."

"You'll have all week with the kids. Please, this is important."

Laura sighed. "Okay. For a few minutes."

Laura went over to her mother and whispered in her ear. Peg Whelan looked much younger than fifty-nine. She was trim and shapely with strawberry blonde hair naturally highlighted by the sun. Turning toward Steve, she nodded, but Steve saw the start of a frown in place of her usual sunny smile.

"Where you going, honey?" asked Carl Whelan as he juggled Natalie and Patrick on his lap. He was a tall man, distinguished looking at sixty-five with gray hair just starting to recede. Gentle by nature, he had always been supportive of Steve, but now he glanced coldly at his son-in-law.

"We're going out for just a few minutes," Laura said, approaching the front door.

Neither of her parents had yet spoken to Steve. The look of disapproval in Peg Whelan's eyes had a chilling effect making him feel deep remorse. The Whelans had always treated him like a son, and the truth was that Steve was much closer to them than to his own family — his dad — back in Traverse City, Michigan.

Laura was the oldest of the three Whelan siblings and the only one living in Florida, just an hour and a half away from her parents' home in Sarasota. Janet, two years younger, lived with her professor husband in Paris, and the Whelans saw her only one week a year, in Paris or Sarasota. So far, they were childless and the whole family knew that Janet was becoming increasingly desperate to have a baby. Ted, the youngest, now thirty-one, was a Jesuit missionary priest stationed in Uganda. Although so proud of him, they also worried about him as Idi Amin's dictatorship in Africa turned more and more ruthless.

Both Steve and Laura's dad were die-hard Detroit Tigers baseball fans — had been all their lives — and that shared passion gave Steve a sense of belonging in the Whelan family. Not that they got to see much of the Tigers anymore, but whenever possible Steve and Carl would take the kids to Bradendon for spring training. Suddenly, Steve realized if he lost Laura, he'd lose the Whelans too.

"Looking forward to seeing Billington play soon," he said to his father-in-law, but Carl acknowledged Steve's awareness of the baseball player's move from Cincinnati to Detroit with only a shrug.

"Let's take a ride over to the park where we can talk," Steve said to Laura as they stepped outside.

"All the way to the park?"

"It's just a couple minutes away, c'mon." He took her arm and led her to the Ford Fairlane. To his relief, she stepped in when he opened the door. "We'll get some ice cream."

As he parked under the shade of an old willow at the park, Laura broke the awkward silence that had filled the car. "So did you go to Busch Gardens?"

"Yeah, but the kids didn't have a great time. Not like when we've been there before. I've been thinking a lot and really —" he reached over and touched her knee, "we owe it to them to stay together."

"The kids'll be fine," Laura answered, removing his hand. "But what are you going to do about getting a job?"

Steve stared openly at his wife. "You know, I guess I can even understand why you did it. You had a good reason to be totally pissed at me for what I did."

Laura stared back. "Did what?"

"Come on, I know you told George." Steve had apologized for doing it with Kim, and now he expected an apology from Laura for getting him canned. "He sort of let it slip."

She frowned. "I can't believe you just said that. I haven't spoken to him in months. And I can't believe you'd make up a lie like that."

"Look, have it your way. I'm fired, okay? I need to come back home and start looking for a job."

"My God, Steve, you think this is some kind of game? This is our life. I agree you'll have to find a job, but I've decided to talk to a lawyer about a permanent separation and divorce. You'll get visitation rights for the kids. I'm not even asking for child support."

"Divorce? Laura, c'mon, it doesn't need to be this way."

"Yes it does. Now that I've had a couple of weeks to think about it, I realize that we've been living two separate lives for I don't know how long. You at the station. Me at the hospital. We've been avoiding each other for years. We never make love. Sex, maybe, but love, no. The only thing we have in common is the kids, and I know I can be a better mother if I'm on my own. Besides the way you feel about the twins — Anyway, it's fine with me to keep alternating weekends, but we'll have to go to court and get the whole thing finalized."

Steve's face tightened. "Sounds like you've got everything figured out. Except for me. What about me?"

"Please stop."

"Laura," Steve went on, "we've been married for fifteen years. We have five kids who need two parents. I'm living in a dump, and I have no job."

Laura sighed. "Look, we're not getting anywhere with this. Just take me home."

"C'mon, we need to talk about this. Let's take a walk, get an ice cream."

"I don't want any ice cream. If you won't take me back, I'll walk."

Steve's face clouded as he turned the ignition key. "Promise me one thing. No more talk about a lawyer. The least you can do is give me some time to find a job. Cut me a little slack here."

"No," she said through clenched teeth. "I need to move forward with my life now."

"Laura, please. Don't back me into a corner."

CHAPTER SIX

Alone in the small apartment all week long, he'd had plenty of time to think. For the first time in his life, Steve had had to do his own household chores and the place was a mess. Dirty dishes scattered about, the same unwashed sheets on the bed. There was a mildew smell in the closet and that circle of scum building in the bathroom sink. After lying around watching mindless TV all day, each night he'd gone back to the Bayside Saloon.

Midweek, he'd stopped by the newsroom to pick up his belongings. That prick George had been "in a meeting," and "couldn't be disturbed." Kim was packing up her side of the office, too busy with her plans to move to Atlanta that weekend to even have lunch. What a bitch she'd turned out to be. Last night Steve had driven by her place thinking that maybe he could get her to change her mind. Kim hadn't even been home. So where was she? With that "dangerous" boyfriend of hers? The one he was supposed to be so scared of? Well, he wasn't scared. Pissed, yes, but not scared.

That morning, Steve had stopped at the Barnett Bank. No questions asked, he had withdrawn all but $942 from his and Laura's joint savings account — $51,942. Guess she hadn't gotten a lawyer yet. He took the money as cash in hundred dollar bills, placing most of it in a safe deposit box under his name only. Steve and Laura had been one of those rare, lucky couples who never argued over money. They spent what they needed to maintain the household, a little extra for Steve's "television" clothes, and they rarely entertained. Although Laura's income exceeded Steve's, they both contributed to their combined savings and checking account and wrote checks as needed against the healthy balance.

Laura picked up the phone on the first ring when Steve called the following Friday night. "I'm coming for the kids tomorrow at eight," he announced, not even giving her a chance to say "hello."

"No, tomorrow's not your day."

It always annoyed Steve when Laura used that brazen tone of voice. "You had them last Saturday. Besides, we're going to the beach tomorrow for Dad's birthday."

"They see plenty of your family. I've made plans. It's only fair. You have them all week."

"You know our agreement. Alternate Saturdays and Sundays every other weekend. Right?'

"No, not 'right'. 'Our agreement' was your decision. Who are you to make 'our' decisions?"

"Please, Steve, don't give me a hard time. You know it's fair."

"Not seeing my kids is fair?" Steve knew his voice was rising, but where did she get off sounding so goddamned sanctimonious. He was standing at the kitchen counter and he felt like slamming his fist, but the place was so cluttered with dirty glassware he'd have sliced his hand. So he raked one hand through his hair while gripping the phone with his other. "What I know is that they want to see me more."

"Of course they want to see you."

Laura was trying the "let's everybody be reasonable" move now. She was a pro at that one, trying to make him out to be a fool who couldn't do shit.

"We have to give them some sense of structure, some kind of reliable schedule."

Steve couldn't help grimace at the thought of being excluded by his in-laws. He'd always had a good time with the Whelens. The old man was a sports fan, and Laura's mom had offered him unconditional love. Something his own mother never had. "Okay, you want 'structure'? So let's give them structure. Let's all go down to Sarasota together — as a family."

"That won't work. We all have to adjust to us living separately."

He didn't have to take this kind of shit. "If you won't agree to have the kids ready, you give me no choice. I'll just call the boys separately. They'll come with me." Steve knew they would. They loved to fish off the bridges. Maybe he'd even rent a boat. "If you want to take the girls to your mother's, I don't care."

"Just this once."

Steve thought he was hearing things. Laura? Backing down?

"I'll switch my on-call schedule. And if you take the boys, you take the girls. They'd be heartbroken if they thought you didn't care. Aren't they going through enough already?"

"Aren't we all?" Steve countered, still congratulating himself on his victory. "You're the one who kicked me out. It's still not too late to do what's right."

"I am doing what's right. I have an appointment with a lawyer next week."

"No lawyer, Laura. I mean it." Steve could feel hot anger implode in his chest. How dare she threaten him? "We don't need a lawyer."

"I think we do. At least I do."

Steve looked around at the clutter, the overflowing trash can, the dirty dishes piled in the sink. Hell, he'd married Laura when he was only twenty-one. Before that he'd lived at home. How could he be expected to live by himself? Maybe for a few days, but forever? No, a divorce sounded so final. A divorce was out of the question. The best way to handle Laura was through the kids. She'd never give up those kids, even for an overnight. And they wouldn't give up him. That he knew, especially little Patrick. The kid was only eight years old and already he was complaining about Laura's treatment.

"And another thing," Steve said to move the conversation to territory he could manipulate. "You gotta stop being so strict with

Patrick. He said you wouldn't let him watch *Starsky and Hutch* last week."

Laura sighed. "Let's not start using the kids as pawns, okay? It'll only make things worse."

"Fine for you to say. You're the one making things worse." Steve slammed down the phone.

Rolling over to turn off Tammy Wynette's "Stand by Your Man" piping through the clock radio at seven the next morning, Laura was surprised to find herself alone in bed. Since Steve had left, she had usually awakened to find that Natalie or Patrick or both had crept in beside her. Pleased that the kids must be doing better, she lingered under the covers until seven forty-five before heading to Mike and Kevin's room. The kids would need a decent breakfast before Steve picked them up. Once she woke them all, she'd make waffles, a favorite weekend treat. The door to the boys' bedroom was open, the two twin beds empty and unmade. She sighed, knowing as usual that she'd have to send them back up to make their beds. Why even try to make them make their room look neat? She wondered what had gotten them up so early; on weekends those two never got up before nine.

Laura crossed the hall to the girls' frilly pink room. Pushing aside the pile of stuffed animals they so loved, she found both canopied beds empty. A few pieces of clothing were scattered about and she stopped to pick them up. It was odd; the girls usually made their beds first thing. Patrick's small cubbyhole room, decorated with Miami Dolphins paraphernalia, was also empty. That was strange. Funny, she couldn't hear the television on downstairs.

"Where is everyone?" she called. But there was not a trace of sound. She called out again, louder. No response.

Had Steve said he was picking them up before eight? She remembered last night's conversation, decidedly unpleasant, but Steve had specified eight o'clock. And what would they do so early anyway? Laura was already anticipating a tough day at the hospital. She'd called a colleague last night for a last minute switch of

schedules and learned she'd be covering for four staff surgeons today on top of other duties. As she wandered downstairs, Laura reviewed her day: rounds on at least thirty post-op patients, admitting
any surgical cases that came in through the ER, supervising all
emergency operations. And, she recalled, she'd agreed to meet with
that attorney, Sam somebody, at Roxanne's insistence, but against
her own better judgment.

Laura walked through every room downstairs. No sign of
breakfast in the kitchen, no blaring television, no scattered toys.
She headed out the front door, scanning up and down the street for
any sign of her children or for anything unusual. She did note that
the front door was unlocked. Certainly she'd locked it last night,
but, of course, Steve had a key.

"Call a locksmith," she mumbled to herself.

She went back in and checked the back door, which was still
locked. Dressed only in her faded blue dressing gown, still wearing
her glasses, she walked across the yard and headed toward Marcy's
apartment over the garage.

"Good morning," Marcy called out over the flower boxes she
kept under each window. She was an early riser and had already returned from 7:00 a.m. Mass. "Thought you'd be out of here already
you've got such a full day."

"Well, I . . ." Laura faltered. "I was looking for the kids."

"You're a few hours late. Guess you didn't wake up when
Steve came?"

"What time did he pick them up?"

"Around five thirty. In a station wagon. They all left with their
little tote bags."

"They're not staying overnight." Laura felt a prick of panic as
her heart picked up speed. *A station wagon? Could it belong to the guy
who's apartment Steve is staying in?*

Marcy shrugged. "Maybe he's taking the kids swimming or
something."

"Maybe. Steve said he had plans, but I didn't ask him what
they were. Tell you what, I'll call you if I'm not going to be home

by seven. Or you page me if the kids come back before then, and I'll see if I can get home earlier, okay?"

Though Marcy nodded in agreement, Laura worried all day. Something was not right.

By noon, Laura had made post-op rounds with the residents and med students. She felt nauseated and hadn't had a thing to eat — refusing even a Snickers bar, her favorite. Scattered throughout the morning there'd been three surgical admissions from the ER, but only one requiring immediate intervention, an appendectomy in a healthy young man, which she supervised. Counting her own patients and those of her four colleagues, she had five in the ICU to watch over. One — not hers — had gone into kidney failure following the repair of a dissecting aortic aneurysm that had required all day heroics just to keep him alive on a ventilator. The others were in critical condition following major surgery, but when all was said and done, they were doing well.

At four o'clock she headed reluctantly to the small alcove next to the chapel for the meeting with Mr. Sanders. Roxanne was already there sitting next to the tall, gangly attorney. Unexpectedly, Louis Ruiz, in a wheelchair, was seated on her other side. Both legs, still in casts, were elevated and protruding forward. Wearing a teal and black striped silk bathrobe with a gold sash, his jet black hair was combed neatly over his ears, his sad eyes seeming brighter. Laura looked from him to Roxanne as she hesitated at the threshold of the room and noted the tasteful décor in comforting muted patterns of beige and maroon. She made a mental note to use this room on those occasions when she had to deliver painful news. Focusing on the situation at hand, she felt irritated. Roxanne should have told her that Mr. Ruiz would be here too.

"Dr. Nelson," Roxanne began. "You remember Louis Ruiz?"

"Of course," said Laura. "I hope your recovery is going well."

"Thank you, doctor, it is. Allow me to apologize for being so rude the last time we met."

"Please," Laura said quickly, "I understand."

"And this is Mr. Sanders," Roxanne went on. "I know you've exchanged a few words, but let me introduce you properly."

"It's Sam, Dr. Nelson." The attorney rose and held out his hand to Laura. He held her gaze without a waver. "Appreciate your meeting with us. We know how busy you are."

"Of course. I should warn you that I am on call." She took a seat in the chair nearest the door and placed her beeper on her lap.

"Then I'll save time and be perfectly blunt," Sam Sanders began. "Mr. Ruiz was the victim of a horrendous accident. He lost his wife and two daughters. He's left with three sons to bring up on his own and two are still in this hospital. His medical insurance is inadequate. The driver who hit him was legally intoxicated. He's had prior DUIs. He'll go to jail, but that won't help Mr. Ruiz. The guy has no insurance and has no assets to attach. The only way we can help Mr. Ruiz cope is by suing this hospital for negligence in treating his oldest daughter, Wendy."

Laura stiffened. She could still see the small form, could hear the clink as her forceps hit the shard of glass in the aorta so near to the heart. She could hear the dying blip of the cardiac monitor as they lost Wendy. The same frustration engulfed her as it had that night. The ER should have called her in earlier. The excuse of the fracture in the cervical spine and the chaos in the ER that night was just that, an excuse. There had been too much blood in those chest tubes, and she'd told that doctor from the ER that. When Laura had looked at the electrocardiograms afterwards, there'd been evident signs of cardiac tamponade, signs that should have triggered immediate chest surgery.

"The point is, Dr. Nelson, we know what you told the ER resident about the delay in calling you in for surgery that night."

"Still, I'm not certain —" Laura couldn't continue. How would she feel if the medical system had failed her ten-year-old daughters? She looked directly at Louis Ruiz and couldn't ignore the tears he was attempting to hide. She watched Roxanne reach over and gently caress his hand. Taking a breath, she turned to Sam Sanders.

"Listen, I wasn't in the ER that night, and I will stand by my statement that I should've been called in for Wendy earlier. I'm not certain whether that would have made a difference. There was a hole in her aorta —" She forced herself to keep looking at the attorney, not at Mr. Ruiz, "—she had a broken neck, and no matter what, she would have been paraplegic had she lived."

"But she might now be alive," Sam quickly concluded. Turning to his client, who was now weeping openly, he added, "I think that's enough."

Exhausted by six thirty, Laura called Marcy for the second time from a corner in the hospital records room. Because the kids weren't home yet, she decided to stay to sign discharge notes and deal with the endless paperwork that plagues all physicians. She had two remaining charts in front of her.

"Still quiet here," Marcy said, "too quiet. Why don't you just stay and finish what you're doing?"

"Okay. But call me the minute they get home, okay? And one more favor. If Steve brings them home before I get there, would you mind going over so he can leave before I get home? I really don't feel like fighting with him tonight. I have all day with the kids tomorrow. I just want to relax with them, take them to the beach on Anna Maria Island with my parents. Anyway, I'll only be here another forty-five minutes or so."

Home long before midnight, Laura's concern escalated from annoyance to a mix of panic and rage as the night wore on. She called Steve's number three times, each time reaching the answering machine Steve still had, compliments of Channel Eight so that he wouldn't miss any news-related calls. The first message she left on his machine was polite; the second, irate; the third, anxious.

She lay fitfully on the living room sofa. The family room furniture was a lot more comfortable, but after what Steve and Kim had done there, she just couldn't relax in the room. She couldn't focus on the old Elvis movie on the TV either — *Viva Las Vegas*. She clicked off the TV set. She tried to read the new novel her mother had left for her, *The Thorn Birds*, the kind of sweeping saga that usually stole her attention completely, but she couldn't concentrate. She could not eat; had not eaten all day. Anger grew as she realized that Steve had simply defied her by keeping the kids overnight in his small apartment. Marcy said they left with bags, right? They must be sleeping on the floor. You'd think he would have at least called. She could not wait to see that lawyer next week; things with Steve were getting out of control. Eventually she went into the kitchen and put the kettle on for tea. Her stomach growled and she rummaged through the refrigerator for that last slice of cherry cheesecake. But what if they'd had some kind of horrible accident — like the Ruiz family? While the water heated, she paced, saying one Hail Mary after another. One more look up and down the street, then she settled on the sofa to wait and, finally, she dozed.

Waking at dawn, still slumped over the arm of the sofa, Laura felt groggy and disoriented. As she massaged a vague pain on the left side of her neck, she noticed that the hall light was still on. Could Steve have dropped off the kids while she slept? Rushing upstairs with false hope, she faced the empty bedrooms. Damn Steve. Damn him.

She picked up the phone in the hallway, dialed Steve's number and got the same recording. She left a fourth message: "Get the kids home now. I'm taking them to Mass at Sacred Heart before we leave for Mom and Dad's."

When the phone rang at nine, Laura leapt to answer it. It was only Marcy, calling to say that she was going to visit her sister-in-law in St. Petersburg and would Laura be okay. Laura tried to sound reassuring.

At noon, Laura called Steve's apartment again — a furnished one bedroom in the lower floor of a house on Oregon, between Horatio and DeLeon in Tampa's Old Hyde Park section. Again, no answer, and this time she left no message. She then called her mother and postponed the day's trip to Sarasota, asking her to make apologies to her dad. They'd planned a beach picnic to celebrate his sixty-sixth birthday.

The Whalens were a close-knit family. After finishing med school in Detroit, Laura had chosen Tampa for her internship and residency so she could be close to her mom and dad. With her marriage breaking up, she now needed their reassurance, to hear from them that she'd be okay. That she wasn't a failure. That somehow this wasn't all her fault. That she was doing the right thing. If only Janet, her sister, could be there too. Janet was two years younger than Laura and as kids they'd been inseparable. Even through med school with Laura living so far away in Detroit, they'd remained close, but since Jan married a French professor five years ago and moved to Paris, they'd drifted apart. Laura hadn't seen Jan for two years, and she hesitated to burden her with her problems.

Then there was Ted, her younger brother. Her problems, Laura was sure, paled against those he experienced in the poor, remote village in Uganda where he'd been stationed — there was a cholera epidemic there. If Ted were here, would he disapprove of her walking out on a marriage? She'd have to try to explain what happened between her and Steve and hope that he'd understand. As a Catholic priest, he'd have to support the sanctity of the marriage vows, but as her kid brother, he'd always trusted her. Deep down, she knew he'd take her side. If only he were here, he'd be such a positive influence on the boys, especially now. The girls needed some TLC too, but they'd always been closer to her than to Steve.

Lately Laura spent more and more time thinking about the twins. Steve had a problem with them and it was getting worse. She'd never faced it head-on. Always making excuses, hoping that as the girls grew older the shadows of the past would recede, but the truth was that Steve was finding it more and more difficult to mask his ambivalence toward the little girls. An ambivalence that to an outsider may appear barely perceptible. Everyone always declared that the Nelson twins were images of their mother with their blonde, wavy hair worn shoulder length and faces the same heart shape as Laura's. Everyone also claimed that they couldn't tell the girls apart, and wherever they went Natalie and Nicole attracted attention. When they were toddlers Laura had started to part their hair on opposite sides as a helpful clue to babysitters, but whoever got to know the Nelson twins quickly appreciated that their personalities differentiated them. Natalie, sweet and compliant. Nicole, aggressive, the ringleader. Laura usually dressed them identically, which they'd always loved. Hardly a day went by that a stranger wouldn't stop them on the street just to gaze in fascination or say a few admiring words.

Laura realized that most men would dote on such charming young daughters, but Steve remained aloof and only she and Steve's father knew why. Steve, too, had been an identical twin and his daughters were a constant reminder of a horrible childhood scar. At the age of ten — the girls' age — Steve had uncharacteristically shoved his brother, Philip, during a fight in their tree house.

Philip had tumbled to the ground, his neck snapping on impact, dying instantly. For months Steve's mother had been hospitalized with major depression, never resuming a nurturing relationship with Steve, her remaining only child. Her life became recurrent panic attacks, leaving her socially debilitated. It did not matter that the tragedy had been an accident.

Laura and Steve had been married almost five years before she learned the truth. After this revelation, which came not from Steve but from his Aunt Hazel, Steve refused to discuss the accident. Since the birth of Natalie and Nicole, Laura had repeatedly tried to get Steve to confront the impact of the accident on his feelings toward his daughters, but to no avail. Even after his mother died when the girls were five, Steve would not face it. If only he'd gotten psychological help, things would be so different. Not that Laura had that much confidence in therapists; she'd seen her share of incompetents; but Steve's mind was locked in concrete and there was no key.

As these thoughts flooded her mind, Laura wandered through

the house, straining to hear a car pull up in the driveway. She tried calling Steve's apartment several times, but there was no answer, just the answering machine. Where could they be? How horrible, how unforgivable, not to call. Certainly there could be nothing wrong or she would have heard. Repeatedly, Laura tried to tackle the stack of accumulating medical journals on her desk, but she couldn't focus. Where could they be? Where could they possibly be?

CHAPTER SEVEN

Frank Santiago adjusted the incline of the passenger seat to accommodate his lanky frame. "So, Ritchie, what do you tell your kids when they ask you what kind of business you're in?"

Ritchie Noval drove the forest green Lincoln Town Car across Alligator Alley heading for Tampa. They'd just come from a meeting with the big boss, Carlos Tosca, in Miami. Despite the deeply tinted windows, both wore dark wraparound glasses. Ritchie was in his early thirties, a clean-cut Hispanic with massive shoulders, a cherubic face, and jet black hair worn in a neat crew cut. In preparation for the job ahead, he wore dark blue khakis, a short sleeve Polo shirt also in dark blue, and black Rockports.

Frank, ten years his senior, looked ready for Madison Avenue in a charcoal gray Armani suit — the jacket precisely folded atop the backseat — a baby blue shirt stiffly starched, a silk patterned tie of cobalt blues, and gleaming Bruno Magli dress shoes. His coal black hair worn slicked back off his forehead and the debonair style aptly camouflaged the taut, tough muscles that lay underneath the expensive veneer.

"They're too young. Haven't asked yet," said Ritchie with a grin. "Whaddaya think I'm gonna say? Your old man's a soldier in the Mafia?"

"'Organization,' got a classier ring to it," Frank stated. "Can't wait for the day I have boys big enough to follow in the old man's footsteps."

"So you're plannin' your own family, eh, boss?"

"Sons, to take over the business some day."

"Right. I got two and one little girl."

"Girls, you gotta take care of 'em. Four boys, that's what I want. The more the better. I got three sisters I took care of till they finally landed their hombres. Shit, thought it would take forever. Boys, they take care of themselves. Once they know what they're doin', that is."

"I can see it," Ritchie nodded. "You're just the guy to show 'em, Frankie."

"Damn straight."

"That mean you're gettin' married soon or what?"

"Me and Kimmie." He paused. "Soon, real soon."

Ritchie laughed. "She's one sweet piece."

"Yeah, that's right," Frank grumbled, "and you keep your fuckin' eyes to yourself. Noticed you couldn't keep 'em off those twins last night."

"Hey, we're in Miami, there's not one but two sets of amazing knockers for the taking. Whaddaya expect me to do?" Ritchie accelerated to pass a lumbering eighteen-wheeler.

"Business comes first, that's all."

"Frankie, man, I am all business." He stifled a yawn. "So let's talk business. Like, whaddabout your clothes?"

"What about my clothes?" Frank asked, reaching down to his trousers to pick off a trace of lint.

"Those pretty shoes of yours are goin' to get all fucked up on this job. And the million dollar suit ain't gonna look too classy splashed with blood and who knows what."

"Nice to know you're so worried about my threads. I got coveralls in the trunk, we'll stop at Kimmie's and I'll change." Frank checked his Patek Phillippe. "It's four now and we're only fifty miles from Temple Terrace. Plenty of time to make it to the docks by six fifteen."

"Carlos ain't gonna like it," Ritchie said. "He said to change cars once we got to Tampa and don' let nobody see us."

"Carlos don't need to know," Frank said with finality.

"I hear that, boss. Besides, the point is the fucking Mexicans, right? We're not taking no shit from those faggots. Show them who's who, them movin' in on us. We own South Florida. Once we get our hands on that blow, Tampa'll be ripe for months."

Frank smiled. "That's the idea. Now lay it out for me again."

"Just like we said. We take 'em out on the narrow strip. I got all the stuff in the van. Wait till you see the fake old man, looks fuckin' real. He's in these rags, even got a gray-haired ponytail! Gonna look like the old *mierda* passed out pushin' his fuckin' shopping cart across the road, bags and shit falling out. Driver's gonna have to slow down no matter what, gotta figure out whether to run over the old *mierda* or go around him. Not a good choice because the road's so skinny and rutted. We'll have 'em in our crosshairs."

"Nice," said Frank as he fingered the nine millimeter Glock he'd removed from its holster. "You gotta respect how Carlos gets the inside information on the shipments, right down to the map the faggots are usin' to get off Hooker's Point. If they got only one fool ridin' shotgun, shouldn't need more than this, but I also got my throwaway." He reached down and patted the lump on his ankle.

Carlos Tosca, underboss for organized crime in South Florida, had received word that a shipment of high-grade cocaine was due into Tampa Harbor lined up for some Mexicans. That wasn't supposed to happen since the "big boss" had brokered deals with Latin drug groups: Costa Rica, Peru, Ecuador, Puerto Rico, and Mexico, to control cocaine coming into the country. But now, just like the Asians, the Mexicans and South and Central Americans were trying to cut them out and go it alone. "Take care of it," he told Frank. "Fuckin' ingrates. Take 'em out. That'll teach 'em to fuck with Carlos Tosca."

"Me and Ritchie'll handle it, boss. No problemo."

Frank then charged Ritchie Noval, his second in command, to work out the details to surprise the Mexicans just after they'd loaded the packages and as they headed off Hooker's Point away from the Port of Tampa. Nobody else was in on the job — just the two of them. They'd stash the stuff, dispose of any bodies, then disappear from the city for a couple of weeks.

Frank could have assigned the job to his underlings, but he'd come up through the system and liked getting back to basics. Besides, he'd just been in Miami with Tosca for three weeks and was anxious to get back to Tampa. He'd missed Kim Connor. Not that there weren't plenty of women in the Miami clubs, but just thinking of her gave him a hard-on. Sure, she was a beauty, but so were dozens of others. She just made him feel so goddamned good. He knew that she used to be a drug addict and he admired how she stayed off the dope and went easy on the booze. He'd never known a woman like that, so classy, smart, sexy. Truth was, maybe she scared him a little. And Frank's reaction to that was — and always had been — bad. With Kim, he kept telling himself, he had to keep himself in control. Maybe he could slap his other women around, but not Kim. He knew it as soon as he'd hit her.

She'd avoided him the following day, disappearing that night with some story about how she lost her keys. He wanted to believe her, but what about that Nelson prick? The kid at the station saw them leave together, but so what. She came back to the station after she figured out she lost her keys, that's what happened. Then Frank had to leave for Miami.

Kimmie. She was different, so different that he'd even discussed some of his plans with her. And, yeah, it was time to take a wife and have sons to take over the business when he got old. Kim Santiago. He could see it clearly — Kimmie and a bunch of little Frankies and Kimmies.

Of course, she'd have to quit her television job. And change her mind about having kids.

Kim lived in a modest two-story townhouse in Temple Terrace, on the outskirts of Tampa. All the houses looked alike — creamy stucco with green shutters and red tile roofs – but they were all nicely maintained and the neighborhood looked safe and pleasant.

"Here we are, boss," Ritchie poked Frank, disturbing his reverie. "Ain't that where she lives?"

Frank scowled. "Yeah, that's it. Where the fuck is her car? Just keep driving till you find a pay phone."

"Right now? I mean, we got business —"

"Right now means right now. Quit your bitchin', I'm just gonna leave a message on her fuckin' answering machine."

After he'd left a phone message, Frank and Ritchie drove on according to plan and exchanged the Lincoln for a white unmarked van at the designated warehouse. There, Frank carefully removed his clothes and shoes, donned a pair of coveralls and sneakers, and they headed down to the Port of Tampa on Hillsborough Bay. Since it was a Sunday and the location remote, they would make the hit shortly after the blow had been unloaded from the ship into the panel truck. There'd be the driver and one, or maybe two, security guys. Using the dummy to confuse the driver, they'd simply spray them to pieces. Ritchie would drive the truck to a warehouse nearby, and then they'd both disappear.

"Let's do it, Ritchie." Frank Santiago's voice sounded like steel. "There's the fuckin' panel truck, just like Carlos said. Fuck, they won't even know what hit 'em."

Ritchie grunted. Each man, one on each side, stood under cover of the thick palmettos that encroached upon the deserted road at its narrowest point.

The gray panel truck slowed to a stop in front of an overturned grocery cart blocking its way. An old man in ragged clothes lay sprawled on his side next to the cart — only the form was a mannequin. Strewn around him were half-open plastic garbage bags that had presumably tumbled out of the cart. As the bewildered driver focused on the body in the road, Frank stepped forward, his eyes locked on the man in the passenger seat who warily swung his gun in an arc around the perimeter of the cab. Glock in hand, equipped with silencer, Frank fired point black at the swarthy passenger's head. There was a pop, and the man's head exploded into pieces. On the driver's side, Ritchie had already leapt onto the road before firing at the driver. Then the two men jumped into the truck just long enough to assure themselves that there was no one in the back with the blow. Frank shoved the dead passenger to the floor, went back out, and hastily hauled the dummy over to the truck and tossed it inside while Ritchie pushed the dead driver to the side, engaged the gears, and pulled out. By that time Frank had jumped back out of the truck.

No way should Frank stop before returning the van to the warehouse, but he was filled with a nasty feeling about Kim — a nagging, sick premonition that he couldn't shake. Why wasn't her yellow Firebird parked out front of her place like it always was? Had she come back and picked up his message that he was going to come by just for a few seconds for a quick kiss? Then he clenched the wheel so tightly that his knuckles turned white. What if the little bitch thought she could walk out on him? If she ever tried that, what choice would he have?

Frankie felt the rage build in that familiar way and he shook his head from side to side. Part of him wanted to beat the shit out of her. The other part warned him not to lay a hand on her. With an up-and-down nod of his head, he made up his mind. No matter what, he'd promise her everything. Hell, they could get married right away. They'd leave right away, go to a safe place while things at the Port of Tampa cooled down. Yes, he nodded his head more vigorously now. Vegas would be perfect.

When Frank pulled up to Kim's place, heart beating excitedly with this new plan, he felt his body lurch forward in the seat. He arrived just in time to see Kim climb into her Firebird and drive away. He followed.

CHAPTER EIGHT

By six o'clock Sunday, Laura's frustration was uncontained. The phone hadn't rung all afternoon. Even though she was not on call, someone from the hospital or some patient's relative usually got through the switchboard, something that would distract her from her missing children and defiant husband, but nothing.

After waking on the sofa that morning, Laura had changed into a pair of faded cutoffs and her favorite, tattered "Michigan" T-shirt. She'd splashed cold water on her face, but hadn't wanted to chance missing a call by taking a shower. All day she'd done nothing but pace back and forth from the kitchen door to the front door, climb the stairs to again and again check the empty rooms, and open and shut the refrigerator, taking nothing out. Accelerating fear competed with blinding rage as Laura paced, unable to sit, unable to think. Could they have had a horrible accident? No, of course not. Somebody would have notified her. Steve was doing this just to aggravate her, the selfish bastard. Had they really come to this? How hopeless, draining, depressing.

She called his apartment again. That stupid answering machine. Another hour. She looked up at the clock on the kitchen wall over the refrigerator. She went back to her desk. Sat down. Got up. She went back upstairs and made her rounds of the bedrooms once again, stopping to straighten Mike and Kevin's room. She thought about fixing something to eat, but decided on donuts instead. Three chocolate donuts that she didn't even taste.

At seven with fumbling fingers, Laura flipped through the

Tampa phone book's white pages searching for Kim, or Kimberly, Connor. No such listing. She called information. Learning that Kim had an unlisted number, Laura pushed herself to call George Granger. She desperately needed to find her kids.

"Hello, George," she said, trying to sound calm when he picked up on the first ring. "It's Laura Nelson. How are you?"

"Well, what a surprise, Laura. I'm fine."

"And Melanie?"

"Oh, she's great. She was able to catch up and finish fourth grade with her class. You'd never know she'd been that close to — well, Laura, we owe you everything."

Laura knew quite well that Melanie had fully recovered. She was on the same Little League team as her own girls. "She's such a lovely child, George."

"Thank you. You know, I wanted to talk to you about Steve. I knew he'd take it hard, and I told him I'd try to help any way I could. I hope you understand that with Kim moving to Atlanta, we really couldn't keep him on as anchor. The decision was out of my hands."

"You did what you had to do, George. I understand. He'll just have to pull himself together and find another job."

Laura didn't know whether George was aware of their separation or about the night with Kim Connor. She'd called him impulsively, not knowing how she'd approach him to get Kim's number. Her stomach began to hurt.

"Whatever I can do, Laura. Just let me know."

"Actually, George, I do need a favor. Steve asked me to call Kim and ask her to drop off some photographic equipment she'd borrowed." Laura felt her body stiffen, a reaction to the blatant lie. "He's away for the weekend and I thought I'd get on this. Could you give me her home phone?"

"You just hang on while I get it," George said. A few moments later, he read off the seven digits. "She's moving, as you know. It might be this weekend."

"Great. Thanks, George, and give my love to the family. See

you at softball one of these days. Your Melanie and my Nicole take the game much more seriously than my Natalie."

He chuckled. "I know what you mean. Okay, Laura. Nice talking to you."

"Same here. Good night now."

Laura took a breath and dialed the number. It was seven fifteen. Could Steve actually be at that woman's house with her children? It's not possible, she thought. Laura assumed that Kim had no use for kids, but she might act like she did if she wanted Steve badly enough.

"God, I just don't know what else to do," she said aloud.

Three rings. A click. Of course. Like Steve, Kim would have an answering machine too.

"Hi there. Sorry I can't take your call right now, but please leave a message and I'll get back to you just as soon as I can." No identification, but it was Kim's voice all right, her sexy public voice.

"Kim, this is Laura Nelson. I'm looking for my husband." Laura didn't know what else to say. "Listen, I don't want you anywhere near my children. I'm warning you. Stay away from them."

She hung up, glancing for the hundredth time out the front window. There was still plenty of light for the late June evening as Marcy's car pulled into the driveway and headed toward the garage. Should she tell Marcy the kids still weren't home? No, she decided. Surely they'd be home soon. She called Steve's again. The damn answering machine. She slammed down the phone.

That was it. She was going over. Marcy could keep an eye out for them in the meantime. She picked up the receiver and dialed the phone once more. "Hi, Marcy." She struggled to sound cheerful. "Have a nice day in St. Pete?"

"I did, but I'm ready to get into my robe and plunk down in front of the TV."

"Sounds good. Listen, can I ask a favor? I have a little emergency in the ER that should just take a few minutes." Another outright lie. "Would you watch out for Steve and the kids and tell them I'll be right back?"

After Marcy agreed, Laura hung up before the housekeeper could ask any questions. Hot angry tears spilled down her cheeks as she backed the Olds wagon out of the garage. She hadn't bothered to touch up her hair or lipstick. Trance-like, she drove past Tampa City Hospital and across the bridge that connected Davis Island to Tampa's mainland. An ache in her throat, she noted that Steve's billboard had been replaced with a car dealer's ad. The thermometer near the bridge registered eighty-one, and it had started to drizzle. Before reaching Steve's downstairs apartment on Oregon, she pulled over to dab at her eyes, blow her nose, and wipe the sweat off her brow. If the kids were there, she didn't want them to see her such a mess.

It was eight ten, still plenty of light outside as Laura approached Steve's place. Parking behind a late-model yellow Firebird she found vaguely familiar, she silently advised herself to remain calm. Once she got the kids home safely, she would figure out what to do about Steve.

Despair and panic eclipsed anticipation as she walked to the front door and pushed the doorbell. Did it even work? This was not exactly the high-rent district. The house needed a lot of work. The roof was sagging on one side and the cement stairs had begun to crumble. The houses on the block were built close together and she noticed that they were in much better repair than the one Steve occupied, which needed a paint job badly. Two stories high, these were much older than the homes on Davis Island. As she glanced around, she saw a child in an upstairs window next door looking at her. A girl with pigtails and a cute, inquisitive face. About the age of the twins, Laura guessed. She did not want to embarrass the child by waving, so she proceeded to knock on Steve's door. No response. She knocked again before trying the doorknob, which turned easily. Stepping inside, she walked across the empty living room. There was a sofa and two matching chairs in a faded plaid pattern. Newspapers, dirty dishes, and empty beer cans were scattered about.

Disgusting, she thought. How could a person so meticulous about his personal appearance be such a slob? What a bad influence on the kids. The last month must have been much easier on Marcy without him around. One less person to pick up after.

"Hello?" she called.

She picked her way through the hallway and looked into the room on the right, a bedroom. Besides the unmade bed and clothes strewn about, only a bureau filled the room.

Down the hall, she stepped into the kitchen. What a mess there too — it seemed that Steve had not washed a single dish since he'd moved in. Completely repulsed, Laura fumbled in her cluttered purse for her car keys, nearly tripping on the foot before she noticed it.

A human foot. Only inches away.

The body of a woman lay on the kitchen floor. Blank eyes stared at the ceiling and feet — nails painted a fiery red — protruded from spiked high heels. Laura gasped as she took in the black eyes frightfully wide open, the short, dark hair neatly combed behind her ears exposing diamond cluster earrings shaped like starfish. She wore a sleeveless cobalt blue dress above tanned bare legs and the sling-back heels precisely matched the dress's color. But it was her chest that riveted Laura's attention — the gaping wound in her chest, the blood that was everywhere.

At a glance Laura knew the woman — and she *knew* the woman — soaked in a pool of blood on Steve's tiled kitchen floor, was dead.

Kim Connor was dead.

Nevertheless, Laura knelt down beside the body, feeling for the carotid artery with her right hand, trying to find a pulse. She knew she wouldn't find one even though the flesh was warm. Ripping open the top two buttons of the dress with both hands — the blue cloth was warm and sticky, drenched with blood — she reached in. The chest was immobile, no trace of respiration. Should she try manual open-chest cardiac massage? As she inched closer to make absolutely sure there was no pulse, her left hand, sticky with blood, landed on something cold and metallic nestled against Kim's hip. She ignored it, never taking her eyes from the woman's chest. Finally, she stood up.

Kim was dead. Who had killed her? And here, on Steve's kitchen floor? Steve? Could he have done this? And the kids? Had they been here?

Help. She needed to call for help. That's when Laura heard footsteps behind her.

Two uniformed cops had let themselves in while Laura stood mute and unmoving. They'd been cruising the Hyde Park area when the request came through to respond to a call from a female who had reported hearing a gunshot from upstairs at this Oregon address. The front door had been open and unlocked, and at precisely 8:13 p.m., the officers let themselves in, planning a cautious walk through.

"False alarm," Belinsky, a big-bellied Tampa veteran, mumbled just before he heard the wheezy voice of Parker, his younger partner: "Freeze. Police."

Darting toward the kitchen, Belinsky entered a scene that looked like a staged tabloid. Hands bloody, a blonde female stood staring down at her apparent victim: a familiar looking, petite female with short dark hair lying in a pool of blood on the tile floor, a Colt thirty-eight beside her. Parker's .45 was locked on the blonde's back. Belinsky started blankly at his partner for only an instant before drawing his own gun. He felt cold sweat trickle down his neck and down his forehead into his eyes as the blonde started to turn.

"Hands up," Belinsky barked, his gun taking aim at the center of the blonde's chest. She seemed dazed and disheveled. Maybe a crazy?

"Lady, hands up," Belinsky repeated more slowly as he inched closer. "Easy now." Signaling his partner to stay still, he said evenly, "Let's nobody get hurt." His warning too late for the young woman bathed in blood on the floor.

In slow motion, Laura lifted her hands up into the air.

"I got her," Parker said in a high-pitched wheeze.

"Okay, man," Belinsky said as he inched close enough to reach down and grab the piece that lay on the floor with his handkerchief. "I got the weapon."

Belinsky placed the thirty-eight on the Formica counter, moving quickly to slip the handcuffs off his belt. Clamping them shut over Laura's bare wrists, he was careful not to smear her bloody palms as he pulled her arms behind her back. She had not moved.

"Stay put, lady," Belinsky grunted, "Parker, keep watching her."

Kneeling over the bloody body, he carefully checked for a pulse, respiration, any sign of life. "Dead as dead can be," he announced. "Parker, ambulance first, then the station. There's a phone in the living room." Belinsky turned toward Laura as Parker walked out. "Name," he demanded.

"What," Laura whispered.

"Your name, lady," Belinsky repeated.

"Laura Nelson," she whispered almost inaudibly.

"Do you live here?"

"No." Again almost inaudible.

"Speak up. Do you know who does live here?"

"My husband," Laura answered a little louder this time.

"You don't live with your husband?"

"No — not anymore," Laura managed. She was shaking now, all traces of color drained from her face.

"Do you know this woman?" Belinsky demanded.

The younger cop returned and started in with his own questions as he pointed to Kim's body. "Do you know who she is?"

"Yes."

"Well, are you going to tell us or do we book you first?" Parker grabbed Laura's arm.

"Ms. Nelson," Belinsky said in a conciliatory tone, "why don't you just answer the questions. For starters, who is that woman?"

"Kim Connor," Laura answered simply.

Belinsky whistled. "Connor? The Channel Eight News lady. Thought I recognized her."

"Doesn't look so good blood soaked, does she?" Parker commented. He let go of Laura's arm with a little shove. "Wasn't she on with some guy all the time? Both their mugs are plastered all over town."

"That's my husband," Laura said quietly.

CHAPTER NINE

Heading north on I-75 Sunday night, the kids finally fell asleep. Relieved, Steve drank the silence in. He had to clear his head, come to grips with what was happening. Back when he was a social worker, he would often counsel his clients to simplify their view of whatever situation was troubling them. That small act, he saw again and again, was the first step toward making any terrible reality more manageable. Well, maybe now he could do the same for himself. He had to. Had to think this through, but how? The problem was, he didn't know where to start. With himself? With Kim? No, that was way too much at this moment. Easier to start with Laura.

Both hands drumming the steering wheel, he imagined her reaction to the empty house. She'd be shaken up. One thing anyone would say about Laura was that she was devoted to those kids. He had woken them at dawn on Saturday and hastily packed their duffel bags with clothes and toys, before herding them into a rented station wagon as quietly as he could. Originally, he had only planned an overnight trip to Clearwater Beach while the brakes on his Ford were being replaced, wanting to show Laura not to mess with him, acting like she could just kick him out with no job, no house, no nothing.

But that was before.

And now, after she learned that he'd taken them far away, she'd follow, and then they'd all be back together. That was pretty simple, right? It was a plan, he needed a plan. He and the kids would head for his father's house in Traverse City. Laura would follow, and they'd have time to work things out. She would have no choice. It was his plan: it could happen.

It really could. It had to. What happened with him and Kim was just that, an unfortunate mistake.

Still, when he and the kids were in the movie theatre, what had possessed him to check his answering machine? He inhaled sharply, sucking in the silence as if it were oxygen. Before the kids had finally fallen asleep in the car, they had peppered him with questions.

"How long are we going to be gone?" Kevin asked.

"We'll see."

"When are we going to get there? Can we go fishing?"

"Kevin, shut up with all the questions," Mike demanded.

Steve attempted a smile, though he could not keep his fingers from drumming even then. "Relax, Mike. It'll be an adventure. There's fishing, and hunting —"

"But Mom doesn't even know we're gone," Mike said. "We were supposed to go to the beach today for Grandpa's birthday. Does she even know that your dad is sick?"

"You let me worry about your mother. Like I said, Grandpa Nelson's got the flu and he lives by himself so it's good that we're headed up there."

"But we don't even know him," Mike argued.

"We'll fix that," Steve said.

"Hey, Dad, Mom always packs our clothes for an overnight," Kevin added. "She'll be mad that you just threw stuff in a bag."

"I'm hungry," Natalie complained.

"We'll eat later," said Steve. "Can't stop now. Besides, Patrick's sleeping."

"But Dad —" Natalie tried again.

"I said no, not now. Everybody be quiet — don't wake up your brother."

"I'm hungry too," Nicole complained. "Do you want us to starve to death?"

Steve turned to flash a stern look. "Stop being so sassy."

One by one, the rest of the kids eventually fell asleep. When Kevin stirred and asked what time it was, Steve told him midnight, though it was really two fifteen. After driving two more hours, Steve finally checked in at the Roadside Motel in Forsyth, Georgia, just north of Macon. There were two double beds in the drab room, which was warm and smelled like mildew, and although Steve adjusted the air-conditioning, it didn't get much better. Steve, Mike, and Kevin crowded into one bed, and Patrick and the twins slept in the other.

After setting the clock alarm for 6:45 a.m., Steve fell into a fitful sleep. He woke the kids at seven, and packed the car. By the time they ate breakfast at a Waffle House off the interstate, the kids were clamoring to call Laura. Climbing back into the car, Steve told them she was on call and promised he would call her later at the hospital.

"Dad, can we call Mom at home right now?" asked Kevin. "Maybe she hasn't left for the hospital yet."

"Bet she's worried about us," Mike added.

Steve drummed the steering wheel. "How many times do I have to tell you to let me worry about your mother? I told you I will call her later. You know how she is at the hospital. Now, no more talking. I need quiet to think."

"I still don't see why we have to go all the way to Michigan," Nicole whined. "Why can't we just go home?"

"I just told you why," Steve said sharply. "It's time we spent time with my side of the family."

"But what about Mom?" Natalie went on.

"Look, Mom'll come up as soon as she can," Steve shouted. "Now I want you to stop whining and shut up! Mike, get me the map out of the glove compartment."

They drove in silence toward Michigan. Just after ten, Steve stopped at a gas station in Dalton, just south of the Georgia-Tennessee border. While the kids used the bathrooms, he called his father from the phone booth. He wanted to let him know where they were now, and when they would get there tomorrow. It was over a twenty-hour trip and they would take it in pieces. Unlike last night, Steve told himself, tonight he'd get more than a few hours sleep.

He went into the restroom and doused his face with cold water. Even with the air-conditioning on at full blast, he'd been sweating profusely.

"My children are missing." Laura sat slumped over the bare metal interrogation table. It was after ten, almost two hours since they'd found her with Kim Connor. Her head ached. Her eyes burned. "Don't you understand? I was looking for my children."

Why wouldn't they stop badgering her? First those policemen back at Steve's house. Then these two detectives who showed up at Steve's and led her off in handcuffs to police headquarters on Tampa Avenue. In a blur, she was fingerprinted, probed, and photographed. They took away her purse, inventoried the contents, made her sign something, and removed the shoelaces from her sneakers. She was still wearing a tee shirt and cutoffs, and the air-conditioning made her shiver as she tried to answer the onslaught of questions. It was all being tape recorded. They told her that. The room was a perfect square with enough room for only a small table and four ancient chairs. The walls were painted a darkish green, reminding her of bile, bare except for a smudged rectangular mirror. The lone light fixture in the center of the ceiling was yellowed and chipped, making the light dim and uneven.

Detective Randy Goodnuf, the younger of the two detectives, was in his mid-thirties with thin sandy hair surrounding a patch of scalp that looked jaundiced in the bad light. Too skinny, he seemed extremely tense, tapping his feet, checking his watch, twisting his navy blue tie as he paced.

Detective Ramiro Lopez, the senior of the partners by several years, was his opposite, sitting quietly across the table from Laura. Jet black hair feathered back from his tanned, smiling face, he exuded charm. Dressed in an expensively tailored suit, he looked more like a successful Hispanic businessman than an aggressive homicide detective. Tonight the detectives led with Lopez's disarming charm, but as the night wore on, everyone's tone changed.

"With all due respect, Dr. Nelson, we do have a dead woman to deal with first," Goodnuf snarled.

So far all they'd gleaned from the interrogation was a fragmented story. Found the body. Knew the victim. Was looking for her husband and children. Separated from husband. Wasn't her gun. Didn't own a gun. Didn't know who did own the thirty-eight that lay by the body. Blood on her hands from trying to assess the victim.

Lopez held up two fingers — the victory sign — to his partner. "Okay, Dr. Nelson," he said, "we understand that you're concerned. I have two boys of my own. Now, your husband picked up all five kids early yesterday morning, while you were still asleep. Is that right?"

"Yes." Laura nodded weakly.

"Where do you think he took them?"

"I don't know. I thought they might be at his apartment. That's why I went there. I left several messages on his answering machine."

"Answering machine?" Detective Lopez's eyebrows shot up. "Uh-huh, we'll follow that up."

"So where were you before you went to your husband's apartment?" Goodnuf pressed.

"Just a minute, Randy," said Lopez. "Let's try to help Dr. Nelson with her kids first."

Goodnuf stepped back. "I've had enough of this runaround."

"My partner's getting restless," Lopez said as he rose from his chair, rolling it back against the wall and stretching his legs. "Now where do you think Mr. Nelson might be?"

"I told you —"

"Name all the places he might take the kids," Goodnuf snapped.

"I've tried," Laura said, pressing her hand to her temple. "The only place I can think is my parents' in Sarasota, but they would have called me."

"We'll call them," Lopez said. "Has your husband ever done this before? Taken the kids away?"

"No, never."

Goodnuf frowned. "Do you think he'd try to leave the area with them? He could be almost anywhere now. It's been about forty hours — according to your story, that is."

"I . . . I don't know. I guess so." She paused. "No, I don't think so."

"Dr. Nelson, who was close to your husband?" Lopez sat down again. "Who would he go to?"

"I just don't know. He lost his job and the only —" She stopped herself from saying that his closest friend had been Kim Connor.

"The only what?" Goodnuf demanded.

"I . . . I don't know."

"Dr. Nelson," Lopez said quietly, "does your husband have any relatives?"

"His father lives in Michigan."

Certainly, Steve would not head there. She hadn't even considered that. They'd hardly had any contact with his father since his mother died five years ago. Jim Nelson was a nice enough man, but a passive one, refusing to travel, preferring his own company. Why would Steve take them there? Then she remembered that remark in the park only last Saturday. "Don't push me into a corner," Steve had said. Had that been a threat?

"Okay, why don't you tell me where in Michigan, so we can check it out?"'

Laura recited the Traverse City address of Steve's father.

"Anybody else in Michigan?"

"No, we used to live in Detroit, but that was almost eight years ago. There's no one there."

"Okay," said Lopez with a reassuring smile, "we'll check that all out. In the meantime we have to ask you some other questions. Before I do, I want to remind you again of your right to remain silent, to have an attorney present, and if you can't afford one, the court will appoint one."

Laura was impatient. "I don't need an attorney. I'm a doctor. I was trying to help. I've already told you that."

Lopez handed her a printed Miranda warning and recited it again slowly and completely for the benefit of the tape recording. "I'd like to ask you to sign this. Just a formality."

She glanced at it and signed without hesitation. Anything to get out of here.

A slight smile crept across Lopez's face. "Okay, now. First, would you tell us again why you went to your husband's place tonight?"

Laura sighed. "Because I thought my kids might be there."

"I'm tired of this bullshit thing about kids," Goodnuf broke in. "Why did you kill Kim Connor?"

For the eleventh time during the interrogation, Laura denied killing Kim, but this time she also offered more. As she gripped the table with both hands she said, "My husband was having an affair with her. That's why we separated. I didn't know that Kim would be there. I called her apartment and she wasn't home, but I did not know that she was at his."

Then Laura slumped back into the chair and let her head sink onto the table, oblivious to her own wracking sobs.

Lopez and Goodnuf exchanged a "got-it" expression. They had plenty of evidence and now they had motive. Enough to hold her for the D.A.

"So why don't you just tell us exactly how it happened," Goodnuf pressed. "When you found out this woman was involved with your husband, you decided to track her down and kill her?"

"No," Laura cried, "that's not true! I told you she was dead when I got there."

"But only your prints were on the gun," Lopez bluffed. The print results would not be back until the next day.

Lopez sat silent as Laura stared into his dark eyes, her face entirely pale. "That can't be possible. I want to call a lawyer."

"Of course," he replied.

"Just one more question you can think about on the way over to the county jail," Goodnuf went on. "If you didn't kill her, who did?"

CHAPTER TEN

Greg Klingman strode toward the Hillsborough County Jail wondering what his client's story would be. Cliff Casey from Tampa City Hospital — for whom he'd done a lot of legal work — had told him that a woman doctor had been charged with murder and found with the actual weapon right beside her. She'd even volunteered a motive. How the hell had a smart woman like this, a doctor no less, had the recklessness to blabber to the police without legal representation? How foolish people could be when caught off guard. And then there was the question of the missing children; the woman was nearly hysterical about them. On the phone, she said she hadn't committed the murder, of course. But, the celebrity girlfriend of her celebrity husband? Greg could plead her, but she'd probably still do time. Tough with all those kids.

The Nelson arraignment would be early, somewhere around nine o'clock, and Greg wanted to talk to Laura in person, hear her tell her story again before anyone else did. No doubt she'd pay for her careless loose tongue the night before. Now that the D.A. knew about her husband's affair with the deceased, he'd want murder one, and he'd want it to stick.

Greg walked into the county jail at eight, having stopped for a bagel and coffee on the way to his office to clear any urgent issues of the morning. He wanted to get to the courthouse as soon as its doors opened at nine to find out who would hear Laura's arraignment, and when. Thinking he'd have some time to question Laura in a holding cell, Greg was surprised to find that she'd already been transported to the courthouse. So he had no choice but to plead her innocent as she'd insisted on the phone.

At forty-two, Greg had sandy, prematurely silver-streaked hair, slate gray eyes, and a strong face slightly marred by a smattering of shallow pocks from adolescent acne. He was six feet tall with an athletic build just starting to show traces of a paunch, and dressed the part of a successful lawyer. Until he met his fiancée, Celeste Marin, eighteen months earlier, he'd been a popular Tampa Bay bachelor.

Arriving at the massive courthouse at the intersection of Madison and Jefferson, Greg passed through security and learned that the Nelson case was assigned to Judge Stanley Potter. Greg knew him well. A big man, just past middle age, tough by reputation, especially with frequent offenders, but even his critics had to concede his sense of fairness. Greg recalled with some relief that the judge had a daughter around Laura's age, and that she had six children. That might bode well for Laura, as well as the fact that she was a solid figure in the Tampa medical community.

Greg soon learned that her case was first on the docket. So the district attorney's office had given it priority, not surprising since it was a sure media event. Potter's court held to a tight schedule, which meant all Greg could do was accompany Laura as they led her in to enter her plea. His client wore cutoff shorts and a tattered T-shirt with a large stylized 'M'. University of Michigan, Greg surmised. As her handcuffs were removed, he looked down from her messy, ponytailed hair to the worn and laceless sneakers on her feet. This plumpish, disheveled blonde in clunky glasses was a hotshot thoracic surgeon?

"The State of Florida vs. Laura Nelson," permeated the silence as Greg and Laura stood together in front of Judge Potter's bench.

Assistant D.A. Sandra Mulloy had risen from her seat to state the charges. All eyes shifted from the defendant's table, where Laura sat listless, to the statuesque woman who turned toward the judge.

Sandra, independently wealthy and aggressive, was the dread of Tampa defense attorneys. About Laura's age and single, she had yellow blonde hair that framed a sharp, narrow face. The A.D.A. had made her reputation by taking a particularly tough stance against women. Typically assigned to middle-class female defendants, she rarely failed to win a conviction.

Sandra's confident voice addressed the judge as she ticked off the salient points of the case. Found with a dead body. Found a Colt thirty-eight next to her. Just minutes earlier, test results had confirmed that only her fingerprints were on the gun. Motive established. "The State enters the charge of first degree murder, your Honor."

"Defense Council, how do you plead?"

Judge Potter turned his bulky, robed body toward Laura, waiting for a response on her behalf from her attorney.

As they rose, Greg whispered to her, "You're sure?"

Panic crossed Laura's face as she nodded. Terribly pale, she rubbed her hands, now free of handcuffs, together.

"The defendant pleads 'not guilty,' your Honor."

As Greg and Laura sat down once more, the judge scrutinized Laura before proceeding. "On the matter of bail —" he began.

"The State requests no bail, your Honor," Sandra interjected. "The charge is murder in the first degree and the defendant is an obvious flight risk. As a doctor, she's had an ample income which would afford her the means to flee."

Greg jumped up. "Objection, Your Honor. My client is a prominent member of the medical community in this state with never so much as a traffic ticket. She certainly poses no flight risk. Her entire family is rooted in this community, her parents, her children. I see no reason for any bail whatsoever in this case."

Judge Potter again studied the defendant.

"The State reiterates the request for no bail," rang the voice of Sandra Mulloy.

"Rather severe for someone with no prior arrests." Judge Potter said simply.

"Not for murder one, Your Honor," Sandra said again. "Under no circumstances should bail be set for less than one million dollars."

The judge then looked up as Jake Cooperman, the D.A. himself, strode into the courtroom and took a seat at Sandra Mulloy's table. All eyes followed his path, his presence a signal that the prosecution intended to take this case seriously. Over the past twelve years, Jake had built his reputation on a politically astute winning streak. He selected his high-profile cases carefully and worked in the limelight of the media, looking more like a Brooks Brothers model than a practicing D.A.

"That's preposterous, Your Honor," Greg said. "My client's record in this community is unblemished."

Judge Potter cut him off. "Bail will be set at five hundred thousand dollars."

Among a shuffle of chairs and buzzing of voices, Laura was handcuffed once more and ushered out of the now-crowded courtroom.

An hour later, Greg was led into the small, dingy holding area of the Hillsborough County Jail.

"Dr. Nelson," he began as soon as the matron had locked the cell door behind her. Laura had brushed her hair and now wore the tan prison-issue shirt and pants that fit tightly over her frame. She was still pale with deepening circles below her eyes.

"We have a lot to talk about, but first we need to clarify my representation. I hate to go over it now, but if you want me to represent you, I'll need a retainer of thirty thousand dollars. Depending on what happens, the fee may be much higher, but we would negotiate anything further as we go."

"Do you believe I didn't kill that woman?" she asked quietly.

"Yes," Greg said, surprised that he did believe her.

"Thank you." Laura leaned forward in the metal chair. "My children, no one's told me anything. What about my kids?"

"We'll find out as soon as possible, but first we need to agree on fees and the matter of bail," he said. "Is it possible for you to come up with my retainer plus fifty thousand for the bail bondsman?"

"I'll pay whatever is necessary. Can you get me out of here today?"

"Of course," he said gently. "Now let's get started. First thing, bail."

"Steve and I have a joint savings account. About fifty thousand dollars in there and a checking account that we keep almost tapped out. You'd think we'd have more with both of us working and all," she said with a sad smile, "but we do have some equity in the house."

He nodded. "That's a start. It'll just cover the bondsman and get you out, but you'll need more. Your parents?"

"I could never ask them. They've worked hard their whole lives and now they're both retired." Laura shook her head. "I do have somewhere around twenty thousand dollars in accounts receivable from the hospital for surgical cases, but that comes in slowly from third-party payers."

Greg nodded again. "That should help."

"Fine. I'll pay you as soon as I can, Mr. Klingman."

"Call me Greg. Because we're going to be seeing a lot of each other."

"And call me Laura, Greg."

Before he left, Laura gave Greg authorization to access her bank accounts. He promised to get her out that day and reassured her that he'd do everything he could to help find her children. Unexpectedly, he meant it.

CHAPTER ELEVEN

"Listen," Greg said after the matron led Laura back into the dingy holding cell at noon, "I've got good news and bad news."

Laura did not speak until the matron locked the door behind her. "Tell me the bad news first." Then she gasped, "My kids?"

"No, no," Greg said quickly, "your husband. Last week he all but emptied out your joint savings account. There's nine hundred forty-two dollars left. I've spoken with the hospital to see if they can give you some kind of an advance. As it stands now, they've agreed to ten thousand."

"What? How could Steve do such a thing? I can't believe it."

"Believe it. I saw the bank statement. Now let me tell you the good news. You were right — your family was on the way to Michigan. Cops here put a call into your father-in-law to notify the Tampa station in case your husband turned up there. Turns out he was on his way. Anyway, he's flying in for questioning from Chattanooga."

"What about my kids?"

"They're fine. They'll all be back in a few hours. I'll meet the plane when the flight gets in."

"Oh, thank God. You can take them home, can't you? My housekeeper will be there."

"No problem. The kids can head home while the detectives talk to your husband —"

"Do they think he had something to do with it?" Laura gasped. "I admit I did at first too, but —"

"I can't answer that — being on the road with five kids." He paused. "But I don't know what his actual itinerary was. Or why he emptied your bank account and fled the state."

"Dear God, Steve's not a murderer." Laura let out a deep breath. Kim's body had still been warm — she couldn't have been dead that long — so it couldn't have been Steve. Somehow that realization comforted her.

"I hope you're right. In the meantime, we're still stuck with getting your bail money. I'll talk to your husband about it as soon as they land, but if we can't pull it together in time that means another night here for you. I'll do my best to get you a cell to yourself again, but I can't promise." He reached over and patted her hand.

Laura slumped back in the hard-back, steel chair. "Just make him give me the money to get out of here."

Greg Klingman recognized the familiar face of Steve Nelson and headed toward the cluster of Nelsons as they deplaned. Steve was flanked by two blonde boys, one a teenage version of his father and the other obviously younger, with floppy bangs. Twin sisters, also blondes, wore matching turquoise outfits. They each held the hand of a smaller boy with chestnut hair. Two plainclothes sheriffs shepherded the family to the central terminal as Greg attempted to introduce himself.

"Mr. Nelson," he called, "I'm Greg Klingman, your wife's attorney. I need to talk to you. It's important."

Greg was surprised that the good-looking guy who was always perfectly groomed on TV looked so sloppy, in rumpled khaki shorts and a worn tee shirt. But then, he'd been on the road with five kids. Even so, it was irksome when Steve Nelson merely glanced at him, making no attempt to respond.

"Not now, mister," one of the sheriffs responded. "We're headed directly to headquarters."

"Certainly I can talk to him for just a few minutes," Greg said. "I do represent his wife."

"Yep, you can, but only when the detectives are finished with him."

Greg looked at Steve again, who just shrugged.

"What about the kids?" Greg went on. "I have Dr. Nelson's permission to take them home. Your housekeeper is waiting for them there."

"I want to go home," one of the little girls said.

"No," Steve said sharply, "everybody stays with me."

"But Dad —" the floppy-haired boy whined.

"I said no," Steve repeated.

"It's okay, Mr. Nelson, if you'd like your kids taken home." The officer's face softened as he looked down at the group huddled around their dad. "They look pretty beat."

"No. They stay with me," Steve said stubbornly.

Greg tried again. "It would be no problem —"

Steve shook his head. "No."

"Then I'll wait for you at headquarters. It's imperative that I speak with you just as soon as possible."

"Fine," Steve finally said.

It was almost nine when Greg returned to the jail. Laura's hair was combed, but greasy. Her face scrubbed. Her eyes less bloodshot under her glasses.

"My kids?" she asked.

"Safe and sound." Greg explained that they were home with Mrs. Whitman, neglecting to tell her that they'd been detained for more than four hours with nothing to eat or drink. The kids waited in a drab interrogation room equipped with only a conference table and a few chairs while a pair of Tampa detectives interrogated her husband in another room. Pending substantiation, they'd accepted Steve's alibi — he was on his way to Michigan with five kids in a rental car during the time of the murder. Steve had learned that his father was sick and decided to drive to Michigan.

"That's why he took them away?" Laura asked in disbelief.

"Apparently the police pressed him on this, and he did admit that he was upset with the way you'd tossed him out. And something about how busy you were with your career. He figured since he wasn't working anyway, you could use a break."

"And what did Steve tell you?" Laura asked dully.

"Well, I didn't get a chance to talk to him until after they all got home," Greg said. "Said he was tired and couldn't even think straight when I explained that you needed fifty thousand to post bail as well as a retainer for me."

"And?" Laura pressed both hands to her temples.

"He said he was worried about your state of mind. Thinks that you might do something, and I quote, 'foolish' if you were out. He wants to talk to you first."

"What? Are you saying he won't give me the money for bail? That's my money too! I've got to get out of here." Laura started to stand up, but then seemed to remember where she was. She fell back and stared at one of the cement walls for a few moments. "I find a dead woman on his kitchen floor, and I'm the one who ends up in jail? Can you have Steve come talk to me?"

"Yes, but brace yourself, there's one other thing. It seems that Steve thinks you actually killed the Connor woman. His theory to the police is that you were insanely jealous. That you killed her so he would come back to you."

"What? That's absurd," Laura began. "He knew I planned to file for a separation, a divorce. He tried to talk me out of it, but —"

"Well, he's putting out that 'crime of passion' and all. I only wish he'd talked to me first."

Laura's fist slammed against the table. "I can't believe this. He's just trying to get back at me."

"Maybe, Laura, but I detected more than that. Maybe an ego thing. Like the image of you being jealous enough to kill his girl-friend feeds his ego?"

Laura frowned. "And the kids? What did Steve tell them? And the police, what did they tell my kids? I mean, about me?"

"Best I know, they were told there'd been an accident. That you were all right, but you were needed for lots of questions. Hell, it's in all the papers. He'll have to tell them something soon. And, apparently Channel Eight wants to do an interview with him tomorrow. I advised him to just keep quiet, but he seems to have a need to explain what he thinks happened. Maybe he just wants his face back on TV."

Laura's frown deepened. Again she started to get up before slumping back into the chair. "Can you stop him?"

"I tried, but he seemed insistent — self-righteous. I suspect you'll have better luck talking him out of it."

"My parents?" Laura asked faintly.

"I called them too. It's obvious they'd do anything for you. They're coming in tomorrow, to your place. Maybe they can talk some sense into your husband."

"God, I hope so. I'm so ashamed that they have to go through this." She covered her face with her hands.

Greg cleared his throat. "In the meantime, we have to figure out how to post bail. I'm sorry you'll have to spend another night in here."

Laura looked up with a grimace. She'd been so numb she could only remember the coldness, the toilet in the corner, the smell of urine leaching out through the pervasive odor of Lysol in her cell.

"I just don't believe Steve would deliberately make me stay in here."

"I can't see that either, but just in case we've already talked about the hospital. You parents? What about friends, Laura? Think hard."

Laura shook her head. "Please give my parents another call will you, Greg, and tell them that I'm okay and that I didn't do it."

"I'll tell them anything you like. Of course, they know you didn't do it. So am I going to ask them if they can raise the bail bond as well?"

"No, don't do that."

"Then how are we going to get you out of this jail?"

"Steve just has to change his mind. We have enough money for bond."

"And if he flat out refuses?"

"There is one possibility," Laura said quickly. "I never thought I'd use it, but —"

"Let's hear it."

"There's a safety deposit box in the Tampa National Bank on Dale Mabry. A money market fund. Two hundred thousand plus accumulated interest for the past few years. I'm telling you this in strict confidence, Greg. Attorney-client privilege, is it not?"

"Yes it is." He nodded for her to go on.

"A long time ago a very dear friend of mine died and left me the money. Steve doesn't know it exists and he must never know. I'm absolutely adamant about this. Not Steve or anyone else."

"I see. Is this money legal?"

"Yes," Laura said without hesitation. "I've kept it in a tax-free fund so it doesn't show up on our income taxes. All statements go to a post office box I keep exclusively for this account and the statements are in a locked drawer in my office."

"Man, you're not kidding about not wanting Steve to know."

"No, I'm not." Her eyes locked onto Greg's. "If Steve persists with not paying the bail, you can get the file key tomorrow from my secretary."

"So we'll use that as a backup. I'll also need the key to your box at the bank. Power of attorney —"

"The key to the box is in the file."

"You'll need to sign the paperwork to get this going."

"As long as there's no hint to Steve as to how I got the money. Just get him to come see me first thing tomorrow. And reassure my parents that financially I'm okay, will you please?"

"Of course," Greg replied. There was a lot to be done. First, he needed to call his fiancée, Celeste. It was already too late to join her for dinner. He'd be lucky to get to her place by midnight and she was leaving for a big job in Atlanta in the morning.

"And Greg, now that I can pay you, help me, will you?"

Greg looked back at Laura, her clear eyes clouding over. "I'm trying to. I'd intended to juggle my accounts to cover your bail. Now, though, I'm realizing that if you're willing to use this money, we can even afford a top-notch private investigator."

"A private investigator?"

"His name's Chuck Dimer, and he's the best in South Florida. I'll call him tonight. As soon as we get you out of here, I'll introduce you to the whole legal team. There's lots to be done."

"All I want is my life back."

"I know. That's why we'll be digging into everything. Police reports. Autopsy results. Fingerprints. The victim's background. Like I said, Chuck is the best."

Laura gazed at the matron, who was now standing outside the door. "You do whatever you need to do. Just get me out of here tomorrow."

Greg nodded and Laura forced a glimmer of a smile as she was led away to her cell.

Heading for the bank of phones at the end of the hall, he planned first to call Celeste, next Laura's secretary at her home to arrange meeting her at the Medical Arts Building, and then Chuck to set up a meeting for first thing tomorrow. As he waited for Celeste to pick up the phone, his thoughts were still on Laura. Why had she hidden the existence of that money from him, and why was she hiding it from her husband? As Celeste answered, Greg wondered whether, when they were married, they would have such secrets between them.

CHAPTER TWELVE

Steve was still groggy when he awoke the next morning. He'd tossed and turned until three o'clock, his mind everywhere. Why the hell had Kim shown up at his apartment that night anyway? He never got to find out whether she was really leaving that Santiago clown and coming to him or maybe just coming to say good-bye. And the gun. The cops told him that Laura's fingerprints were on that gun. Laura hated guns.

She'd carried a thirty-eight once, at his insistence back in Detroit. But once they'd moved to Tampa, Laura admitted that she'd dropped the gun into the Detroit River the night she'd gone to her med school graduation party on one of those party boats. Had she lied about that? Steve grimaced at the memory. He'd been too busy getting the family ready to move and she'd gone to the party alone. When she finally told him that she'd gotten rid of a perfectly good, if unregistered, gun, he'd exploded in anger. Laura had cried and when he couldn't stand the tears anymore, Steve promised to forgive her. And that was the last he'd heard about that gun. But that gun had been a Smith and Wesson and the one at Kim's place was a Colt. Traceable? The cops didn't know yet. And Laura did have a motive, didn't she? Wouldn't everybody feel sorry for her? Kim — the other woman — had completely disrupted their life. And he had — what about what he had done?

Too much. It was all too much.

Finally, Steve decided to take a sleeping pill, one of those Seconals Laura kept around for the times she worked all night and had to get some sleep during the day in a noisy household. As he was lulled to sleep by the barbiturate, he struggled to come up with a plan. He would confront Laura directly, in jail, first thing in the morning. He would bail her out. That was the least everyone would expect, he decided.

The house seemed eerily quiet as Steve showered and dressed in neatly pressed tan slacks, a buff Oxford shirt, and a maroon sports jacket. Heading downstairs to the kitchen, he was surprised to find Peg and Carl Whelan there, grief etched on their faces. Get ready, he told himself, they're going to try to blame me for this whole mess.

But Peg got up from her chair at the kitchen table and hugged him. "We didn't know whether or not we should wake you," she said. "It's after nine."

"Trouble sleeping," Steve mumbled.

"How you doing, Steve?" said Carl. He rose and clamped an arm around Steve's shoulder. Honest and kind, Carl had retired twelve years earlier from the Fisher Body car plant in Grand Rapids, Michigan, when Laura was still in med school. He and Peg moved to Florida where baseball, gardening, and golf kept him busy while Peg taught first grade in the Manatee County Public School system until her recent retirement.

"All right I guess. This is all so terrible," Steve said, glancing down at the table. He saw the headline in the *Tampa Tribune:* RENOWNED TAMPA SURGEON SUSPECT IN CELEBRITY MURDER.

He picked up the paper and read: "Dr. Laura Nelson, wife of Steve Nelson, former coanchor of Channel Eight News at Eleven, pleads not guilty to charges of the first-degree murder of Kim Connor, her husband's former coanchor." The article followed with the story of Steve leaving the station and Kim's plan to move to Atlanta. It quoted a Tampa City Hospital spokeswoman saying that Laura was a successful surgeon with no prior criminal record. It ended with speculation of a love triangle. Photos of all three lined the right column of the third page. At the top, a casual shot of Laura, looking a little chubby and smiling brightly in a white lab coat, a stethoscope dangling around her neck. Next, a full-body shot of Kim, microphone in hand, looking professional yet alluring in a dark suit with a short skirt and a low cut V-neck blouse. At the bottom was Steve, a studio shot of him at a podium, well made-up, a serious expression.

Steve dropped the paper on the table, shaking his head. So the whole world would know about him and Kim. His clean-cut reputation was shot to hell, but so what? He'd already been fired. Then he sank into a chair and held his head as a momentary flash of panic seized him. What about Santiago? Kim's words, "insanely jealous" pounded in his head. Laura had blabbed to the cops about Kim. Nothing he could do about that. Santiago would see the paper. He would — my God, would that mobster come after him?

"Steve, are you sure you're okay?" Carl asked again.

"Yeah, just thinking." Steve massaged his temples.

"What are we going to do? We feel so helpless." Peg wrung her hands. "We got a call from her lawyer yesterday. We have to get her out of that jail."

Steve slumped farther down into his chair. "I'm going down there after breakfast. Do you know anything specific about what happened? Did she say anything to you?"

"We haven't talked to her since —" Carl answered quietly, indicating the newspaper. "She'd already told us about you and Kim Connor."

"And that she wants a permanent separation," Peg added.

"It's true that Laura and I had separated," Steve said slowly. "Even though it was her decision, she must have been, well, having second thoughts."

"I don't know what you're trying to say. She made it perfectly clear," said Carl. "But that's not so important now. What is important is to get her out of that jail and home to us and the children."

"Listen, I haven't even talked to her yet," Steve cut in. "I got back late last night after being questioned nonstop by the police for hours. This is all quite a shock."

"Of course it is. What can we do, Steve?" Carl asked.

"I'm not sure."

"Mr. Klingman already called this morning," Peg offered. "He wants you to call him right away. Said you could see Laura this morning. We asked if we could see her and he said no, not this morning, but that he'd have her home this afternoon."

"Of course I'll call him," said Steve. "Where are the kids?"

"Marcy took them to Lowry Park," Peg said. "She'll keep them out as long as possible to give us time to work all this out."

"We decided it was best — before they saw the morning paper," Carl said.

"They looked scared, Steve," Peg added. "What will you tell them?"

"I . . . I don't know, Peg, but I'll figure it out. First thing is, from now on, I don't want them going out anywhere without me anymore."

The Whelans exchanged looks as Steve got up and poured himself a bowl of cornflakes and some coffee. Carl reached for the paper and Peg began washing dishes.

"I'll call that lawyer now," Steve said when he was done. "I wonder if he's the right one for Laura. Based on yesterday, the guy's pretty cocky, pretty aggressive."

"In this case, aggressive is good," Carl said.

"We'll see," countered Steve as he headed upstairs, went into the bedroom, and shut the door.

"Mr. Klingman," Steve said as Greg picked up the phone, "this is Steve Nelson. I'm calling about my wife. I want to get her out of jail. I don't want her to spend another minute in there."

"Good, Mr. Nelson," Greg replied. "There's a lot to discuss. It's important that I meet with you as soon as possible."

"Of course. Channel Eight is coming over for an interview at noon."

"Interview, Mr. Nelson?" Greg stifled a gasp. "I already told you I don't think it's wise. At least wait until you've had a chance to meet with Laura. She needs to see you. Can you come down right now?"

"And I need to see her. It's just things are so strange — surreal — right now. Did you see today's paper?"

"Mr. Nelson, you really need to talk to your wife before you talk to anyone."

"You're right, of course I do." Steve cleared his throat. "I need to hear her side of the story."

Steve had decided as he'd showered that he should know exactly what had happened when Laura went to his apartment rather than risk coming off badly on TV. Not that he had anything to loose. His ass was already fired. Now that Laura had blabbed about his relationship with Kim, it wasn't likely that he'd be getting a job in the Tampa Bay area. If she'd have just kept her mouth shut. Then Steve felt his body heat up under the warm water and he reached to adjust the temperature to cool. As he stepped out of the shower and toweled off, he couldn't seem to cool down. A sheen of sweat persisted on his forehead despite the chill of the air conditioner. A gnawing sensation made him stop and stare in the mirror. And then he realized the source of this queasy anxiety: the world now knew about him and Kim. And that included her scary boyfriend. Yes, he must proceed with this interview so he could get the best spin on the story, one that would best protect him and Laura.

When he went back downstairs, Peg and Carl looked up expectantly from their seats at the kitchen table.

"I'm going down to see Laura now," he stated.

"About bail," Carl asked, "do you have the money, Steve, or should we raise it?"

"Don't worry, I'll handle it."

Steve let the door slam behind him.

Greg met Steve just past the guard station inside the dismal receiving alcove of the Hillsborough County Jail. After a perfunctory handshake, Greg began, "Mr. Nelson, I need you to help me help your wife beat this murder charge."

Steve nodded. "That's why I'm here. My thought is, won't Laura be better off just telling the cops what happened? That she found Kim and I together and that led to, well, a crime of passion. It happens all the time, doesn't it? Not cold-blooded murder, just an irrational jealous rage – not premeditated. Won't they let her off easy? Probation? Community service?"

Greg recoiled. "Mr. Nelson, are you saying you believe your wife killed Kim Connor? She said she didn't do it."

"Honestly, I don't know what to think." Steve's words came rapidly. "I can't imagine Laura killing anybody, but, I mean, what about the gun being right there?"

"How would your wife get a gun?" Greg asked.

"I can't honestly say. They say it was a Colt thirty-eight. I do have a gun collection, but no Colt."

"What kind of weapons?" Greg asked.

"Shotgun for birds. Thirty-ought-six rifle for deer. Thompson Contender 50-caliber pistol for game, and a Browning twenty-two for target practice. Never carry concealed. Always locked up." Steve nodded as he ticked off the four guns on one hand.

"Quite an arsenal," said Greg.

"You can believe that the first thing I did when I got back last night was to check them over. They were all as I left them. Unloaded. Untouched."

"You told all this to the police?"

"Of course."

"Does Laura ever handle your guns?"

"Never," said Steve, shaking his head. "She hates guns."

Greg frowned. "I see. And what can you tell me about Kim Connor showing up at your place Sunday night? That she got there at the perfect time to meet her demise?"

Steve stared at him. "What are you talking about? Are you trying to say that I had —"

"Think about it. I believe that Laura didn't do it, which means somebody else killed Miss Connor." Greg paused, scrutinizing

Steve. "Or somebody had her killed. You knew the victim well. You must have some idea of who could have done this."

Steve wiped beads of sweat off his forehead and shook his head. "I don't."

"Fine." Greg leaned in. "Before you talk to Laura, however, you've got to agree that everything said between you and your wife and between you and me is held in strictest confidence. It's called privileged communication. Do you agree?"

Steve waved a hand dismissively. "Yes, of course. But Laura's never been in any trouble before. They've got to cut her a break, right? It's your job to make a deal with the prosecutor, the district attorney, whomever."

"If she's innocent, now why would I do that?" Greg shook his head. "What else did you tell the police last night?"

"I told them the truth, that Laura found me with Kim. Only once. It meant nothing, but Laura lost it and threw me out. That explains why I was staying in that apartment, and why, well —"

Greg shook his head. "And why did you take off with your children Sunday without telling your wife that you were taking them to Michigan?"

"Look, my father was sick. I thought Laura was working." Steve again wiped the sweat from his brow with the back of one hand and hardened his voice. "Now, Mr. Klingman, I'm here to see my wife."

"Just one more thing," Greg said icily. "Emptying your joint savings account last week has already caused Laura hardship — an extra night in jail. As I've told you, she needs fifty thousand for the bail bondsman. Do you have it?"

"Yes," Steve hissed. "Look, I don't have a job. Neither does she, I imagine. I need money to pay the bills. The fact is, we can't afford expensive attorney fees."

"I see. So you let her spend another night here so you can stick to your budget? Do you realize what it's like in there?"

"I'm here to see my wife."

"Of course. But I'm sitting in."

Steve did not object so Greg led the way.

They were escorted to the interrogation room by a rail-thin male guard who wore heavy tinted glasses. Laura sat alone at the sole square table, supervised by a prison matron stationed at the door's threshold. She wore baggy brown pants and an oversized smock the same dull color. She had showered and shampooed, her hair neatly pulled back in a ponytail, her pale face absent of any makeup.

"Steve," she greeted him dully.

Greg motioned for him to sit across the table from Laura and then he nodded to the matron, who stepped out to stand guard just outside the room. Greg leaned against the edge of the table.

"Disgusting," Steve said as he took in the yellowing cement walls and chipped gray floor tiles. "Look at this place — and those clothes."

"I have to get out of here. Last night I was locked in a cell with two prostitutes. I guess I was lucky, they pretty much left me alone. Steve, please get me out of here so I can get home to the kids."

"I . . . I have to say I'm glad they can't see you right now," he answered, shaking his head.

"Just get me out of here. This is all a mistake."

"Mistake?" Steve echoed. His eyes were bright. "I knew you were jealous of Kim, but —"

Laura's mouth fell open. "You think I killed her? I didn't kill her!"

Steve was sweating profusely now. "Laura, it's me," he glanced at Greg, "and your lawyer. You can tell us the truth."

"I am! I can't believe this. Kim was dead when I got there! For God's sake, Steve, I'm a doctor, I know when somebody's dead."

"But what about the gun? They said they found you with a gun."

"It wasn't mine! You of all people know how I hate guns. How many arguments have we had about your owning guns?"

"But they found you with it, there's no denying that."

"That's because it was there on the floor, and I accidentally touched it before the police showed up. I went to your apartment because I was frantic, trying to find the kids. Kim was on the kitchen floor already dead. But newly — her body was still warm. And what about you? What was she doing at your apartment? And why did you empty our bank account? Why were you taking our kids to Michigan? You must know who killed her." Laura glared at Steve and pounded her fist on the table, "You must know something!"

Steve shook his head, ignoring Laura's questions and wiping his sweat away. "All I'm saying is to tell the truth. They'll go easy on you if —"

Laura slumped back in her chair and looked helplessly at Greg, who was taking in the conversation in stony silence. "He thinks I did it. Steve, what have you told the kids?"

"Just that there's been an accident and you're being questioned. Marcy took them over to Lowry Park to distract them today, but I'll have to tell them later. It's all over the news. The station wants me to give an interview today too."

Laura began to sob. Steve stood and stepped closer to Laura and clamped a hand on her shoulder. Looking at Greg, Steve said, "Don't worry about it. It's better that I face this head-on. I'll just say that, yes, something happened between Kim and me. That this is really all my fault. That I never thought it would lead to this. Something like that."

Laura looked up at her husband in horror. "How could you think I did this? Steve, I'm telling you, somebody else killed Kim. Just think for a minute. Who could have done it? How about the boyfriend you said beat her up?"

"But they found you there, not him."

"What boyfriend?" Greg cut in.

"I didn't do it!" Laura cried. "This is all to get back at me, isn't it?"

"Face the facts, Laura." Steve took his hand off her shoulder. "You're the one who told the police about me and Kim. About how she threatened our marriage, at least you thought she did."

"Oh, my God," Laura sobbed, elbows propped up, head in hands, "Oh, my God."

Later, Steve watched the six o'clock news on the big TV in the family room with Laura's parents, who frowned throughout the broadcast.

"I tried to take as much blame as possible," he said as he clicked off the set. "So much of this was my fault."

"How could you," Peg finally sputtered, "when that reporter asked you whether you thought Laura killed Kim, you didn't deny it. Laura could never kill anyone! Why didn't you just tell them that?" She burst into tears.

Carl reached over to comfort his wife. "Not now," he whispered to her. To Steve he said, "You made the world think she did it."

"How can you say that? This hasn't been easy for me either, you know."

"I don't know anything at this point," Carl said.

"Look, Carl, we're all upset, and I need some time alone. Marcy can handle the kids when they get back. Why don't you and Peg go home; get some rest yourselves."

"We need to be here for our daughter when she comes home," Peg said stonily.

"Well, we don't even know when that will be," Steve said, walking to the back door and blatantly holding it open. "I'm sorry. With all this, I'm not a good host."

As soon as Steve closed the door behind Laura's parents, he picked up the phone and dialed and hung up a few times before finally calling his own father.

Laura jumped out of the shiny black Porsche as it slowed in front of her house at seven thirty. She had waited in the jail holding cell with no food or water for four hours, though the matron had allowed her to change out of prison garb into the same cutoffs and tee shirt she had worn Sunday night. Her clothes smelled like a mix of body odors, but it was much better than being in that cell with Sheila, a hardened prostitute, and Bobbie, a young girl picked up for shoplifting. It was seven by the time Greg had arranged for her release, once Steve provided the money for bail.

Without waiting for Greg, Laura bolted to the front door and rushed inside, nearly colliding with Steve, clad in gray sweatpants and a white tee shirt, who was carrying a bottle of beer across the hall into the family room.

"Where are the kids?" she asked anxiously.

"Uh, still out."

"I thought my mom and dad were here."

"They left." Steve set down the bottle and glared as Greg Klingman trailed Laura into the house.

"Where did my parents go?" Laura insisted. "They left a message at the jail that they'd be here."

"We have to talk. Alone," Steve said. He'd made no move toward, her but stood frowning at her disheveled appearance. "Why don't you shower and change. Put on your contact lenses."

"Mr. Nelson," Greg said, "we do have to talk."

"You might as well come in and watch my interview," Steve said, "both of you. I recorded it when it ran at six. Then we'll talk."

Laura and Greg followed as Steve walked into the family room and inserted a videocassette into the VCR.

The interview was sandwiched between the AMA convention in St. Louis proposing a resolution calling for voluntary physician curbs on escalating fees, and the birthday of fifty-year-old Mickey Mouse.

Amy Katz, a young, attractive reporter with overly styled brassy hair, had that strangely upbeat air of the interviewer as she peppered Steve with serious questions. She was pictured sitting next to him on the patterned brocade sofa in the Nelson living room. Steve wore brown slacks and a yellow and white striped short sleeve shirt open at the neck. His hair was combed back and sprayed to stay in place, and he'd insisted on studio makeup. He looked young and disarmingly innocent.

Ms. Katz began, "Mr. Nelson, I know how difficult this must be for you. I don't want to seem intrusive at such a sensitive time, but since you and Kim were so well known across the Tampa Bay area, it's a big story."

"That's okay, Amy. Please, call me Steve."

"How did you feel when you first learned that your wife had been arrested for the murder of Kim Connor, your former coanchor here at the station?"

"Absolute shock. I was with our kids." He paused as the camera zoomed closer.

"Do you think she did it?"

His brow crinkled. "I just don't know. Anything's possible, I guess, but Laura's such a wonderful person."

"Could this be a crime of passion," the reporter asked quickly. "Are the rumors true that you were having an affair with Kim Connor?"

Steve exhaled with resignation. "I'm saddened to admit it, but yes, Kim and I did have a brief, well, indiscretion. But it was over, completely over. I'm committed to my family. Besides Kim was moving out of Tampa."

"One more question, Steve," Amy's upbeat voice continued. "Your wife is a very successful surgeon at Tampa City Hospital. What impact will this charge have on her career?"

"I . . . I don't know," Steve stammered. "I guess this is all my fault, really. None if this would have happened if I hadn't had that one indiscretion. I really do blame myself."

"What about the children? You have five kids, isn't that right?"

"Yes. We'll have to manage," Steve said quietly.

Amy Katz thanked Steve with a faint smile. Then the new anchorman – the one from Memphis — thanked Amy before announcing the upcoming clip on Mickey's Mouse's birthday cele-bration, to be followed by sports and the weather.

"You're a damn fool, Nelson." Greg shot up and faced Steve, who sat quietly reflecting on his performance, oblivious to his stunned and ashen wife.

Pale, Steve drained his bottle before rising to eject the cassette. "What?"

"Do you realize what you've done? Condemning your wife in front of the entire Tampa Bay viewing audience?" Greg stepped back abruptly. "I've never seen such a blatant betrayal of a spouse. What are you trying to do, man?"

"What right do you have —"

Greg raised one hand in a "stop" gesture. "Your wife's charged with murder, for God's sake." He turned to face Laura. "We'll make the best of this."

"Hey, you think it was easy, making that confession about Kim? All my fans think of me as an all-American family man. Now —"

Laura finally stood up. "You think it was easy, spending two nights in jail? Worried out of my mind, not knowing where my kids were? Finding a dead woman on your kitchen floor, how easy do you think that was? And if I didn't kill her, because I didn't, who did? You still haven't answered me."

Wordlessly, Steve sat down again on the sofa, sweat starting to seep through the underarms of his tee shirt.

"Try to stay calm, Laura," Greg said softly. "Mr. Nelson, you didn't do your wife any favors with your performance."

"I know my wife better than you do," Steve countered. "Now why don't you just leave so Laura and I can talk things out."

"Fine. You should know that I've instructed your wife not to discuss the case with anyone. Not even you."

"That's the most ridiculous thing I've ever heard. I'll help her through this, but I'm not sure I want you for her attorney."

Laura stepped in front of the TV, both fists clenched. "Well, I'm sure."

Before Steve could respond, there was a loud knock at the front door. Laura sprang toward it as Steve followed.

"Laura," a familiar male voice called from the front hall.

"Dad!" She raced toward him. "Oh, Dad, Mom, thank God you're here!" She threw her arms around them both.

"We had to see you, honey," Carl Whelan said, eyeing Steve accusingly. "We got a bite to eat then we stopped at the jail. They said you'd just left, so we came right over."

"Might as well come in," Steve grumbled.

"Oh, Laura, we were beside ourselves with worry," her mother began, wiping away fresh tears. "How could anyone accuse you of this? What can we do?"

"Mom, I don't know. Just stick with me and help with the kids."

Peg glanced around. "Are they back?"

"No," Laura answered. "They don't know what's happened yet."

"Listen, folks, I'd like to make my introductions and then leave you," Greg spoke for the first time, addressing Laura's parents once he'd entered the room. "I'm Greg Klingman, Laura's attorney."

"Mr. Klingman, please forgive us," Peg Whelan began, "we're just so upset." She extended her hand to Greg.

"These are my parents," Laura said simply as her father reached for Greg's extended hand and grasped it firmly.

"We've spoken. Good to finally meet you," Carl said. "Why don't we all go on inside?"

"I'm on my way out," said Greg, "but Laura, remember, no talk about your case."

The Whelans nodded in unison.

"And that warning extends to you, Mr. Nelson. Laura is not to discuss anything. It could jeopardize her defense. She's stated that she didn't kill Kim Connor, that she's innocent, and that should be good enough for you."

Everybody looked at Steve, but nobody said a word.

CHAPTER THIRTEEN

The next morning Greg got out of bed and tiptoed to Celeste's walk-in closet to rummage on his side for a suit, dress shirt, and tie. Last night they'd had a late dinner, and this morning he hoped she'd sleep late before her flight to Atlanta. As partner in an exclusive interior design firm specializing in luxury hotels, she was about to begin an assignment at a new skyscraper hotel. That might be for the best, since the Nelson case threatened to be all consuming. Greg always slept better in his own place anyway, a sprawling clapboard beach house right on the Gulf of Mexico, in Palm Harbor. Its casual décor — or lack of it, as Celeste liked to quip — relaxed him, the sound of the surf and ocean breezes lulling him to sleep. Its wraparound porch and creaky plank floors made him feel more at ease than her Carrollwood Lake townhouse in Tampa, filled with so many expensive artifacts he always feared he'd break something. But either place was lonely without Celeste, Greg decided, dressing as quietly as he could.

As for the Nelson case, his associates had spent yesterday gathering the basic facts on the crime scene from the police, unfortunately corroborating Sandra Mulloy's statement about Laura's being the only prints on the gun. That was about all Greg himself knew, aside from the sketchy information he got from the police once they'd questioned Steve and inspected his gun collection. At this point, it was clearly convenient for the state and the police to have made such a sensational arrest, which meant it fell to the defense to find

convincing evidence to create enough reasonable doubt to success-
fully defend Laura. If she didn't kill Kim Connor, and Greg
believed she did not — it was his job to find out who did. Today his
legal team would meet Laura and start to pursue all avenues of her
defense.

Greg founded Klingman Law Associates nearly five years after
he graduated from Notre Dame Law School. That was twelve years
ago, and the firm seemed solid at a staff of ten, including paralegals
and secretaries. He prided himself on keeping the firm small, yet
dynamic, and so far had held back from promoting either of his
other two attorneys to full partner, reluctant to give up full control.
But soon, in order to keep them, he knew he would have to.

His right-hand man was Rob Wilson, a thirty-eight-year-old
Yale Law grad who had been with him now for three years and was
well liked by both staff and clients — especially female clients. Still
single, with dark hair untouched by strands of gray and a physique
that proved his passion for pick-up sports, Rob had maintained a
boyish style that Greg had initially found disarming. Although he
was a brilliant strategist, Greg worried that Rob lacked actual street
experience, so in this investigation Rob would manage the face-to-
face encounters with the police, Judge Potter, and the D.A.'s office.
He would also be responsible for tracking the crime scene, the autopsy, and any witness reports.

Greg's right-hand woman was Carrie Diamond, a talented
attorney out of the University of Miami Law School who'd been
with the firm for nine years. Carrie usually handled lower-profile
cases, those that left her more time for her husband, Don, an insurance agent, and their congenitally deaf eleven-year-old daughter,
Elizabeth. Carrie's strengths included her professional judgment,
her knowledge of case law, and maturity beyond her thirty-seven
years. She was attractive with dark brown shoulder-length hair
usually pulled back behind her ears, dark violet eyes, and a sincere
smile. Even though Carrie made no pretense about her family
taking priority over the firm, Greg felt she'd be invaluable to this

case. He sensed that Carrie and Laura were alike — both professional women and mothers, both smart and assertive — and predicted that a kind of synergy would develop between them, which would only help the case. And if, God forbid, it ever came to court, Carrie always exerted a positive effect on juries with her grounded demeanor, which would play well in contrast to Sandra Mulloy's flamboyance.

Finally, and most important to Laura's team, was Chuck Dimer. If Laura didn't kill Kim Connor, they needed the best private investigator in the Tampa Bay area to find out who did, and that meant Chuck. It was a good thing Laura had that mysterious pot of money, because Chuck's fees were legend, but so was his scorecard of success.

"Honey, you're up already?" Celeste peeked out from beneath the ivory satin sheet.

"I've got to go in early." Greg bent over his fiancée and kissed her on the forehead.

She smiled sleepily. "I love that gray suit." She reached over and stroked the herringbone-patterned fabric she'd had imported from Hong Kong.

"And I love you." He smiled back.

"I love you too," she murmured, "Listen, call me later at the office. Maybe lunch before I leave for the airport?"

"Absolutely," he said, knowing full well he'd never be able to spare the time. "Go back to sleep, darling."

"That's about all we know," Greg concluded, looking at the serious faces assembled around the polished oval table in his well-appointed conference room. "I can tell you that my first impression was to plead her. I mean, finding the gun right there, but I've done a one-eighty. I don't believe Laura Nelson killed Kim Connor. Once you meet her, I think you'll agree. Anyway, it's our job to get her off."

The walnut paneled room was lined with shelves of bound legal texts interspersed with assorted artifacts that Celeste had chosen to make the place feel more comforting, less intimidating. He got up to pour himself another cup of coffee as the others scribbled on notepads.

"What happened Sunday night is still hot Wednesday morning," Chuck Dimer whistled, glancing at the *Tampa Tribune* featuring a picture of Laura leaving the jail with Greg.

Chuck was six foot six, with the bulky build of a linebacker, a physique that served him well in his line of work. He had deep blue eyes and salt-and-pepper hair that he wore in a flattop crew cut, a tough guy façade he enhanced by dressing mostly in black — pants, shirts, loafers. Chuck owned and operated Dimer Investigations, a highly respected firm in the Tampa Bay area with an extensive network across the country and even beyond it. He'd been one year ahead of Greg at Notre Dame Law and had joined the FBI after graduation, staying with the bureau for ten years before coming back to Tampa to care for his aging mother about a decade ago.

"The celebrity aspect will keep this one in the papers for a while."

"You're not kidding," Carrie said. "Her own husband goes on television and all but convicts her." She got up and selected a cranberry muffin from a platter of baked goods after refilling her coffee cup. "I can't imagine Don doing that."

"Soon to be ex-husband, don't forget," added Rob. "Just vindictive, or does he really think she did it?"

"Could be vindictive, but I think it's ego," Greg mused. "He was a big TV guy, lost his job, and now he's trying to pump up his own self-image. After talking to him, I think he may really believe that she did it to get him back. It's like the guy's arrogance is clouding his grasp of reality. 'A crime of passion,' he keeps repeating like some kind of a mantra. Laura absolutely denies she wanted him back."

"I wouldn't want a jerk like that either," Carrie said with a frown. "Those poor kids."

"Dr. Nelson is here," announced an officious female voice over the intercom.

"Okay, Betty, please show her in," said Greg. To the group before him he said, "Let's get to work."

Betty Harmon, a buxom woman with a square face surrounded by a halo of white wavy hair and large round glasses, ushered Laura into the conference room. Flashing a smile, Greg's longtime secretary was assuring Laura that Klingman Law Associates had assembled an excellent contingent of lawyers. Rob Wilson rose as he offered her the remaining empty chair.

Greg could only stare. Laura looked so different. So wholesome, so "California." Shoulder-length blonde hair now clean and shining instead of tied in that scraggly ponytail. Her complexion was clear of blotchy patches, and he suspected that she wore makeup, though it was not obvious except for the tinge of eye shadow and mascara that highlighted her now luminous green eyes. Gone were the glasses that made her look so bookish. With tailored gray slacks and a simple white shirt open at the collar, she seemed a different woman from the one he'd left last night in wrinkled shorts and tee shirt. Right, he could finally see her as a professional. Quite a beautiful professional in fact.

"Everyone, this is Dr. Laura Nelson." Greg made formal introductions. Betty Harmon, prim and proper as usual in a black linen suit and frilly white blouse, poured coffee into a blue porcelain cup for Laura before closing the door behind her.

"Laura," Greg began, "we've got a lot to do. Not only do we have to find who really killed Kim Connor, we also have to focus on your defense. Since we'll be pursuing several paths in parallel, we'll need your absolute cooperation on all fronts. Right now, Rob is digging into the police work. He'll be working with the D.A. and law enforcement. You and I and Carrie and Chuck, will explore everything that you know about Connor. That's our first priority, okay?"

"Of course. I don't think I have much to tell you about her though," Laura said. "Steve would know more. One thing Steve did say was that she had a boyfriend who beat her up."

"Right," Greg said.

"There's a good start," Chuck nodded. "Wonder what the cops know about this guy?"

"We'll find out soon," said Rob. "It'll be tops on my list."

"There is something else before we go on," Laura said. "I need to know where I stand with the hospital. Have you spoken with the CEO, Cliff Casey, at all? I have cases, a surgical schedule. Not only will my patients be waiting, it's my week for emergency back-up."

The members of the legal team exchanged glances. Laura had obviously not been informed that her hospital privileges would be suspended until the case was cleared up.

Greg shook his head. "No, I haven't heard from him."

"Chances are they've put you on leave pending resolution of the charges you're facing," Rob ventured.

"Perhaps, but I'm three lung resections behind, two for cancer and one for TB, plus whatever comes in through the ER today. I need to verify that everything's being handled."

Greg looked at Carrie, who stood up. "Dr. Nelson, let's go to my office right now and call the hospital to see how they want to handle this. It's Cliff Casey we need to speak with, right?"

Laura nodded, also standing. "He'll be upset. There's really no one else qualified to do these difficult thoracic procedures."

Laura followed Carrie into her cherry-paneled office and sat across from the desk as Carrie dialed the phone. When she identified herself as Laura's attorney, Cliff Casey picked up immediately. After they exchanged greetings, Cliff asked how Laura was.

"She's fine. She's right here as a matter of fact —"

"As well as all over the newspapers and television," he interrupted. "You can appreciate the scandal for the hospital. I've always admired and supported Dr. Nelson, but now —"

"Dr. Nelson would like to be assured at this time that her schedule has been reassigned —"

"That's been taken care of, of course, Ms. Diamond," he said quickly. "If and when this murder charge is cleared up, we'll have to reconsider Dr. Nelson's contribution to the hospital. As you can imagine, we can be seriously discredited by such an ordeal."

"I understand," Carrie went on in a calm, complacent tone. "And we as her defense team need her undivided attention, so we appreciate anything you can do to lighten Dr. Nelson's responsibilities."

"Did you hear what I said? That's been done already. Tell Laura not to even step a foot into the hospital until this is cleared up."

"Of course, that's our intention, to clear it up. Right now, I'll let her know that the hospital is behind her, and that you'll arrange for her receivables to be sent promptly to her."

"Agreed. One more thing, Ms. Diamond," Cliff added, "tell Laura that any discussions with plaintiff attorneys are off-limits while she's officially suspended from staff privileges."

"Meaning?" Carrie asked.

"Just tell Laura to stay out of the Ruiz case. I know she's been talking to Sam Sanders, that son of a bitch ambulance chaser. He's got no ethics — just a goddamned predator. Tell her to stay out of it."

Laura was holding a framed picture of Carrie and a dark-haired girl in a frilly white dress when Carrie hung up the phone. "Your daughter?"

"Yes, Elizabeth. It was her First Communion."

"She has your eyes," Laura said, putting down the picture. "How old is she?"

"She just turned eleven."

"I've got ten-year-old twin girls," said Laura, checking her watch distractedly. "I promised them I'd be home mid-afternoon."

"Then let's get to work. About the hospital, all your surgical cases have been reassigned, so you don't have to worry. Until this is over, your hospital privileges are suspended. It's procedure. Mr. Casey will facilitate your receivables promptly so that you don't even have to go in."

"I see," Laura said sadly. "Well, thank you."

As they walked toward the conference room, Carrie almost brought up the Ruiz case warning, but one look at Laura's anguished face stopped her.

At noon, Rob left for police headquarters in search of any new evidence files, and Chuck took Laura in his custom Chevy van to Steve's empty apartment to reconstruct the murder scene. Steve had moved back into their Davis Island house, and the police tape had been taken down around the house on Oregon. The front door was locked, different from that night when Laura had just let herself in. She tried hard to focus on other details: Which rooms she had walked into. What she had seen. How she had stumbled upon the body. The feeling of the gun as her hand touched it. How the police found her standing there. How she had reacted.

"Did she see anybody? Could anybody have seen her?" Chuck kept asking.

Something kept trying to play in the back of her mind, but she couldn't get it into focus. Somebody she'd noticed that night, but she couldn't remember and just wanted to get away from there. Finally, Chuck drove her back to the law office.

Sandwiches and salads had been ordered in and they ate as they waited for Rob to return. They reviewed the crime scene report and the preliminary police notes, and when Rob arrived, the autopsy findings. Then the trio of lawyers and Chuck peppered Laura with questions. What did she know about Kim? Who could have killed her and why? What was Steve's part in all this? Laura had no answers, and at five Carrie suggested that they break until morning.

As Laura turned the shiny brass handle of her front door, still struggling to find the right words to make her children understand everything that had happened, a deathly quiet and a sickening sense of dread confronted her. The children were gone, she knew it. Flinging down her purse, she ran upstairs, just like the first time, frantically searching through each bedroom. This time there were signs of hasty packing, items of clothing strewn on the floor, dresser drawers open and half empty.

And they were gone.

Blind with panic, she flew down the steps looking for any sign as to where they might be. This time she'd follow them. But how? To where?

She saw the white envelope. It had been placed conspicuously on the kitchen table anchored by Marcy's favorite coffee mug, the one with the butterflies Patrick had made in art class. With shaking hands and a plunging heart, Laura tore open the envelope. She immediately recognized the handwriting on the notepaper as Marcy Whitman's neat block lettering.

> Dearest Laura,
>
> Please try to understand. Right after you left this morning, Steve told me he was taking the kids to his father's in Traverse City. He already had the plane tickets, including one for me. I told him there was no way I'd go, that I was not going to pick sides, that I was loyal to you both. He said that if I went with him the kids would have someone to watch out for them because his father's not well. Please trust that the reason I'm going is so I can be with the children and help them understand that you love them and that there's absolutely no way you would ever harm anyone, no matter what. That you have spent your whole life helping and healing people. Please believe me when I tell you that I am completely dedicated to you and I believe in your innocence.
>
> All my love, Marcy
>
> P.S. When I asked Steve if he was going to tell you where he was taking us, he said I could. Also, the police were here to question me about that night. I had

to tell them what you said. About where you were
going. An emergency at the hospital. I hope that's
okay.

Laura sat at the table, tears falling freely as she struggled to
think. Did she have any options? It was slightly past six. She picked
up the phone.

"Hello."

"Oh, Greg, thank God," Laura said.

"I'm just on the way out. What's happening?"

"My husband took off with my children."

"What?"

"I went directly home from your office," she sobbed, "and
they were gone."

"Do you know where —"

"Steve's taking them to his father's in Traverse City. The
housekeeper left a note."

"Bastard," Greg breathed. Did Steve have the right to remove
the kids to Michigan? His alibi at the time of the murder had been
confirmed by the police. He had left Tampa well in advance of the
murder. All confirmed by the kids. So he was not a suspect and, yes,
he probably did have the right under these circumstances.

"Okay, Laura, if they left this morning they're already out of
state and there's nothing we can do."

"Nothing we can do? My children are my life. I've barely had
the chance to talk to them about what's happened. I need to go —"

"There's nothing we can do tonight, Laura. Tomorrow we'll
get a custody expert and develop our options."

"We're still married. That means we share custody equally,
right? I was supposed to see a divorce attorney yesterday. Obviously, I never made it."

"That's too bad. Starting the proceedings might have helped.
Regardless, what you need to remember right now is that you're out

on bail. If you leave Hillsborough County, they'll put you right back in jail."

Laura shuddered at the memory. "But what if Steve is telling the kids that I killed that woman?"

"Laura, we'll work this out tomorrow. It'll be complicated because they're with their father and grandfather and you have no special custody rights."

"Custody rights? I'm their mother. I need to do something now. The last time he took them, I just waited around and didn't ask for help and look what happened."

"You can't leave Tampa."

"Then will you go?"

"We have to wait until morning. Now tell me that you're going to be okay. That you'll just stay home, get something to eat, and rest."

But she couldn't. Instead, Laura just hung up the phone and began wandering through the empty house, lovingly touching the kids' things. There was Mike's baseball bat, Kevin's model planes, Natalie's menagerie of stuffed animals, Nicole's collection of Barbie's, Patrick's Tinkertoy constructions. Unable to eat, unable to sit, unable to even pray anymore, she paced and paced the house until she heard pounding on the front door.

Greg had called her parents.

CHAPTER FOURTEEN

Jim Nelson waited for Steve at the Cherry Capital Airport three miles from his home in Traverse City, Michigan, a charming, tourist town tucked in the crook of Lake Michigan's Grand Traverse Bay. He held a copy of his son's itinerary — a United Airlines flight from Tampa to Chicago, then a two engine prop to Traverse City.

"Hey there, kids," he called as soon as he spotted Steve, looking sporty in tailored tan slacks and a tangerine golf shirt. Following him were five kids, whom he hadn't seen in five years, along with a middle-aged woman with salt-and-pepper hair pulled back in a bun.

Jim shifted nervously, blowing his nose into a handkerchief, and running his fingers through his own thinning gray hair. Neatly pressed Bermuda shorts, a short-sleeved summer sports shirt open at the neck, and sneakers without socks made him look more like a tourist than a native. "Wow, you've all gotten so big, I wouldn't recognize you."

"Yeah, Dad," Steve said as slung an arm around his father's shoulder, "it's been too long."

"Son, you look great."

"And you look better than you sounded on the phone. That flu better?" Without waiting for an answer, he turned to introduce Marcy, who stood grasping the hands of the twins. "Dad, this is Mrs. Whitman, my housekeeper."

"Marcy," she said as she extricated her right hand from Nicole's and offered it.

"Jim here. Glad to meet you," he said. "Thanks for coming, be needing your help with all these young ones. I am feeling better, but still sniffling a bit."

"Sorry you've not been well," Marcy said.

The kids all offered awkward hello's.

It was Cherry Festival time and the airport was crowded with visitors, forcing the Nelson entourage to make their way slowly through the small airport to the baggage claim area. Jim and Steve walked together with Patrick trailing closely behind. Mike and Kevin followed, silently hoisting backpacks and looking glum. Marcy and the twins were last, their hair braided and dressed in matching candy-stripe pinafores, their usually bright faces downcast.

"How's Laura doing, son?"

"Like I told you on the phone, Dad, she's a wreck, meeting with her lawyers day and night. That's why I had to get the kids out of there. That, and the media's everywhere."

Jim frowned. "I just hope they don't follow you here."

"So do I. How're you doing?"

"Better. You know, I haven't seen you since your mother's passing almost —"

"It's five years ago. I know, Dad. You've never come to Florida."

"I've got your mother's roses to care for. Last winter we had so much snow I couldn't have come anyway. But you —"

"I know. It's been hectic with my job and the kids and, of course, Laura's always on call. I know it's a lot, us landing on you like this, but I've got a plan. I'll take the boys camping in a few days, and Marcy can help with the girls. That's why she's here."

His father frowned. "Steve, Laura called."

"Not now, okay?" Glancing back at the kids, Steve picked up his pace.

Initially, Steve brightened when they arrived at his father's street. The neighborhood looked unchanged, homes all in good repair, plenty of beautiful shade trees. Neighbors sat on porches enjoying the perfect summer temperatures, the sweet aroma of roses climbing on trellises, and rhododendrons in full bloom. Halfway down the block, now painted the color of celery with slate gray shutters, with the old wraparound front porch, was his parents' house, where he and his twin, Philip, had shared a large bedroom upstairs with full-size poster beds. They spent most of their playtime in the tree-playhouse Dad had built to match the big house. Stepping from the car, Steve looked from the tree stump up into the air where the tree house used to be.

He had been ten years old, the age of his own twins when it happened.

In those rare moments when Steve allowed himself to reminisce about growing up with his identical twin brother, he ruminated over the biggest difference between them. Philip was the aggressive one, making all the plans, pretty much telling Steve what to do. Much like the role of his daughter, Nicole, while Natalie was more like him, the follower. And how Nicole irritated him because of it. Even though he'd resented Philip's control, he still loved him, depended on him. Nobody would ever know the depth of his pain as a child and his lingering grief still. The day of the accident the boys had been arguing over which twin their Black Lab puppy, Lucky, liked best. Steve had angrily shoved Philip out of the tree house and he'd ended up dead. It was an accident.

An accident.

Once Marcy took over the kitchen to make lemonade and chocolate chip cookies, and the kids discovered the swing beyond the back porch, Steve and his father sat nearby under an oak tree. Jim Nelson brought up Laura again.

"Maybe you should call her and let the kids talk to her."

"I don't want them mixed up in this. No calls to or from the kids. I'm trying to get them away from all her troubles."

"But Steve, I told her I'd have you call. You know that I haven't always agreed with Laura. Your mother never did understand why she was hell-bent on going to medical school instead of staying home with the kids. But over the years, I've come to believe she's a good mother. And you said yourself that this was all your fault. Because of — well, you and that dead woman — what you did."

"Dad, I made a mistake. We all make mistakes, right?"

Jim Nelson nodded sadly.

"Before that Laura and I were very happy. Now we have to give her time to work with her attorney. She needs a break from the kids."

"That's not what she said," his father said shakily, "and I did tell her I'd make sure you called."

Steve acquiesced. "I'll call her later, okay? Now let's not worry about Laura."

"And Steve," he continued, "how are we all going to manage in this small house?"

"I'll sleep with the boys in the spare bedroom and Marcy can stay with the girls in my old room. And like I said, I'm going to take the boys camping in a few days, so it's only a couple nights."

"But we don't have enough beds."

"Sleeping bags will be fine for the kids. Really, Dad, it'll be okay."

It was a struggle to talk to his father now, because Steve had become irritated as well as preoccupied. Coming back home, he realized he saw Traverse City as a security blanket, one that was more than a thousand miles away from Frank Santiago. Though Steve had tried to avoid thinking about it, the reality was that Santiago was one violent — and dangerous — son of a bitch. The mob! It was everywhere, wasn't it? Were they looking for him right now, here in Michigan? A personal vendetta because he had screwed the woman Santiago wanted to marry? He sank deeper into his chair and stared up at the sky as he wondered why he hadn't thought more about all this when he agreed to do the goddamned TV interview.

Because he was in shock, that was why. Kim. That gun. Laura. That night was all too much.

Well, he'd lay low in northern Michigan. He'd be able to think once he got to the Upper Peninsula. Not only did he need to calm down, he needed a plan. A long-term plan.

Late Sunday afternoon, Mike picked up the phone in his grandfather's kitchen on the first ring. As he'd so hoped, it was Laura. "Mom," he breathed, not daring to talk too loudly. He'd heard his dad tell Grandpa Nelson when they'd arrived on Wednesday that the kids were not to talk to their mother.

"Mike, is that really you? Oh, honey, how I miss you all. How are you?"

"Not so great, Mom. We're supposed to go camping, but Dad doesn't want to take the girls. Dad's sending Mrs. Whitman home too."

Laura paused. "Yes, Marcy just called to tell me."

"I tried to get Dad to take Natalie and Nicole, but he says it's a guy trip."

"Honey, I'm going to try to get you all back to Tampa as soon as possible, but now Dad doesn't even want me talking to you guys."

"Dad says that you don't have time for us, that's why we have to stay up here."

"Of course I have time for you. I'm frantic with worry about you. I can't think of anything else except how to get you home."

"Then why don't you just come and get us?"

"Mike, I'm not allowed to leave Tampa. It's legal stuff. Otherwise —"

"I didn't know that. Kevin and I were wondering why you didn't come."

"Mike, of course I would if I could. The problem is, I can't. Honey, will you please try to make the younger ones understand?"

"Sure, Mom, but I gotta hang up. I think Dad's coming."

Before the connection was broken, Laura heard Steve in the background, "Mike, how many times have I told you —"

*   *   *

Laura had walked the streets of Davis Island Sunday afternoon following a thunderstorm that temporarily cooled the humid Florida summer air and left a cloying smell of jasmine. She reflected on the dreadful week since she'd stumbled upon Kim Connor's body — the end of her marriage, the nights in jail, the absence of her children. Roxanne Musing called every day with hospital news, but Laura's practice, her patients, her entire professional life so quickly seemed unreal, something from the past. Even Roxanne's reports on the Ruiz family served only to remind her of the night she'd found Steve with Kim.

After her walk, Laura had returned home determined to talk to her children. She'd put the call in to Traverse City and to her relief Mike had picked up. And before Steve yanked the phone away from him, she'd learned more distressing news. What was Steve trying to do to her? Now he was taking the boys camping, but where and for how long? And why was he sending Marcy home? Why wouldn't he send the girls home with her rather than leave them alone with his father in Traverse City? It wasn't that she didn't trust Jim, but he apparently had some kind of medical problem. Surely he wouldn't want that responsibility. A guy who never even bothered to visit his son and grandchildren?

This was just so wrong, so unfair. She needed to do something. She needed to be with her children, but she was trapped, helpless to do anything to get them back.

Once she'd finally stopped shaking after talking to Mike, Laura dialed Greg's home number. It was July first, a Sunday. What had he told her? Was he going to Atlanta to see his fiancée or was she coming to Florida? Please be home, she prayed.

"Hello," a woman's upbeat voice answered.

"Hello," Laura said faintly, "is Mr. Klingman available?"

"I can hardly hear you. Can I say who's calling?"

"It's Laura Nelson."

"Oh, Dr. Nelson," the voice cooled. Celeste had just poured

two glasses of Chardonnay to tide her and Greg over as the sword-fish marinated in olive oil and orange juice. "It's Celeste Marin. May I take a message?"

"Oh yes, Celeste. Please, will you ask Greg to call me tonight? It's important."

"Surely, I will."

But it wasn't until after they'd finished dessert, pecan pie with French vanilla ice cream and their second cup of coffee that Celeste mentioned that he'd had a call from Laura Nelson.

"When did she call?"

"About six." It was now nine forty-five.

"On a Sunday night? I should have gone into taxes or con-tracts." Greg reached over to the phone on the table behind the couch and dialed Laura's number.

She answered on the first ring. "Greg, is that you?"

"Yes, Laura. What is it?"

"Sorry to bother you, but there's something I need to tell you. Steve's going away with the boys."

"What do you mean, 'going away'? He's already away."

"Camping. He's leaving the twins with his dad and sending our housekeeper home. And he won't let me even talk to any of them. Greg, I'm frantic."

"I see. Will the girls be okay with his dad?"

"It's just that Jim Nelson is like a total stranger to the kids, Greg. The way Steve's neglected the twins, they'll be so upset. Isn't there something you can do to get them home?"

"Neglect to abandonment," Greg grumbled. "Listen, first thing tomorrow, we'll intensify our look at custody issues. So far we've just gotten the runaround on jurisdiction — Michigan versus Florida. I'll get Chuck involved. You can meet us at the office at eight, okay? Oh, that reminds me. I got a call from Carrie this week-end. She mentioned that Cliff Casey brought up another case — a malpractice case — that you're involved in. A Wendy Ruiz? What's your involvement?"

Laura let out a long breath. "Nothing, really. I was contacted by a lawyer who was interested in representing her father."

"For what purpose? What's your role?"

"I was called in for emergency surgery. I said I would tell what happened to Wendy," Laura admitted. "The ER neglected the patient's chest wounds, and they called me too late to save her. The child died."

"Does that mean you'll testify against the hospital, against other doctors? That's pretty sticky, especially given your present circumstances."

"Look, I just can't —"

"I hope you reconsider. My firm does the defense work for the hospital. If I'm defending a client who's a hostile witness to another client, it'll be a perceived, if not real, conflict of interest. Do you understand?"

"Well, not really. But I don't want to cause problems for —"

"Does that mean you'll drop out as a witness for the plaintiff?"

Laura inhaled. "Would that be right? I mean, the reason I agreed to help was because of all that poor family has been through."

"With all due respect," Greg said gently, "you have to worry about yourself right now. Agreed?"

"Okay, Greg, if that's how it has to be. I do apologize for calling you at home. I . . . I just didn't know who to call."

"Hey, just stay put. Promise?"

Laura hesitated. "I will," she said. But no promises, she thought.

CHAPTER FIFTEEN

When Laura arrived at Klingman Law Associates at seven thirty the next morning, a sleepy security guard let her in. She paced the reception area until Greg's arrival just before eight, her mind filled with images of the kids, what they must be going through — especially the girls. They'd be confused and scared. And not only that, did they think she was a killer?

"Morning, Laura," Greg greeted her. "Aren't you the early one?" He walked into his office suite and carefully hung his jacket in the closet before joining her at the window where she stood staring out at the clump of coconut palms in the courtyard below.

"I couldn't sleep," she said.

"Well, come on in."

Greg motioned for her to take a seat on the burgundy leather sofa in his private office before stepping out to the hallway's utility cabinet to start the coffee maker.

"I've scheduled an update meeting first thing," he said. "We'll focus on this new situation first. Then we'll go over your case. So, tell me what you think your husband's doing."

"Besides running away, you mean?"

"I am sorry. Will the kids will be safe where they are?"

"I guess so. I have no idea where Steve is taking the boys, but the girls should be okay at Jim's."

"We'll get Chuck to check their whereabouts and we'll develop our options. Carrie'll dig into disputed custody issues —"

There was a knock on the door and Betty Harmon poked her head in. "Morning. Just wanted you to know that Mr. Dimer has arrived. Ms. Diamond and Mr. Wills are waiting in the conference room."

"Thanks, Betty. Tell them we'll join them in a moment, please."

As Greg and Laura walked into the conference room, Chuck Dimer stood out among the business attire with his black jeans, black tee shirt, and loafers.

"Morning, everyone," Greg said. "First, let me brief you on Laura's most recent problem." He brought them up to date on Steve's activities.

"I'm on it," Chuck said, leaving the room to place a call to Michigan. If he could prove that the girls had been left behind with their grandfather, it might sway a judge on custody.

Carrie leaned over and squeezed Laura's hand. "I'm sorry. If it were my kids —"

"Thank you. Just help me get them back."

"Chuck is the best. You'll see," Carrie murmured.

"Now let's get down to work," Greg said. "We have a lot of ground to cover. First, Rob will summarize the police details. Rob?"

"Right." He opened the file before him and glanced across the conference table until Laura looked up at him. "To recap what we know. When the police arrived, they found Dr. Nelson standing over the body beside a gun, a Colt thirty-eight, not traceable. Whoever it was maybe carries one of those around "just in case." My guess. Officers Parker and Belinsky arrive in a squad car exactly nine minutes after the call from upstairs. Neighbor says she heard a gunshot, didn't see anything unusual."

"Or hear anything. Like an argument, any voices?" Carrie asked.

"Just the shot. Cops think it's maybe a car backfire, no biggie. All else is just like you told us, Laura."

Laura grimaced.

"But no other prints on the thirty-eight," Greg confirmed.

"Only Laura's."

"No other prints on the scene, except the obvious — Steve Nelson's," Carrie added, "and an unknown. Presumably the guy Steve's renting from, considering they're all over the apartment."

"Right," Rob went on, "easy to check out."

"And Steve's alibi?" Carrie queried.

"Sounds solid. He was on the road with five kids. Stayed overnight in the Roadside Motel near Macon. Receipts check out," Rob added, glancing pointedly at Greg. "So far, nobody seems to think he's connected in any way."

"Was there a forced entry at the apartment?" asked Greg.

"None at all," Rob answered. "But remember, Laura said the door was unlocked when she got there."

"That's right," Laura offered. "I remember it distinctly."

"So maybe Kim had a key? Or maybe Nelson doesn't lock his door?"

"Lots of maybes. There's a lot we need to find out about Steve and Kim," said Carrie, "but go on, Rob."

"Okay. There's no doubt that the gun beside the victim, the one with your prints, Laura, was the murder weapon. Ballistics, a perfect match. I asked about a residue report. It's not in the file, but sometimes the lab holds off before running it. Sandra Mulloy said she'd check into it."

"What does that mean?" Laura asked.

"Standard routine," Rob answered. "They check your hands for gunpowder residue, to prove that you actually shot the gun. Without a positive residue, the fact is, they don't have much of a case."

"They did take my fingerprints, but that's all I remember. There was blood on my hands that they swabbed off —"

"You think they somehow screwed up and didn't get it before they let her wash her hands? Or are they playing games?" Greg wondered aloud.

"Your guess is as good as mine," Rob said. "Anyway, the autopsy confirmed cause of death. Bullet ripped through the left ventricle. But, Laura, there's something else that came up: you told them that you didn't own a gun?"

Laura turned two shades of red. "I know that was a mistake," she said, looking away. "It's true I don't 'own' a gun. I guess I never thought they'd find out about Steve's. He grew up with guns in northern Michigan. All the boys from there hunt." She turned to face Rob. "Does that mean they think I'm a liar?"

"Let's say it didn't help your credibility." Rob admitted.

"Is there anything else we need to know, Laura?" Carrie asked. "Anything that they know and we don't can only hurt you."

"Lies," Laura said. "They always come back to haunt you, don't they? Yes, there are a couple more. One, I told my housekeeper that I was going to the ER that night I went to Steve's. I simply didn't want to upset her. And I told Steve's former boss, George Granger, that I needed Kim's phone number to drop off some photography equipment — another lie. He gave it to me and I left that message on her phone."

"They know about the housekeeper. She said as much in a statement. But nothing from the other guy, so we'll let sleeping dogs lie. Only a little white lie anyway." A miniscule grin flickered on Rob's face. "I do have good news. They're looking into the abusive boyfriend you told us about. Turns out nobody's seen the guy around lately. Lopez and Goodnuf checked around. Interviewed the victim's friends, acquaintances, didn't get much."

Laura flinched at the mention of the detectives that had ruined her life. "You mean they're still investigating? That's a good sign, right?"

Rob shrugged. "They're just covering all the bases. Routine, they say, but Lopez did tell me that they knew about Santiago's occupation, so to speak. They're checking him out with RICO, but it's not likely they're going to share anything about that with us."

"What's RICO?" Laura asked.

"Racketeer Influenced and Corrupt Organization Act. The

focus is on organized crime, and this Mr. Santiago is obviously part of our own Tampa mob."

"Steve said that Santiago beat Kim up and that she needed help," Laura offered. "It was his excuse for her being at our house the night I found them together."

Greg frowned. "Some kind of help."

Chuck walked back into the conference room. "Things are in motion. I've got a guy on the way to the Nelson house in Traverse City."

"What will he do when he gets there?" Laura's hand flew to her neck as she turned to face Chuck.

"He'll be discreet, confirm that the girls are there, that they're okay, and wait for instructions from here."

Chuck's authoritative baritone reassured Laura and she let her hand fall into her lap.

"He'll let me know the minute they make contact."

"Good," Greg said. "Meantime, we're talking about this Santiago character. What have you found on him?"

"Francisco Ramiro Santiago. Age forty-two. Born in Cuba. Grew up in Miami. Now in Ybor City runnin' narcotics. The guy looks like a Latino version of Wall Street. Expensive clothes, slick operator. Those in the know — who are willing to talk — say he made his way up the ladder in a nasty way. Also iced a few cops in his illustrious career, including the partner of our own Detective Lopez back when he was on the street."

"The mob?" Carrie went wide-eyed. "As in *The Godfather*? Here in Tampa?"

"The mob is alive and well in 'Cigar City'," assured Chuck. "The name Santo Trafficante Jr. mean anything to you?"

"No," Carrie said.

"Well it scares the shit out of anybody in Mafia circles and aggravates the hell out of the FBI. Feds have been tryin' to entrap him forever."

"I've read about him," said Greg. "Didn't he make some big donation to feed the masses or something like that?"

"Yeah, right across the bay in St. Pete. But no way those hand-outs are gonna compensate for the bad shit. Excuse my language, ladies."

"You're scaring me," said Carrie as she reached for the coffee pot. "Anybody else?"

"I'll take a refill." Greg held out a maroon Buccaneers mug.

"So how does this *Godfather* person relate to Santiago?" Carrie continued.

"Santiago is like a captain or lieutenant to an underboss," explained Chuck. "A player not far down the feeding chain. There are several Latin factions apparently. Sometimes they work together, sometimes not. That's when you get blood baths. Guy by the name of Carlos Tosco out of Miami runs him. Our boy Santiago may be dapper, but behind that pretty façade, he's a dangerous creep."

"That is scary," said Laura. "I wonder how much Steve knows about him and those connections."

"For his sake, let's hope, not much," said Greg.

"Steve may be in over his head," Laura said, cringing at the thought.

"So where's the creep been?" asked Rob. "The cops can't find him for questioning."

"So Santiago could be the killer?" Laura mused.

"We're still digging for a true time frame," Chuck said. "The closest lead I have is a friend of Connor's, a Carmen Williams from Ybor City. Says that Santiago was in Miami around the time of the murder. Maybe she's right on it, maybe not. She's got a drug habit. Wants no part of the cops, but she's pretty broken up about Connor. I'll keep pressing her for details."

"I wonder if Steve knows her?" Laura looked absently toward Chuck.

"I need to talk to him," Chuck said. "If Connor used him as a confidant, that bastard — oops, sorry, Laura — must know more."

"I'm sure he does," said Laura. "But since he's so sure I did it, he won't even talk about looking for who really did."

"We'll see about that. Rob, anybody see anyone going in or out of the Oregon place?" Chuck asked.

"Police have covered all the neighbors. Nobody saw anything. Kim's Firebird and a station wagon — presumably Laura's — were mentioned, but no other strange cars. The lady upstairs, the one who called in, did see Kim come in at least five minutes before she heard the shot. Couldn't see if she used a key, but none was found. Didn't see Laura come in though or anyone else."

Chuck nodded. "I'll follow on the heels of the uniforms. The lady upstairs is my first stop. Sometimes, people remember things later."

Laura looked at him intently.

"Damn. Somebody must've seen something," said Greg. "It was a Sunday night for God's sake. It was eighty-five degrees, people linger outside."

"Yeah, only problem, it was raining. Don't worry, I'll be all over this," said Chuck with confidence.

"That's right, it was raining," Laura added quietly.

"Now, as for Kim's place," Rob said, glancing toward Laura. "They have a recording of your call to Kim about an hour before she was killed. We have the transcript."

Laura winced. "I was so upset I can't even remember what I said."

Rob read aloud the brief message she'd left. "They're trying to make it out as a threat, you warning her to stay away from your kids. But it's weak."

"What about the messages I left on Steve's machine? They must have those too, right? I called at least four times looking for the kids."

Rob frowned. "Actually, Laura, there's a notation from Detective Lopez on that point. It looks like you brought this up in the initial interview, but when they retrieved the answering machine, there weren't any messages on it."

"What? That can't be. That means Steve — or someone — must've gotten the messages and —"

"Erased 'em?" offered Greg. To Rob, he said, "Is it something to worry about?"

Rob shrugged. "I can double check. But to be honest, the cops — well, they don't tend to believe Laura's story."

"They think I'm making it up," she mumbled. "Just another lie."

"Hmm. Well, anything else at Kim's place?" Carrie asked.

"Boxes. She was ready to move. The movers were scheduled for the next morning." Rob paused and checked his notes. "That's about it," he concluded, "although they didn't do much of a neighborhood check in my opinion."

Chuck nodded again. "I'll be digging in over there."

"My question is: what was Kim doing at Steve's place to begin with? According to the folks at Channel Eight, she ignored him at the station when he came back to collect his things," Carrie said.

"'Cool as a cucumber,' wasn't that the exact quote?" Rob asked.

Carrie concurred. "So why was she at Steve's house that night? The abusive boyfriend is back in town and she goes over to Steve's for safe haven?" She looked around at the ponderous faces.

"So the guy follows her over and he snuffs her," Chuck offered.

"Whatever happened," Carrie went on, "he got out fast without leaving a trace of evidence."

"Carrie, you're getting good," Chuck said lightly. "Want to take over my role?"

The lawyers laughed as Greg looked at Laura, his smile waning. "What do you think?"

"I don't know. I really don't know."

"Well, it seems to me," Greg said, getting up to stretch his legs, "that we need more information from Steve about this gangster boyfriend."

"Yeah," added Chuck, "enough on this creep to convince the State to open up a more intensive investigation."

"So far the cops have nothing to connect him with her that night," Rob said. "Uh, Laura, do you remember them taking fingernail scrapings, at the station? They'd test for signs of struggle to connect you that way," he explained.

"I . . . I don't remember that."

"Good enough. Well," Chuck said, "I'll start in Old Hyde Park, and then move on to Connor's medical records, including emergency rooms. Could be more abuse."

"Good, Chuck," Greg said. "That Connor woman was playing with fire. Wonder if the boyfriend found out about her liaison with Steve. And what about drugs? Chuck, you said she has a friend who's an addict? Could this be about drugs?"

"I don't think so," said Chuck. "The word in Ybor is that Connor helped Williams with rehab and such. The rumors — not substantiated — are that Connor used to be a user, but she's been squeaky clean now for years."

"Steve ever dabbled in drugs?" Greg asked Laura.

"Never. Alcohol yes, but usually in moderation."

Greg nodded. "Well, guys, we've got our work ahead of us. The Mafiosa. Certainly adds another dimension."

"No question," Chuck said. "I've got someone in Miami to track 'em down. The big boss down there is a Carlos Tosca. He'd be pulling Santiago's strings. "

"My bet's on Santiago," Carrie offered. "But I don't want to go anywhere near him if he's so dangerous."

"I hear you," replied Chuck. "In the meantime, I gotta dig up something to show the cops they got the wrong person now."

Greg started to gather up his notes. "Okay, everyone, let's get to work. Laura, you okay with all this?"

"I want to see my kids."

For a moment, nobody said a word. "Yeah, I hear you," Chuck said kindly. "Once we have all the facts, we'll find a way to get them back."

"It'll be okay, Laura," Carrie said, leaning over and squeezing her hand again.

"Right," agreed Greg. "Carrie, what's up with the custody statutes, both Michigan and Florida?"

"I've got local counsel ready to file in Michigan and we'll file in Hillsborough County tomorrow. Since the kids are physically in Michigan, well, we'll see."

For the rest of the day, Greg, Rob, and Laura sat around the conference table poring over endless details. Carrie had gone off to work the custody angle, and Chuck to organize his contacts working out of Tampa, Miami, and Traverse City. When Chuck returned later, Laura jumped up, anxious for any news of her children. Chuck explained that he'd commissioned a P.I. firm in Grand Rapids to cover the Nelson house in Traverse City without initiating contact. Chuck didn't want to alert Steve until they'd established their legal options.

Meantime, Laura took two calls. The first from her parents who offered to travel to Michigan to see the kids. Laura told them what she knew — that Steve told the boys he was taking them camping, and that the girls would stay with Jim Nelson. The second call was from Roxanne Musing at the hospital. News had already traveled back that Laura had withdrawn as plaintiff witness in the Ruiz case. Laura told Roxanne that she couldn't discuss it just then, that they'd have to talk later. Roxanne tried to object, but Laura cut her off and hung up.

In the late afternoon, Carrie came in to request Greg's participation in a conference call she'd set up with a local law firm in Traverse City. Chuck and his Grand Rapids man would also be on the call to set the strategy for extricating the twins. Reassuring Laura that the girls seemed fine and that nothing more could be done that night, Greg sent her home.

Collapsing in the lounge chair in her bedroom, Laura sipped a cup of ginger tea and ignored the cheese sandwiches that Marcy had left. She drifted into exhaustion and fell asleep, still sitting up. When the doorbell rang, Laura catapulted up and ran downstairs.

Roxanne and a small boy with big black eyes, smooth olive skin, and jet black hair in a neat crew cut were standing at the door.

"Come on," Roxanne said, "we're going over to Bayside Park." She leaned over and patted the child's head. "This is Jose Ruiz. He's our kid for tonight. Let's share him and go watch the fireworks."

Laura looked down into the boy's shining face. "Only after I get Jose here one of my big lollipops. What's your favorite color, Jose?"

"Red," he said, a wide smile crossing his face.

"Mine too!" For an instant, Laura felt her heart lighten as she followed Jose and Roxanne outside into the warm evening air.

CHAPTER SIXTEEN

Laura spent the week at the mercy of the civil courts' agonizing pace. Because Wednesday was the Fourth of July, the courts were closed. Then there was the issue of jurisdiction for custody. Was it Grand Traverse County, where Steve was visiting his father? Or as Greg and Carrie argued, Hillsborough County, Florida, the Nelson family's permanent residence? Neither Laura nor Steve had filed divorce or separation papers, so either parent could legally take them anywhere. But because the twins were no longer in the care of their father, Laura's attorneys argued that she could legally retrieve them and bring them home. Except that she could not leave to do so personally, and so far Judge Potter had not ruled to let her do so.

In the meantime her lawyers did not want to serve Steve's father with papers and risk Steve's abrupt return to take the girls. Rather, they wanted everything in place to allow the twins' release to Laura through a legally appointed agent, namely Chuck Dimer.

On Tuesday, through local counsel in Traverse City, briefs had been filed in that jurisdiction in support of returning the girls to Laura in Florida. Late on Thursday, a Grand Traverse County judge ruled that they could be released to the mother or her authorized agent pending notification of the father. If the father filed no dissenting papers with his court within twenty-four hours, Jim Nelson was to release the girls to their mother's legal agent for transport to Hillsborough County, Florida, where that court would then assume definitive jurisdiction.

By the time the court order arrived by courier at the Nelson home in Traverse City, Steve had already left with the boys. Jim Nelson signed for the delivery of the notification because he had no other option — and he had no idea where Steve was. If Steve got in touch with him, it'd be up to Steve to decide if he wanted to try to block Laura. If he didn't, Natalie and Nicole would be free to leave Traverse City at 5:00 p.m. Friday, July sixth.

"Okay, Laura, here's where we are." Carrie Diamond sat down at Laura's kitchen table with a cup of tea Thursday evening. "Chuck is arranging to bring the girls home tomorrow night or Saturday morning, depending on flight availability. So far Steve has not responded to the court order so it's unlikely, although not impossible, that he'll intervene in time. So that's good news. Hopefully we'll have them home tomorrow night."

"Oh, I just can't wait. Thank you, and thank Greg and Chuck and Rob," Laura blurted. A hint of hope crossed her ashen, drawn face. Not eating very much for days now, she'd dropped several pounds.

"And there's more news," Carrie continued. "Possibly not related — and definitely morbid — but it turns out that following the night Kim was killed, a couple of dead bodies turned up in Tampa."

Laura abruptly set down her cup of tea. "What's that got to do with Kim?"

"I'm not sure, but Chuck and his P.I.s came up with a possible connection."

Laura frowned. "I'm not following."

"Well, the dead guys were Mexicans. The police found traces of high-potency cocaine in the truck they were found in. The same grade of cocaine that they're now finding on the street in Ybor City."

"I'm still not getting the connection. Does this have something to do with Kim's drug addict friend that Chuck talked to?"

"Maybe. Ybor City is Santiago's territory, and maybe he had

something to do with the drugs — and the dead guys. Apparently trouble's been brewing between the drug elements in South Florida for a while. Anyway, it gives the police another reason to want to find him."

"Oh, that's just too bizarre," Laura shivered. "Steve so close to the mob? I can't believe he knew anything about it. He's always been so conservative."

"Chuck's going to question him whenever he gets out of those Michigan woods. But in the meantime, he thinks that Detective Lopez is buying Santiago's tie to the drugs."

Laura nodded. "I see. Detective Lopez was the more reasonable of the two detectives that night. Do you think that he actually wants to help me?"

"Who knows," Carrie said, "but the more resources the police commit to trying to find Santiago, the better for us."

"At least they're looking for someone else. Thank God. Listen, do they know yet?"

"What?" Carrie looked confused. "Does who know?"

"Natalie and Nicole? That they're coming home. Has anyone told them?"

"No," responded Carrie carefully. "Nobody thought it wise to tell them before everything's settled."

"Can I talk to them at least?"

"That might be a bit risky." Carrie hesitated. "But since their grandfather already knows he has to release them to the court order —"

"I'll call right now. Jim will be okay with this, I'm sure."

After Carrie agreed, Laura dialed Michigan.

Jim Nelson answered in a cautious tone. "Hello?"

"Jim, it's Laura. I'm so sorry about all this. And about saddling you with our problems, but I miss the girls so much. Could I talk to them, please?"

"Of course, Laura. You know I'm sorry about all this too, about you and Steve. But enough, the girls miss their mother. Hold on."

"Mom!" Nicole was first to grab the phone.

"Nicole, oh, honey, how are you? I miss you so much."

"Mom, Natalie and I want to come home. Dad doesn't want us around and I don't want to live here. When can I come home?"

Laura laughed. "Oh, it's so good to hear your voice. You're coming home soon, honey, very soon. Okay?"

"When? We miss you." Nicole hadn't stopped for a breath. "You better talk to Nattie, she's crying again. She'll be okay as soon as we get home."

"Honey, thanks for taking such good care of your sister. I'd better talk to her now, okay? I'll see you soon. I love you."

"You're not in jail or anything are you?" Nicole asked.

"No, honey, I'm not in jail. I'll be right here when you get here, okay?"

"I love you, Mom. Here's Nattie."

"I love you, sweetie."

Natalie was barely coherent as she took the phone from her sister. "Mommy," she managed between sobs, "Mom, I miss you. I want to come home. Why can't Nicky and I come home?"

"Natalie, I love you so much. Listen, honey, you and Nicole will be home real soon, okay?"

"But Dad said you were going to jail."

"That's not true at all, Natalie. I'll be right here when you get back."

"Promise?"

"Promise." That she could do.

CHAPTER SEVENTEEN

Greg, Carrie, and Rob spent all day Friday in Greg's office working out preliminary trial strategy. They wanted to stall the Nelson case as long as possible to give the real killer time to make a mistake, to somehow reveal himself. Meanwhile things were starting to shape up in Laura's favor. Kim's troubled relationship with Frank Santiago, followed by his total disappearance from the Tampa Bay area, had caused the police to intensify their efforts to question him. Lopez and Goodnuf also told Rob that they wanted to question Steve again, this time more specifically about Kim's relationship with Santiago. Chuck had been right; the more they learned about Santiago, the more obvious his connection with the Miami and Tampa Latin mob became. Now Santiago's disappearance on the heels of two dead Mexicans turning up in a cocaine-laced truck, the D.A.'s office had to be sweating it. District Attorney Jake Cooperman would be astute enough to jump ship if he smelled political risk.

"It's almost six," Greg finally announced. "Let's call it a day."

"Good," said Carrie.

Greg saw the relief on her face. He reminded himself not to work her too hard. Carrie had a tough time balancing work and family. Her daughter, Elizabeth, was deaf and mute, and Carrie was dedicated to providing her with every advantage. As Greg had predicted, however, Carrie and Laura had developed a bond between them, and Carrie was pushing herself too hard.

"I want to talk to Sandra Mulloy on Monday," said Rob,

sounding optimistic. "Try to put some pressure on her to suspend charges against Laura while they track down Santiago. May not work, but it's worth a try."

"That'd give her more flexibility to move about," said Carrie. "To say nothing about boosting her morale."

"I agree," said Greg. "Maybe by then Chuck will have more on Santiago. My guess is he's hiding out in Miami."

Rob nodded, packing up his files. "So, heading out on the town tonight?"

"Going home to an empty house. Celeste's staying in Atlanta this weekend."

"I got a bunch of guys coming over for poker. Want to join?"

"No thanks, buddy. How about you, Carrie? Plans?"

"The usual. Kids. My daughter's school's having a fund-raiser, a carnival with a picnic, tomorrow."

"How's she doing?" Rob asked.

"Elizabeth is fine, thanks. Doing well," she said quickly. Any solicitous attitude toward Elizabeth annoyed Carrie.

The intercom buzzed. Chuck was on the phone at Cherry Airport with the twins.

"Things are going according to schedule with Chuck," Greg announced as he hung up. "All's well that ends well, eh? Let's regroup Monday around noon. And Carrie," he added, "can you swing by Laura's Monday morning to make sure everything is okay with the girls. My guess is she'll be feeling 100 percent better just to have them home."

Chuck Dimer had booked himself and the Nelson twins on the Friday seven p.m. flight from Cherry Airport through Chicago's O'Hare to Tampa International. They'd arrive late, but getting the girls home to Laura as soon as possible was his goal. The release paperwork at the Grand Traverse County Courthouse had gone smoothly, and he waited in Jim Nelson's driveway so he'd be right there at five when they all returned home after the foray to the mall.

*   *   *

Laura sat on the edge of the sofa in the family room of her empty house, too wound up to focus on the latest issue of the *New England Journal of Medicine*. She wore a yellow cotton shirt open at the neck, fitted tan slacks that were now baggy, and soft brown loafers. Her hair hung loosely to her shoulders, giving her a look of innocence, even vulnerability.

It was almost eight thirty. At nine, she planned to drive to the airport. Calmly, she kept reminding herself. It was only a twenty minute ride, and she would be there at least an hour early to meet the ten thirty arrival. Soon, so soon, the girls would be home. She could wait that long.

CHAPTER EIGHTEEN

On Wednesday, the Fourth of July, a drenching rain had convinced Steve to delay leaving his dad's until late afternoon. Jim Nelson had helped Steve load everything into his rented Ford station wagon, strapping the rest up on top, before Steve headed out with his three sons toward the Mackinac Bridge connecting Michigan's Upper and Lower Peninsulas. When they reached Wilderness State Park just south of the bridge that night, they set up their tent, made a fire, and cooked hot dogs and beans. There were no fireworks allowed in the park, but Steve let the boys light sparklers as long as they were careful to dispose of the glowing ends.

They stayed at Wilderness for two nights. The weather was chilly, but the family in the next tent had boys the same age as the three young Nelsons and they all played baseball, fished, collected frogs, even went swimming in the frigid Lake Michigan waters. There was a pay phone at the office, but Steve took pride in "roughing it," savoring the isolation from worries encroaching upon him from all directions.

It was wise, very wise, to be far away, and now, out of sight.

On Friday, Steve packed up camp and headed to Mackinaw City. He tried to relax and bought the boys fudge before heading to the Starline Ferry bound for Mackinac Island. The kids were thrilled by the island without cars, and Steve rented bikes so they could explore. As they made their way to Fort Mackinac to watch the rangers fire the historic muskets, Steve noticed that Patrick was having trouble keeping up.

"Pat, you okay?" Steve asked after the third time his son lagged behind.

Patrick wheezed, "Yeah, Dad."

Steve sat down on the curb next to his son. Why was he breathing so fast? Like he was having trouble catching his breath. Laying his hand lightly on the child's thin chest, Steve gasped at Patrick's fast, wild heartbeat.

"Come on you guys, " yelled Kevin. "The fort's up there on that hill!"

"Yeah, let's go," shouted Mike as he bicycled in circles around his brother and dad. "To the fort!"

"Pat's resting," said Steve. "Slow down, will you?"

"Pat's a sissy," taunted Kevin. "Sissy, sissy, come on, let's go."

"Am not," countered Patrick, attempting to get up off the curb, but quickly sitting down again.

Steve was worried now. Patrick had been born with a heart murmur — a hole in his heart. They had said it was nothing to worry about, that Patrick had no physical restrictions, but —
"Okay, boys," he announced, "let's pack it in. We've seen the island, we're going back now."

"Aw, Dad," complained Mike, "you said we were gonna see the show with the guns. You said, after lunch."

"Yeah, and the horse and buggy ride," Kevin added.

Steve got up, hoisted Patrick to his feet, and started walking their two bikes slowly back toward the rental shop.

"Pat's sick. Let's go," Steve called.

"He's just a spoiled brat," Kevin said to Mike, loud enough for Steve and Patrick to hear.

Instead of heading directly to the new campsite back on the mainland, Steve drove to the small town of Cheboygan on the shores of Lake Huron, about thirty miles away. Without telling the kids where he was going, he suddenly pulled into a parking lot.

"Where are we?" Kevin asked, looking up at a red brick building with a wide circular driveway.

"It's a hospital," muttered Mike, waking up from a snooze in the backseat.

"Look, you two just stay in the car for a few minutes," Steve said. "Pat, you come with me."

"Dad," whined Patrick, "I wanna stay with Mike and Kev."

"Come on, Patrick," Steve insisted.

A half hour later, at three thirty, Steve came out to get Mike and Kevin. Before he could say a word, Kevin blurted, "Dad, are you having a heart attack?"

"What? No, of course not."

"Is Pat really sick?" Mike asked.

Steve led them toward the emergency room door where an ambulance partially blocked access to the double automatic doors. "I'm sure he's fine, but the doctor's checking him out right now, and I want you here in the waiting room. No fooling around, you hear me?"

"We haven't even had lunch," Kevin complained.

In the waiting room, Mike started pacing. "Kev, come over here," he whispered from across the room. "You can hear them talking about Pat in there. Listen."

"I don't understand, Dr. Pope," they could make out Steve saying. "He's just a child. He's got nothing to be anxious about."

"Some children are high-strung by nature," they heard a gravelly male voice coming from the treatment room. "Their bodies overreact, resulting in a rapid heartbeat like the one we have here."

"But the tiredness? He just can't keep up. I told you, it's not normal when an eight-year-old child can't even walk a hundred feet without having to stop and his heart racing so."

"Probably just nerves," the doctor said. "Maybe some passive-aggressive acting out."

"My son is not a nervous type. I'm telling you."

"I'm not a pediatrician, Mr. Nelson, but I'm telling you, there's no emergency here."

"His blood count is normal?"

"Perfectly. He's not anemic. No abnormal white cells and a normal hemoglobin. I suggest you take him to your family doctor to do a more thorough check-up if you still feel that something's wrong."

"Fine. I'll take him in to see Dr. Chambers then," Steve said.

"Dean Chambers? Been to a lot of meetings together, the Northern Michigan Medical Society. Say hello for me," Dr. Pope said.

Mike and Kevin exchanged looks and scurried away from the door as Steve came out holding Patrick's right hand. In his left was a large green lollipop.

"So what happened?" Mike asked as they all settled back in the car.

"My heart was going too fast," Patrick answered. "But there's nothing wrong with me, is there, Dad?"

Steve attempted a smile. "The doc said it's nothing, so we're heading up to the U.P., guys."

"Doesn't Pat have a hole in his heart?" Mike asked.

Steve glanced quickly at Mike in a shut up way.

"No way," Patrick blurted. "There's nothing wrong with me."

"Well, let's call Mom," Mike went on. "She'll know what to do. Did you tell that doctor in there that our mom is a doctor, Dad?"

"Listen Mike, just quit it. This is a camping trip for us guys. Right now my plan is to cross the Mackinac Bridge and stay at one of those cabins on Trout Lake tonight. Then tomorrow we can fish in the morning and leave for Tahquamenon Falls State Park, the place I told you guys about."

"Hey, Dad," Patrick said, "I just wanna go fishing."

"We're all gonna starve to death first," said Kevin.

Steve smiled genuinely for the first time all day. "Maybe I should make you catch your lunch, huh? But you're in luck, there's a place to stop just before the bridge."

*   *   *

After eating deli sandwiches, they crossed Mackinac Bridge, the largest suspension bridge in the United States, and reached the Trout Lake Cabins just at dusk. There were fourteen small cabins situated in a horseshoe pattern, lacking any amenities except for telephones. Steve chose to stay the night there, off Route 123, rather than set up the tent, in case something did happen with Patrick. He parked the wagon behind their cabin, unloading only what the kids would need for the night as well as the ice chest with the sandwiches they'd bought at a small store after they stopped at St. Ignace for ice cream.

He returned to the cabin amid complaints that that there was no TV. In fact, there were only two double beds, a night table, and a phone. He sent the boys outside and called his father. Learning of Laura's latest antics — that she'd gotten a court order to have the twins returned to Florida as a result of his absence — Steve began to wonder how much detail the girls would remember of their Michigan trip. Another of his growing bag of worries.

Later, after a game of cards, he slept with Patrick in one bed, and Kevin and Mike shared the other. In the middle of the night Steve heard a muffled sound — Kevin crying. Turning over he whispered, "Kev, you okay?"

"Is Pat going to be okay," Kevin whispered back.

"I'm sure he will," said Steve.

"What's anxiety?"

"It means nervousness."

"But Pat's not nervous," Kevin snuffled. "I wish Mom was here to check him."

"He'll be okay, Kev. Some people may not act nervous on the outside but they worry on the inside, you know."

"Yeah," agreed Kevin. "I'll try to be nicer to him."

"Good idea for all of us, son," said Steve.

CHAPTER NINETEEN

In the pinkish-gray of predawn Saturday, Laura awoke. For a moment, she could not move and panic started to seize her. As a rush of feeling followed, she remembered ecstatically: the twins, they were home! At the moment, one slept peacefully on either side of her, having pressed themselves completely against her as they all went to sleep in Laura's big bed the night before. Breathing a sigh of huge relief, she thanked God for returning the girls safe and sound to her. Maybe this was a sign that everything would work out, that their lives could finally get back to normal, that everything would eventually be all right.

She needed this sign. She needed to believe this, she repeated to herself like a mantra, until it finally lulled her back to sleep.

Laura crawled out of bed just before seven. Later in the kitchen, she checked the clock over the stove as it ticked toward eight, picked up the phone, and dialed.

"Mom, did I wake you up? I waited until eight."

"Laura?" Peg Whelan sounded excited. "I've been dying to call, but I didn't want to —"

"They're home! We got back just before midnight — too late to call."

"And are they all right, honey?"

"Absolutely! We all slept in my bed, talked half the night. They're still asleep."

"Oh, I can't tell you how happy I am. No problems on the Michigan end?"

"No, thank God. Chuck had the court order, so Jim had to turn them over. Chuck said he seemed relieved actually. You know, I'm going to give him a call later today. I don't want any hard feelings between us. He's a nice man and always has been good to me."

"Um hum." Peg paused. "Strange situation though — Steve's relationship with his family. I mean, Jim's never visited you down here, and you've never taken the children to Traverse City, except for when Helen died five years ago. Well, I don't know, it's none of my business anyway. So how are my granddaughters?"

"They really seem fine. You should have seen us at the airport. All crying at once. Poor Chuck must have been embarrassed. Later today, I'll have a talk with them, see if I can find out what's really going on. Like why would Steve just take off with the kids? Why the sudden urge to see his father? Is Jim seriously ill?"

"I think Steve just wanted to punish you," Peg said not unkindly. "To teach you a lesson, that he can take what's most important to you. Using the kids to get back at you. I just don't understand Steve anymore."

"He's like a whole different person," Laura sighed. "I just want to get my life back together."

"Honey, have you gotten around to actually filing for a divorce?" Peg asked. "All these custody issues need to be squared away. You've got to get the boys back with you too."

"I know. Haven't done it yet," Laura admitted. "Need to talk to Greg about it. We've all been so focused on getting the charges dropped. My custody chances have to be better once I get out from under all this. Anyway, that should be soon."

"Certainly there can be no doubt?" Peg sounded surprised. "Custody always goes to the mother."

"Not if the mother is accused of murder," Laura said. "Not such a minor detail."

"Honey, Dad and I will be there later this morning. We can't wait to see Natalie and Nicole, but we're expecting a call from Ted today. We think he's still in Uganda, and Idi Amin's on another rampage. After kicking out the Orientals, missionaries are supposed to go next."

"Geez, Mom, I am so sorry to add to all your worries. You've got enough on your minds without all my stuff. You know I pray for Ted's safety every day. When are those Jesuits going to send him home?"

"Don't forget to pray for your sister too, honey. She and Kenneth are still waiting for that baby. She can't leave France right now or the adoption might be put on hold. Anyway, you know how much both Ted and Janet want to be with you, but —"

"I know, Mom. You'd better hang up so you don't miss Ted's call. We'll see you and Dad later."

"Mom!"

Laura was flipping through an AMA journal munching her third peanut butter toast with orange marmalade when Natalie and Nicole, still in their nightgowns, bounded down the stairs.

"I had to pinch Nattie," Nicole announced as she darted toward the refrigerator and pulled out a half gallon of orange juice. "We couldn't believe we were home when we woke up!"

"Oh, I missed you oh-so-much!" Laura jumped up and hugged them both. It felt so incredibly good to have her little girls home again. The house had been deathly silent until their return, but still there was an anguished void. The delightful banter of her daughters only served to highlight the ache in her heart for her sons. When would they all be together?

As Laura made the twins' favorite breakfast, pancakes with strawberry syrup and bacon, she pondered how to approach a discussion of their father, about his plans, his motivations.

Nicole preempted. "Mom, Dad said that you were too busy trying to stay out of jail so you didn't have time for us. I kept telling him that that was a lie. I mean, of course you wanted to talk to us, right? He was the one who didn't want us to talk to you."

"Nicole, you shouldn't talk about your father like that," Laura felt obliged to say.

"Dad's always mad at me anyway," Nicole said. "He's always liked the boys better than us. Like, why didn't he take us camping with him?"

"That's not true, Nicky. You just like to make him mad," Natalie said. "We even said that we didn't want to go camping. Yuck. No bathrooms. Sleeping in a tent. Bugs. Snakes."

"Yeah, well, why did Dad make us all go away in the first place?" Nicole said. "When we left that night, he said it was because Grandpa Nelson was sick. He didn't look sick to me when we got there. What do you think, Mom?"

"You know, that's what I was going to ask you two," Laura countered. "Did Dad say anything about how long he plans to stay in Michigan?"

"Nope," said Natalie, "even though we all kept asking him — especially Mike. He wants to be back here for baseball real bad, but Dad kept saying that you don't want us with you."

Laura stroked her daughter's hair. "You didn't believe that, did you honey?"

"No, I didn't," Natalie insisted, though she sniffled a bit. "None of us did."

"Boy, he's really gonna be mad when he finds out we got to come home," Nicole grinned.

"Let's not worry about that, girls. I just wish the boys were here too," said Laura. "But, hey, guess what? Grandma and Grandpa will be here later this morning."

"Let's make a cake for Grandpa!" Natalie suggested.

"Yeah!" Nicole added. "We had to leave with Dad instead of having his birthday party like we were supposed to that day."

"I remember," said Laura, as she once again pondered the details of that dreadful weekend.

"Jim, this is Laura. I wanted to just say that I'm sorry that yesterday things had to happen the way they did."

Laura had waited for the twins to go back up to their room to choose a board game. It was one of those rare monsoon-like days that drenched South Florida, otherwise the girls would be out in the neighborhood checking on their friends.

"It's not your fault, Laura." Jim Nelson sounded tired. "Though Steve is very angry indeed. He called a while ago from a campsite in the Upper Peninsula. It's got one of those long Indian sounding names I can't pronounce. I wouldn't be surprised if he gave you a call."

"That's good, Jim. I need to talk to him to tell him that charges against me are being suspended."

"Oh, is that so? Maybe that'll change things. You know, I still don't know why he's hell bent to keep the kids away from you. I keep telling him that the kids need their mother. They really want to go home, you know. Not just the girls, the boys too. Oh, well, Steve's put his foot down. I never remember him being this stubborn."

"I know what you mean. So Jim, how are you? You've been ill?"

"I'm fine," he said. "Had the flu right before Steve arrived with the kids, but I was better by the time they got here."

"Good. I'm glad you're okay."

"Well, you take care. Tell the little girls that I miss them, but that I'm glad they're back with you."

No sooner had Laura hung up with Jim Nelson than the phone rang. It was Steve.

"How did you manage that?" The snarl in his voice made Laura cringe. "I leave for a couple of days, and you send some kind of agent in to scare the hell out of my dad? Some stranger drags off my daughters when I've left them in the care of their grandfather. I never suspected you'd stoop so low."

"No stooping, Steve. It was all legal," Laura said evenly. "Court order."

"Right. Well, I gotta give it to you and your lawyers. God, I can only imagine how much this is costing. With neither of us working, we can't afford all this legal stuff."

"It shouldn't go on much longer," Laura announced. "The D.A. here is getting ready to suspend the charges against me. All I know is, I'm going to be free very, very soon."

"What? You're getting off? How?"

"You sound like you don't believe it," Laura said. "But the police have another suspect. It's that guy Kim Connor was dating."

"Suspect?" Steve's voice went hoarse. Less hostile and angry — more shaky, concerned. "What do you know?"

"They won't give me any details, but they do want to talk to you. Remember how you said the guy beat her up? They think she must have told you stuff about him that might help them locate the guy."

"I don't know a damned thing about that creep."

"Unfortunately, I now know about how cops operate. Like how they press people for details that lay folks just aren't even thinking about."

"Exactly. You just tell them that I know nothing."

"And Chuck Dimer," Laura went on, "the private investigator that Greg hired, wants to talk to you too."

"And how can we afford a private investigator?" Although Steve's comment sounded petulant, Laura detected underlying panic. "No way I'm talking about Kim to anyone. I don't know a goddamn thing about her personal life. She's already caused me enough trouble. My marriage. My job. No more."

"I can tell you that the police are going to insist. And so is Chuck. Because when they catch this guy and indict him, then I'm off the hook. Period. Charges go from being suspended to being dropped. The sooner the better. When are you coming back to Tampa?"

Steve's side of the line was silent.

"Did you know that the mob is involved?" Laura pressed.

"For God's sake, Laura, of course not."

"Well, Frank Santiago is a major figure, and the Tampa cops are hot to bring him in. So, Steve, your theory about me and my crime of passion just isn't going to fly. You've got to tell the boys.

According to the twins, you still think that I pulled the trigger on that gun. Now will you explain this to the boys?"

There was a long pause. "Are you sure about all this?"

"Completely," Laura said. "Now will you explain it to the boys?"

"Yeah, sure."

"Can I talk to them?" Laura asked.

"No, we're at a state park in the wilderness. Kids're in the rec room."

"They're all okay?"

"Having a ball. Fishing. Hiking. Sleeping in tents. All that father-son stuff. Listen, there is one thing," he continued reluctantly. "I had to take Patrick to a doctor on the way up here. In Cheboygan. Turns out it was nothing."

"What?" Now Laura heard panic in her own voice. "What's the matter with Patrick?"

"Nothing. Just nerves."

"Nerves? No way, Patrick's the most happy-go-lucky child I know. What kind of symptoms did he have? Tell me, Steve."

"Hey, don't get so uptight. The doctor said it was nothing. Just a rapid heartbeat and he wears down easily. But they did blood tests and everything checked out."

Laura's medical mind scanned the possible causes of fatigue and tachycardia in an eight-year-old. All conjured the specter of dread. Was it his heart? But she'd had his heart murmur thoroughly checked out by a pediatric cardiologist — it was only a patent foramen ovale. In most children a small, slit-like opening between the upper two chambers of the heart closes off after birth, but in some it stays open. If that was the only defect, as in Patrick's case, it was of no clinical significance.

So Patrick's basic blood work had been okay. That must have included a CBC — complete blood count. Any type of anemia or even leukemia would be unlikely. Was it anxiety? Could all this be affecting Patrick to the point of physical symptoms? Her most carefree child, who basked in Steve's attention, and laughed off the occasional accusation that he was spoiled rotten. Could he be that disturbed? Better that than a real physical illness, thought Laura, yet her concern mounted.

"Give me the doctor's phone number, and I'll call him just to check everything out."

"That's unnecessary. I'll check with Dr. Chambers, my old family doctor in Traverse City, if he has any more symptoms. I'm just having him take it easy."

"Steve, I insist."

"Look, I said he was okay, and I don't have the phone number. Name's Pope. Cheyboygan."

"Hey, Mom," Nicole yelled. "Can Nattie and I go over to Alison's?"

"Hang on, Steve," Laura said, not sure that she wanted her daughters out of her sight even if it was just across the street.

"Why don't you have her come over here?" she suggested.

"She doesn't even know we're home yet," Nicole hollered back from somewhere upstairs. The sounds of her girls back home filled Laura's heart — but back to Patrick.

"Please, Mom!"

"Okay, just for a few minutes, then come right back. Grandma and Grandpa are coming."

"Can Alison come over?" Natalie had bounded down the stairs and now stood next to her. "Who are you talking to, Mom?"

"Dad," Laura said. "Of course Alison can come over."

"Can I talk to him?" Natalie asked.

"Yes, you may, but don't hang up. I'm not through talking yet."

"Hi Dad, how're you doing?" asked Natalie.

Laura stood nearby, only half-hearing Natalie's side of the conversation. Could Steve be right about Patrick? Just nerves? A normal reaction of an eight-year-old to the type of stress he'd had heaped on him these last few weeks?

"Yeah, it's good to be home," Natalie went on. "Nope, we got home late. Almost midnight. But Alison's coming over. Are the boys okay? Okay, Dad. I love you. I'll go get her." She put down the phone and yelled up the stairs. "Nicky! Dad wants to talk to you!"

"I don't want to talk to him," Nicole called back.

"Come on, you're gonna hurt his feelings."

Nicole whizzed down the stairs. "So what? So why'd he go off and leave us, huh? He didn't have to go off camping and leave us alone with Grandpa Nelson."

Natalie walked back to the phone. "Dad? Uh . . . Nicky's busy doin' stuff. "But Mom wants to talk to you again. Here."

Laura reached for the phone.

"So Nicole won't even talk to me?" Steve began. "What's she been saying anyway?"

"Saying?" Laura repeated. "Saying about what?"

"About — Never mind. Is she okay? Has she said —"

"She's fine. Just upset that you chose to leave her and go off with the boys. A natural response if you ask me."

"The girls would hate being off in the woods and you know it. Besides, you've got them now. Isn't that what you wanted?"

"You know as well as I do that all the kids belong here with me." She came close to blurting that she'd see to a permanent custody order very soon. "But are you sure Patrick's okay?"

"I think so," Steve answered. "I'll take him to Dr. Chambers if he doesn't perk up."

"Bring him home, Steve. If Patrick has something wrong with him, he belongs here with me. Maybe it's his heart."

"Hey, the specialists we saw said that he'd be fine, that the heart murmur wasn't serious. Remember?"

"But —"

"Look, I'm sure Pat'll be fine."

"Promise to call me if he's not, okay?" Laura needed to talk to Greg. How soon could she get to Michigan, and do whatever she had to do to get all her kids back?

He hesitated. "Okay. And when we get back to Dad's, let talk, Laura, really talk. I've been thinking. Now that they're going to drop those charges. Maybe if we moved. Somewhere far away. Away from all these bad memories. All of us."

"Move away from Tampa?" Laura was taken aback. Things

were bad, but never once had she thought of running away.

"Look. I screwed up. I know that. What I did — Kim. How I left you alone in Tampa. How I doubted you when you said you didn't, you know, shoot Kim."

Laura realized that this was the first time he'd admitted this. "That really hurt me. And when you took off with the kids —"

"It was a bad mistake. I — thought maybe you couldn't cope with the kids with being indicted on those charges."

"Well, it almost destroyed me," Laura said as tears gathered and she realized that for the first time since the night she'd found Steve with Kim, they were really talking to each other. Tentative, primitive, but talking.

Steve's voice softened. "I'm sorry, Laura. For everything. I'll do anything to get my family back, but I can't come back to Tampa for a while."

"Why not?" Laura asked.

"It's nothing," he said. "I screwed up, that's all."

"So let's work out a visitation schedule so the kids see us both, but I'm not moving away from Tampa. In the meantime, can't you just bring the boys home?"

"It's not that simple," Steve mumbled.

"Why not?"

"I can't explain. I've got a lot to think about, but I'll talk to you soon."

"Okay. Bye, Steve."

For a long time Laura sat at the table in the kitchen alcove. She'd been so sure she wanted a separation from Steve. A divorce, eventually. But did she? Did she really know her own heart? Or had she been so humiliated by that night with Kim that she'd selfishly put her anger ahead of what was best for her kids and maybe even best for her once time had passed? Or had her instinct that next day been right, that she and Steve had already drifted too far apart? That they would both be better off if they were free to live their lives separately and work out shared custody of their children? Roxanne had suggested a counselor. Maybe they should see a counselor.

CHAPTER TWENTY

Laura was still thinking about her conversation with Steve when the phone rang again. Greg.

"Hi, Laura! Heard that Chuck and the girls got back just fine last night. Wanted to check in and make sure everyone's all right?"

"Oh, hi, Greg. Thanks, the girls are great."

"That's a relief. Listen, Chuck's going to run a neighborhood blitz on Oregon tomorrow night. He's got a few guys lined up to question anyone and everyone who may have seen something the night of the murder. We're looking for a break with Santiago's name on it."

"That's good. Whatever I can do, you just let me know."

"Of course. Someone did kill Kim Connor. Even though the cops are looking for Santiago, the D.A. still hasn't given up on you. They'll backpedal once we get something solid, you can bet on that. They won't want egg on their face."

"And all I want is my life back — my freedom and my kids."

"Your freedom and your kids matter more than anything," he said firmly. "So tonight we're looking for a connection that ties Santiago to that night, before every lead goes stone cold and we end up in court. I want you cleared long before that."

"What can I do?"

"At the moment, just sit tight. You've got the girls home now, and they've been through so much. Be there for them."

Following his initial interviews a week and a half earlier, Chuck

Dimer had assembled a small network of private investigators to thoroughly canvas Steve's neighborhood. The plan was to try to talk with every man, woman, and child in every household, and to identify anybody who might have been present in the area surrounding Steve's rented house. Located in an old section of Tampa, the Old Hyde Park houses were close together with small brownish lawns and few ornamental plants. Steve's was so worn down, even its cement stairs were crumbling.

The P.I.s were given a checklist and instructed to probe into anything unusual regarding that night, anybody who'd been seen or heard in the vicinity, descriptions of all cars. They were given pictures of Kim, of Laura, of Steve, of the Nelson kids, and of Frank Santiago and a few of his mob contacts.

"Okay, Greg, we're all set up," Chuck announced as they met at Bucky's on Swann Avenue for a quick breakfast the following morning. "I've got three guys going house-to-house in a ten-block radius of Nelson's apartment. Time of the murder was around eight so we'll ape that, more or less. I'll take the immediate vicinity myself."

"You got all the pictures?"

"Yup." He reached into his pocket and pulled out a stack of photos.

Greg stated the obvious as he picked up the shot of Santiago. "Focus on this guy."

"Gonna look under every rock."

"Yeah. Wonder if you're gonna find Nelson under one. Can't see why a woman like Laura would marry such a jerk."

"Women are strange," Chuck answered. "Wonder why Celeste is marrying you?"

Greg's head jerked up.

"Just a joke, buddy. Anyway, I've never shaken the suspicion that Nelson's involved with the Connor killing myself."

"So you think he's hiding something or he's just a son of a bitch?"

"Good question. At first I thought the former, but now I'm not sure. Something came up in one of my interviews — that friend of Connor's I talked to right off, Carmen Williams. Turns out that Connor left Carmen all her earthly belongings, so I went back and talked to her again last week. She's really not a bad kid. Trying to pull her life together. Well, her being involved was in the back of my mind. Connor didn't have much, but to Carmen, who had nothing, maybe if she knew she'd inherit —"

"You think she's a suspect? Why didn't you say so?"

"Thought she might be, but after talking to her again, I'm thinking otherwise. She's so shook up. Connor had stuck by her all these years, her only friend. Besides, that Sunday night she was hanging out at a club in Ybor City. I had it all checked out."

"Oh." Greg sounded disappointed.

Chuck nodded. "And the girl is scared of Santiago. I sensed it the first time I talked to her and even more the second. Like she wanted to tell me more about him, but was afraid to."

"What does she know about Nelson and Connor?"

"They had a one-night thing. Connor told her about it the next morning and Carmen warned her to stay away."

"Stay away? Why?"

"Because Nelson was a married man. Because of her job at Channel Eight. Because of her boyfriend."

"Santiago?"

"The same. Said Connor wanted to break up with him, move to Atlanta. That he was jealous by nature. I couldn't get her to say that he'd ever hit Connor. Claimed to know nothing about what he did for a living, clammed up. Let's not forget how dangerous these guys are."

"Connor and Mr. Steve Nelson and Santiago," Greg mused. "What's it add up to?"

"After tonight's blitz, I'll talk to her again. Maybe she'll loosen up. You know, boss, Carrie's theory still holds up for me. Connor goes to Steve's for comfort, whatever, Santiago follows her and boom."

"Not much solace for Connor there." Greg shook his head.

"Someone must've seen something over there on Oregon, Chuck. We're running out of time on this. It's already two weeks later."

"Hey, it is Sunday, Greg. Keep sayin' your prayers, my man."

On Davis Island, Laura's parents came over late morning, and in the early afternoon, the Nelson home had three unexpected visitors: Carrie Diamond with her eleven-year-old daughter, Elizabeth, and Roxanne Musing. Oddly, they arrived at the same time.

"Roxanne! Carrie! And you must be Elizabeth," Laura exclaimed as she met them at the door. The child looked so much like Carrie with her violet eyes and brown hair — Elizabeth's in pigtails. Seeing the pigtails brought the shadow of a memory back to Laura, but she couldn't force a clear picture into her consciousness. Then she remembered that the girl couldn't hear her and she bent down to shake her hand. "What a beautiful dress," she said carefully so that Elizabeth could see her lips. She ran her hand over the pretty plum sundress, then she pointed to the child's eyes. "It matches your eyes."

Elizabeth smiled brightly at Laura, and her hands began to move in sign language.

"She says 'thank you,'" explained Carrie. "I hope I'm not barging in, but I wanted to see how you were doing before we went over to the school. They're having a fund-raiser, and Elizabeth's in a skit." As Carrie spoke, she automatically signed to the child. To Laura, she said, "The twins got back last night, right?"

"Right," Laura said. "Thank God. Let me introduce you to everyone. Come on in, Rox."

After saying hello in the living room, Peg and Carl took Elizabeth and the twins into the kitchen for milk and cookies. The twins insisted Elizabeth come upstairs to play with their legendary collection of dolls and stuffed animals as Peg started to make coffee.

"Do you like dolls?" Natalie wanted to know.

When Elizabeth didn't respond, Nicole stood up from her seat at the table and stood directly in front of Elizabeth. She repeated the question.

Elizabeth nodded vigorously.

With a squeal, all three girls went running upstairs.

"If I'd have known you'd be here, I would have brought Jose over," said Roxanne to Carrie.

"Jose?" Carrie asked politely.

"Remember that case at the hospital," Laura explained, "Ruiz?"

Carrie squinted. "The malpractice?"

"Yes. Roxanne's been taking care of the smallest boy, who's five. He was the only one in the family that wasn't seriously injured, and he had nowhere else to go."

"What happened to the parents?" Carrie asked. "I remember talking to you about dropping out of that case."

"The mother died," Roxanne said softly, "and their baby girl died. But the case was about Louis's ten-year-old daughter, Wendy."

"The father?"

"Louis is still in the hospital, and Jose's two older brothers are still there too. They're going to be okay."

"Still see them every day?" Laura asked.

"Yes, and I'm pretty worried. I mean, how are they going to survive this financially? Louis is a strong, proud man, but with the hospital bills, not being able to work —"

"What an awful situation," Carrie said slowly.

Laura nodded. "I explained to Rox the reason I had to drop out as a witness, Carrie, but I don't feel good about it."

"I can understand," said Roxanne. "Things haven't been easy for me at the hospital since they know I'm involved. The truth is, I'm worried about my job."

"What? Cliff Casey would never let that happen," Laura protested.

"I'm afraid he would. He's not happy about you either. Any doctor who even thinks about testifying against the hospital is considered a traitor."

"You know," Carrie said, "it's a shame about the Ruiz family, but as Laura's attorney, I have to say she has way too much to worry about right now."

Roxanne reached for Laura's hand. "Right," she said.

"Before I go, there's something about your case that I'd like to discuss." Carrie looked from Laura to Roxanne.

Laura read Carrie's cue. "Rox, whenever I talk legal stuff, I have to be alone with my attorneys. Maybe you could wait in the kitchen with Mom and Dad?"

"That's okay, honey, I've got to run." All three women stood and Roxanne hugged Laura. "Call you later."

"I'm glad to meet you, Roxanne," said Carrie. "I am sorry we can't do more for the Ruiz family."

After Roxanne left, Carrie said, "Laura, the main reason I came by is to tell you that Greg and Rob have been working all weekend on a motion to take to Judge Potter. There's good news. You know that residue test — the one that shows if you actually shot that gun?"

"Yes." Laura held her breath.

"Results came back negative," Carrie announced with a broad smile.

"Thank God. I mean, I knew it would, but still —"

"The prosecution will try to make light of it," Carrie cautioned, "because of the blood that contaminated your hand, but overall it'll give us something to work with."

Laura sank to the couch. "At this point I — it all seems so unreal. Seeing Roxanne. Thinking about my career. I worked so hard. Sacrificed so much. Will they ever let me back in the hospital? Will I ever be able to pick up my life?"

Carrie stepped closer and squeezed Laura's shoulder. "Laura, you're a strong woman. Your daughters are back and you have three young sons who need you, no matter what. More than ever."

"How can I even face them?" Laura bolted up. "Steve's telling them I'm some kind of monster. A killer. I haven't seen them in almost two weeks, haven't even been able to explain. And now something's wrong with Patrick —"

"Laura, I wish I could tell you that everything will be okay. I'm sorry, I really do have to get going." She squeezed Laura's shoulder once more. "What you need to do is stay as calm as possible, okay? Let's go up and fetch Elizabeth."

"Oh, she's a delightful child. I just wish —" Laura grew silent, choking back tears.

CHAPTER TWENTY-ONE

Chuck had timed the investigative blitz for early evening to simulate as much as possible the scenario of two weeks earlier. The weather was humid and in the high eighties, similar to the night of the murder, but it had been drizzling that night. Chuck personally questioned the older woman living upstairs from Steve, who had called the police. He had interviewed her previously and this time, although cooperative, she had nothing more to add. He then planned to interview the neighbors on either side and the house directly across the street, along with the two houses flanking it. They all had the most direct view of who came in and out of Steve's apartment and the best chance to have heard anything unusual.

The neighbors directly across the street had been away that entire weekend. When they'd approached Oregon Avenue at ten thirty, it had been blocked off and they had difficulty getting through the police barricade to their home. This was substantiated by the police reports that Chuck had repeatedly scrutinized. To their right lived an older couple in their seventies, who relayed the details of the TV programs they had watched that Sunday evening from their family room in the rear of the house, denying even glancing out their front windows.

On the other side of Steve's, a middle-aged housewife delayed preparations for the family's dinner so Chuck could question her and her two teenage sons. Her husband had also been there, but he'd left that afternoon for a sales conference in Miami. Consistent answers. Nobody saw anything that shed new light. The older of the boys recalled seeing Laura's light blue station wagon parked right behind Kim's canary yellow Firebird. He remembered thinking that the wagon was parked too close to the Malone driveway and that old man Malone would be pissed, maybe enough to even clip it with his ancient pickup. He estimated the time to be minutes, maybe ten, maybe twenty, from when he'd noticed the two cars to when all the action started. None recalled any other unidentified parked vehicle. Nobody saw Laura or Santiago enter the house or noticed any type of commotion or noise. Nobody — except the woman upstairs from Steve — heard the gunshot.

Next, Chuck revisited Matt Malone, a widower with a mean-tempered reputation, who lived alone in the gray, two-story house on the left of Steve's.

"Who is it," the scrawny, white-haired, elderly man growled as Chuck rang the bell for the third time.

Chuck could smell the hint of whisky on his breath, but the old man seemed coherent. First time Chuck'd stopped by Malone's, he'd merely heard, "I didn't see nothin', and that's what I told the cops." This time Chuck came prepared with a fifth of Jack Daniels, which he hastily pushed into the man's veined hands.

"I'm not the law, Mr. Malone, I just need answers about that poor woman who got killed next door. Pay you back a little for helping me out."

Malone took the amber liquid. "I dunno, guess we could talk some. Sure you ain't a cop?"

"Absolutely sure." Chuck walked into the surprisingly neat living room. Everything was in place. Lace curtains, embroidered doilies on the end tables. Probably just as the deceased Mrs. Malone had left it.

Malone motioned for Chuck to take a chair. "You know I talked to the cops. Got nothing more to say."

"If you'll indulge me. You were here on Sunday night two weeks ago?"

"I'm always home Sunday night. Got nowhere to go."

The TV in the living room was blaring beside a small air

conditioner set in a window. It was placed in the corner so that Malone could watch from the well-worn recliner. The angle of vision beyond the TV overlooked the front-curb parking spot that Laura had used.

"Mind if I turn the volume down so we can talk," Chuck asked amiably. The old guy certainly couldn't have heard anything that night with the TV so loud.

"Go ahead," came the gruff reply.

Chuck headed to the set and turned the dial so he could hear himself speak. Then he walked across the room to confirm the recliner's view of the street. "Okay, Mr. Malone, we did this before, but it'd help me to go through everything you remember from that night."

Malone, still cradling the whisky bottle, began to loosen up. When Chuck exhausted his list of questions, Malone got out of his chair, walked into the kitchen, and returned with two glasses. He poured out three inches of the whisky in each and offered one to Chuck.

Chuck never drank while in the throes of an investigation, but he accepted the drink now. He was hot and sweaty from his efforts so far, and wanted to encourage the cooperation of this old man who, he had learned, had grown up in this house on Oregon and who knew every inch of the neighborhood.

"Everyone around here thinks I'm a crank. That's fine by me. Since Estelle passed I just wanna live out my time. Neighbor kids get on me, but one, little Molly Palmer from a couple doors down, she brings me stuff she made at school, cookies her mom makes. She don't care if I'm an old grouch. We sit on the porch and don't say nothin'. Poor kid's a deaf mute. Guess when it comes down to it, she's the only living thing I care about. Got no kids, no dog, no nothin'."

"I know what you mean," said Chuck, rising from his chair. It was just past eight, about the same time Laura had arrived at Steve's. "Mr. Malone, will you let me sit in your chair for a minute?"

"What the hell for?"

"Humor me. Step over to the window here and tell me if there's anything different about what you see out there now and what you saw that Sunday night."

"Well, that's about the dumbest thing —" Malone got up slowly, walking to the window as Chuck lowered himself onto the worn recliner. If he stared directly at the flickering TV set, he couldn't see much of the street. He would have to sit bolt upright and crane his neck severely to the right to see the outline of the curb. Anything routine in the street would probably go unnoticed by the old man. He got up and joined Malone at the window.

"I always keep an eye on what goes on around here, even if I don't go out much. Station wagon was parked too close to my driveway that night, I remember that. Meant to go out and give the owner a piece of my mind, but then I heard the cop cars and all hell broke loose over there."

"But you didn't see anyone, man or woman, go into the house?" Chuck showed him the photos.

"Nope, no cigar. Don't recognize nobody."

Discouraged, Chuck offered his thanks and stood for a moment in front of Nelson's Oregon apartment. So far, nobody had seen anything but a few cars. He wondered how likely that was and then wondered how many times Kim Connor would have to show up in this neighborhood before she was recognized. Had it been only once? He was still uncertain about why she had come. Maybe Carmen Williams could answer that.

With a heavy step, Chuck moved to the last household on his list, the Palmer residence, a white clapboard house with green trim, next to Nelson's. A tall, rugged looking man in his mid-thirties with deep blue eyes and wavy light brown hair answered the doorbell after the first ring, giving Chuck just enough time to wipe the sweat from his face with his handkerchief.

"Good evening, Mr. Palmer," Chuck proffered his hand, "sorry to bother you again. Chuck Dimer, private investigator heading up the investigation on the incident next door."

"Good God, Dimer, how many times do we have to go through this?" Dirk Palmer stood solidly blocking the front door.

"It's two weeks tonight since the murder, Mr. Palmer," Chuck said matter-of-factly. "If you don't mind, there are some new questions I'd like to ask you. You and Mrs. Palmer." Remembering that Malone had mentioned a daughter, he added, "and your daughter."

"Look, mister, all we want is to raise our daughter in a safe neighborhood without being badgered by the police or people like you."

Chuck hadn't expected this belligerence. Dirk had seemed amiable and cooperative when they last spoke a week ago, and his wife, Sally, seemed all too anxious to unload any neighborhood information, real or otherwise.

"Just a few minutes with you and your wife would really help. Is she here?"

"She's already gone to bed."

"So early? It's only —"

"Who is it, dear?" came a singsong voice from within before Dirk could shut the door.

"Damn," Dirk grumbled. "It's not important," he called inside, finally closing the door behind him. "Now what do you want?"

"There are some details, Mr. Palmer. Uh, maybe we can include your wife?"

"She's busy, but go ahead and ask me what you want."

The front door flew open, practically knocking Dirk aside as Sally Palmer, fully dressed in a tailored blouse and an A-line skirt, appeared. She was almost as tall as her husband, with short auburn hair and large brown eyes. "Oh! Sorry to interrupt."

"Get back inside," her husband ordered. "It's that private investigator."

"You're not interrupting, Mrs. Palmer," Chuck hastened. "In fact, I'm here to talk to you too."

"No, no, I can't."

"Mr. Dimer —"

"Is it about next door? Did you find out something?" Sally Palmer blurted.

"Not yet. Maybe your daughter could help us."

There was no mistaking the look of alarm passing between Dirk and Sally Palmer.

"There's no way I'll have you harassing my daughter," Dirk said, anger intensifying on his face. "She's gone through enough."

"I don't want to harass her. I've got some photos —"

Sally shook her head. "Mr. Dimer, our daughter couldn't talk with you if she wanted to. Unless, of course, you know sign language."

"I'm sorry," Chuck muttered. Not knowing what else to say, he quickly pulled out the pack of photos and mechanically ran through his list of questions. Dirk Palmer answered the questions curtly, barely glancing at each picture as Chuck presented them.

With the front door still open, Chuck saw a young girl peer through the pane of a narrow window in the entry hall. She wore a long, mint green nightgown, her dark brown hair worn in two braids down her back. She looked at Chuck only momentarily, but the look seemed plaintive, expectant. How could he get past her parents to her? And even if he could, he'd need an interpreter.

Carrie Diamond.

CHAPTER TWENTY-TWO

The Nelson defense team met early Monday morning, only to face the disappointment of the previous night's efforts. It was clear, after the debriefing of Chuck's men, that nothing new had emerged. A few strange cars parked around the four-block area. Vague descriptions. No license plates. No positive I.D. of Frank Santiago or anybody else who seemed suspicious. Chuck's vague discomfort with Dirk and Sally Palmer's response was the only thread of a lead. Greg and Rob found Chuck's assessment of the Palmers' reaction intriguing. How could they approach the child to find out whether she'd seen anything relevant to Kim's murder?

Carrie was strangely silent until Greg asked, "What do you think, Carrie? I trust your instincts when it comes to legal ethics."

"Molly Palmer goes to the Tampa School for the Deaf," Carrie said slowly. "I don't know the child well. She's in the sixth grade, not in Elizabeth's class, but I've met the parents."

"And —" Rob pressed.

"They're outgoing, quite active in the school. I think she's secretary of the PTA. Yes, she is."

"And how they treated me last night," Chuck asked, "does it seem out of character?"

Carrie nodded. "Sally is a nonstop talker, and Dirk has always been quite friendly."

"Well last night he was downright hostile."

"Carrie, is there any way we can get to talk to the girl?" Rob ventured. "Perhaps at the school?"

"I don't know," Carrie replied. "The Palmers sounded like they were adamant. We'd have to be very careful to avoid any real or perceived exploitation, especially with such strong parental objection."

"It could be important," Greg said. "Carrie, could you take the assignment to try to reach the child in a way that would not compromise us or the school?"

"I'll give it a try. I realize how important this might be to Laura. But you know, if this were Elizabeth —"

"Thanks, Carrie," Greg said quickly. "Call Chuck if anything comes up."

After passing the security cameras that flanked every corner of the main building, Carrie Diamond walked through the open door into the principal's office at ten o'clock. She found Randall Franklin poring through a thick, black binder full of charts and tables of numbers. A big man in his mid-fifties with black bushy eyebrows behind wire-rimmed glasses and a triangular beard that made his face seem too long, he looked formidable, yet he was known for his compassion. Carrie stood silently a few moments until the big man looked up with surprise.

"Why, Mrs. Diamond —"

"I didn't mean to startle you. You just looked so engrossed."

"Ick, budgets," he said with a smile as he rose from the swivel chair at his desk. "Didn't think I'd see you again so soon. Wasn't yesterday just grand?"

"Absolutely. Elizabeth was thrilled being in that skit. It's such a confidence builder for the kids to perform in front of an audience."

"Great turnout. Hope you parents know how much I appreciate everything. The proceeds from an event like yesterday let us do so much more for the kids, especially during our summer sessions when we can plan these types of performances."

"It was fun," answered Carrie. "It's great to spend time with the other parents. We have a lot in common."

"Of course. So how can I help you?" the principal asked,

raising his bushy eyebrows. "Elizabeth seems to be doing well — excellent grades and a great attitude. Is there a problem? Here, sit down."

"I don't know, Mr. Franklin . . ." Carrie hesitated as she settled into the chair opposite his desk, "how to go about this, so I'll just be as honest as I can. There may be a problem, but it's not about Elizabeth."

"Go on, please." Randall Franklin removed his glasses and looked closely at Carrie.

"It's about Molly Palmer."

"Oh? Her father called me this morning, reluctant to send her to school. Said she'd been having some stomachaches."

"Oh? Anything else?"

"He asked me about our security. I reminded him that in addition to a morning and night patrol, our buildings are equipped with security cameras operating twenty-four hours a day. A little bit later, Mr. Palmer arrived with Molly and escorted her to her classroom. It was odd."

"Hmm. Have you noticed anything else unusual," Carrie paused, "about Molly?"

"Well, now that you mention it, at the picnic yesterday, the Palmers seemed rather protective of her." He stopped abruptly. "Is something going on that I should know about?"

Carrie exhaled. "My law firm is representing Dr. Laura Nelson, the woman accused of shooting Kim Connor, the television newscaster, a couple of weeks ago. The murder took place next door to the Palmer's home. I wonder if the child may have seen something that's frightened her."

"I see." He paused. "Well, maybe you should talk to Janice Meyer. She's Molly's teacher. If the child is upset, we need to work with her parents."

"I understand. If this were about Elizabeth —" Carrie's voice trailed off, "well, I would appreciate help."

"I'll have Janice come over during recess." Franklin looked at his watch. "Which is in ten minutes."

* * *

"Mrs. Diamond, how nice to see you." Janice Meyer smiled as she rose from the table in the teachers' lounge and smoothed her red dress.

Carrie knew Janice from the volunteer work she'd done to help orient new families to the school. An attractive woman with red-brown hair and a creamy complexion, she was in her mid-forties with a deaf child of her own.

"I didn't get a chance to talk to you yesterday," Janice said. "Elizabeth was great in that skit."

"Thanks. She had a wonderful time."

"So what's happening? Randall said you wanted to talk to me about Molly Palmer?"

"Can we go outside?" Carrie anticipated the influx of teachers who'd all want to say their hellos, particularly Tammy White, Elizabeth's young, enthusiastic teacher.

"Sure. There's an alcove over by the garden with plenty of shade. Let's grab a coffee or a soda first." She filled her ceramic Tampa Bay Buccaneer mug with hot coffee while Carrie chose a Diet Coke from the vending machine.

Outside, they settled at a small wrought iron table tucked under one of the portico overhangs in a small garden amid a blaze of crimson azaleas.

"Randall said to help you the best I can. What's happening?"

"First, I want you to know that I represent Laura Nelson, the local surgeon accused of killing her husband's colleague, Kim Connor, the TV newscaster."

"Quite a story."

Carrie nodded. "I'll say. Did you know that Molly lives next door to Steve Nelson, Laura's husband, where Kim Connor was shot?"

"Uh, no." Janice's brown eyes narrowed. "Remind me, when did this happen?"

"Two weeks ago yesterday. On Sunday night, around eight. The police have investigated, of course, and talked to all of the neighbors. Nobody saw anything."

"So what has this have to do with Molly," Janice asked softly, "if nobody saw anything?"

"Yesterday, her parents seemed strangely unwilling to cooperate with our investigator. It didn't seem like normal behavior for them. My instincts tell me that Molly might've seen something that's frightened her."

"That might fit with the behavior I've been seeing," Janice mused. "Molly hasn't been herself. When I mentioned it to the Palmers yesterday, they just brushed me off."

"I can understand their concern. But if the child saw something, if she doesn't confront it, well, I don't know how healthy that is."

"So you think that what she may have seen would help your client?"

"I don't know. That's why I came, to try to find out."

"What would you do, if it were Elizabeth?" Janice asked. "Expose her to the world of the police and criminal investigations? A court trial, maybe? Nobody wants that for their child. These kids are so vulnerable."

"Believe me, I've thought about that. But, you know, at some time we have to teach our kids right and wrong and encourage civil responsibility even if there might be some risk." Carrie let it go at that, choosing not to add, "Risk as in this case with a mob connection" or "Though I might want to keep Elizabeth hidden, out of it altogether."

"Well, I know you wouldn't be here, Ms. Diamond, if it weren't important. I've read about the Kim Connor shooting, and I can't believe that that nice woman doctor with all those kids did it, even if that woman was having an affair with her husband."

"You're right, my being here is important."

"So, how do you propose we go about this?"

Carrie breathed easier on hearing the 'we.' "Maybe you could talk to the child. Ask if anything is wrong, anything she wants to talk about."

"I don't know if that would get anything out of her. My guess is her parents have told her not to talk to anyone about that night," Janice speculated. "But, you know, kids talk much more readily to other kids. How about Elizabeth?"

"Elizabeth? She's not in Molly's class."

"But they know each other. I was thinking that if you explained some of this to Elizabeth and she talked to Molly, maybe it would come out and Molly herself would volunteer to talk to you. I can get Elizabeth and Molly together alone over lunch."

"You mean have Elizabeth just come out and ask her if she knows anything?"

"Sure. Have her explain to Molly that her mother is trying to help another mom who's in big trouble over what happened to the lady in the house next door. The truth. Right?"

Carrie nodded.

"If Molly wants to tell her anything she knows that might help this other mom and her kids, fine. If not, fine. But if she does know something, Elizabeth could suggest that she tell you. That way, there'll be no chance that you can be blamed for inappropriately approaching her."

"Will it endanger the school?"

"You're the lawyer, but if it's Molly's choice to confide in the mother of a classmate who just happens to be a lawyer, what's the harm done?"

"Okay," said Carrie with a sigh. "Let's give it a try. Can you get Elizabeth out of class so I can talk to her?"

Molly and Elizabeth sat in a small alcove off the cafeteria with their lunches arranged on orange plastic trays in front of them. Molly was a thin child, tall, like her parents, with her brown hair in braids, with huge brown eyes, her face sprinkled with freckles. Elizabeth was plumper, with porcelain skin, her mother's violet eyes, and curly brown hair. The girls interspersed eating with facile sign language as they settled in across the table from each other. Carrie sat inconspicuously at an empty table just outside the alcove, but she had a clear visual angle on the girls' signed conversation — she also noticed two security cameras trained on the girls from the alcove walls.

Janice Meyer had offered no explanation to Molly, but she had brought over extra chocolate chip cookies to go with their bagged lunches. Elizabeth had been happy with the surprise visit from her mother and told her that she'd always liked Molly Palmer, but since they were in different classrooms and rode different school buses, she didn't know her that well. Yesterday, after leaving Laura's, she'd had so many questions about the nice lady she'd met and her twin girls, who'd both been really nice to her. Now she was excited about being able to help the lady, so, sure, she'd ask some questions.

Elizabeth started by admiring Molly's earrings, telling her by sign that she was trying to get her mom to let her get her ears pierced.

Molly said that she'd had pierced ears since she was a baby and that she had a whole collection of pretty earrings.

"You're lucky," Elizabeth signed. Then she relayed her mother's request.

"I saw those kids go over next door before," Molly signed. "Some boys and two girls about our age. I thought they were twins. I wanted to play with them, but they were outside playing catch with their brothers." Then she added, "Plus, they wouldn't know sign language."

"Did you see the kids the day the TV lady was killed?" Elizabeth prompted.

"No. I saw the blonde lady come that night. Then later all the police cars showed up, all the red lights flashing. You know the guy that lived there was a TV news man?"

"Yes, he was on TV with the killed lady," signed Elizabeth.

"I used to watch him go in and out from my bedroom window. That's where my desk is, where I read or do my homework. And the lady that was killed, I saw her go in that night. I never saw her come before, but I know her from the pictures in the newspapers and on TV . . ." she hesitated, "I didn't know the man who moved in next door was married to the blonde lady."

Molly seemed eager to share this information with Elizabeth, but then Carrie noticed a shadow darken Molly's face.

"My mom and dad told me not to tell anybody." She leaned forward toward Elizabeth. "I saw someone else go into that house too. He had dark skin, but not a black man," she clarified. "He went in a little before the blonde lady, but I never saw him come back out."

"He didn't come out?"

"Not through the front door. I didn't mean to spy on them, but nobody famous ever lived next door before."

"Me either. Then how did he get out?"

"Maybe the back door?" Molly signed. "I can't see it from my window."

"Did you tell this to the police?" Elizabeth asked.

"No way, but I wanted to. I told my mom and dad and they said that it wasn't important and not to talk to anyone about it. I don't get it. They say I should always tell the truth, so why did they say not to tell the truth to the police?"

"I don't get it either. But would you tell my mom since she's trying to help the lady — the one with the kids?"

"I don't know. My parents would be mad at me."

"My mom's very nice. She'll explain to your parents."

Molly considered this. "Okay," she finally signed. "I'll tell your mother if she'll explain it to Mom and Dad."

CHAPTER TWENTY-THREE

By Tuesday, Steve was worried. Very worried. Somehow he'd imagined that fishing with his sons in the remote streams of Michigan's Upper Peninsula would reward him with a plan. But the reality: he was at a loss. Almost six weeks since that night Laura had walked in on him and Kim. More than two weeks since Kim died. Now Laura was no longer a suspect, and the cops had zeroed in on Santiago.

And the cops and everyone else wanted to talk to him about Santiago's whereabouts? How the heck would he know where Kim's mobster boyfriend hung out? And what about Santiago himself, now that he — and the whole world — knew that Steve had boinked Kim. What would a mobster do? Would he want revenge? Steve's paranoia that Santiago would come after him was rapidly escalating. Was he safe in Michigan? Should he leave the country? Could he get the kids out with him? None of them had passports. Should he take off with the boys? Leave the girls with Laura? Could he convince Laura to come with him? Maybe to Canada? Or should he just go back to Florida, work things out with Laura, and take his chances?

These questions pounded in his head, making it throb with pain. He'd searched their supplies for Tylenol, but he must have forgotten to pack it. The weather had turned miserable, rainy and cold and depressing. Cooped up in a leaky tent, Mike became sullen and Kevin's high spirits decelerated to outright grumpiness. But it was Patrick who scared him. The little boy could hardly walk from the tent to the outhouse.

"Hey, Pat, wanna go out and have a catch?" Kevin stuck his head inside the tent and yelled. "Rain's stopping."

"Okay, yeah," Patrick said as Kevin barged inside and reached out to pull Patrick up from a sitting position.

Alarmed, Steve watched as Patrick had to catch his breath before following Kevin out of the tent's flap door.

"Come on, Mike," Steve said, grabbing two gloves, tossing one to Mike. "Let's go out with them."

"Okay, Dad, but —"

"Dad, come quick!" Kevin screamed from outside.

Steve and Mike rushed outside to see Patrick sprawled on a wet bed of pine needles. Kevin was trying to pull him into a sitting position.

"Just a minute," Patrick rasped. "I'm okay."

"Kev, what happened?" Steve asked.

"Don't know. Pat musta fell down."

"Did you slip on the wet needles?" Steve crouched down and held the little boy in his arms.

"Yup. I'm okay." Patrick's breathing was rapid and shallow.

For the first time Steve noticed the bluish hue of Patrick's skin. Was it the light filtering through the thick clouds? Steve turned to his oldest son. "Mike, start packing up the campsite. We're heading back to Traverse City."

"Right away, Dad."

"Pat, we're bringing you to see Dr. Chambers," Steve said as he carried the child toward the small, dank tent. "He was my doctor when I was a kid. You're going to like him."

"No more doctors, Dad," Patrick said weakly, his little arms around his father's neck. "Just call Mom."

"Nice work, Carrie," Greg said as Laura's defense team gathered in the conference room on Wednesday morning. "That child's ID of Frank Santiago is solid."

"Thought we'd never get the parents' okay for the affidavit," Chuck said, "but Carrie talked them from suing the pants off all of us into full cooperation — as long as their daughter is protected."

"Can you really protect her?" Laura asked quietly. "I'd be worried sick if it were my child. And she sounds like such a sweet girl . . ."

"She is a sweet girl," Carrie agreed. "I've already talked to the police about it."

"I'll take the affidavit to the D.A. right away," said Rob. "They'll need to verify it, but with an eyewitness putting Frank Santiago at Nelson's place — even if it is a kid — they'll be sweating bullets."

"Wonder how long that'll take. Of course, they'll have to question Molly Palmer," Carrie sounded nervous. "I'm just sorry she'll have to go through that again."

"If there's anything I can do," Laura offered, "Molly's done so much for us already . . ."

Greg nodded. "Thanks, Laura, you just sit tight." To the others he said, "Once the D.A. smells vulnerability, he'll squirm out and concentrate on spin control. You can be sure that Jake Cooperman, our esteemed D.A., will come out smelling like a political rose."

"Not until they find Santiago," said Rob. "Jake won't want to go public before they nail a new suspect. But with the kid's affidavit they'll issue a warrant, I'm sure."

"Rob, double-check about security for Molly. The cops have the real responsibility here," Chuck said, reaching for a bagel and smearing it with cream cheese, "but I'm thinking of backup. Maybe put a bodyguard on her right now. What do you think, Greg?"

"Maybe, but let's see what the cops can offer first."

"Santiago's buried pretty deep out there these days," Chuck went on. "They'll have to turn up the heat to flush him out. My guess is he's left the country."

"That's the speculation at police headquarters," said Rob. "And let me tell you, jurisdiction's a hot topic. Tampa wants the collar — quite a coup for them. Now that we have Molly's ID, the

Feds want in to grab the glory. Lopez and Goodnuf still lead the investigation, but who knows where this will go?"

"Infighting as usual," said Greg, "but it's our job to get Laura off. You take care of things downtown, Rob. Meantime, I'll finalize the new motion. I'd love to see the look on Jake's face when Sandra recommends dismissing the case. Knock him right on his —" He glanced at his client. "Right off his soapbox, I mean."

"So we're going for a dismissal with prejudice and because of extenuating circumstances, an immediate hearing with Judge Potter," Carrie explained to Laura, who sat quietly, an uneaten corn muffin before her. "You know, I just realized you've lost a ton of weight."

Laura managed a small smile.

"We'll settle for dismissal without prejudice," added Rob. "That'd be enough to let Laura come and go at will."

"Laura, we're getting there," Greg reassured.

The phone rang and Greg picked it up with a curious look — he'd specifically put all calls on hold. "Laura, for you," he said. "A Dr. Chambers? From Traverse City."

Laura reached for the receiver, her face suddenly pale.

"Dr. Chambers —"

"Yes. Dr. Nelson?"

Laura nodded, but remained mute.

"Well, Steve suggested I call you directly and explain the situation, since you're a physician."

"Is this about Patrick? Have you seen him?" Laura breathed deeply. So Steve had followed her advice and taken him to see his own family physician. Good.

"Yes, I have. I hate to be the one adding more to your troubles but, Dr. Nelson, I admitted him to the hospital here this morning."

Laura let the receiver slip then recovered it, jamming it against her ear as she let out a gasp. "You did? What's wrong?"

"We don't have a diagnosis yet. We're doing tests. EKG, blood work, cardiac ultrasound, lung scan, respiratory function, for starters. He presented with tachycardia, tachypnea, and slight cyanosis. No obvious signs of infection."

"Oh, no." Laura's mind raced through a differential diagnosis of these ominous symptoms in an eight-year-old.

"Dr. Nelson, is there any history of congestive heart failure with the child? Steve said he'd always had a heart murmur. No activity restrictions, so I assume nothing serious?"

"Patrick has a patent foramen ovale, grade-three systolic murmur at the left sternal border. It's been worked up thoroughly. Right, no functional disability." Her mind reeled as she attempted to mentally navigate the thick *Textbook of Pediatrics* that served as her bible in dealing with children. Patrick had a minor congenital defect. Nothing that would cause the kind of symptoms that Dr. Chambers had described.

"So," he went on, "any family history from your side that I should know?"

"Family history," she repeated.

"Of course I'm familiar with Steve's side, and there's nothing cardiac there."

"Uh, no, nothing relevant on my side either," she said. Had he said anything about heart disease? About anything else medically important? Had she missed something when Steve had told her about Patrick's symptoms over the weekend? Could she have prevented this?

"I'd like to get a pediatric consult right away," he went on. "And Dr. Nelson, I'd say that you'd better get to Traverse City to see for yourself. Unless the local pediatrician feels differently, I'd like to transfer him to the University of Michigan in Ann Arbor as soon as we can make the arrangements."

"I'll try," Laura jumped up and faced Greg, "to get there as soon as I can."

"Good. We'll attempt to make a diagnosis in the meantime, but I sense something very serious is going on with the child."

"I'll be there as soon as I can." Laura hung up the phone and turned to the three concerned faces.

"There's something wrong with Patrick, my youngest son," she blurted. "He's in the hospital in Michigan. I have to get to him right now."

"Oh, Laura!" Carrie sprang up. "Greg, let's call Judge Potter, get an emergency hearing. With our new information, the D.A. might be willing to let her go. Compassion for a sick child and all."

"Get on it, Carrie," Greg agreed. "Laura, give us time to get you out of here."

"I'm going. Now. I'm not waiting for any permission to see my son. There's something really wrong with him, and I need to be there!" She started gathering her belongings.

"If you go now, they'll just arrest you. Give us time to get this thing settled legally this afternoon so you can leave tonight," Greg said firmly. "I'll go with you."

Thunder and lightning halted all air traffic all night in and out of Tampa — the lightning capital of the world. So it wasn't until Thursday morning with the twins safely at home with Marcy Whitman and the Whelans that Laura, accompanied by Greg, departed Tampa via a nonstop Delta flight to Detroit with a transfer to a small commuter twin engine to Traverse City.

Rob had met with Sandra Mulloy on Wednesday afternoon as planned. He'd convinced her not to object to his motion to allow Laura to leave Hillsborough County to travel to northern Michigan in the custody of her attorney, and Judge Potter had signed the order. Initially balking at testimony from a minor, Sandra had reluctantly agreed to evaluate Molly Palmer's affidavit and to look into matters of police protection for the child.

The next step, Greg hoped, would be immediate suspension of the charges against Laura. The P.R. machine in the D.A.'s office would then take over, obsessed with finessing the politically correct way to preserve Jake Cooperman's reputation. If a mob figure like

Frank Santiago was ultimately convicted, the D.A. would come out
a hero. In the meantime, Greg was charged with Laura's custody.

*   *   *

Calling from the Tampa airport, Greg breathed a sigh of relief when
Celeste answered at the design site. "Darling, I'm so glad I got you.
I tried the Peachtree, but you'd already left."

"Oh, Greg, it's so good to hear your voice. My client is making
me crazy — a new fabric here, a new twist there. I need a break."

"Likewise. Listen, the judge has put Laura Nelson into my
custody. I've got to escort her to Michigan to see her sick child, but
I'll be back tomorrow night. It's a long story that I'd love to explain
in person. Will you come home this weekend?"

"I'd better. I think I'm going through withdrawal here."

"Withdrawal? What kind?"

"Your kind. I miss you so much. I'll be home by seven."

"Ah, that's the best news I've heard all day. This weekend it's
just you and me. And the sun and the moon and the stars. I miss
you, darling."

"Glad to meet you, Dr. Nelson. I'm Dean Chambers." The rotund,
balding man rose to greet Laura as she and Greg entered his cubbyhole office at Traverse City Community Hospital. He invited them
to sit on the two wooden folding chairs positioned across from the
ancient desk. This was the first time in almost six weeks that Laura
had stepped into a hospital, and to be called "Dr. Nelson" evoked
a sudden and sad recollection of her professional life before Kim
Connor's death. For a split second she almost forgot that the patient
she was here to see was her own son.

She quickly introduced Greg and the two men shook hands.

"Here, let me move these charts aside," Dr. Chambers suggested. "I'm behind, as usual, in my discharge dictations."

"Thank you for seeing us," Laura began. "What's the latest on
Patrick? I'd like to go right in and see him."

"I thought it wise for us to talk first. He's a bright eight-year-old and will surely hammer you with questions. Mainly, he wants to get out of here."

"Can't say I blame him," Greg murmured.

Dr. Chambers ignored Greg's comment. "Dr. Nelson, we did an ultrasound yesterday. The results are — disturbing."

"What do you mean?"

"We think he has some kind of a tumor. In his chest."

"Chest," she repeated. "Lungs?"

"We're not sure. Probably not. We think that it's in the heart, but we don't have the sophisticated equipment to be definitive. We've had consultations from pediatrics, cardiology and pulmonary."

Laura realized that Dean Chambers was a general practitioner with extensive experience but no specialty training that would equip him to manage much more than the day-to-day ailments of a small city practice. She found, however, that given his obvious candor she trusted him implicitly.

What could it be? Something related to the congenital heart defect that had worried her so before he'd had the reassuring cardiac catheterization as an infant? Not likely. A tumor in an eight-year-old with normal blood work? Lymphoma? Sarcoma? Tuberculosis? Laura's mind recycled the differential diagnosis. What type of tumor could this be? Something very rare.

"We'd like to send him to Ann Arbor for evaluation," Dr. Chambers continued. "Of course, we need parental consent, and arrangements have to be made."

"Is Steve here?" Laura asked.

"Not at the moment. He went home for a nap after spending the night in a chair in Patrick's room."

Laura sank back against her own chair. "Oh, this is all too much."

Dr. Chambers smiled kindly. "Do you want to see Patrick now?"

"Of course. I guess I'll tell him that he has to go to another hospital."

"You'll find him resting comfortably, but we do have oxygen

running with nasal prongs. We're keeping him in bed, giving him Lasix for congestive failure, and a lidocaine drip as prophylaxis for ventricular tachycardia."

"What does that mean in English?" Greg asked.

"It means that Patrick has a serious heart problem. A tumor that's blocking the normal blood flow," Laura explained.

"Like a heart attack?"

"No, but with the same complications," Dr. Chambers offered. "Heart failure, arrhythmias."

Greg's eyes were wide. "But he's just a little kid."

Laura walked shakily beside Dr. Chambers to the small pediatric ward, Greg trailing behind. There were only five beds and two were empty. Patrick was propped up, working on a puzzle laid out haphazardly on his tray. On each side of him was a crib with a baby. One about three months old lay quietly sleeping, the other older, red faced, crying furiously as he struggled to free his left arm which was securely connected to an IV board.

"Patrick!" Laura ran toward him.

"Mom!" A huge smile spread across his face.

"Am I ever glad to see you!" She threw her arms around his small body, taking care not to disrupt the IV catheter taped to his left arm and the EKG leads that she knew were connected to electrodes on his chest.

"You too, Mom." He looked tentatively at Greg. "How's it going?"

"Good, honey," she said, tousling his chestnut brown hair. "What about you, how are you feeling?"

"I wanna go home. Can you tell them to take all this stuff out of me? They won't even let me get up and walk around." He took several short breaths. "I missed the All Stars game last night."

"You didn't answer my question, honey," Laura said. She held his face in her hands. "How do you feel?"

"Good. Get me outta here, Mom." He lowered his voice. "These babies are driving me crazy."

Laura smiled. "Here, let me check you out." She gestured toward the stethoscope in Dr. Chamber's pocket and he silently handed it to her.

"Shush for a minute, honey."

" 'Kay, Mom."

Laura pulled up the child's blue hospital gown, careful not to disturb the electrodes taped to his chest. She moved the stethoscope across his thin frame, pausing at the pulmonic area in the right upper chest, the aortic area, left upper chest, and the apical area on the left side below the nipple, listening for irregular heart rates and abnormal heart sounds.

Laura tried to steady her hands as she auscultated his lungs, calmly asking her son to take big breaths in and out. His struggle to do so was more than evident. Laura's hands trembled as she silently handed the instrument back to Dr. Chambers.

"Just one more thing, but I'll have to crank your bed up a little." Laura carefully inspected Patrick's neck, looking for and finding marked distension of the jugular veins. Then she palpated his abdomen, taking special care to note with escalating concern the enlarged liver as it sank too far beneath the rib cage on the right side, but also to see with some relief the absence of a distended spleen.

"New murmur, grade four, systolic," she said, looking to Dr. Chambers for confirmation. "Normal rhythm on lidocaine, definite signs of CHF."

"Right. Full-lead EKG and ultrasound reports in the chart."

"What's CHF?" Patrick demanded as Laura cranked the bed back to a sitting position and plumped his pillows.

"Oh, just doctor talk. You've heard me talking funny like that about my patients, right?"

"Yup." He gulped air. "Mom, what's wrong with me?"

"Well, Patrick, we still have to do more tests and stuff, but first we're thinking about taking you to another hospital. We have to make some phone calls first."

"No way. I hate hospitals. I wanna go home."

"Soon, honey. Listen, my friend here, Greg, is going to stay and talk to you a while when I talk to your doctor. He's from Florida, and his favorite thing is sports — baseball, football, you name it." She hoped she was right and that Greg wasn't one of the minority of males who hated sports.

Greg nodded. "You bet."

"Be right back." Laura pulled up the lone visitor's chair, and with her eyes pleaded with Greg to sit down before she and Dr. Chambers left the ward.

Patrick took the bait. "What about basketball? Did you think that Washington would beat the Sonics for the championship?" He grabbed the plastic prongs going into his nose and pushed them down around his neck. "I hate these things."

"Yeah, I did. Did you?"

"Naw. Anyway, baseball's my favorite. I like Sparky Anderson." He paused, struggling to breathe. "I got his autograph once when my dad and grandpa took us to see the Reds for spring practice. You like baseball a lot?"

"Oh, man. How about Pete Rose and his three thousandth hit?"

"Yeah! Pete's one of my favorites." Patrick was gasping.

"Hey, buddy," Greg said, "don't you think you should put those things back in your nose? I think they help you breathe."

"Yeah, okay," said Patrick. He struggled to put the nose straps in place again.

"How do you think the Bucs are gonna do next season?'

"I'm for the Dolphins," Patrick said. "Bob Griese is the best quarterback in the —"

CHAPTER TWENTY-FOUR

What to do? Where to turn? Laura potentially had access to any medical expert, any medical center, but where to start? Where should she go to get the best medical care for her son? First she called the local pediatrician and adult cardiologist who had seen Patrick at Dr. Chamber's request. They reiterated Patrick's presentation: irregular, rapid heartbeat; runs of ventricular tachycardia, which could result in sudden death; an unusual cardiac outline on his chest X-ray; some kind of a mass on two dimensional echocardiography, most likely in the heart itself; a loud heart murmur typical of severe aortic stenosis with obstruction; obvious clinical signs of congestive heart failure presenting as easy fatigability, the shortness of breath on exertion that Steve had described. Could any of this be related to the preexisting patent foramen ovale?

Where would they have the most experience in cardiac tumors in kids? Of course, she'd fly him anywhere. Then she remembered a name from the past. A surgical resident with whom she'd trained back in med school in Detroit. He'd gone on to pediatric cardiac surgery at Children's Hospital in Philadelphia. He would know where to turn.

Laura had Tim Robinson paged during post-op rounds at Children's Hospital.

"Laura? Is this the ravishingly beautiful Laura Nelson I'm talking to?"

"Hi, Tim. Yes, it's me, but things aren't too good."

"Tell Uncle Tim all about it. Better make it snappy though. I've got a bunch of residents waiting on me. I'm an associate professor here, if you didn't know. Miracles do happen."

"I'm glad. Listen, Tim, my youngest son has some kind of a cardiac tumor. He's eight. I need help."

"I'm sorry, Laura." Tim's characteristic frivolity gave way to grave professionalism. "Tell me all about it."

Laura explained what she knew. Patrick's symptoms, his past medical history, the EKG, the echocardiogram. "What could it be?"

"Several possibilities. A tumor? An aneurysm? Hypertrophic subaortic stenosis? Infectious disease? Like tuberculosis, ecchinococcal cyst? Doesn't seem related to the PFO. Hell, Laura, I can't tell from here."

"They think it's a tumor. What can you tell me about cardiac tumors?"

"First, they're rare and they present much like your son's story — arrhythmias, signs of congestive heart failure. Eighty percent are benign. They're usually attached to the left ventricular wall or septum. Somewhere about three to five centimeters in diameter. They can compress the endocardium causing arrythmias and block the aortic outflow. Usually operable." He paused for a breath.

"What about sarcoma, rhabdomyosarcoma, or some kind of metastatic malignancy?"

"Eighty percent are benign, rhabodmyomas, myxomas, fibromas. Where are you anyway? In Tampa? Shands, in Gainesville?"

"No, I'm in Traverse City, Michigan."

"Oh boy, out in the sticks, medically speaking. Listen, here's what we'll do. I'll get on a plane tonight and find my way to Traverse City. Never been there. Bet it's beautiful this time of year. Don't they have lots of cherries up there? If your son needs surgery, there's no better place than CHOP. We have the best, I mean, *the best*, pediatric facilities and surgeons anywhere."

"What about the University of Michigan? Ann Arbor is so much closer."

"They're great, but I'm telling you, Children's Hospital here in Philadelphia is where you want to be. I'm here, but more importantly, so is George Kamen. He's the best surgeon in the world for this kind of situation. "

"Okay, Tim, I trust your judgment. But please, hurry up and get here."

Laura spent some time with Patrick before saying a temporary goodbye when *Happy Days* came on TV. Patrick idolized "The Fonz."

She found Greg in the corner in the visitor's lounge at the lone pay phone.

"Your fiancée?"

"Yes. I mean, no," Greg said as he replaced the receiver. "No answer in her hotel room. Probably gone to dinner."

They walked down the corridor toward the nurses' station. Laura hurriedly briefed Greg on her telephone conversation with Tim and the change of plans, asking him to make sure she had the clearance to travel to Pennsylvania with Patrick. She asked if he could arrange transportation by private medical jet.

"What about your husband," Greg said skeptically, "will he agree to this?"

"What about him?" Laura shrugged as she handed Patrick's chart to the desk clerk. "This is a medical emergency. What say does he have?"

"I don't really know," Greg considered. "So far he's thrown every obstacle imaginable in your course."

Laura frowned. "I guess I'll see him soon enough. Right now I'm going to donate some blood to the hospital on Patrick's behalf, and then we'll head over to Steve's dad's house. I haven't seen Mike and Kevin in over two weeks."

Kevin was the first to spot Laura as he sat perched on the glider on his grandfather's wraparound porch. It was cool in the shade of the leafy maples that graced the front lawn. The air smelled fresh after a brief shower and the yellow roses climbing the trellis were fragrant.

"Mike," he yelled through the screen door before rushing to meet his mother as she jumped out of the passenger side of Greg's rental car, "Mom's here!"

As Kevin reached the bottom step, Mike raced out of the house toward Laura. Both boys hugged her ferociously. Jim Nelson emerged from inside, and Laura introduced them all to Greg as they settled in the shade of the spacious front porch.

Laura clung hungrily to her two sons and for a few minutes all three dissolved into tears. It had been fifteen days since the boys had left home with Steve with no advance warning, no chance to say good-bye. They peppered her with questions. About Patrick, about the twins, about herself. About how much they wanted to go home.

"Stay for dinner, Laura," Jim urged when the boys slowed for a moment. To Greg, he said, "You too, of course. Laura, I'm making a macaroni and chicken casserole and you look like you need a home-cooked meal. You've gotten so thin!"

"Oh, Jim," Laura said, "that sounds great. I just gave some blood at the hospital and I have to admit, I'm feeling a bit weak."

"Good. Why don't you sit down. You know how sorry I am about Patrick."

"I know, thank you. We want to transfer him to Philadelphia in the morning."

"I see. Well, Steve should be back any minute from the grocery store," said Jim. "Mike and Kevin have been eating like horses, and they're holding up like champs. Right, boys?"

The boys shrugged, trying to hide their embarrassment.

"I'm pretty good in the kitchen," Greg offered. "Mr. Nelson, let's go see to dinner and give Laura some time with her boys. I could use some coffee, how about you?"

"Thanks, Greg," Laura whispered.

"Okay, guys," Laura began once the others had gone inside. "I don't know how much time we'll have together, but I want you to know how much I love you, how much I want you home with me."

"But Dad says you're too busy for us. That's why we have to stay here." Kevin strained to look up at her, his blonde bangs now long enough to cover his eyes.

"What? I want to be with you more than anything," Laura pledged. "All of you. You and Mike and —"

"Mom, are you going to jail?" Mike interrupted. "Dad says you are."

Laura hugged him. "No. The police in Tampa made a mistake. At first they thought I shot the gun that killed that Kim Connor, but, of course, I didn't." She looked at each of them squarely in the eye. "I needed to tell you face to face it wasn't me. Someone else was there at your dad's place right before me, but I was the one who found that poor woman. The police arrived just then, and because they found me there, they made a mistake and thought I did it. You must believe me."

"I believe you, Mom," Kevin blurted.

"So do I," Mike rushed to add, "but Dad told us that you did it because you were jealous and you wanted him to come back home."

Laura jerked. "I know, but he's not thinking that anymore. The police have a suspect. Now listen."

Laura explained that Patrick was sick and might need surgery and had to go to another hospital in Philadelphia. As she spoke, the rented Ford station wagon pulled into the driveway. Steve got out, looking rumpled and tired and badly in need of a shave. It was obvious to Laura that he'd dropped at least five pounds.

"Hey, Laura," he said, walking slowly toward the porch where they sat. "I'm surprised they let you come."

"Why? I told you I was coming. That the police have another suspect."

Steve put the groceries down in front of the door and stood with his hands on his hips. "So what's wrong with Patrick? The pediatric cardiologist you took him to when he was little said that heart murmur was nothing to worry about, right?"

Using words she hoped would not upset Mike and Kevin, Laura explained that she'd brought in Tim Robinson and that he wanted to transfer Patrick to Children's Hospital of Philadelphia.

Steve frowned. "Isn't he the guy we knew when you were in med school? Dated your cute little friend, Rosie?"

Laura nodded. "Yes. He's a pediatric heart surgeon now."

"Uh-huh. I never did like the way he looked at you," Steve grumbled.

"Oh, come on, Steve. Not now, don't —"

Before he could answer, the screen door opened and Greg appeared.

Steve frowned. "What's he doing here?"

"Helping your father with dinner," Greg said matter-of-factly, "which is ready."

Though they tried to keep the conversation going, no one said much during the meal. When Jim removed what was left of the casserole, Greg offered to drop Laura off at the hospital where she planned to spend the night on a cot next to Patrick's bed. He'd be staying at a nearby hotel. In the morning, they'd all meet Dr. Chambers at the hospital after Tim Robinson had completed the preliminary tests on Patrick. Steve would be there, then they'd decide what to do.

Laura could not suppress her tears as she said good-bye to Mike and Kevin. One of her contacts had slipped and she fiddled with her eye to resituate it as she promised she'd see them the next day.

CHAPTER TWENTY-FIVE

Laura, Steve, Greg, Tim Robinson, and Dean Chambers all crowded around the small conference table in the hospital on-call room on Friday morning. Laura had stopped by her father-in-law's earlier to spend some time with Mike and Kevin, knowing that if Patrick's transfer to Philadelphia were immediate, she'd have no time to come back to say one more heart-wrenching good-bye.

"You can just drop me off in front of the house," she told Greg as he approached the house.

"You okay? I can wait, and you can drive in with me."

"I'm fine, Greg. The meeting's at nine, so it's easier just to drive in with Steve. Why don't you get some breakfast and I'll see you there?"

Laura headed for the front door. She rang the doorbell and Steve answered, still in his bathrobe and slippers, still unshaven.

"You really have lost weight, haven't you?" Laura said.

He grunted. "Likewise. You look great. Let's sit out here so we can talk." He plopped down on the wicker loveseat. "How's Pat?"

"The same," she said, leaning against the porch railing. "The tumor is putting pressure on the heart valves and causing serious arrhythmias. He needs surgery soon, but we'll go over all that when we meet with the doctors."

Steve was frowning. "Hasn't enough happened already? He's gonna be okay, right?"

"God, I hope so," she said, sitting down next to Steve. "We'll have to see what the specialists say."

"He's a spunky little guy, isn't he?"

"Yes," agreed Laura. "He is."

Steve shifted his position so that their arms touched. "So bring me up to date on your legal situation. What's this new evidence?"

"There's a witness who saw a man at your place that night," Laura blurted. She stopped herself from saying more — this was still confidential.

Steve jerked forward. "Huh? Who?"

"I really can't say more. It's not supposed to be public knowledge."

"Oh, c'mon! You can't tell me?" His jaw clenched.

"No, I can't. Besides, we've got Patrick to worry about right now."

"That's right. And the girls? Safe and sound with your parents, I assume."

"Fine. I'm going to call Mom and Dad after we know what's happening with Patrick, and ask them to fly up with the girls."

Steve hesitated. "Then we'll all be together again. A family, just like we've always been." Steve hesitated. "Laura, please, let's get back together. Move away from Tampa, away from all the painful memories."

"No," Laura said firmly. "I belong in Tampa, and so do the kids."

Steve sighed. "I wish you'd reconsider." He steeled himself. "But, just so you know, I'll never give up my sons. You could keep the girls, but I'll never let you take the boys."

Laura glared at him. "What? Abandon the girls just like that. You know, I'd agree that you've been a good father to the boys, but that doesn't make up for how you've treated your daughters. Just because they're identical twins and they remind you of what happened to your brother."

"That's the most ridiculous —"

Laura watched Steve's whole body stiffen.

"What happened to Philip was not your fault, yet you've transferred all your mistaken guilt to the twins. You take the boys camping and dump the twins with your dad just to get rid of them — and punish me while you're at it."

Steve's hands curled into fists as he started to get up, but then he stopped himself, staring at his wife. "That's enough, Laura." Steve's chin jutted forward. "Of course I left the girls with my father, because they didn't want to go! No toilets, no running water — they hated the idea."

"You should never have taken off with the kids."

"What? You think all this has been some kind of picnic for me? My wife, arrested. My job down the tubes. My son with some mysterious illness that you should have known about."

"How can you say that?" Laura turned sharply to face him.

"Damn, that's not what I meant!" Steve turned in the loveseat and took her head in his hands. "Laura, look. Let's just try to get our lives back together. Be a family. We'll start over. Remember the old Laura and Steve? We had it all. We've been through so much together. Now that you're not going to jail."

She reached up and took his hands, placing them between hers on her lap. "Not now, we don't have time. But I have been thinking — we need to talk. Once Patrick is out of danger. Okay?"

"Good, honey, that's what I hoped you'd say. Now I have to go get dressed."

"I want to say good-bye to Mike and Kevin before we leave for Philadelphia." She glanced at her watch. "It's after eight already, and we have to be at the hospital at nine."

Steve finally stood up. "Don't jump to conclusions about Philadelphia. U. of M. is closer and Dr. Chambers recommended —"

"Let's wait until we meet with the specialists," Laura suggested. "At least where Pat's concerned, let's act like a team, okay?"

Steve hesitated. "Okay. Mike and Kev are out in the back having breakfast with Dad. Go on out. I'll be down in a few minutes."

Laura walked away.

*   *   *

Tim Robinson was obviously happy to see Laura. He was taller and broader than Steve, his thick brown hair combed straight back, his golden brown eyes behind eyeglass frames that matched his eyes. More sexy than handsome, his ready smile, quick wit, and prestigious medical appointment made him a favorite among the single females in the Philadelphia medical community. He'd been ahead of Laura in med school, and he'd known Steve socially when he'd dated Laura's anatomy partner and friend, Rosie Santangelo. He'd gotten himself in hot water with both girls when he'd propositioned Laura once at a surgical meeting he'd attended with her in Montreal. When Rosie found out, it had been the end of that relationship. As far as Laura knew, Tim had never had a serious relationship since.

"Hey, Laura, it's been a long time."

"Graduation, I think," she said, smiling slightly as he kissed her on the cheek.

"Though it's nice to see you both," Tim said, shaking Steve's hand, "I'm sorry about the circumstances. So if you don't mind, let's get focused on your son. Dr. Chambers has provided me with all the test results and I've examined Patrick."

"Yes," the Nelsons said simultaneously.

"Good morning, Steve, Dr. Nelson." Dr. Chambers greeted them as Tim ushered the trio toward the large rectangular table in the hospital conference room. "Mr. Klingman is already here."

"Does he need to be here?" Steve stared suspiciously at Greg.

"I'd like him to stay," said Laura.

"Okay, let's get started," said Tim. "Here's what I think. Patrick has some kind of cardiac tumor. Probably benign," he hastened to add. "It's impinging on the aortic outlet causing an obstruction severe enough to induce CHF and arrhythmias —"

"What's CHF?" Steve interrupted.

"Congestive heart failure. That's why he's been so short of breath," Tim explained. "Anyway, we need more sophisticated tests, but the echocardiogram here is pretty good quality and I think the tumor is resectable." He paused to address Greg's quizzical frown. "Meaning it can be surgically removed. When we go in, we'll do a frozen section — that's a quick biopsy while the patient is still on the table. Pathology will give us a read on the tissue type and hopefully, according to the numbers, it'll be benign. We remove it, patch things up, and he'll be just fine."

Steve was the first to speak. "That sounds good, Tim, but I don't want to send him to Philadelphia for this. Ann Arbor's much closer, and Dr. Chambers says they have a good pediatric surgical department."

"That's true, Steve," Dr. Chambers interjected, "but Tim here is the real expert. They have the best pediatric surgeons in the world at CHOP. Dr. George Kamen is world renown. I've been in the library reviewing the series of these types of cases. They're rare and there's no doubt in my mind that Patrick should be operated at CHOP. And soon."

"I've made all the arrangements for transportation," Greg offered quickly. "The tests can be done over the weekend with surgery on Monday. The MediJet can be here this afternoon."

Steve glared at Greg. "It's not up to you to make decisions about my son."

"I think you should let Dr. Nelson make the decision. Chest surgery is her area of expertise," Greg countered.

"Now, Steve," Dr. Chambers turned toward Steve with a look of concern. "I know you're anxious and want what's best for that little boy. You know, you and Laura were really wonderful to adopt him, what with four kids of your own and you two with such busy careers. I don't recall your father even telling me. I'm sure everything will work out. I've got all the transfer documents ready to go."

"Adopted? Nobody told me that," said Tim.

Steve's eyes opened wide. "What are you talking about?"

"How much do you know about the natural parents' family history anyway? I didn't think to ask you that earlier, Dr. Nelson," Dr. Chambers went on. "Can this be something hereditary?"

"Hereditary?" Steve echoed.

"Well, I assumed you adopted him."

Steve looked at the elderly physician as if he were a doddering fool. Laura, sitting next to Steve, turned a chalky white.

"Simple matter of genetics. Your blood's been A/B negative for as long as I can remember, Steve. Very rare, that's why I remember. You and your — anyway, Laura, yesterday's bloodwork showed you to be B neg. Dr. Nelson offered to donate yesterday and well," he glanced over at her, "two negatives just can't make a positive. Since Patrick is O positive, I just assumed —"

Steve stared at the older man as a look of abject horror crossed his face.

"Doesn't the child know?" Dr. Chambers asked. "Children should be told right off, as young as possible, so there aren't problems later. That's what I tell my families who adopt."

"You're saying that my son is not my son?" Steve swung slowly around and looked at Laura who sat rigid in the chair beside him. "Laura, what's he saying? This is all a big mistake. Laura?"

Laura would not look at him. He stared at his wife. A long moment passed.

"No, no, no. It can't be!" Steve suddenly bolted out of his chair, lunging toward Laura, grabbing her by the shoulders, shaking her. "How could you — you whore!"

Greg and Tim jumped up. Each gripped one of Steve's arms as Laura sat frozen, not moving a muscle to defend herself. Dean Chambers remained in his chair, head bowed into his hands, as Steve struggled to free himself.

"You take your bastard wherever you want," Steve spat at Laura, "but don't you even think about getting near my real sons again."

"Steve, Steve, let's not be so impetuous," Dean Chambers managed. His kindly face registered confusion and regret.

"Let go of me!" Steve ignored Dr. Chamber's plea as he writhed to free himself. When Greg and Tim finally released him, Steve abruptly left the room, on his way crashing into a supply cart and a dozen stainless steel emesis basins clattered to the floor.

*   *   *

Children's Hospital of Philadelphia, known throughout the pediatric medical world as CHOP, sent a fully equipped MediJet to Traverse City. It arrived at one thirty on Friday and was scheduled to leave within the hour. The day was bright and sunny and they'd estimated three hours for the return flight. As the medical officer in charge, Dr. Tim Robinson checked all the medical supplies and instruments as he waited for the arrival of his passengers. The manifest he'd prepared for the return flight to Philly included both Laura and Steve. It would be a full flight with himself, the pilots and co-pilot, and an intensive care nurse.

After the nightmare scene in the conference room, Laura forced herself to pull it together. Her focus had to be on Patrick right now, and with Tim and Greg's help the arrangements were finalized to transfer him to CHOP. As she sat with Patrick, Laura tried to make the trip sound like an adventure, but he was apathetic. She reached for the chart on the hook at the foot of his bed and flipped through the progress notes to the lab results, searching for the latest blood gases. As she noted the steady fall in arterial oxygen levels, she withheld a gasp and immediately inspected her son more carefully, taking in the bluish discoloration of his lips and nail beds.

Patrick squirmed. "What's wrong, Mom? Where's Dad?"

Laura didn't know what to say. What to tell him about Steve? "Listen honey, your job is to wait here while everybody gets ready for your trip. I'll be right back," she said, "then we leave with Dr. Robinson."

Patrick made a face. "I want Dad."

Laura found Greg by the telephone in the visitor's waiting room about to place a call.

"Greg, can you take me to Steve's father's house? Right now?"

"One second, Laura. I've got to call Rob back about Judge Potter. We have to make sure it's a 'go' here." He glanced at his watch. "We have less than an hour."

"Now, please. It's only a five minute drive, and I have to go now," she pleaded. "Patrick's worse. He wants his father."

Greg hung up the receiver and started to follow Laura out the door. "Do you really think Steve will —?"

"He's got to be there for him. I've got to convince him that none of this was Patrick's fault. It would be devastating for the child to lose his father, especially now. I don't know what to do, but I'll do anything."

"Laura, what are you doing here? After . . ." Jim Nelson stammered as he stood blocking the front door. "How could you do this to my son? To all of us? I know things have been tough for you and Steve, but I've always trusted you, defended you. You know how much Steve loves that little boy."

"I'm so sorry, Jim." Of course she was sorry that she had hurt her family, her husband, and especially Patrick, who she feared would pay the price. But the truth was, she would never be sorry about that one night and she would never, never tell a living soul about it. This she had solemnly vowed over seven years ago, before leaving Detroit forever.

"Is that all you have to say?"

"It's that things were awful between Steve and me at the time." Laura could think of absolutely nothing else to say as she made up this response. "Please understand."

There was a prolonged, uncomfortable silence. Finally, Laura said, "Please, tell Steve that I need to talk to him."

Jim Nelson shook his head. "He's very upset. I'm not sure you want — Steve came home from the hospital all in pieces. I had to call Dr. Chambers to find out what happened. He's just beside himself for bringing it up at all."

"Jim, I really am sorry that it happened this way, but Patrick needs Steve. He's getting worse and he's calling for his dad."

"Steve, Laura's here," the older man called inside, still not letting Laura across the threshold.

In a moment, a disheveled Steve appeared beside his father.

Blonde hair falling out of place, his eyes red and puffy, the neat slacks and shirt he'd worn to the hospital rumpled.

"What do you want?" he stared at her, sadness mingled with fury.

"Steve, we have to talk. You can't just abandon Patrick at a time like this. He's just a little boy. He idolizes you. It's not his fault, and he's so sick right now —"

Steve turned away.

"Please, Steve."

"Son, why don't you let her in? Sit out on the back porch. Try to talk things out." Jim led them back through the shade of maples and the smell of roses. Silently she and Steve followed, taking a seat next to one another on the back porch swing they had always loved when they were young. "None of us are perfect, son," said Jim Nelson as he closed the door behind them.

"So, what? You're here to tell me what happened over eight years ago back in Detroit? Which one of those doctors knocked you up?" Steve moved as far as he could to the edge of the swing.

"It was so long ago, I don't —"

"You don't remember?" Steve cut her off. "What? There were so many you don't remember who you fucked? And you give me grief over one fucking single mistake like you're some kind of canonized saint? My God, this is — I can't believe this. All these years —"

Laura's hands rose up in a "stop" gesture. "You don't understand, Steve. It's not like that."

"Then you tell me what it is 'like.' I keep going back to 1970. I thought we were happy. Sure, we had a tough year with you being pregnant with the twins and all that trauma around their early birth, but after that I actually thought we were fucking happy."

Laura remained quiet.

Steve's eyes were wild as he ran his fingers again and again through his hair. "I have to admit that when you got pregnant with the twins, I suspected something. Naw, you're just being paranoid,

I kept telling myself. But there was my beautiful wife, a med student, spending nights and days with all those fucking doctors. On call. Medical meetings. All that shit. And I talked myself into trusting you. What a goddamned fool. Maybe I should be blaming myself for being so stupid instead of blaming you for betraying me."

Tears flowed down Laura's cheeks. "You can blame me, Steve, just don't blame Patrick. It's not his fault."

"No, it's not, but you know how the child always pays for your 'sins'? God, look what happened to my mother — and me — after my brother —"

"Steve, it's not — I was raped," Laura said quietly, her eyes downcast.

"What? Raped?" Steve lifted her chin with one hand so he could look into her eyes. Lying eyes, like the song, flashed though his mind.

Laura was silent.

"'I was raped'?" he echoed. "And where was I? We'd been married for seven years by then. And now what, nine years later, when it's convenient, you tell me that you were raped?" He jerked his hands away from her head.

"It's the truth, Steve," Laura spoke so quietly that Steve had to lean in to hear her. "I never reported it. I never told you — or anyone."

"Didn't tell anyone that you were raped? You expect me to believe that? Sure you do. You've taken me for a fool all these years."

"No. I was afraid. I thought you'd make me quit school back then. I didn't want the shame. Then when I knew I was pregnant I didn't know. I still thought — prayed — the father was you. I mean, if it weren't for that blood test, I still wouldn't know."

"What a fool I am. I've got four kids with blue green eyes, and one with brown — or hazel, as you've always insisted. You knew all the time. How can you sit there and lie to me like this?"

"Steve, I did it for Patrick. I didn't think it would be fair to him to ever let him find out. Please, don't tell him."

"I won't." Steve's voice turned hoarse. "He's not my son. I'll take care of my real sons, but I can't face Patrick. That's it."

Laura burst into new tears. "Please, can't we all be together again?" She took Steve's hand, expecting that he would pull it back, but he didn't.

He looked down at her hand. "What? I don't see how you can even ask me that."

"The last time we talked you said you wanted us to all go away," she said in a rush. "Start all over, you know, fresh."

He stared at her. "That was a lifetime ago. And remember, you said, 'no'."

"I've . . . I've reconsidered." Laura squeezed his hand, pleading now. "We can put our lives back together."

His hand squeezed back. "Truth is, Laura, we've both made mistakes. What I learned this morning was a shock, an affront to my manhood. I don't know how I'll live with it. But, I admit I've done things, things I'm not proud of, and I wish we could just go back to those happy years. Remember when we'd sneak out here after Mom and Dad had gone to bed and just talk away the night under the stars?"

Laura nodded, sniffling, pulling out a pack of Kleenex, blowing her nose.

"Remember how thrilled we were when Mikey was born? And then Kev? We survived on loans and scholarships, but, as the song goes, we had the world on a string. Remember how we'd splurge and go out and buy every one of Elvis's albums. Go to all his movies. Even the crummy ones."

"Yes, I remember," said Laura. "We were so much in love. What went wrong?"

"I don't know," he continued, now stroking her hand with his free one. "Busy careers. More kids." He paused for a long time. "I guess now we know — not enough trust."

"Steve, about the rape —"

"No, let's not go into that again. You need to get on your way, and I have to take care of Mike and Kevin." He placed her hand back on her knee, patting it gently.

Shaking her head, Laura glanced at her watch. "I do have to go. Please, Steve. Change your mind about Patrick."

He rose from the swing and turned to Laura, clearing his throat. "I hope the surgery goes well. You're right about one thing — this is not Patrick's fault."

With a deep sigh, Laura stood up. "Okay. Look, I have to say good-bye to Mike and Kevin."

"The boys are very upset, Laura. I don't want them to see you like this. They're upstairs. I told them not to come down."

She wiped away tears, hand shaking, but careful not to dislodge her lenses. "Just to say good-bye."

Without another word, Steve headed into the house through the back door. Laura heard the slide of the bolt. She grabbed the porch rail to steady herself, quickly drawing back as a rusty nail pierced the palm of her hand. A large drop of blood oozed out and with her free hand she reached inside her purse for the one remaining Kleenex and started dabbing the blood away.

Blood. Oh, God, how could she possibly have just given blood without a thought to these consequences?

Greg stood to the side as the MediJet pilots completed their checklist. He'd finally gotten in touch with Rob and learned that the news from Tampa was good: Judge Potter had given verbal permission for Laura to travel from Michigan to Pennsylvania with her sick child. As if answering his wish, the judge had not specified a custodial escort, so there was no necessity for Greg to accompany her, and in his pocket was an airline ticket to Tampa. Celeste would be arriving home from Atlanta, and he had just enough time to make the flight once he saw Laura off. As that time neared, however, he doubted he'd make it.

Laura had returned to the car devastated after talking with Steve. She kept shaking her head, sobbing, "He won't come, he won't come."

"Give it some time," Greg advised, worried now that Laura, always so strong, was not going to hold up.

"He won't even let me talk to Mike and Kevin," she sniffled. "God, would he be able to take them away from me, Greg?"

"I really don't know. It's complicated, as you know, but Carrie's working on it. In the meantime, Steve's very angry right now. Hurt and angry," was all Greg could think to say as they sped back to the hospital.

"But how can he just reject Patrick? He's always loved him the most of all the kids, and Patrick's so sick. He'll never understand this terrible rejection. Greg, I told him I'd go back with him, move wherever he wants. My God, I'm desperate."

"After all these years," Greg said slowly, "I guess it was quite a shock." He didn't go on to say, 'How would any man feel finding out nine years later that his wife had fucked another guy?' So far she'd not given him so much as a hint as to how to solve the mystery of Patrick's paternity, and it was obvious that Dr. Laura Nelson was not exactly who she seemed to be. What he did say was, "And both of you are under an incredible amount of stress. Try to remember that you, both of you, are only human."

The team of white coats had just completed all the connections for the flight — the intravenous lines, the oxygen flow meters, the EKG leads. Then they pushed the small stretcher toward Laura and Greg, who said, "Right now, Laura, you have to concentrate on that little guy over there. Let's get on that plane."

Laura's eyes brimmed with fresh tears along with a flicker of hope as she looked into his. "Are you coming with us?"

"Well, there's an extra place now."

"But I thought —"

"It's okay," Greg glanced around and saw Dr. Chambers and Dr. Robinson heading toward them. Did he have time to call Celeste? No. Besides she'd be in the air by now.

"Dr. Nelson, I'm terribly sorry about this morning," Dean Chambers said apprehensively. "I just assumed that, well, I am truly sorry."

Laura nodded as Tim approached her and affectionately put his arm around her. "Come on, honey, let's get this show on the road. Where's our boy?" he called within earshot of Patrick, who lay propped up by several pillows looking nonplussed by all the nurses' attention.

They walked over to Patrick's stretcher and Tim reached out and squeezed the little boy's shoulder. "Our man here is hooked up to oxygen, and we'll keep it flowing throughout the flight, right Pat?"

Patrick nodded.

Tim also nodded, speaking now to the nurses. "We'll hook up the EKG on board for constant monitoring. We've got all the records and we're ready to roll."

Dr. Chambers formally shook Patrick's hand — the one without the intravenous line hooked to the bottle of clear colorless fluid suspended from the metal hook overhead.

"Have a good trip, buddy," he said.

"Okay," Patrick replied. "Do I still have to wear this thing?" He pointed to the plastic oxygen prongs secured below his nostrils with a strap around his head.

"Afraid so," said the kindly physician.

"That's part of the deal," added Tim, ruffling the child's chestnut hair.

"Where's Dad, Mom?" Patrick asked Laura.

She tried to smile as she lied, "He'll meet us at the hospital just as soon as he can, honey."

"'Kay."

As they boarded the MediJet that would take them to Philadelphia, Greg silently promised to call Celeste the minute they touched down.

CHAPTER TWENTY-SIX

The minute Greg walked into his room at the Sheraton Hotel, located directly across the street from Children's Hospital in west Philadelphia, he phoned Celeste in Tampa. She'd said she'd be back by seven and it was already eight, yet her phone just rang and rang. He'd promised her the moon and the stars when they last spoke: cocktails at her place, followed by dinner in Clearwater. They'd drive to Palm Harbor and spend the weekend at his place, waking up to the sound of the Gulf and a leisurely breakfast on the terrace. He'd been so determined to take the weekend off, to make up for lost time with Celeste.

Sitting alone on the edge of the king-size bed, he hoped he'd done the right thing by accompanying Laura to Philadelphia, and that Celeste would understand. As he tried her line again, he thought of the marquis-cut diamond he'd given her eighteen months ago, and of his utter elation when she'd accepted it. Yet they still hadn't set a wedding date. Could it be that she really didn't want to marry him? Maybe they both were too dedicated to their careers. Maybe marriage wasn't right for them? He knew he wanted a family, and she said she did too. But with her constant traveling and the intensity with which they both approached their work, was it possible? He promised himself that after the Nelson case, things would change. He'd promote both Rob and Carrie to senior partner and let them share his responsibilities.

As soon as he'd set the receiver down, the phone rang.

"Celeste?" He assumed that she'd been in the shower or

stepped outside or something before he remembered that she didn't even have his phone number. Didn't even know he was in Philadelphia.

"No," a familiar woman's voice said. "Greg, is that you?"

"Yes."

"Greg, it's Carrie. You okay?"

"Hey, Carrie, I'm fine. Any news?"

"Wanted to bring you up to date on what's happening down here. Rob told me you were headed to Philly," she went on, "but I thought you were coming back —"

"Made a last minute decision. I was supposed to be meeting Celeste tonight, but I can't reach her. She was flying in from Atlanta for a beach weekend."

"Uh huh. Well, we just had one of those Tampa specials, you know, summer storm complete with booming sound effects and a spectacular lightning show. Her flight was probably delayed. It's okay out there now, but the streets are flooded, so she'll be late for sure."

"Damn. She takes a direct flight from Atlanta to Miami, then a small prop to Tampa. She hates flying in perfect weather, so a small plane in a storm —"

"I'm sure she's okay."

"But she doesn't know I'm stuck here," Greg went on. "She's got Betty's home phone, but I feel like a jerk for standing her up."

"Hey, she's a smart lady. Just keep trying her, she'll forgive you. Now what's going on with Laura and her son?"

"Well, I'd say she's about as well as can be expected what with a seriously ill son and a failing marriage. I need you to intensify your look into custody and jurisdiction issues in case Nelson really tries to take Mike and Kevin away from Laura."

"I don't know how she can deal with all this."

"I don't know that she can, to tell you the truth.

Carrie sighed. "So, are you planning to stay in Philly?"

"I don't know. I'll stay at least until the surgery on Monday. Carrie, they think the child has a tumor in his heart."

Carrie gasped. "Cancer?"

"They don't know, but they will on Monday. I can't really leave her. You won't believe what's happened. You and Rob have to know this, but I hope we can keep it away from the Tampa gossip machine."

He then related to Carrie the jarring scene with Dr. Chambers and Steve's reaction.

"It just goes from bad to worse. But I agree, you'd better stay with her," Carrie responded. "Did she give any explanation at all, I mean, about the child's father? I mean, how could that doctor be so sure?"

"Blood types. Genetics 101, I guess."

"But to find out now. Doesn't that seem, well, unreal?"

"You know, Carrie, she didn't say a word." Greg paused. "Nothing to her husband. Nothing to me. She certainly didn't deny it."

"What a horrible time for it all to come out. At least things are on the upside here. We've made good progress with Sandra Mulloy and the judge. We'll be working all weekend on the motion to dismiss. We want to set it up so the D.A. won't resist it."

"What more do we need?"

"Well, the D.A.'s office has jump-started an official investigation — the Organized Crime Task Force shaking down Ybor City."

"All eyes on Santiago."

"Who's nowhere to be found."

"Still, it's enough to get them to suspend charges. Good work, you guys."

"Best to thank Chuck. But," she went on, "I'm worried about security. Though the D.A. came through and had the Tampa police send an officer to the Palmers, they're still worried. Santiago's a mobster, for heaven's sake. What if word gets out that Molly Palmer can ID him? She could be in real danger."

"You've got a point. The D.A. has to keep her affidavit confidential, but with all the police involvement, there could always be a leak."

"We've got to get her better protection. Greg, I promised, that's how we got this far."

"I know. I think we should get the family out of Tampa." Greg was quiet for a moment, rubbing his forehead with one hand. "Got it. We can use Celeste's condo. It's on Amelia Island near Jacksonville. Chuck can set it up. They'll need an assumed name to start with."

"How does that work? What can I do?"

"Let Chuck handle it, he knows the drill. We used it once before as a safe house."

"Sounds good to me. So who'll talk to the Palmers?"

"You do that. Just be sure to emphasize that secrecy is critical. They're to tell no one, absolutely no one, including the police. The only ones who know where they are will be Chuck and me. Just tell the Palmers that it's a safe, comfortable place a few hours away. Okay?"

"Okay, Greg. Makes me feel better, though I wonder if Sally Palmer can possibly keep a secret. In the meantime, Chuck's got people in the street here and in Miami after Santiago."

"Right. Carrie, here's what I've been thinking: how much danger could Nelson be in? I mean, Santiago did show up at his place, right? After he takes care of Connor, he's thinking that Nelson was Connor's confidant and that she told him things she shouldn't have. What'd he do then? Run it by Chuck, would you? I don't give a shit about the bastard, but he's got Laura's two older sons."

"Will do. I've wondered about that too. I thought maybe he'd go after Steve Nelson right after it happened —"

"In a jealous rage," Greg finished her thought. "Wonder how much that had to do with Nelson trekking up to Michigan that night. How much, and what, did he know?"

"Exactly. I'll talk to Chuck about it, and about the Palmers. I'll go see them tonight and arrange for them to leave in the morning. And you'd better get over to the hospital with Laura," Carrie added. "Sounds like about now, you're all she has."

*   *   *

"Hey Carlos, it's Frankie. What's shakin' in Miami, man?" Frank Santiago had been waiting by the phone and finally made the call himself. He was barefoot and wore swim trunks with small gold-colored diamonds against a plum background and a matching top as he tried to lounge inside the beachfront cottage. He hadn't even been able to show off his stylish swimwear on the beach. It was Saturday. Tomorrow would be three weeks since the Mexican heist and he was losing patience.

"No matter to you. You where you supposed to be," a heavily accented Hispanic voice rasped.

"Sweet fucking island, but I gotta get outta here. Saturday night and I'm sitting here doin' fucking nothing. Got business to take care of."

"Too hot in Tampa," said Carlos Tosca. He sounded authoritative and annoyed.

For fifteen years Carlos had controlled the Cuban arm of the South Florida mob out of Miami. He was a self-made man, now sixty-three and thinking of his successor. He had three daughters that he'd sent to the Ivies — and that he'd kept isolated from the family business. He had no sons, and over the past year he'd been grooming his captains for the top job. Frank Santiago was one, and nine months ago, Carlos sent him up to Tampa to expand the Ybor City operation into the larger Tampa Bay area.

"They got a manhunt goin' down and you the man," barked Carlos from his mansion in Miami's South Beach. "Like I don't got nothin' better to do than cover your fuck ups. How many times I tell you. Just you and Ritchie, get to Tampa, do the job, don't make no stops, don't let nobody see you. And whaddaya do instead? Go chasin' after pussy, then you even off the bitch."

"Carlos, that's not what went down — but the job got done, right? That blow's raking it in now and I gotta —"

"Shut the fuck up," Carlos sneered. "Listen to me real good. I'm callin' the shots to keep your ass outta the slammer. You stay outta sight, you hear me? Ain't anybody gonna find you there. Sanibel's a quiet, family-type island. Droppin' you by boat at night means nobody saw nothin' so long's you stay inside. You got that?"

"I'll go loco in this shit of a paradise," insisted Frank. "I gotta get back to Tampa."

"Ritchie's takin' over."

"Ritchie don't know shit. I got stuff all set up."

"Yeah, you're all set up. That why the pigs crawlin' through Tampa lookin' for you for buryin' that stupid bitch."

"Shit, I'm telling you that nobody can finger me."

"That the fact? Then why you got somebody singin' 'bout you, asshole. Word is they gonna drop the charges on that lady doctor. That leaves you in a bad place, so you fuckin' stay put. Down the line we may hafta get you outta the country fast."

"Drop the charges? What the fuck —?"

"I'm hearing that someone saw you, Frankie. I know you've been like a son to me, but you're not leavin' me too many choices."

"I swear, nobody saw nothin'."

"I gotta go," rasped Carlos. "Ritchie'll stay in touch. He's in charge now, and you do what he tells you. No more fuck ups."

Santiago slammed down the phone, grabbed a beer, and walked out into the humid South Florida air, gazing with contempt at the aqua blue waters of the Gulf of Mexico. He detested islands. They made him feel like he was in a prison. Especially this one, accessible only via a toll bridge connected to Fort Myers and, of course, by small boats. He needed to get back to business in Tampa and fast. Before that prick Ritchie dug too deep in his business. Didn't everybody skim a little off the top? But if Richie ever found out, he'd go straight to Carlos. Frankie knew what would happen next. He'd sent his share of bodies to the bottom of Tampa Bay. He went back inside.

There wasn't much time. Frankie began to sweat. He stripped off his shirt. Forced himself to sit down on the bed. Forced himself to think. To list his problems. First, Ritchie. The kid was smart, as in mathematically smart. The money reported to Carlos was light by 3 percent — enough to get him iced. He had to get back before Richie figured this out.

Second, what Carlos said about that night? That somebody saw him at Nelson's shithole? He'd been so fucking careful, parking his Caddy two blocks away. Left no prints. Took the back door out. But somebody musta seen something 'cause they were droppin' charges on the Nelson bitch. He knew the rule. Better to take a soldier out than let him sing inside the joint. Carlos already figured he'd iced Kim and was fucking pissed. He could think of only one way to handle this mysterious witness — Manny Gonzolas.

Finally, there was Steve Nelson. Free as a bird out there. Frankie sank back against the pillows, reliving that night. Tears pricked his eyes as they had off and on since he'd lost Kim. This weird sign of emotion confused him. Tears because he missed her? Or tears of sheer anger? How could she betray him for fucking Nelson? And what did Nelson know about his scheme? He had told Kim, hadn't he? Trying to impress her with how smart and how rich he was. So many pretty woman out there, and he'd finally chosen Kim to be his wife and she —

Frankie wiped away the tears, his face hardening into a tight grimace. Had to be Nelson pointing the finger. Why else would they let his wife walk and the law be out looking for him? Pigs found her right there. Yes, Nelson had to be iced and soon. "And that will be my pleasure," Frankie said aloud as he stripped down to take a cool shower.

CHAPTER TWENTY-SEVEN

Greg spent most of Saturday at the hotel, either on the phone with Rob or Chuck, or riding up and down elevators to the lone fax machine in the so-called business office of the Sheraton. Laura was across the street with Patrick as the poor kid endured CAT scans, ultrasounds, and other torturous procedures that Greg had never even heard of.

Rob was in the office putting the finishing touches on the motion to persuade Judge Potter to dismiss the murder charge still officially pending against Laura. Sandra Mulloy had been informed, so that when the motion made it to the judge on Monday, the D.A. would not feel blindsided. They were so ultrasensitive to P.R. that Greg thought it best to give them time to evaluate their political options. When the judge dismissed Laura's charges, the D.A.'s office would have to publicly expose Frank Santiago as the new prime suspect. How they handled that would be their problem and that of the police to finally arrest the guy. But it did make Greg feel better that little Molly Palmer would be safely sequestered three hundred miles away on Amelia Island.

In between telephone marathons with Rob and Chuck, Greg had repeatedly tried to call Celeste. Alone in the hotel, he missed her terribly and still had not been able to explain his snap decision to go to Philly with Laura. He'd tried her townhouse in Tampa, his beach house, and then, the Peachtree Plaza Hotel in Atlanta just in case, but there was no answer at either residence, and no message waiting for him at the hotel. Although Greg knew that Celeste would not object to their using her place, he was anxious to let her know it was happening.

After meeting Laura for a quick dinner in the CHOP cafeteria, he returned to the hotel and headed to the bar. Nursing a glass of tawny port, he wondered whether Celeste's absence was a sign that he should have gone home instead. Sipping the second port, Greg finally begun to worry, not so much about Celeste's safety, but about their relationship. He didn't deserve her, and his decision to go to Philadelphia with Laura just proved it. Back in his room, he called her condo once again. No answer. Celeste had sacrificed her own professional goals to spend the weekend in Tampa with him and he'd stood her up. No wonder she wasn't answering the phone. These were Greg's thoughts as he'd tried to drift off to sleep long into the early hours of Sunday morning.

Around nine in the morning, Greg's phone rang.

"Carrie calling," she announced as he said 'hello.'

"Morning. What's up, Carrie?"

"Well, I need your opinion on something. It's important."

"Shoot."

"It's the Palmers. Chuck and I set it up to get them to the house on Amelia Island this morning as we discussed. The thing is, they want to take Elizabeth as a companion for Molly seeing they'll be so isolated. Don says it's up to me whether to let her go. What do you think?"

"I see." Greg paused. "Carrie, the truth is I really don't know what I'd do if I were you. She's your daughter, only you can decide. What I can tell you is that we'll make sure Chuck takes every conceivable precaution in terms of security, but in the end I guess it boils down to how you feel. Do you know?"

"I feel that I got Molly into this and that it wouldn't be right if I didn't let Elizabeth go with them. But still, I'm scared."

"I don't blame you. You know, not to change the subject, but I really need to get back to Tampa. If Elizabeth goes with the Palmers, I wonder if you'd be able to replace me here, stay with Laura for a few days. I hate to leave without one of us here."

"Let me see, Greg. There's so much up in the air, I'll talk to Don about it."

"Good. Let's talk later then," he said, hanging up the phone. *Where was Celeste?*

From his resort prison on Sanibel Island, Frank Santiago finalized his plan Sunday morning. In the middle of summer, Sanibel was a sleepy, family-type place known for its perfect seashells. Kids chased each other in and out of the surf, the usual Florida crowd of grandparents nearby. It looked like every generation on the planet collected buckets of those stupid shells from the endless supply the sea dumped onto the wide, white beaches. Watch it happen for one more day and Frank knew he was gonna lose it.

Fact was, Carlos was going to hand Tampa over to that fucking Ritchie if he didn't get back there. Well, he'd worked too hard to let that happen. Besides, Ritchie couldn't hold a candle to him. All because of Kim, he could lose everything. Back and forth, Frank paced the humid living room as Channel Eight News reported the Nelson update like they had a fucking exclusive, making as much as they could of their former anchors, Kim Connor, now dead, and Steve Nelson, soon to be dead — if Frank had his way.

He'd just had a call from Ritchie Noval. Carlos was gettin' more uptight. This stupid island was bad enough, but what if he had to leave the country, like Carlos had said? Columbia? Costa Rica? That unnerved Frank more than the fucking Tampa man-hunt. Cops in Tampa had turned up the heat, crawling all over his haunts in old Ybor City, hell-bent on finding him, asking questions about Kim, about him and Kim.

Frank's bowels loosened. Fucking Nelson. First, the fact that Kim had actually fucked him. And now, the actuality that Kim coulda blabbed that shit he'd told her. Why had he introduced her around? He knew the answer: because it felt so good to have a gorgeous, intelligent, sexy lady on his arm to show off to the fucking world.

"Carlos wants to know what Nelson knows about our operation," Ritchie'd accused.

"Nothing," Frank told him. "Prick don't know nothing. Why's Carlos talkin' to you about this shit? Why don't he call me?"

"Cause I'm callin' yuh. I'm in charge now 'cause you fucked up."

"Nobody fuckin' saw me. How many jobs we do together? I'm a pro, you asshole."

"Yeah, that's why every pig in Tampa lookin' for you, man. Fact is, somebody saw you goin' into that guy's house. My brother-in-law, Remy, got ties into the D.A.'s office. Positive ID, he said, but he don' know who fingered you. Pigs keepin' it real quiet. Gonna drop the charges on the Nelson bitch, that's why they lookin' for you. Carlos probably gonna be wantin' you in Columbia sooner than later."

"Ritchie, you tell Carlos I'll take care of it. Ain't nobody gonna finger me."

"You fuckin' sit tight, let Carlos handle it his way."

"Right," said Frank as he hung up the phone. "While I'm sittin' here on my ass till Carlos decides to ice me."

He paced for a few minutes more, then made a call.

The phone was picked up in a tiny office in downtown Clearwater. Frankie had never been there, but he pictured an empty room except for a desk and phone as per the business card: Mr. Manuel Gonzolas. Financial Consultant. By appointment only. Only address, a P.O. Box. This phone number.

"Yeah, Manny, course I know about the shit goin' down. Reason I called."

Frankie listened as Manny explained, like he had the last time Frankie'd hired him. He operated as an independent. No ties to nobody. No jobs connected to the organization. Respects Carlos Tosca. Respects Santo Trafficante, Jr.

"You guys take care of your own. That's my motto," he repeated.

"Look, Manny, this is private. Me. Not the organization. Like the last job. Carlos wants me takin' care of this myself."

"Sure you cleared this with the boss? I don't need trouble from Carlos."

"Yeah," Frankie lied. "And I got the money."

"Okay, I'm listening. Lay out the job."

Frankie told him what he knew about a witness who could put him at the Nelson place on Oregon. "Use your connections downtown, my man. Just take this fucker out. Nice and clean."

Frankie heard Manny whistle over the phone. "Gonna cost you big time, amigo. Prices are up from the last time. My informants are buried deep in Tampa police headquarters. I'm gonna need a hundred big ones. Half to get started. Plus all expenses."

"Shit, that's way more —"

"Take it or leave it. I gotta lay out ten K just to get my man to open his mouth."

"Okay, just get on it right away," Frankie said. "Shit, I ain't got much time."

"Gotta see the money, touch it, count it," Manny said.

"I'm good for it," Frankie tried to keep the tremor of desperation out of his voice. Deal from a position of strength, he told himself. You've got all the money you scammed. Money motivates Manny. "Be a fool to stiff you, right? But just to show my good faith, I'll throw in an extra ten for you."

"That's one ten, plus expenses — you got a deal."

"Then you'll get right on it," Frankie breathed relief.

"Oh, yeah, but I wanta see that money. Half tomorrow. Half when I tell you I'm done, where I tell you."

Once Frankie hung up the phone, he began to pack a small satchel, checking his Glock before tucking it into his jeans and strapping his money belt into place. He knew that the matching cottage next door was empty and that in its garage was a white Cadillac, several years old with Florida plates. Wearing dark glasses and a baseball cap pulled well over his forehead, he could pass without suspicion across the two-lane bridge connecting the barrier island to Florida's mainland. Tomorrow night, he'd meet up with Manny Gonzolas in Ybor City. Manny had surefire connections inside the pig world. On the street, he was a real pro — one with a head on his shoulders. As for Nelson, Frank'd take him out in person. The prick was in Michigan at his father's according to the news. No risk of recognition up there. Frank had never stepped foot in Michigan.

At seven thirty Monday morning, a pimply young orderly appeared in Patrick's room. Laura had spent the night in a cot beside his bed and was still wearing the green scrubs Tim had found for her to sleep in. Patrick had already been sedated, and the orderly gently lifted him onto the gurney as Laura fussed with his hospital gown, making sure the IV tubing was not disturbed. As they wheeled her son toward the wide swinging doors to the operating suite, Laura stayed beside the gurney and approached the door as though she'd walk right in.

"That's as far as you go, Dr. Nelson," Tim said formally as he stopped the procession and gently motioned for her to wait in the family lounge.

"Tim, I can't just wait out here. I need to be in here with him."

"Honey, there's a whole team in there for him."

"I won't get in the way, I promise. Just to observe —"

"Laura, it's out of the question," Tim said firmly. "You know we can't do that."

"But he's my baby —"

"That's exactly why you can't come in." Tim squeezed her shoulder. "Today, you're a mother, not a surgeon. I'll come out and let you know what's what as soon as I can, but I've got to warn you, it's a long procedure. Could take up to twelve hours. He'll be on the heart/lung machine, we'll have to place a Teflon prosthesis, probably replace the mitral valve. It's complicated, and it'll take time, so try to be calm." He smiled. "You know, like you tell all your patients' families."

Laura winced, tears in her eyes. "Of all people, I know how

dangerous this surgery is." She bent over the small gurney to kiss her sleeping son's head. "Tim, I just feel so totally out of control, like nothing I do matters."

"Ah, so not true. Your son needs you here, just not in the OR."

Laura nodded. "You're right. Tim, Patrick's in your hands. Thank you," she stammered as they pushed the child's gurney toward the bright lights of the operating room. As she turned away and began to walk toward the lounge where she hoped and expected she would soon be joined by her parents and the twins, Greg bounded toward her, a wide grin on his face.

"Laura, I've got good news! The charges against you in Tampa have been officially dropped."

"What does that really mean?" Laura asked quietly.

"It means you're free to come and go as you please," he said, smiling. "And that there's a manhunt on for Frank Santiago."

"But they haven't found him?"

"No, not yet."

Laura frowned. "That's too bad. I mean, I guess I'm having a hard time believing what you're telling me. That I'm actually free."

"Little Molly Palmer's story did it. For a young child, she is very sure of herself. I.D.ed Santiago going in before you got there. Of course, she didn't hear the shot, but the timing lines up with the call from the lady upstairs."

"Thank you, Molly," Laura breathed.

"She's one strong and credible young lady."

"So I'm free," Laura said as Greg gave her shoulder a squeeze. "Greg, does that mean you'll be leaving to go back to Tampa?"

He paused. "Yes, but I'll try to get Carrie to come up and stay with you. Okay?"

"But isn't she working on getting the boys back to me?"

"Carrie's on it. But I don't think you need to worry, especially now that the charges have been dropped.

"Oh, I can't tell you how much I hope you're right. I feel like what's happening is all my fault. That what's happening to Patrick should be happening to me because of what — I did."

CHAPTER TWENTY-EIGHT

Laura stared at the hands of the large wall clock in the family waiting room. Never had time crept so slowly. Nearly seven hours in the operating room and still no word. Why couldn't they send somebody out with a progress report? They must be having problems. Maybe they couldn't get at the tumor? Maybe the tumor had destroyed the delicate electrical circuitry that keeps the heart beating? Maybe in trying to get it out they damaged the aorta? The pulmonary arteries? The lung? Was it malignant and spread out of control? If only they'd let her in there, she wouldn't have to endure this agony of not knowing. She'd promised not to interfere, not to panic. Now all she could do was pray that Tim would send someone out.

And where were her parents and the twins? Certainly enough time had passed for them to have taken a second flight, in case they'd missed their first, out of Tampa. No sooner had she thought this, when a wonderful, familiar voice rang out from the corridor.

"Mom! Mom!"

Nicole, dressed in a navy and white striped sundress, burst into the room and ran straight for her. Natalie, dressed identically, followed.

"Mom, it's us!" Nicole cried as Laura jumped up and seized them both, her parents right behind them.

"Nicole! Natalie!" Tears streamed down Laura's cheeks as she held them tightly.

"Hi, honey," her father eventually said. "Patrick?"

"Oh, Dad, Mom!" Laura finally let go of Nicole and embraced her parents. "He's still in surgery. Oh, how can I ever thank you for bringing the girls to me?"

"We can't tell you how happy we were to do it," said Peg, her arm around her daughter's shoulder as they sat down, each twin seemingly attached to one of her daughter's knees.

Laura beamed, but only momentarily. "It so good to see you — I haven't heard anything."

A knock on the door distracted them. Tim Robinson walked in wearing a knee length white coat over blood-spattered green surgical scrubs. "I'm interrupting —"

"Tim!" Laura jumped up, leaving the girls with her parents, and rushed over to him. "Patrick?"

"We're not finished yet, but so far, all is okay," he said. "We're going to be able to resect the whole tumor, it's just taking longer than we expected. Dr. Kamen is personally doing the surgery. I'll fill you in on all the details later. But right now, are you ready for some really good news?" He barely paused for a reply. "I just got back from pathology, checked it out myself. The tumor is a benign cardiac fibroma. Totally benign. Okay?"

As the relief spread across Laura's face, he smiled. "Now I've got to go scrub back in. It'll be another few hours before we close. See you then. Here's to the good report, huh?"

"Oh, Tim. Thank you."

Laura's mind raced through her checklist. The girls, now safely with her. Tentative, but good, news on Patrick. No malignancy, but would they be able to repair the physical defects caused by the tumor? Would he have a fatal arrhythmia, or end-stage heart failure? Mike and Kevin were physically well, but totally alienated from her because of Steve. Greg would help protect her against him. For a moment, Laura saw nothing. There was nothing — at the moment — she could do to stop Steve.

Marcy Whitman returned to an empty house. In all the years she'd worked for the Nelsons, living in the apartment over their garage, she'd never been totally alone. Steve and Laura rarely vacationed, and when they did, she'd invite her sister over from St. Petersburg. After the girls left that morning with their grandparents, she'd tidied up the house and treated herself to a movie. Last year's academy award winner, *Annie Hall*, starring Diane Keaton. She didn't care for it, but figured she was just too set in her ways. When she returned home, she fixed linguini and clams and made a small salad. After cleaning up, she decided to watch *Charlie's Angels* on the big screen TV in the family room of the main house. All five kids loved this show, but it depressed Marcy as she glanced around at the kids' toys neatly shelved in the room. *Star Wars* stuff. Matchbox cars. Matching Baby Wet and Cares. Maybe music and a book would be more relaxing.

Marcy got up, switched off the TV mid-episode and headed to the stereo. What to choose? Not Elvis, she heard too much of that when Laura was home. She and all the kids groaned when either Laura or Steve decided to listen to their enviable collection. She smiled at the Eagles's *Hotel California*. Not her cup of tea, but Mike was getting into them and the Bee Gees. She chose Barbara Steisand's *Evergreen*, but as she went to place it on the player, she noticed a shadow lingering outside the nearby window. Low, maybe a big dog? Or was it her imagination? Nothing was there now as she looked more closely. Shivering in the air conditioning, she put on the music, adjusted the temperature, and picked up a fat book that Laura had left on the coffee table. *War and Remembrance*. She hoped that Laura wouldn't be peeved if she'd read it first. Marcy had so loved *The Winds of War*.

Settling on the couch, Marcy twisted and turned, trying to get comfortable with the heavy book. "That's it," she finally announced. "I'm going to my place."

When she went back to the stereo to turn it off, she peered once more out the window. Nothing.

The tome tucked under her arm, she checked the lock on the

front door and went out the back, remembering to lock the door, remembering how she'd always had to remind Steve and the kids to lock doors and turn off lights.

Not wanting to waste electricity, she walked in the dark, looking back once when she thought she heard a rustle. She did not see the figure, all in black, lurking behind the rose trellis off to the side of the back porch.

"Steve, don't do it," Jim Nelson said. "It's never good, running away." Together they'd cleared the dinner dishes Monday night and stacked them in the sink before Steve asked his father to sit down at the kitchen table for a cup of coffee.

"I've got the tickets, Dad. We're leaving tomorrow."

"Son, work it out with Laura. Don't take the boys right now, don't do anything you may regret. Think about it, Nicole and Natalie need a father too. I know I haven't been much of a role model, but you —"

"I have thought about it. I just can't forgive what Laura did."

Jim slumped in his chair. "Now, Steve. What about you? With that woman who was killed?"

"A mistake. I've said it a hundred times. But Laura — after all these years." Steve ached to share his real fears with his father. His fear of Frank Santiago. The wrenching feeling that he had to get as far away as he could. What had possessed him to let things get out of hand with Kim that night? She had warned him that Santiago was dangerous, that he was insanely jealous. Even if the cops ever found Santiago, would he ever be safe? No, these were things he could not share with his father.

Jim Nelson cleared his throat. "Son, remember when your Aunt Hazel stayed here with us, after your mother was admitted to the asylum that first time?"

Steve sighed. "I remember. Aunt Hazel was so different from Mom."

"Yes, she was. You were too young to know, but she and I — well — while your mother was away." He blushed. "I'm ashamed to admit it, but we all make mistakes. It's only sometimes that we can correct them."

Steve smiled a thin smile. "Dad," he said slowly, "I knew. I used to say my prayers that Aunt Hazel would stay with us. She made you smile, even laugh. Then when Mom came back, and Aunt Hazel left, nobody was happy. Did you ever think that maybe you and she could have made it together?"

His father blushed again. "That's what I mean, son. Once you've made a mistake, you have to do everything in your power to correct it. You can never make it go away, but you can try to do the right thing. For me, that meant staying with your mother. I don't regret it, and that's why I'm asking you to give this some time to work things out with Laura."

Steve stiffened. "Uh, there's nothing to work out. The boys'll be better off with me. She can have her illegitimate child and the twins too. Nicole already resents me. And Natalie is too dependent on Nicole to go off with me. They'll be better off with their mother."

Jim Nelson frowned. "Steve, do you think much about your twin brother?"

"What?" Steve sputtered. "Of course not. That was so long ago."

His father's frown deepened. "That's another one of my mistakes — letting you take all that stress, not taking your side. So protective of your mother that we never even talked about Philip. It was like he'd never existed once we had the funeral. Now that you have your own twins, they must remind you of yourself and Philip when you were their age."

Rising from his chair, Steve stared at his father. "Dad, I really don't have time for this right now. I have to pack." Why was his father bringing this up now, twenty years later? No, not now.

"I'm so sorry, Steve. I never meant to abandon you as I did . . . I . . ."

Steve put a firm hand on his father's shoulder. "You didn't — and I'm not either. Are you going to help us pack? We need some stuff from the attic."

"I just don't want you to do anything you'll regret," Jim Nelson said hoarsely. "My only regret is that I abandoned you."

Steve stepped away. "Please, Dad, don't," he said sharply. "Right now I've got to save what's left of my family. I've got a job interview with the TV station in Fairbanks, and you know as well as I do that I need that job. We're going tomorrow."

"Still, Kev and Mike need some stability."

"And that's exactly why we're going, so we can get stable."

"But now that Laura is no longer charged, she can get her job back and —"

"No way. Not after what she did. Before — you know — I asked her to come with us. She refused. Then I find out about what she did. I just want to get far away from here. Away from Laura. Away from everything that happened in Tampa. I'd appreciate it if you'd drive me over to pick up my rental car in the morning. I'll drop it off at the airport in Detroit."

Jim sighed and stood up. "It's up to you, son. But I still think you should sleep on it."

"Look, Dad. Mike and Kev are all I have left. I won't lose them to Laura. Now that she's so-called 'free' again, you can bet her high-priced lawyer will try to take the boys away from me. Besides, I think we'll all start to feel a little better when we get some hunting and fishing in."

"Have you told the boys?" his father asked sadly.

Steve shook his head. "I'll tell them now so they can get packed. I didn't tell anybody before because I didn't want it getting back to Laura."

"Maybe you should wait until tomorrow. No use upsetting them prematurely. Maybe you'll change your mind by morning."

"I'm going up to talk to them now."

Steve found Mike and Kevin sitting on his bed, the airline tickets in Kevin's hands. He tried to cover them up as Steve walked through the door, but he recognized the colorful logo of the Traverse Travel Agency.

"What do you have there, Kev?"

"Uh, nothing," his younger son mumbled.

Steve opened his hand and waited until Kevin handed him the tickets.

"Dad, we heard you talking to Grandpa about taking us away," admitted Mike. "We just wanted to know where."

"Fair enough. We're going to Alaska. First to San Francisco, then on to Fairbanks."

"Alaska!" Mike bolted off the bed, shaking his head. "That's so far away. We don't want to go there."

"Mike, sit down. You're too young to understand. You don't know what's best for you, and I've decided that we're moving to Alaska. I already have a job interview lined up at the TV station there. It'll be great. Just what you guys like: camping, fishing, and hunting when you're ready."

"Only us?" Kevin gulped. "What about everybody else?"

"Nattie and Nicky? And what about Pat, isn't he getting surgery right now?" Mike added. "We can't leave the country —"

"Leave the country? Alaska's part of the United States, guys."

"You have to go through Canada to get there," Mike reasoned.

"Well, like it or not, we're leaving tomorrow so let's get packing. We'll hit the attic where Grandpa keeps his camping and hunting equipment. I still have some of my old stuff in boxes. We'll take all the heavy stuff since it does get cold up there."

Kevin started to cry quietly, but he couldn't suppress his sniffles.

"See what I mean, boys," Steve said sharply, "you guys have to stop being such mama's boys and toughen up."

"But we need to talk to Mom and make sure that Pat's okay," Mike insisted.

Steve frowned. "Boys, we're a team now. We're what's left of this family, and we're starting a new life. Now let's go. Let's get Grandpa and go sort out what goes and what stays."

As the Nelson men climbed the stairs to the attic, Mike excused himself to go to the bathroom.

"Mrs. Whitman?" Mike struggled to keep his voice low after he dialed his Tampa telephone number, which rang in her apartment. "Kevin's in the attic with Dad and Grandpa. They're —"

Carmen Williams missed Kim. Didn't matter that she now had money. Money from Kim's small nest egg and Kim's awesome wardrobe and jewelry collection. Didn't matter that she could now afford places like the bar at the Columbia Restaurant in Ybor City. A classy place where Kim used to take her. A place where Kim used to go with Frankie Santiago.

Carmen approached the bar, aware of the looks. She looked great, and she knew it. Kim had been much tinier that she, but Carmen had found a seamstress that had done magic. The red halter dress — Kim's favorite color — was snug, but sexy. Her luxuriant auburn hair was clipped into place with a ruby — probably not real — studded clip and she felt like quite the lady in red strappy heels.

"What'll you have?" asked the bartender, a hefty man with salt-and-pepper hair clipped military style. He had been there most times she and Kim had come in.

"Perrier with lime," she said after a noticeable hesitation.

"On the wagon or what?" he asked.

"Yeah, I'm trying. Guess I shouldn't be here, but I'm so lonely. I sure miss Kim."

"You two were such good pals." He blinked as he poured the bubbly water into her glass. "I miss seeing her too. She was a perky one. Channel Eight's never been the same since she left." He nodded to the TV monitor over the bar. The news was on. The anchor couple from Memphis.

"Duds," Carmen said.

"But you're lookin' like a million bucks," he said. "You doin' okay?"

New patrons had arrived, so he took off without a response.

Carmen went back to her drink, but was soon distracted by a familiar sounding voice. She turned to look as an older man with longish gray hair and dark glasses nodded to the bartender. The guy

looked out of place in this swanky lounge –cheap baggy pants that
hung to the floor, a faded teal Miami Dolphin tee shirt, worn sneakers. Curious, she watched as he headed up the steps leading to
private rooms and offices, carrying a worn canvas gym bag.

"Who was that?" she asked the bartender when he came back
her way.

"Hell if I know," he said, shrugging his shoulders. "Knew the
code, so I let him up."

He must be used to characters, Carmen thought. Everybody
knew that the Columbia was a hangout for the mob boys. Even
the big boys came here. Guess that's why Frankie kept taking
Kim here, she figured. Then she choked on a sip of Perrier. That
voice — Frankie's raspy voice.

There was a ladies' room upstairs next to the private rooms.
Carmen bolted out of her chair before even thinking.

"Carmen?" the bartender asked.

"Gotta use the can," she said, rushing toward the stairs.

"One's down here," he said, scratching his head, but she was
halfway up.

Carmen knew the cops were all over Tampa looking for Frank.
So why was she following him? Did she want that Detective Lopez
and that jerky Detective Goodnuf all over her again? Shit no. She
stopped abruptly at the top of the stairs just as two men went into a
room. The bummy looking one who sounded like Frank and, to her
horror, a guy with a bushy moustache, coal black hair clipped close
to his head, dressed in slacks and a black polo shirt. A guy she knew
from the old days when she'd turned tricks. A high strung, slight
man, who liked his sex routine missionary. A john who'd used her
twice and that was it until the night she'd been in this very restaurant with Kim. Kim had leaned over and whispered, "That's Manny
Gonzolas. He's a hit man. Frankie told me. Lives in a mansion on
the beach in Clearwater. Hangs out here all the time."

Carmen shook with fear then, and she did so again now. Frank
and a hit man?

Instead of going back to the bar, she ducked into the ladies' room next door. Putting a cold paper towel to her forehead, she strained to hear conversation from the next room, but of course, she couldn't.

"C'mon, Manny, give it up," Frank snarled as he accepted a shot of tequila.

Manny sipped his beer. "You got the cash? Half now, half when it's done. Hundred grand plus."

"I got it, but you ain't seein' it till I get the plan. C'mon already, I gotta get outta here."

"Don't fuck with me, Frankie. I got a reputation, don't take no gang stuff. Don't want no complications with Miami."

"Won't be any. It's just gotta happen fast. So what did you find out?"

"My man's expensive, but he's good, long as I take care of him."

Frank reached down and lifted a worn athletic bag onto his lap. He carefully removed the dirty socks and underwear he'd brought with him from the Sanibel hideaway, revealing neatly packed rolls of hundred dollar bills beneath a sheet of plastic.

"Now you're talkin'. Ten grand for my informant. It ain't cheap to get inside like this. Maybe another five for expenses. One ten for the job itself. That's one twenty-five, my man."

"Yeah, I'm good for it. Now fuck it, Manny, what'd you find out?"

Manny dug out a piece of paper from his pants pocket. "It was the kid next door who fingered you at the Nelson place. Palmer. Turns out she's deaf and dumb, goes to a special school for the deaf."

Frank scowled. "A kid? *Mierda*. Not a fucking kid? How the fuck —"

"Nelson's lawyer called the cops 'bout what the kid saw. A woman lawyer. Turns out she's got a deaf kid too. Name's Carrie Diamond."

"Okay, so Diamond's a lawyer," Frank repeated.

"Firm hired a P.I. Big guy with a big rep, he got results. D.A. had nothin' on you till this Palmer kid shows up. Cops put a uniform at the house for protection once the kid pegged you, but over the weekend they got a call to hold off. So I figure maybe they split."

"Whadda mean? You gotta find this kid."

"Did a little walk around the neighborhood early this morning, but nobody's home at the Palmer's. Neighbor thinks they're on vacation, but doesn't know for sure. Not like them to just leave without tellin' the whole neighborhood. Apparently the missus is big on blabbin'. Knows everyone's business, tells everyone hers."

Frank drummed his fingers on the table. "Yeah, yeah. What else?"

"Followed up with the school the kid goes to, see what I can find out. Is the kid absent is the bottom line." He pointed to himself. "Make like I'm a prospective parent, right? I ask to see the school roster, there's the 'absent' or 'present' columns right there. I see the kid's gone. Also, the Diamond kid is 'absent.' What a coincidence, eh? Security cameras all over the place so I start asking questions about that. Managed to nab last week's tape by the time I left."

Frank grunted. "And?"

"Spent the rest of the day on fast forward with it, and bingo, caught the day Diamond showed up and then a half-hour later there's one kid having a conversation with another kid — fitting the description of the Palmer kid. Got a sign expert. Bingo again. She's the one fingered you, amigo."

Frank slammed his drink down on the table. "A fucking kid. No way. I can't believe it."

Manny watched him. "Yeah, so?"

"A kid. Takin' a kid out —"

"Job's a job. You want it done or not? The kid ID'd you, that's the word. If you want my advice —"

Frank scowled. "Hey, gimme a minute to think, a kid. Ice a kid?"

"Whatever you decide," Manny took a long swig of beer, "half that money's mine. Already did a ton of leg work."

"Shit, what am I gonna do?" Frank squirmed. "So the kid disappeared?"

Manny lit a fat Cuban cigar. "Vamoose. But I have my ways. You know how the females are. That Diamond bitch'll lead us to those kids no doubt. So, is it a go?"

"Fuck it, Manny. You took the job, you fucking do it." Frank scratched the stubble on his chin. "No way around it."

Manny nodded. "Just so ya know, my inside didn't turn up anything linking you to that Mexican hit."

Frank checked his watch. "Tell me something I don't know. So what the fuck did you find out about Nelson?"

Manny smiled. "Put a bug in his place on Davis Island last night. Easy stuff. And it already paid off."

"What's that do for me?"

"Your guy's leavin' for Fairbanks, Alaska, tomorrow. Takin' off in the middle of all this shit with two of his kids. So you better get on him pronto. Unless you wanta freeze your ass takin' him down in the tundra."

Frank stared at his empty shot glass. "Now why the fuck would he do that?"

"You tell me, I'm only the hired help. Your lady was killed at his place, right? He's gotta figure sooner or later you're on his tail so he tries to disappear in Alaska, I dunno. Do know the info's on target, checked out the airlines. Northwest flight out of Detroit with a connection in San Francisco."

"Detroit," Frank groaned. "Easier take-out than fucking Traverse City."

"Figured. I already booked you. Set up a car at the airport through a guy I know. There's a piece in it."

"*Bueno*. Fucking Nelson." Frank stood up.

"Forgettin' something, Frankie?" Manny pointed to the bag of cash.

Frank shoved it at Manny as he fumbled in his pants pocket for a key that he put in Manny's other hand. "Once I hear the job's done, the rest'll be where we agreed."

Manny opened the door. The two men lingered as Manny slapped him on the back. "No worries, it's in the bag. Nail Nelson in Detroit. And amigo, when I'm done with the job you won't be seein' me around for a while."

"Same."

As the men said good-bye, neither noticed the young woman in a short red halter dress lurking just inside the open door to the ladies' room.

CHAPTER TWENTY-NINE

As the sun began to set beyond the hospital windows, Laura sat between her parents, the twins playing checkers in the corner. While the minutes crept by, she vowed to remember the agony of those waiting when she operated again — if she ever did. At the moment, presiding over a surgical procedure seemed about the furthest thing from reality.

Twelve hours had passed since Patrick was wheeled into the operating room; the only feedback Tim's visit five long hours ago. His report had been a huge relief, but still so many things could go wrong. If it hadn't been for her parents' and the twins' arrival, Laura didn't think she'd get through this ordeal.

For a moment, she shut her eyes. When she opened them, Tim was striding into the room.

"Tim!" Laura rushed toward him.

The surgeon smiled a tired smile as he took Laura's hands in his. "He's going to be okay. They've taken him to the ICU. Still on a ventilator, but —"

"Oh thank God! Can I see him?"

"Right now the surgical team's meeting in the conference room, and we'd like you to come in. Being a surgeon, we thought you'd like all the details and Dr. Kamen himself is handling the debrief."

"Of course. Thank you."

Four men in surgical greens stood up as Laura entered the room with Tim. Among them was Dr. George Kamen, the venerable head of pediatric surgery at CHOP. Tumors in the heart were very rare in kids and of all pediatric surgeons in the world, he had the most experience excising them.

"Dr. Nelson," his deep, booming voice greeted her, "we had ourselves quite a case here, but your little guy's quite the fighter."

A big man of sixty with bushy eyebrows and curly gray hair, he shook her hand. "It's an honor to meet you, my dear. I didn't expect you to be so young, or so beautiful."

A touch of color permeated Laura's pallor as she held out her hand.

"You've made quite a name for yourself in Florida," he went on, "but I am so sorry that we meet under these circumstances. I'd just returned from a pediatric surgery conference in Moscow, when I learned about your son. Because it's such a rare condition I did the procedure personally."

"I'm so grateful, Dr. Kamen. Such an overwhelming tumor. I should have been more vigilant," Laura replied as the elder doctor took his place at the head of the cluttered conference table and waited for her to take a seat. "I'll never be able to thank you all enough," she said to everyone.

"Young lady, that's what surgery is all about, you know that. Now let's review your little boy's status. As you know," Dr. Kamen continued, "our objective was to resect the whole tumor since the child presented with such severe symptoms. If we couldn't get it all, we'd go for palliation, or worst case, have to wait for a heart transplant..."

"A heart transplant. So drastic." Laura sucked in her breath.

"We were able to get the tumor out, but it was not well circumscribed and it extended into both ventricles, practically destroying the mitral valve, so we put in a prosthesis —"

Laura stifled a moan. Tim had predicted this, but she'd hoped it could be repaired. Recalling the favorable statistics on valve replacements in children, however, she sighed with relief.

"We had to go to cardiopulmonary bypass. The OR was equipped with intraoperative radiation and —"

"But Tim said the lesion was benign," Laura interrupted. Then she covered her mouth with her hand.

"Yes, my dear, it was a typical fibroma. Abundant fibroblasts arranged haphazardly in interlacing bundles," he patiently explained, "but we were prepared in case there were malignant cells."

Laura nodded, mentally reviewing the pediatric texts she'd scoured and the stack of case reports from the medical library. Yes, this was good news. The cytology Dr. Kamen was describing meant that the tumor was benign, which meant it would not come back, and it would not metastasize to other organs.

"Of course. I'm so thankful." Laura stammered. "Excuse me for interrupting, I'm just beside myself with worry."

"It's understandable, Dr. Nelson," the kindly surgeon went on. "So after the valve replacement we reconstituted the anterior wall of the left ventricle with autologous pericardium and used as much pericardium patching as we could along with direct suture. But for the most part, we relied on Teflon strips." The doctor glanced at Laura. "You've probably used these extensively, Teflon buttressed sutures for closure. And that, my dear, is why it took so long and why I'm so exhausted and will now leave your son in the capable hands of Dr. Robinson here."

"Thank you, Dr. Kamen. May I just ask, what complications do you expect postoperatively?"

Dr. Kamen sighed. "In my experience, ventricular arrhythmia is our main worry. Right now we can only monitor him. He's on high doses of beta-blockers. In a couple of months we'll do programmed electrical stimulation and see if we can take him off. Antibiotic prophylaxis, of course, is routine for a prosthetic heart valve, but the good news is that the myocardium is basically healthy and we expect no residual heart failure."

Newly relieved, Laura was about to thank the surgeon yet again when a knock on the door interrupted her.

"Sorry, I have an urgent call for Dr. Nelson," a pert, young assistant explained.

Laura rose from her chair to follow the young woman. "Excuse me, please."

"Take it in here," the assistant said as she led Laura back to the waiting area where Peg stood gripping the phone. She handed it to her daughter with a worried expression on her face.

"Hello," Laura whispered.

"Laura, thank the good lord I got you," blurted Marcy Whitman in an anxious, high-pitched tone.

"Marcy?"

"It's me. Laura, I'm so sorry I have some bad news —"

"It's Mike and Kevin," Laura cut in. It was more statement than question.

"Yes, Mike and Kevin. Steve has plans to leave with them for Alaska tomorrow. The boys saw the plane tickets."

"To Alaska?" Laura's knees buckled and she grabbed the desk for support.

"Mike called a little while ago. I warned him not to let Steve know he told me. The boys are really confused — scared."

"Marcy, did you say *tomorrow*?" Laura felt her world swirling. She was losing Mike and Kevin. She started to sway and Peg reached to steady her.

"That's what Mike said. Can you get your lawyers to stop him? Alaska's so far away it's easy to get lost. I remember my cousin's kid went there when he got in some kind of trouble and nobody ever heard from him again."

"My lawyer is here in Philly with me," Laura spoke as calmly as she could. "I'll call him right away. I can't let Steve take them. Oh, Marcy, thanks for being there and for letting me know."

"We're all praying for you, Laura. I'm here, if there's anything I can do."

Laura hung up the phone and whirled around. "Where's Dad?" she asked her mother, panic flashing in her green eyes.

"He just took the girls down to the vending machines," Peg explained. "Tell me what's happening."

"I've got to see Greg. Steve's taking Mike and Kevin to Alaska!"

Peg gasped. "What? Can he do that?"

"Tomorrow, Mom. Greg's working at the hotel. Can you call him and tell him to come right over? I need to check on Patrick now, but I'll be back by the time Greg gets here."

Laura stood by Patrick's bedside in the surgical intensive care unit. It was strangely quiet except for the beeping of monitors, the hum of machines, and the occasional doctor's beeper. As she glanced around, she saw how a roomful of children could be so quiet. Most were on ventilators, deeply sedated, others too sick or weak to even babble or cry. So eerie and profoundly sad. She was surprised to see so many diverse faces — Arab, Indian, Asian, black, and white faces, all with one thing in common: a desperately ill child struggling to emerge from a dangerous yet life-saving surgical procedure. Laura recalled that most of those Siamese twin separations had been done at CHOP, but never in her worst dreams had she ever thought she'd be here, totally helpless, in street clothes no less, by the side of her own critically ill child. Even with that heart murmur, Patrick had always been so healthy, so carefree. Sure, everybody said they'd spoiled him. Steve made no pretense that Patrick was his favorite and for reasons buried deeply in her very being, Laura acknowledged that Patrick held a special place in her own heart. Yet despite this undisguised favoritism, he was just a sweet little boy.

And here he lay, so pale and still. Though his chest was covered loosely with gauze, Laura knew what lay beneath. They'd split his chest from just below the neck to the umbilicus to reach the massive tumor in his heart — and she'd never even suspected a medical problem. Had she been so wrapped up in her own surgical conquests that she'd missed this horrible thing growing in her own little boy? She should have overruled the pediatric cardiologist and had him checked more frequently.

Amid a maze of tubes, all of which Laura recognized so well,

Patrick did not move. The clear plastic endotracheal tube, which extended into the main bronchial tube leading to the lungs, was taped to his face and secured with a strap around his neck, the other end connected to the rasping ventilator. She walked around to look at the settings. Still set on mandatory, which meant that the machine was driving each breath. So far no signs of spontaneous breathing, but it was too early to expect this. Next she checked the gastric tube draining his stomach and found a yellow tinted liquid with flecks of mucus. There was a Foley catheter draining his bladder and the urine in the plastic collection bag looked normal, a clear pale yellow. The wires attached to his flesh were connected to the EKG monitor at the left-hand side of his bed, displaying every heartbeat. As she expected, there was a catheter in the large subclavian vein to infuse blood, antibiotics, and electrolytes and to monitor pulmonary artery pressure and heart function. The insertion was just below the right clavicle and protected by a large, bulky dressing.

Though she knew that her child would still be heavily sedated, she wasn't prepared for the awful stillness — except for the wheezing of the ventilator and the heart monitor's beeping. Surrounded by the frenetic activity so characteristic of ICUs everywhere, Laura stood as if paralyzed.

As she closed her eyes, Tim Robinson's words floated through her mind again: "Laura, I know what you're thinking, but these tumors are silent. Silent until they cause an arrhythmia or heart failure. There's no way that you or anyone would have a clue that he had a serious problem until very late. This has absolutely nothing to do with the patent foramen. Nothing."

"If only I'd taken him in to be checked or gotten an X-ray or an EKG —" she remembered saying.

"You know very well that these things aren't routine in healthy kids. They would have thought you were paranoid."

She heard Tim's real voice then and felt a hand on her shoulder. She opened her eyes.

"Laura, that lawyer is outside the ICU looking for you. Some kind of emergency? I couldn't let him in."

"Greg's here? Tim, I have to see him."

"What's wrong?" He squeezed her shoulder. "That phone call?"

She nodded. "I'll tell you about it later. Can you stay with Patrick, just in case he wakes up? I'll be back as soon as I can."

"Sure. Okay." Tim slid onto the lone chair with a tired groan.

After filling Greg in on Steve's plan to take the boys to Alaska, Laura returned to her son's bedside. Soon after, she slept fitfully in the surgical on-call room across from the ICU. There were four narrow cot-like beds and one unisex bathroom for the house staff that wandered in and out all night, thanks to their beepers. All shared the same shower, and the shelves were kept stocked with clean surgical scrubs. Tim Robinson slept there often and, without official permission, offered the off-limits room to Laura after finding her dozing on her feet by Patrick's bed earlier when he himself awakened in the chair beside the boy's bed. The child was still too heavily sedated to recognize her, but between lapses of fretful sleep, she rose throughout the night and walked across the hall, trying to stay out of the way of the doctors and nurses ministering to the desperately ill children in the beds all around her.

At three in the morning she'd returned to the narrow bed across the hall and drifted wearily back to sleep. Almost simultaneously, three individual beepers sounded, waking the occupants of the other three beds who immediately jumped up and bolted across the hall. A code — cardiac arrest. Patrick! Oh God, no, she prayed. He would be most vulnerable to fatal arrhythmias as he emerged from the heavy sedation, which was why she insisted on being nearby to calm him if he panicked. She jumped off the bed, fumbled for her glasses, and followed the others into the hall, running directly into one of the doctors rushing into the ICU. It was Tim.

"Tim!"

"Not now, Laura."

Laura bolted toward Patrick's bed. Curtains were drawn around his cubicle and she felt her heart lurch as she jumped to the ghastly conclusion that Patrick had died, that they'd already pronounced him while she slept.

She felt a strong arm around her shoulders. "Get a grip, Laura," Tim said sternly. "Patrick's okay. They're just adjusting the ventilator settings, trying to wean him off."

Laura gasped with relief and finally saw the commotion in the opposite corner, crowded with the on-call doctors and ICU nurses. A young girl had coded. The one with Eisenmenger's syndrome, caused by a congenital defect in the heart that produces pulmonary hypertension. If not surgically corrected in time, damage was irreversible. The four-year-old daughter of a Saudi prince had already been cyanotic when she reached CHOP, and Laura and Tim had discussed her pessimistic prognosis despite the heroics of an experimental surgical technique. Laura's professional instincts told her that they'd lose this child, and she was almost ashamed as she thanked God that it was not her son.

Peeking behind the curtains, Laura confirmed that Patrick was indeed stable — as stable as a child could be a few hours after a huge tumor had been carved out of his heart. She stood there watching the respiratory specialist tweak the dials to ensure the precise combination of pressure and gases to support Patrick until he could breathe on his own.

Would God continue to punish Patrick? It was she who should be punished, she prayed. It was she, not her innocent son, who had sinned.

As he strode across his hotel room Monday night to answer the ringing phone, Greg dropped the printed confirmations for the flight back to Tampa onto the bed.

"Hello?"

"Greg, it's Carrie."

"Oh, hi."

"You sound disappointed."

"I . . . I thought you might be Celeste."

"What? Don't tell me you two still haven't made up?"

Greg hesitated. "Carrie, I need to get back to Tampa. I did stand her up Friday night."

"Anything I can do?"

"You know, yesterday I mentioned you coming up here. Have you made a decision yet about the Palmer situation? About Elizabeth going with them, I mean."

Carrie cleared her throat. "She left with them yesterday and I'm a nervous wreck. I just can't see leaving town right now."

"I understand," Greg reassured. "Carrie what you're doing is already over and above. Now that Laura's son made it through surgery, I've decided to head back to Tampa tomorrow."

"So surgery went okay?"

"No cancer, but he's still in the ICU."

"That's great news. And Laura's legal troubles should be clearing up now that the charges against her have been dropped. I was so relieved that Judge Potter came through. The draft press release you worked out with the D.A. today worked like a charm," she added.

"I spent almost my whole day on the phone back and forth with Jake Cooperman himself. Politics. We finally agreed that quote, the defense working with the prosecutor were able to determine Laura's innocence, etcetera, etcetera."

"And the fact that he's going public with Frank Santiago as the new suspect should be all over town by tomorrow. I'm glad we got Molly out of here, but I'm not sure I should have let Elizabeth go."

"Listen, you hang in there. When I get back we'll sit down and figure out how long the girls should stay put on the island."

Carrie exhaled. "Greg, you read my mind."

Moments later, the phone rang again. Greg's heart filled with the thought that it might be Celeste, but it was Peg Whelan. After learning the bad news from Traverse City, he rushed over to find Laura at the hospital and then back to the hotel to immediately set up a conference call with Carrie, Chuck, and Rob to develop a strategy for this new Nelson bombshell. They would retain a Detroit law firm to work with the Michigan courts to get a restraining order in the morning, and Greg would fly directly to Detroit to expedite. In the meantime, Rob would work the custody angles out of Florida, and Chuck would fly to Traverse City to track the boys' whereabouts, ready to take them to Laura if and when they got a court order. Because Rob would be in the Tampa courts all day tomorrow, Greg designated Carrie as the continuity person at the office to coordinate any loose ends and facilitate communications between the courts in Florida and Michigan, and Laura in Philadelphia. As he worked out the schedule in his mind, Greg realized he had forgotten to tell Laura about the subpoena. Sam Sanders, that sleazy attorney for the Ruiz family, was going forward with the case against the hospital and the ER doctor, and he planned to serve Laura with a subpoena as a hostile witness.

It was after midnight by the time Greg hung up the phone for the last time that night. Though he tried several more times, he never reached Celeste.

CHAPTER THIRTY

Tuesday morning at six, Greg's phone rang. He grabbed the receiver groggily. "Celeste?"

"Sorry to wake you so early," Chuck's voice boomed. "I'm at Tampa airport. Got a flight to Chicago, and a charter to Traverse City. Also got the Nelson flight information. Northwest Airlines. Leaves Detroit at eight tonight for San Francisco. Then they change planes to Fairbanks on Air Alaska. I debated as to whether to fly straight to Detroit, but I'd rather follow them all the way from Traverse City. I want them in my sights. I figure if I don't catch them there, I'll take the charter on to Detroit, be there in plenty of time before that flight takes off."

Greg stifled a yawn. "Sounds good, Chuck. I got a flight out of Philly to Detroit at ten."

"And Laura? She coming with you?"

"I don't know," Greg said with a sigh. "I booked it, but as of last night she didn't think she could leave her son at the hospital."

"Guess I can understand that. But it'd really help our end if she were there herself to convince the kids to head back with us. Avoid an abduction scene."

"I know, Chuck. I'll try to convince her to do just that."

"Got it. So if I can't reach you and need an immediate call, who's our point person?"

"Carrie's in the office all day. Timing is tight. All this has to happen in only one day."

"Realistically, boss, it doesn't look good. Hassles over jurisdiction with a twelve-hour window? What if it doesn't work? Want me to grab the boys and worry about the consequences later?"

Greg paused. "That's a 'maybe,' Chuck. I told Laura we'd move heaven and earth to stop Steve from leaving Michigan with her sons, but I'd like to do it legally."

After Greg hung up, he went for a long run to clear his head. Once showered and dressed, he called his Tampa office. His first question was whether Celeste had tried to reach him.

"No, Mr. Klingman," Betty Harmon answered, "no calls since last week." When he then asked to speak with Carrie, she said, "Ms. Diamond isn't back yet. She did come in early, before I even got in at seven thirty. But then she left after she got that call."

"Call? Did she say where she was going? We've got a lot going on today." He filled her in on the Nelson situation.

"I see. No, Carrie didn't say where she was going. She got a call about five after eight from no one I recognized. A Spanish accent, I think. He didn't give a name, but he said he was an old client. I'm sorry, I should have insisted on a name before I put the call through."

"Just try her at her house," Greg directed. "I'll hold."

"Come on, Carrie, I need you at 100 percent today," he mumbled as he waited for Betty to get back on the line.

"There's no answer at her house," Betty reported. "I also tried her husband's office, but he's not there either and hasn't called in. Not yet anyway. He has appointments, so he's expected."

"Shit. Well, get in touch with somebody in Chuck Dimer's office and have them check out Carrie and Don's home. Nothing heroic or drastic, Betty. Just make sure everything's okay there."

"Will do, Mr. Klingman. And well, it's probably nothing, but —"

"Go on, Betty," he urged. "I've got a lot to do before I leave for the airport."

"Well, it's just that Mrs. Diamond left in such a hurry after that call. She seemed upset."

"Did she say anything about Elizabeth?"

"No, but she literally ran out after she hung up the phone."

"How long was she on the phone?"

"Just a few minutes, I'd say. You know, this is just not like her."

Greg checked his watch. It was eight twenty when he left his luggage with the bellman at the Sheraton and headed over to CHOP. He had to talk to Laura before leaving for Detroit. It was important that she understood not only what they'd be doing in the Michigan and Florida courts, but particularly what Chuck would be doing in Detroit, if Laura did not accompany Greg to Detroit. If the boys came voluntarily with Chuck that was one thing, but the question was whether or not Laura wanted Chuck to take them forcibly if they protested and wanted to stay with their dad. They didn't know Chuck from Adam, and at age fourteen and eleven, they were likely to resist physical force.

As he approached the surgical ICU, Greg encountered a cluster of white coats exiting through the swinging doors, young doctors in discussion as they headed toward the elevator across the hall. One of them held back and called to Greg, "Sorry, you can't go in there."

Greg ignored the comment and kept going until he felt a tap on his shoulder. He turned to face Tim Robinson.

"Ah Tim, I'm glad it's you. I need to see Laura. It's important."

"Sorry, the ICU is for immediate family only," Tim replied.

The two men faced each other, the younger draped in a freshly starched white coat with a stereoscope dangling from his neck; the other, seven years older, clad in a charcoal gray pinstripe suit embellished with an expensive silk tie in rich reds and golds.

Glancing at his watch, Greg was the first to breech the silence. "I really do need to see Laura now."

"I understand. But meantime, you'll have to wait in the visitors' lounge."

"But I've got to catch a plane."

Greg watched Tim start to walk away, intending to step

through the ICU doors as soon as the meddlesome doctors were far enough down the hall.

Then Tim turned back. "Okay," he said with a shrug. "I'll go back in and ask Laura to come out."

"If you insist. It seems like such a waste of time."

Tim shrugged. "Rules are rules. It's not like I made 'em."

The last passenger to board, Greg had to take the one remaining seat toward the rear of the plane in the center. He was still fuming about Tim forcing him to wait for Laura. But Greg remained dutifully in the visitors' lounge until Laura appeared about ten minutes later. It was no easy task, but he'd finally convinced her to fly to Detroit. After some effort, he then managed to book her on a three o'clock flight out of Philly with a return flight at nine fifteen with the promise that she'd be back at her son's side by day's end.

Amid all those logistics, there'd been no time to try Celeste at her job site in Atlanta again. There'd been no answer at her townhouse when he tried her just before he checked out of the Sheraton either. Claiming to be Mr. Marin, he'd tried the Peachtree Plaza in Atlanta once more, and he learned that Ms. Marin had requested that they hold her suite over the weekend for an anticipated return on Monday, which had not occurred. They'd requested notice should she need to postpone her arrival, because they needed the room, but received none and as a result they'd packed and stored her things. This was so unlike the Celeste he knew, so meticulous about planning, about showing up on schedule, and he was determined to track her down today.

As Greg made his way down the aisle, he paid no attention to the mustached, overweight man in the watch-plaid shirt and thick black sunglasses, sitting comfortably by the window in first class, sipping a vodka and tonic. If he'd looked closely enough, he might have noticed that the man was wearing flesh-colored surgical gloves as the flight attendant started her spiel: "Welcome to the new passengers boarding in Philadelphia. We're continuing our flight to Detroit for those passengers who boarded in Tampa —"

*   *   *

The plane landed in Detroit at noon, right on schedule. Carrying a phony ID, Frank Santiago was the first to disembark and he headed directly for the nearest men's room carrying a tan canvas overnight bag. He'd checked no luggage, and once behind the bathroom stall door, he removed the plaid shirt and the bulky padding stuffed beneath his vest to create a pot belly. Underneath this extraneous bulk, he wore a light blue pullover shirt that fit neatly over pressed khakis. Next, he yanked off the moustache, replacing it with a trim beard that covered most of his lower face. He changed from the heavy black to wire-rimmed sunglasses. Ten minutes later, he emerged, a trim, neat Hispanic traveler heading out of the men's room with his hand luggage to the parking deck across from the terminal.

There, as he knew it would be thanks to Manny's contact, was a black Ford Fairlane with Michigan plates. Glancing around to make sure he hadn't been followed, he approached the car and deftly slid his hand beneath the driver's side rear bumper. The keys were there. He opened the car door and using the smaller key un-locked the glove compartment. With a satisfied grunt he removed the weapon, a forty-caliber semiautomatic equipped with a silencer, and slid it into his overnight bag. So far everything was working according to plan, but the tricky part lay ahead. He had to isolate Nelson between the time he arrived at the terminal and the time the flight took off for San Francisco. He'd count on the confusion he himself would cause to allow enough time for a clean escape. Then he'd drive to Chicago, lose himself in the crowd, and board a flight to Orlando. From there he'd have an easy drive back to Tampa.

Manny should have taken out the kid by now, which meant Frank would be free and clear. Mother of God, why did it have to be a fucking kid? Without the kid and Nelson, there was no way they could pin Kim's murder on him, and eventually, Carlos would ease up. Frank still could not believe Kim was dead. And what the fuck had she seen in that Nelson prick with all those brats of his anyway? She had told him that she did not want kids. Had she lied about that too? Lousy timing. He had showed too late at the station that night, he coulda tailed 'em to Nelson's and handled them both at the prick's place. But fuck it, he was here now, ready to take Nelson down.

"Count your minutes, pretty TV boy," he mumbled. Soon he'd go back inside the terminal to watch the departure monitors. Last time he checked, the Northwest flight from Detroit to San Francisco was still listed as on time.

The head nurse of CHOP's ICU ignored the rules and allowed Laura to remain at her son's bedside as the critical care team buzzed about checking his vital signs, adjusting his IVs, monitoring his EKG, checking his urine flow, and examining the wound beneath the bulky gauze bandage that covered staples running nearly the full length of his torso. Other than the huge dressing over the incision, Patrick lay naked and still. The many times Laura had tended to such children, she'd never even come close to realizing the helpless agony of their mothers. Dr. Kamen told her that they planned to keep Patrick sedated long enough to stabilize the cardiac rhythm now displayed on the green fluorescent screen at the head of the small bed. Kamen had told Laura that the priority in this crucial postop period was to minimize the risk of fatal arrhythmias, and she listened intently for every blip on the monitor, praying for the normal sinus rhythm to continue.

As the team moved on, Laura's mind drifted to Wendy Ruiz, the child she had lost only six and a half weeks ago. It seemed like a lifetime. At least the Ruiz mother had died and didn't have to suffer through the death of her child. Laura could think of no worse horror for a parent. It must be unendurable, she thought, looking down at her son who lived because of the skill of his surgeons. But what about Wendy's father? He must be so devastated and — she had let him down, hadn't she? Wasn't there something about a lawsuit? Her mind was fuzzy and she pushed these thoughts away. If she'd lost Patrick, she didn't know what she'd do.

*   *   *

"Okay, Greg, I made it to Traverse City about noon," Chuck reported after Greg picked up the phone in Detroit. "It's called Cherry Airport, for God's sake. Anyway, Nelson had already left for Detroit when I showed up at his father's place. His father? Not a happy man. Wouldn't give me any information, but a neighbor said his son left in a wagon crammed with duffel bags, one of those conversion numbers. Had a Budget logo. I'll have someone check it out. Left about an hour ago. Right now, let's see, it's almost one. I held the charter from Chicago in case I missed Nelson here, so I'm heading back to Cherry now. Should arrive in Detroit about two thirty. You name the place."

"Law offices of Youngman, Polk, and Allen. They're in Wayne. It's close to the airport so you'll get here about three. By then we'll have a better idea if the legal system is going to help us out."

"Got it. Too bad I couldn't get here an hour earlier. I'd rather grab the kids in a less public place than an airport, but at least we know where he's heading, flight number and all. So, is Laura with you?"

"I convinced her to take a three o'clock. It'll be tight, but we'll make it work."

"Got it. So what's going on with Carrie? Still AWOL?"

"I was about to ask you the same thing."

"Betty at your place filled in Tracy at mine, so I got a guy checking on her pronto. Haven't heard back, but that's my next call right after we get off the line," said Chuck. "As for the condo on Amelia, I've got a contract guy on surveillance — a bodyguard, really. That security slash concierge service they've got there won't let anybody unauthorized up."

"Tell me about it. I forgot my keys once —"

"I think one guy on the inside is enough," Chuck went on. "Talked to the Palmers a few minutes ago. Everything's fine down there except the girls can't understand why they can't go down to the beach."

"Carrie's being missing still bothers me," Greg mused.

"Well, she can't be there, right? She doesn't know the location. Not from our conversation anyway —"

"And not from mine either. Except that it's on Amelia Island."

"Lot of condos on Amelia Island. It's a big golf resort. Right?"

"But she does know it belongs to Celeste."

"Still. Yeah," Chuck ventured, "how is Celeste about us using her condo again?"

"Uh," Greg said sheepishly, "I haven't told her yet."

"What?"

"I'll handle it with her," Greg said quickly. He didn't want to tell Chuck that she'd refused to answer her phone all weekend. Chuck was a real fan of Celeste's and had often warned Greg to "tie the knot" before she got away. "She's in Atlanta finishing a big design project. I'll let her know. Don't worry about it."

Chuck grunted. "Yeah. Sure wish they'd find El Creepo Santiago and soon. Put him away so the Palmers can go home. And Carrie's kid. You know how she is about that kid. We're not going to be able to keep her away from Elizabeth for long."

"So call me when you land in Detroit."

"Oh Greg, one more thing. Forgot to tell you this morning. Detective Lopez had my office track me down — as in, urgently. So I call him. He wants to talk to Steve in the worst way. I figure that's good, so I let him in on Steve's plan to take off tonight."

"Got his attention, hmm?"

"Completely."

"Any details?"

"Nada. Gotta go, boss. My plane's takin' off."

Until now, Greg had avoided calling Celeste at the Atlanta design firm. He suspected that she'd waited for him Friday night after flying through that torrential storm in some tiny plane. Once she'd gotten over that trauma — she hated flying, even in large planes in good weather — he imagined she'd refused to answer her phone when she realized he'd stood her up and then gone back to her job on Monday as planned. Or maybe she was so mad she'd spent the weekend elsewhere, but Celeste was not the moody type and certainly not given to histrionics. Actively avoiding him for four days now was out of character. He'd inquired about her earlier today with his secretary, yet Betty Harmon said she hadn't spoken to Celeste since last week. But why hadn't Celeste checked back into the Peachtree? Greg was truly worried now, and the reality of needing to let her know that he'd co-opted her condo, without her permission, pressed. That's all he could tell her, he realized as he dialed the phone, he couldn't even tell her who was staying there.

"May I please speak to Celeste Marin," he asked politely as the receptionist answered in a sugary drawl. "She's a consultant designer out of Tampa, Florida."

"One moment, sir."

A male voice came on the line. "You're calling for Celeste Marin?"

"Yes. This is Greg Klingman. Is she available?"

"I'm afraid not. Can I take a message?"

"Well, yes. Will you tell her I need to talk to her? Tell her it's urgent. To call my office and have my secretary put her through to me."

"I'm not sure when she'll be able to return the call," the unidentified voice hesitated. "Can I help you?"

"Do you know where I can reach her? I'm her fiancé. It's very important."

"Oh, Mr. Klingman, I didn't realize. I'm Larry Foster. I'm responsible for the project she's doing here. In fact, maybe you can help me. Celeste left in the early afternoon last Friday. She said she'd be back Monday morning, but so far, no show. No phone call. No Celeste. We're at a critical design phase here and —"

"She hasn't even called?" Greg checked his watch. It was one twenty-five. "Celeste is always so fastidious about keeping her commitments."

"I checked with her hotel," said Larry. "She never checked out, but she's not there either. This is just not like Celeste. She knows the pressure we're under."

"No, this isn't like her at all," Greg muttered. "Let me give you my temporary phone number here in Michigan, and my office phone in Tampa. Please call me immediately if you hear from her. Okay?"

"Fine. And if you talk to her first, please tell her to get in touch."

"Where the hell is she?" Greg said aloud as he hung up the phone. Sure, she had a right to be pissed off at him, but to blow off her job? Where the hell could she be anyway? She could be hurt, ill, any number of things could have happened. A woman, traveling alone. God, why had he let this go on this long? Immediately, he thought of Chuck. Even though he was still in transit, Tracy, his assistant, should be able to handle this.

"Mr. Dimer's office," the cheery voice announced. "Tracy Epstein speaking."

"Tracy, Greg Klingman here. Listen, I just talked to your boss. He's on his way to Detroit and I plan to meet him there, but in the meantime, something else has come up."

"Of course, Mr. Klingman. How can I be of help?"

"I'd like you to arrange for one of your agents to check out someone very special to me. Discreetly, of course, but immediately. Urgently, really. It may be nothing, but I just want to make sure. She's not where she's supposed to be."

Greg gave Tracy the necessary information on Celeste, omitting the part that he'd stood her up over the weekend. While not a licensed P.I. herself, Tracy coordinated the office activities of Dimer Investigations and assigned the most appropriate agent to each client.

"No problem, Mr. Klingman, I'll take care of it."

"I appreciate it. Celeste, being my fiancée, well, I don't want this to look like I'm spying on her."

"I understand. But, Mr. Klingman, while I have you. I know how closely you and Chuck are working on the Nelson case. I got a call a few minutes ago. Let's see. It came in at one twenty. A woman named Carmen Williams. Said she had Chuck's business card, that he had questioned her about Kim Connor and Steve Nelson a couple of times. She was a friend of the Connor woman." Tracy hesitated. "I promised to keep the call confidential, but she sounded pretty scared."

"Go on," Greg urged.

"Well, there was not much else than that. She really wanted to talk to Chuck."

"But she wouldn't say about what?"

"Just that she had information Chuck would want. Information about Steve Nelson was all I could get out of her, but —"

"Leave a phone number?"

"Nope. Refused when I asked," Tracy said with an air of professional competence. "Anyway, I told her to try back later, but, of course, Chuck won't be here."

"Shit. Well, whichever of us talks to Chuck first, better let him know. One more thing, Tracy," Greg went on. "What's the news on Carrie Diamond?"

"Hold just a minute, and I'll get you the latest."

In the silence that followed, Greg's mind lingered on the comment about Steve. What had scared Williams enough to make her call? Was it Santiago? Or was it Nelson? Did that jerk know something potentially dangerous to Santiago? Maybe that was why he was in such a rush to take off for Alaska. Maybe he really was afraid, rather than just vindictive.

"Okay," Tracy said into the receiver. "A couple of neighbors saw Carrie and her husband leave their house between nine and nine thirty this morning. Saw at least one piece of luggage. Seemed preoccupied. Not themselves, according to the next-door neighbor who was puttering with her roses. Offered Carrie some, but Carrie pushed right by her."

"That's it?"

"That's all we have. Except the neighbor did say that the Diamond's daughter was away visiting relatives. She figured they might be going to pick her up, but she was only guessing there."

Greg remembered what Betty had said about a man with a Hispanic accent calling just before Carrie left the office so abruptly. About enough time for Carrie to drive home, pack, and leave.

Celeste and Carrie. Two women, each so professional, both missing. So unlike them to just disappear.

What was the common denominator?

CHAPTER THIRTY-ONE

Manny Gonzolas selected his jobs carefully. He liked technical challenges but refused hits related to the mob. This was his second job for Frank Santiago, a personal vendetta like the last one, and this time Manny demanded top dollar being that it had to come off so quick. So what if the kid was deaf and dumb. Make an easy hit. Sure, if he could find her. Finding them, eliminating them, that's what he did best. He'd find her.

Posing as a deliveryman, he'd gone back to the Palmer's late afternoon Monday and chatted with a few other neighbors on Oregon. Nobody had seen the family all day. A call to Palmer's office, where he worked as a senior accountant, was transferred to a colleague who volunteered that Dirk Palmer was taking time off, claiming sudden illness in the family.

Yeah, right. So where the fuck were they? Manny's gut told him the Diamond bitch would know.

The next morning at six o'clock, he drove up to the Diamond house in a dark blue Mercury sedan with tinted windows. At six thirty, he saw the Diamond woman — the woman he'd seen on the tape he'd lifted — leave the house in a business suit, driving away in a late model silver Olds sedan, the kind with a cloth top. Not five minutes later a dark-haired guy, medium build with a pudgy face, emerged from the front door in jogging gear and headed down Oregon, past DeLeon to Swann. The kid, Manny figured, was not around. Both parents wouldn't leave the house with a kid home alone, and it was too early for her to be in school.

He'd give Diamond enough time to get to her office, maybe stop for coffee or something. Then he'd call her there. It was seven thirty when he parked his car less than a block away from Klingman Law Office and dialed the firm from a pay phone. He simply stated that he was a former client when the receptionist asked his name, and she put him right through to Diamond.

Diamond sounded uptight when she answered the phone. Good, she'd be easy to scare. When he started talking about the kid, he heard a gasp. He said that he knew her daughter was with Molly Palmer, and he knew where they were. He told her that she'd better come and get her kid right away, and come alone. Starting to sob, she'd stuttered something about her husband, but Manny interrupted, saying do it or else, letting his voice trail off before he hung up. Then he waited in the car. When she emerged a few minutes later, he followed her home. Bingo, he told himself, he'd spooked her and now she was gonna lead him to his mark.

He had a good feeling about this job. It seemed simple enough, and then he'd split to his retreat in the islands. After the job, Manny planned an extended vacation. Get the hell out of Tampa until this whole thing blew over. Drive straight to Miami. Charter a flight to Martinique. Spend tomorrow on the beach with his luscious Monique.

But first he had to do the kid.

Manny congratulated himself as he sat in the plush seat of the Mercury. Diamond and the guy in the jogging suit, now dressed in pale blue slacks and an aqua short-sleeve shirt, came out, locking the front door in a rush and loading a large, hard-shell suitcase into the Olds' trunk. Sure that he was unseen, Manny trailed the Diamond car as it headed west on Swann, then north on Dale Mabry to the big-money Carrollwood Lake section. The car stopped alongside the curb in front of a bunch of townhouses set amid a perfectly landscaped lawn dotted with coconut palms and surrounded by clumps of flowers in shades of yellows and reds. Manny's passion was landscaping and he admired the the expensive display of lush plantings as the Diamond woman jumped out of the passenger side of the car and raced toward the front door of one of the luxury units and frantically punched the doorbell.

Manny couldn't see everything, just enough to make out that the woman who opened the door was tall, slim, and had long, dark hair. He could see that she wore a baby blue bathrobe and that her hair looked all messed up, like she'd just climbed out of bed. After a brief conversation, Diamond disappeared inside.

Parking the car, Manny waited.

Celeste Marin was surprised at the unannounced visit of Greg's associate. Had he actually sent someone from the office to check on her? She'd met Carrie Diamond only briefly during a few office social occasions and liked her immediately. She remembered telling Greg that she'd like to get to know her better. Based on everything Greg had told her, Carrie was a bright, talented attorney, but what was she doing here, seeing her so unkempt, still unshowered, hair uncombed, no makeup?

"Carrie? Come on in," Celeste greeted her before registering the clear anxiety etched on Carrie's face. "What is it? What's wrong?"

"I . . . I'm so sorry to bother you, Celeste," she blurted, "but I really need your help."

"My help," Celeste echoed. "Did Greg send you here?"

"No. And please don't tell him I came. You see, I'm just so scared," she stammered, "and only you can help me."

"Me? How? Let's have coffee. I just put on a pot. Gosh, I'm sorry I look so awful."

Carrie ignored the comment, still standing, beginning to wring her hands. "I don't have time. I just pray that you can help me."

"But what is it you think I can do? Here, sit down and tell me." She led her over to the brocade sofa.

In a rush, Carrie told Celeste about Molly Palmer. How she had encouraged the child to talk to the police, to identify the man she'd seen go into Steve Nelson's apartment at the time of Kim Connor's shooting.

"But wasn't that the right thing to do?" Celeste asked. Her kind, inquisitive eyes searched Carrie's suddenly blotchy face.

"I thought so, yes. But now I'm just scared for Elizabeth."

"Who's Elizabeth?"

"My daughter."

"I'm afraid I'm not following." Celeste reached for Carrie's hand, unable to fathom what she could do to alleviate this woman's distress. "You were telling me about a Palmer child? And your daughter?"

"I'm sorry, I'm not making much sense I guess." Carrie paused to take a breath. "When Greg and Chuck decided to take the Palmers to a safe place — it was my idea actually — I never thought the Palmers would ask to take my daughter too. You see, they're both deaf, Molly and Elizabeth, and the Palmers wanted to bring Elizabeth as a companion for Molly. My husband and I didn't want to let them take our daughter, but since I'd gotten Molly involved in all this we thought it only right. And Chuck promised tight security."

"Chuck? Chuck Dimer?"

"Yes, he's the P.I. working on the Nelson case with us."

"I know Chuck, and I'm sure the girls are perfectly safe. Chuck is very good at what he does."

"I know. But this morning I got a call from a strange man." Carrie withdrew her hand from Celeste's and reached into her purse for a wad of Kleenex. "I got scared. I . . . I just want to go get my daughter. I think I made a horrible mistake."

"Oh, Carrie, I can understand. I just don't know why you're telling me all this?"

"Because, well, I thought you knew." Carrie gulped and blew her nose. "The Palmers and my daughter are at your condo on Amelia Island."

Celeste gasped. "What?"

"They needed a safe place, and Greg said you wouldn't mind. The firm will reimburse you, of course," she added quickly.

"Uh, that's fine. But your child's there and you don't have the address?"

"No, for security reasons, they said. But Celeste," Carrie looked at her wide eyed. "I need to find my daughter. The man on the phone sounded so threatening."

"Carrie, I'm sorry. I'm not a mother, so I can only imagine how you feel. All I can really do is tell you how to get to the condo," Celeste decided. "But you must promise me that once you do, you'll let Greg and Chuck know immediately. This is obviously quite serious."

"I will," promised Carrie. "I'm just so glad you understand. They never would. Besides, they're so tied up with the Nelson case. I can't imagine what more could happen to that poor woman. What she's been through. It's unbelievable."

Celeste nodded as she wrote out directions and then led Carrie to the door. "It's ten thirty now so you'll be there by five at the latest. Drive carefully," she said perfunctorily, as her mind was already on Greg.

Would she ever care so much about another? Or have a daughter of her own? These were questions she'd considered all weekend.

Life had taken an unexpected turn for Celeste Marin on Friday night. South Florida was being hit with the aftermath of a tropical storm and her flight from Atlanta to Miami had been a living nightmare. Under the best of circumstances, she hated flying, but the horrendous turbulence that threw the 727 around like a giant roller coaster in a sky ablaze with lightning had completely petrified her. Trapped in that terrible reality with her fellow passengers, she'd stopped breathing, felt everything go black until the plane again lurched and its bottom seemed to drop out in a violent downward spiral. Surprising herself, she began to pray, a prayer so deeply enveloping that she was not even aware of the plane landing until the woman next to her, drenched in vomit, tapped her lightly on the shoulder. Theirs was the last plane to land before all planes were grounded, to her relief, so she'd stayed at one of those airport hotels overnight.

She called Greg, but there was no answer. In the morning she rented a car and drove across Alligator Alley to U.S. 41 North to Tampa. She'd called Greg again, first at her townhouse, where they were to meet, then at his beach house. She'd assumed that he was upset with her for ruining their weekend plans and had probably just gone home and turned off his phone the way he did when he was working too hard, trying to meet a deadline. He'd sounded so sweet last Thursday night — it would be just them and the stars and the moon. Twice Saturday morning, she'd tried his office, but no one answered.

She arrived in Carrollwood at one Saturday afternoon, arranged for the return of her rental car, and looked around the apartment for a note from Greg, assuming he'd been there waiting for her the evening before. Nothing. He must have really been angry. She tried his office again. No answer, and no answer at his place. Impulsively, she left her townhouse and headed for the Courtney Campbell Causeway connecting Tampa to Clearwater.

Celeste had her own key to Greg's spacious house situated on the expansive sandy beaches of Palm Harbor. This was his sanctuary, far enough away from the city and a beautiful commute across Old Tampa Bay. She'd offered to help him with interior design several times, but he'd politely refused, preferring to keep the dated furnishings of the former owners. Though the house was large and comfortable with a pool and cabana off to one side, the furniture and interior design details, although expensive, were outdated and not up to par with Celeste's discerning taste. Certainly nothing of the decorative splendor she'd lavished on her own condo. They often joked that when they got married, they'd have to get rid of both places and build their "compromise" house. But would they? She knew that he loved her and she him. She knew the demands of a law practice and she knew she loved her job. And, she knew that if neither compromised in a lifestyle change, they would never get to the point of a "compromise" house. Nor to what they both wanted, but were maybe afraid of — a family of their own.

Again Celeste searched for a note, some sign from Greg to let her know he was nearby, but there was none. Where was he? This was all her fault. She decided to sit tight and wait for him to come home. She changed into a bathing suit and stretched out on the deck. The Gulf was still pounding from the tropical storm that had delayed her last night. Getting up only to fix herself a Swiss cheese and lettuce sandwich and pour herself a glass of chardonnay, she stayed there well past a glorious sunset off the west Florida coast — all brilliant reds, oranges, pinks and purples.

Finally she got up, showered and changed into one of the sheer nightgowns she kept there along with a scattering of casual clothes and beachwear. It was warm, and she walked outside, strolling along the perimeter decks. Had Greg stayed in Michigan for reasons unknown? The soft breeze off the Gulf of Mexico seemed to speak to her, to urge her to explore something inside herself in this uncommon solitude. When she finally left the moonlit skies and went inside to lie down on Greg's king-size bed, she fell immediately into a deep sleep with only blackness, without dreams.

In the morning, Celeste awoke early with an awesome sensation she could only describe as peace. A sensation so unusual it was alien, really. She could only marvel that something inside her had subdued the usual blinding ambition that had driven her every day from the moment she awoke. Over the next two days, she simply walked in the warm granular sand along the Gulf, and at night she read from the poetry collections Greg kept in the bedroom's bookcase. She did not turn on the television, call her office in Tampa, or the client's office in Atlanta. She felt paralyzed to do so. She did not even call Greg's office again.

She hadn't spoken to him in four days, since Thursday evening. She knew she could reach him through Betty at his office, but she held back. Because she wanted to be totally sure. And now she was.

Hopefully, it wasn't too late.

On Monday night, she returned to her place in Tampa. Resolved. First, she would resign from her job. The excessive travel and demanding clients were sucking up every morsel of her energy. Instead, she'd start her own little business. A small design boutique, which she could manage out of her own home. There would be more time to be with Greg. Maybe it wasn't too late to have a family. The thought of children brought the twinge of a smile. So she booked a flight to Atlanta for the next day, Tuesday. She'd call her boss and tell him she'd return to Atlanta to work out the transition with Larry Foster. Then, when it was all decided, she would tell Greg what she'd done.

If he agreed, they'd set a date, and begin the next chapter of their lives.

A slight smile crossed Celeste's face as she picked up the morning paper and moved to close the door after Carrie climbed back into her car. Then, vaguely, at the edge of her vision, Celeste noticed a dark blue sedan pulling away from the curb behind Carrie's. A flicker of alarm disturbed her reverie. Could that car be following the Diamond's? She scolded herself for her silliness. Was Carrie's paranoia getting to her too? But Carrie had spoken of that strange phone call this morning with such fear.

When Chuck Dimer walked into the satellite law offices of Youngman, Polk, and Allen in Wayne, Michigan a few minutes before three, Greg was on the phone. He motioned for Chuck to sit down and mouthed, "Laura's dad."

After he hung up the phone, Greg turned to Chuck, "Laura's on her way. The sooner she gets here the better."

"I'm with you there, boss. I'll get over there early to make sure I've got the lay of the land over at Detroit Metropolitan. Anything else I should know about?"

"Carrie's still unaccounted for. A couple of hours ago Tracy said one of your guys learned that some neighbors saw the Diamonds leave their place with their bags packed this morning."

Chuck shook his head. "Uh-huh. My thought is she's back-pedaling on having her kid with the Palmers. It's a good thing she doesn't know where Celeste's condo is."

"But she knows it's on Amelia Island. All she'd have to do is call Celeste, but —"

"But Celeste would never give it to her," Chuck interrupted. "She knows we're using it as a safe house."

Greg drew a deep breath. "But Celeste still doesn't know they're there."

"You still haven't told her? Greg, what if she —"

"The truth is, I don't know where Celeste is. I haven't talked to her since Thursday night, which is why I called your office earlier. I asked Tracy to arrange a discreet inquiry. I'm worried about her, Chuck. She didn't show up in Atlanta yesterday for work, and she's not at home. God knows she's a workaholic, and she's in the middle of a big project. Hell would freeze over before she missed a project deadline."

"Sure she's not just in a snit? You been spending a lotta time with Laura Nelson," said Chuck only half-jokingly.

"Probably is all my fault. I must've really pissed her off staying in Philly all weekend. We had plans. She made it home, through a storm no less, and I didn't."

"Sounds like a lover's spat to me."

"I just can't stop thinking there's a connection between Carrie and Celeste. Their disappearance, I mean. I have a bad feeling."

"Tracy'll get back to us as soon as she's got something on Celeste's whereabouts. My feeling is, all will be okay with your little lady if you apologize. Apologize profusely and shower her with all those tokens women like — roses, candy, you name it. But wait till tonight," Chuck hastened to add, "after the airport scene we're creating out here."

"Okay, buddy. See you later and thanks for the romance tips."

After the elevator descended with Chuck on it, Greg realized he'd forgotten to pass along Tracy's message about the call from

Carmen Williams. Though Tracy had said she'd sounded scared, with everything else on Greg's mind, it had just slipped by.

Drop it, Carmen kept telling herself. You tried once. The guy wasn't there. Kim's dead, so it's not gonna help her. No way would she call the cops. She'd had enough of them to last a lifetime. They'd already questioned her three times about Kim. First the uniforms that stopped by her house the night it happened, tracking her down by that message she'd left on Kim's machine about needing a job reference. They broke the terrible news and not in a nice way. Said she'd have to come down to the station in the morning. There Detective Lopez, the slick one, and Goodnuf, the ugly one, asked her all kinds of questions about Kim and Steve and Steve's wife. They asked about Kim's other friends, but she hadn't told them anything about Frankie. About Nelson, she'd told the truth. That Kim did fuck him, but only once. That his wife had caught them and tossed Steve out. No, Kim wasn't hot for Nelson, he was just a safe type of guy to have around. Yes, Kim was moving to Atlanta. Why? For a better job. Did Williams have an alibi that night? That was the worst, that they would ask her that, but the answer was yes. She told them about the club where she'd hung out, where lots of people had seen her.

But she hadn't told them about the gun. She knew she would get into big trouble for that, the unregistered gun she'd scarfed up for Kim after Frankie had hit her. They even asked her if she knew whether Kim had a gun, but she hadn't told them. And she never would.

Later that week someone else showed up. A big guy, but nice, and he had treated her with respect. He didn't seem that old, but he had gray hair in a cute crew cut. Big muscles bulged out of his short-sleeve shirt and she remembered thinking that she'd feel safe if she had a guy like him, but mostly she remembered his kind gray eyes and boyish smile. He'd asked her pretty much the same questions as the cops, but he was a private investigator representing Steve

Nelson's wife, and she'd kept his business card. Charles Dimer. "Chuck," he said, "call me Chuck." He'd taken time to talk to her, to really listen as she told him what a good friend Kimmie had been. Like he really cared.

Then, after a lawyer had called her about Kim's will, Detective Lopez came to the house to ask her more questions. Mostly about why Kim had left her all her money, but also about Kim's "other" boyfriend, Frank Santiago. Pointed questions about how he treated her. Did he hit her? Did he threaten her?

"I don't know," she'd answered, not wanting anything to do with Frankie and his wrath. "He was sort of obsessed with her, I guess," she'd told Lopez. "The funny thing was, he wanted kids."

The detective didn't seem to care about that. "Did Santiago know about Nelson?" he asked.

"No, I don't think so," she'd answered, thinking it was the truth. But now the whole world knew about that night.

It was the very next day that Chuck Dimer had returned. He brought a box of Fannie Mae chocolates all tied up with a yellow ribbon. His questions were pretty much the same as the detective's, but he was so nice about it. She felt bad lying to him, but she was scared. Frankie could easily suspect her if any personal information got out, and it would be real simple to have her killed.

And now, after what she'd seen last night — and heard — at the Columbia, should she call that Chuck back? Nervously, Carmen twisted his card in her hands as she replayed the scene. Santiago dressed like a sloppy street person, meeting with a hit man. She'd strained to hear what they said when they came out of that room. Sounded like, "nail Nelson." Something about Detroit and "when I'm done, I'm going away." She'd been so scared standing in that doorway, that she'd almost wet her pants. But she was pretty sure that what she heard meant that Steve Nelson's name was on a contract. Truthfully, she'd been wondering why Frankie hadn't iced Steve already, what with the way he felt about Kim and Steve's open admission that he'd had sex with her. For a guy that high up in the mob, having Steve killed would be well, expected.

Kim always said that Steve was a nice enough guy, but all involved with his family. With five kids, no wonder. So she'd decided to call that Chuck Dimer. Let him warn Steve. Maybe she was too late. Maybe they did him last night. Finally she said aloud, "What would Kim want me to do?" As she continued twisting Chuck's business card, she decided to try him again. One more time and that was it. That girl who'd answered the phone sounded nice and she'd said to call back.

"Ms. Williams," Tracy said politely once Carmen identified herself on the phone, "I'm glad you called back. Mr. Dimer is anxious to talk to you. He's in Detroit, but I have a phone number. I can patch you in."

"Long distance?" Carmen balked. "Hey, I don't have that kind of money."

"I'll reverse the charges," said Tracy quickly. "Can you hold?"

"Yeah, I guess."

Tracy immediately placed the call to the law office in Wayne, Michigan.

"Greg Klingman here."

"Glad I caught you," said Tracy with a detectable sigh of relief. "Did you locate Celeste?"

"Uh, no, that's not why I'm calling. Not Carrie Diamond either," she rushed on. "I'm trying to reach Chuck on another matter."

"I see. Tracy, you just missed Chuck. Anything I can help you with?"

"I hope so, Mr. Klingman, it's that Carmen Williams calling back for Chuck."

"Patch her through, Tracy. Miss Williams," Greg began, straining to keep it easy, keep the anxiety out of his voice.

"Is this Chuck?"

"No, it's not. Chuck's in transit and he asked if you called to please talk to me. He said it must be important for you to go to all the trouble to contact him, and he hoped you'd trust me. I work with Chuck."

"Trust you?" Carmen said slowly. "Who are you anyway?"

"I'm Greg Klingman and I work with Chuck. Please, just let me know how I can help you."

"I . . . I don't know. I don't want to get in trouble, but I don't want anyone else to get hurt."

"Ms. Williams, has something happened?"

"I saw Frank Santiago last night," she blurted, "in Tampa — Ybor City."

Greg hesitated. "I see. Did you call the police? Does anyone else know about this?"

"Of course not," Carmen snapped. "Oh, shit, why did I tell you? Now the cops'll be all over me. He'll kill me next."

"Please, you can talk to me in confidence," Greg tried to reassure her. "I can promise you that."

"Will you tell the cops? God, I never shoulda called."

"No, I will not tell anyone. Please, fill me in."

But he had already heard the click. She had hung up.

Within a halfhour, Greg's intercom buzzed again as the secretary at Youngman, Polk, and Allen announced that Chuck Dimer was on the line.

"Put him through."

"I'm at the airport. On my way over to Northwest departures," Chuck said quickly, "I wanted to go over the plan."

"Wait, Chuck. I've got to tell you about a call I just got — wait a sec. The intercom."

"Mr. Klingman," the secretarial voice began, "I have a Mr. Rob Wilson. Take it or call back?"

"I'll take it, and put this one on hold. Chuck, stay on the line, will you? It's Rob. Maybe he's got something from the Hillsborough Family Court."

Chuck mumbled "okay" as Greg picked up the other line. "Rob, what's up?"

"Not much, Greg. I've pulled every stop. With the kids in

Michigan with their legal father, there's no way a Florida court will issue a restraining order without a custody agreement in effect. Believe me, I've worked every angle until I hit a stone wall. Well, you know the statutes."

"Yeah, just hoped one of those judges would cut us a break."

"Maybe if the kids were in state, but if it's gonna happen, it'll have to be done in Michigan."

"No way we can swing it here either, Rob." Greg checked his watch. "After three. We're too late. Local counsel did all they could, but not enough time, and Nelson's their father. Kids have been with him uncontested for weeks. Courts here don't know Laura from Eve, and they have the usual local bias. No way they'll give up jurisdiction until at least a preliminary hearing in a Michigan court, and there's just no time."

"Tough all around," Rob commiserated. "Guess it means we have to let those boys go?"

"I'll get back to you. Chuck's at the airport hanging on the other line. Gotta go."

Greg switched lines and briefed Chuck on the disappointing news from Tampa.

"Not surprised," said Chuck. "So the plan's on. You bring Laura over to the boys and voilà! Timing's right. Her flight's due in at six, and check-in for Nelson's flight starts at six thirty. Confront Nelson right there in the airport. If the boys throw a fit about leaving with him, maybe the airline will balk and defer their flight?"

"Could work."

"What's the worst that can happen? A nasty scene? Let's go with it."

"Somehow, I can't see Nelson letting those boys go easily. But if it works, we'll need tickets for the boys on Laura's return flight at nine."

"My money's on the boys going with her. I'll get the tickets right now," Chuck said.

"You're an optimist."

"Always. Okay, boss, see you with Laura around six. Let's get ready for some fireworks."

"Hold up, Chuck," Greg called. "I just heard from Kim Connor's friend, Carmen Williams. Called twice. Very reluctant to talk to me. Sounded scared as hell. Only thing I got out of her before she hung up was that she saw Frank Santiago last night in Ybor City. This girl's really scared. Wants nothing to do with the cops. My guess is she's got more to tell. Can you reach her?"

"So the motherfucker finally came up for air. Let me get right on it, Greg. I've got some calls to make, including Detective Lopez."

"Lopez?"

"Yah, he asked me to keep him in the loop. Funny, he's become a fan of Laura's. Don't forget El creepo Santiago iced Lopez's former partner way back when, so he wants this collar in the worst way. See you later, boss."

CHAPTER THIRTY-TWO

Manny Gonzolas lived comfortably but quietly on Clearwater Beach in a Spanish-style villa surrounded by an extravagant tropical garden. Gardening was his passion and he spent most days puttering about his prize azaleas, gardenias, hibiscus, and stately palms. From time to time, he would drop a flower arrangement off at a neighbors, always in a shy manner and never accepting invitations to come in for coffee or whatever they offered. He purchased Girl Scout cookies and contributed to the various police and ambulance causes. He dressed conservatively, always neat and trim, and attracted little attention. Never married, he lived alone and assiduously isolated his personal life from his business concerns. All business was conducted in Tampa, specifically Ybor City, in a back room of his uncle's club. All mail went to a P.O. Box in Clearwater, where he kept a façade of an office. He always worked alone and preferred to cluster his cases, take care of business, then leave the mainland for several weeks in the islands.

As for his profession, he'd been in it fifteen years. Very successful. Never'd been in peril. This he attributed to careful case selection. He was a pure professional. A hit man simply did his job. No emotion. No moral rectitude. He worked only with clients who paid up front, and who came with the appropriate references. He, not immodestly, considered himself smart and resourceful, priding himself on jobs that involved some strategy, not just simple point and shoots.

When Frank Santiago approached him about this job he'd

hesitated. He'd done a hit for Frank — personal, not mob related — once before and it had gone smoothly. But now with Frank himself the target of a manhunt, he felt leery. But the money was good, and he was a business man. So the "yes" won over the "no" debate. When he found that the mark was a kid, a deaf kid at that, and not only did he have to find this kid, he had to do the job in just one day, he figured he should double the fucking price. He was planning to do just that until Frank began to backpedal about it being a kid. If Frank walked, Manny'd be out fifty grand.

But now, as he followed the Diamond's car, he felt confident. He'd spooked the woman lawyer, and she was leading him directly to his target. Right now they were only two cars ahead of him heading north on I-95. Everything was cool. That was, if his hunch paid off and the two deaf kids really were together.

It was eleven thirty, an hour after Carrie Diamond had left, and Celeste could not shake an ominous foreboding as she paced back and forth in front of the large picture window that overlooked the street in Carrollwood. Had she done the right thing, telling Carrie about the condo? Should she call Greg, admit what she'd done? No, he'd just be upset. Besides, Carrie certainly had the right to know where they'd taken her daughter.

She put down her coffee cup and began to feel queasy — it was the image of that car that had pulled out after Carrie.

Impulsively, Celeste ran upstairs and jumped into the shower. Slipping into jeans and a tee shirt and securing her long dark hair in a wet ponytail, she grabbed her purse and started for the door. Then, stopping abruptly, she retraced her steps to the bedroom, unlocked a drawer in the nightstand by her bed and withdrew a metallic object. It was stupid, she told herself, but she'd already done something stupid by sending Carrie to the condo, hadn't she? Tonight, when she got there, she'd call Greg. Once she knew everything was okay. Tomorrow she'd call her office and resign, just one day later than she'd planned. After all these years, one day could not possibly make such a difference.

*   *   *

Greg had barely reached the Northwest gate at Detroit Metropolitan Airport when Laura deplaned, carrying only a small, canvas shoulder bag. She wore baggy white slacks and sandals, a pale pink pullover shirt with short sleeves, and carried a matching sweater. Looking tired and thin, she tried to pass other passengers in search of Greg.

"You are traveling light, aren't you?" He caught the flicker of relief in her eyes when she turned toward him.

"Thanks for doing this, Greg," she said without breaking her stride.

"No problem." Greg glanced at his watch: 6:11. Chuck should be here soon, and so would Steve and the kids, if they were not already.

"Listen, let's sit down for a moment." Greg took her arm and maneuvered her over to a row of empty chairs near a deserted baggage carousel, where they sat down.

Laura stiffened. "Bad news?"

Greg nodded. "We did everything we could both here and in Tampa to try to get a restraining order, but it didn't happen. That means it's really going to be up to you to convince the boys to go with you. Chuck's already got tickets for them, just in case."

She shook her head. "Oh, no."

"I'm sorry, but it turns out Steve is legally able to take the boys with him anywhere in the U.S. As you know, he's chosen Alaska."

"But how can he do that? They're my sons too!"

"It's too complicated to go over right now, and remember, no matter what happens today, you can go back to court and we'll get them back."

"I don't want to go to court," she said, slamming one hand into the other. "I want them now. Both of them, now. Steve's poisoned their minds against me. I can't believe this is happening. I'll convince them to go with me."

"Just use your instinct and intuition when we approach them. Chuck and I will be there to back you up. If necessary, we'll try to

whisk them away, out of Steve's reach. We can face whatever consequences in court later, but at least we'll have the boys."

"Okay, Greg. What would I do without you?" She squeezed
his hand. "Anything else I should know?"

Should he mention that call from Carmen Williams? No, too
vague. "It'll wait," he replied as he took her arm and led her toward
the escalator.

Don Diamond followed the signs toward the bridge leading to
Amelia Island. An intelligent, affable man, he and Carrie had met as
students at the University of Miami and had married one week after
graduation. Then, he'd taken a job with an accounting firm while
she went on to law school. Because congenital deafness ran in his
family, he and Carrie had gone for genetic counseling before deciding to have a child and when Elizabeth was born deaf, they were
deeply disappointed but not devastated. They had known the risk
in advance and had taken it. They decided to have no more children.

Carrie now directed Don with the help of an old Florida map
they kept in the glove compartment, along with Celeste's scribbled
directions. They had taken the last exit in Florida at the Florida-
Georgia border off I-95 and driven the ten miles to the bridge connecting Florida's mainland to the charming barrier island of white
sandy beaches. It was nearly five and they were now on SR-200,
looking for the turnoff to Celeste's cluster of condos. Carrie glanced
at the street address and the unit number. Celeste had written that
it was on the third floor overlooking the ocean. There was a private
elevator off the lobby that opened directly into her foyer. Carrie was
to take elevator bank 8.

"Wow, this is really posh," Don remarked as they located the
luxury complex, not fully sharing his wife's panic that their daughter was in danger. "I'll bet Elizabeth is having a great time here."

"Well, we're taking her anyway."

"Carrie, honey, let's just hope you're overreacting. How could
that man who called you know where the girls are staying? You said
that Chuck Dimer promised us —"

"I'm not overreacting," she insisted. "He knew that Elizabeth is with Molly. He said for us to get her out of there."

"But Chuck has security stationed here."

She glanced around as the car turned into a parking area near the high-rise facing the beach. "I don't see any security. Do you?"

They locked the car and began walking toward the condo.

"I think that's the idea. You're not supposed to see security people. They sort of blend in."

"Remember, he said to come alone," Carrie said, her eyes darting all over. "You're sure he didn't mean just me?"

Don shook his head. "If all this is real, he means don't bring the police, etcetera."

"I just know it's real. Let's go in."

"I still think we should have called ahead. Celeste gave you the number, didn't she?"

"But it might have scared them into leaving before we got here. I just want to see Elizabeth, then we'll warn the Palmers."

"Honey, I hope we're not making a big mistake," Don said, reaching for her arm and slowing her pace. "Chuck knows his job. Don't you think we should at least have called him? It's not too late."

"No," she insisted. "That guy said to come alone, and Chuck would just hold things up. Besides, he's in Michigan."

"What about Greg? Maybe we should put a call in."

"He's in Michigan too. I'm scared too, Don, but I know we're doing the right thing."

The dark sedan pulled into a parking space two rows away, nicely obscured from view by two sprawling coconut palms. Manny Gonzolas was sure that the Diamond couple had no suspicions that they'd been followed. Nonchalantly, he left his car and sauntered toward the lobby of the opulent condominium. He was wearing jeans, a black polo shirt, a black baseball cap, and dark glasses. He looked casual, easily passing for a resort guest or a service contractor. Through the large, glass picture window in the front of the building, Manny could see the elevator the Diamonds had just used without even stepping inside. It was clearly marked "8," and he could see that once they stepped inside its mirrored interior, they had pushed the button to the third floor. Good, he thought, now to check out all the entrances and exits, assess the traffic patterns, building layout, and most importantly, as best he could, the security system. Checking his pockets as if he'd forgotten something, he returned to his car, ducking into the backseat, and when he was sure that no one was close by, he slipped into the oversized gardener's garb he had ready. Pruning shears in hand, he sauntered out again, hoping to blend in with the tall hibiscus surrounding the building.

Under cover of the lush landscaping, Manny eventually found a spot where he could see the unit's windows. As he studied the four-story building it made sense that the bank of 8 elevators led to the end units on the south side, facing the ocean. Using his small, powerful binoculars, he could see two young girls sitting at a table on a screened-in balcony. They were playing some kind of board game, gesturing with their hands. Bingo — sign language. Yep, he'd found his target. He congratulated himself as he watched the Diamond woman come out onto the balcony and give one of the girls a big hug, the one with the same dark hair as hers. His target was the red-haired one with pigtails, he knew that much. The question was, how was he gonna get to her?

Manny had figured that each unit would have its own key to an elevator that opened directly into the individual unit. He also figured that the concierge had to have a panic button that would bring security, even the cops, if there were any kind of trouble. Rich people who lived in these buildings expected tight security. Methodically, he reviewed his options. There was no way he was going up in the elevator, and it wasn't likely that they'd let the kid play outside anytime soon. He'd have to create a diversion, cause an evacuation, wait for a clear shot at the target. Using his silencer, of course. Do it execution-style. He'd have to act quickly before the local cops — or anyone else — showed. He'd already seen that the condo's on-site security guards were older with no sign of a firearm, which meant they didn't pose any real threat. So far, no sign of private security for the kid, but he'd have to watch for that. Once he flushed the condo occupants out into the open, he'd just pick the kid off. He'd decided on a fire, aided by a couple of loud blasts to speed up the panic. Create terror and confusion, make the hit quick, and get the hell out.

Staying close to the tall hibiscus, Manny slowly made his way back to the parking lot to organize the cache of flammables stored in his trunk. He stopped abruptly at the corner of the building near the lobby as he caught sight of the Diamond couple emerging. They seemed to be trying to shield their daughter as they darted for their car, and he strained to pick up any conversation when he saw the girl signing excitedly to her mother.

"Hurry," was all he could hear Diamond say as she hustled the kid into the backseat of the silver Oldsmobile, climbing in beside her.

Manny knew he had to act fast. The lady was a lawyer, and now that she'd got her kid out, she'd probably try to get more security if she was this nervous. He watched impatiently as the Diamond car headed toward the parking lot exit and then, backing into a clump of palmettos, he slipped out of the gardener overalls, folded them into a small bundle, and strode toward his car. What had Diamond told the Palmers? If she'd scared them into leaving, maybe he could just wait and isolate the target out here, but he couldn't count on that. What if they planned to stay put instead and wait for either the cops or private security? No, he couldn't take that chance.

The Diamond car came to a full stop at the entrance to the resort property. As her husband flipped on the left blinker ready to pull out, a silver BMW turned into the property and braked suddenly, horn blaring. A dark haired woman jumped out of her car and rushed toward them.

"It's Celeste! Don, stop." Diamond rolled down the back window.

"Carrie, are you okay? I . . . I was worried."

"Celeste, what are you doing here?"

Celeste peered into the Diamond's car. "Oh, you have your daughter. I just wanted to make sure everything was okay. I'm glad everything's all right."

"I think so . . ." Carrie faltered.

"Listen, it was probably my imagination," Celeste said as she brushed back a loose strand of dark hair.

"What was?"

"Nothing, really. I don't want you to worry."

"We're fine, Celeste. Here, let me introduce you to Elizabeth. And, here's Don. You met at last year's office party."

"She looks just like you, Carrie," Celeste said, smiling at Elizabeth and saying hello to Don. "Now why don't you go ahead, I'm just going to go up to make sure the Palmers have everything they need. As long as I'm here, there're a few things I want to take back to Tampa with me."

After they said good-bye Carrie called, "Listen, the bodyguard that Chuck hired is up there with the Palmers. Just so you're not surprised."

"We can't check in until six thirty," Steve told the boys as the rented station wagon approached the Northwest departures terminal. "We have plenty of time to unload the luggage. You stay with it right here on the curb while I go return the car, then I'll circle back on the shuttle, got it?"

Neither Kevin nor Mike made a move.

"Look guys, you haven't said squat the whole trip. Get a move on!"

The boys lumbered out of the car. Both Mike and Kevin just stood there as Steve unloaded the stack of bulging duffel bags himself, along with his hunting rifle and his shotgun — the ones he'd used as a teenager in the northern Michigan woods. He'd already placed them, with his hunting knives into a properly labeled container, according to airline regulations.

"Thanks for the help," Steve said sarcastically. "Just wait out here with the bags until I get back."

The boys sulked. Steve tore off in the station wagon.

It was wise to get the hell out of Michigan, Steve thought as he drove away from the airport terminal. Beyond wise, it was essential. So tired of everyone's eyes on him, from those of every stranger to his own father, he was tired of listening to everyone else too, tired of hiding out. Hiding out was for losers. Let him just get on with his life and make the best of it. In the end, what more did anyone ever do anyway? Disgusted, that's what he was, with his life, with all the goddamn secrets, with the fucking world. He'd spent a long night thinking about Laura's offer to reconcile, but he just couldn't face it — face Patrick every day, another man's child. A constant reminder of Laura's rape — or betrayal? He didn't know what to believe, couldn't really believe any of it. And how he'd loved that kid better than the others. No, Alaska would be a new start, a way to get his boys to look forward instead of back, to get away from all the eyes and questions — and Frank Santiago — once and for all.

Pulling up to the Budget Car Rental depot, Steve did a double take. It was that detective, the dapper one, who'd questioned him in Tampa. Detective Lopez stood, chest puffed out, at the building entrance. He'd spotted Steve instantly and was striding over to the passenger side of the wagon. Without invitation he opened the door and slid in next to him.

"Remember me?" Lopez said.

Steve's heart was pounding. "Uh, yes, Detective. What are you doing here?"

"Wanted to talk to you, Mr. Nelson, but you've been very elusive. There've been some developments that concern you."

"I've already given my statement," Steve stammered. "There's nothing more I can —"

"Let me lay it out for you," Lopez said sharply. "Frank Santiago surfaced in Ybor City last night. We know he's on your tail, and that he knows your plans."

Steve had broken into a sweat. "Santiago knows? You mean, he knows I'm here? I gotta get out of here. My boys —"

"Mr. Nelson, calm down. What you're going to do is stick to your plans, head into that terminal and board the plane."

"What? I can't go back in there if that guy's a murderer for god's sake. Look, detective, you gotta help me. I've got two kids waiting for me outside the Northwest terminal. You gotta go back there and get them for me so we can get out of here!"

The detective shook his head slowly as Steve wiped the sweat from his forehead. "Time's running out. You've got no choice, Mr. Nelson. You will go back in there as planned or I'll arrest you for the murder of Kim Connor right here and now."

"What? That's the most ridiculous thing I ever heard!"

"Is it, Mr. Nelson?" The detective ran his palm over his sleek black hair. "What's been nagging me for a long time was your wife's statement that she'd left phone messages for you the day of the murder. Four of them to be exact. That made me wonder how it was possible that your answering machine had no messages on it at all when we retrieved it from your apartment?"

"I . . . I have no idea," Steve stuttered. Both of his hands now gripped the steering wheel.

"Think hard, Mr. Nelson. Answering machines are interesting gadgets. As you know, not many people have them, professionals mostly, like yourselves. You and Kim Connor, that is. So Kim left a message telling you she was coming right over to see you that night. Pleaded with you, actually, that she needed to see to you."

Steve's face had gone gray. "I . . . don't know what you mean."

Lopez smiled. "Come now, Mr. Nelson. You know better than anybody. What I mean is, when I had our techies go back over those tapes, they were able to retrieve the messages from your answering machine tape that somebody thought they'd erased. Almost worked, we missed them the first time. The missing messages that your wife had left — all four — just like she said, and the last message — Kim's message, remember? Now how did those messages get erased, I ask myself. Certainly not by Laura since she's the one who told us about them—"

"Frank Santiago," Steve croaked as Lopez's stare bored into him.

"Now why would he do that?"

"Because. I don't know what you're talking about," Steve muttered.

"That's hard to believe, Mr. Nelson, but there's more," Lopez said. "I've been going over the interviews with your kids very carefully. Can you tell me about the movie you saw the night of the Connor murder?"

"What?" Steve's entire face gleamed with sweat. "Look — okay — just let me go catch my plane. My sons are waiting. I'm in a hurry to catch my flight. I've got a job to get to."

The detective glanced from his watch to Steve. "You're right. We don't have much time if you're going to catch that plane to Alaska."

Wiping his face, Steve stared back at Lopez in horror.

"Speaking of jobs, I've been going over the statements from the Connor murder investigation. Something was bugging me, something that didn't quite fit. I've been a cop long enough to listen to that feeling."

"Look, I said I have to go," Steve cut in, but Lopez was not deterred.

"Your son told us that you left the movie the night of Kim Connor's murder because you had a phone interview lined up."

"Yeah, that's right."

"A job interview by phone on a Sunday night seems a bit far-fetched."

"It's true, goddamn it!"

"Well, who was the interview with, Mr. Nelson?"

"Look, I've got a pending job offer in Alaska. I've already explained that to you. Alaska's three time zones away. You're really going down the wrong road with this —"

"I need a name, Mr. Nelson."

The knuckles on Steve's hands as they gripped the steering wheel had gone completely white. He said nothing.

"Speaking of roads, we interviewed the night clerk at that motel in Georgia. He's willing to testify that you checked in around four a.m., not at midnight as you and your kids said."

"Well, he got it wrong," Steve croaked.

"Is that so? Tampa to Forsyth is about an eight-hour drive. If you left Tampa at eight, well, you do the math."

"You're not making sense," Steve said. "We've been all over this. Look, I have to get back to my sons. They're —"

"And the gun? Was it Kim Connor's?"

"How should I know? You know my prints weren't on it."

"Anybody can wipe off prints. Listen, Mr. Nelson, my theory is that you retrieved Kim's message, left the movie to go home and meet her, and somehow that gun went off. Kim's gun — the one her friend — you know who I mean — Carmen Williams — gave her. The gun that failed the trigger test, it was so far off the scale for hair trigger. So was it an accident? Am I on the right road now?"

Steve scowled, his eyes bright as he blinked desperately at Lopez. "You can't prove anything! If Laura didn't kill Kim, it must've been her mobster boyfriend. He's the one you're looking for, for God's sake! Laura told me you have an eye witness." Steve began trembling badly, sinking back into the seat, abandoning all attempts at bravado. "She said there's a warrant out for Santiago. He obviously followed her to my place that night." Steve let his head fall into his hands, then he looked up to face Lopez. "Kim said that if Santiago ever found out that she had sex with me, that he'd kill her — and me. The guy's a professional killer!"

"That may all be well and true. Always did wonder why you went so public on TV. But the evidence against you —"

Steve blinked back tears. "Just tell me what you want me to do," he pleaded. I don't want to go to jail. I just want to start a new life. Far away from here."

Lopez shook his head. "More than you deserve seeing that you were willing to send your wife to prison for murder. A murder that you committed, you self-righteous bastard."

"I . . . I thought she'd get off easy," Steve rasped. "I figured she'd get probation. Temporary insanity. I wouldn't let her go to prison. I —"

Leering maliciously at Steve, Lopez shifted in the passenger seat, hands tightly clenched. For an instant Steve thought he was going to hit him. "You don't deserve the deal I'm cutting you, you chicken-shit bastard."

Steve pressed his back to the driver's door. What would he do if Lopez hit him? Just sit and take it? Or hit him back?

Then Lopez took a deep breath, held it, and settled back, slowly massaging his neck. "Listen, Mr. Nelson. The fact is, I've got you for murder. Don't think I don't want to put you away. Not so much for killing Connor, if that was an accident, but for what you did to Laura. What you put that poor woman through makes you a piece of scum."

Steve shook so violently that he thought he might be having a seizure. "I told you I never would have let her —"

"Quit the bullshit, you prick. Fact is, Frank Santiago means more to me than you do. I want that son of a bitch. That's the only reason I'm offering you an opportunity to walk away, but don't you think I don't know."

"Why?" Steve asked feebly, "if you think —"

"You're right, Nelson, someone did see Santiago go into your house on Oregon that night, and I'm going to nail him for murder this time. Bastard took out my partner on the street a long time ago. Guy had three little boys. I want this motherfucker. You, I don't give a damn about. Look, we're out of time on this."

After the car had pulled away from the curb, Kevin said, "I didn't think Mom would let us go. Do you think Marcy told her?"

"She said she would," Mike answered.

"Then why didn't she come get us?"

"I don't know, Kev. Maybe she's just too busy with Pat at the hospital."

"I hope he's okay." He paused. "Why doesn't Dad like Pat anymore? He used to let Pat get away with anything."

Mike echoed his father's words. "You're too young to understand. Anyway, it doesn't matter."

"Yes, it does. Something Mom did that made him mad, but why is he blaming Pat? He's just a little kid."

"Wait till you're older. I'll explain it all to you. What Dad thinks Mom did to him."

"Tell me now. I'm not some stupid little kid."

"Right now," Mike said, "we have to get on that stupid plane."

"Are we gonna ever see Mom again?" Kevin rubbed his eye, trying to hold back tears. "Or Natalie or Nicole or Pat."

"Yes. Mom'll find us."

"How do you know? What if Dad won't let her? Anyway Dad says he's got a job with a TV station in Alaska, and that he'll be famous and we'll have a lot of money."

"He's got a job interview, but who cares?"

"Let's just run away. Right now!" Kevin jumped up.

"We'd just get caught. Then he'd be even be madder," Mike said, slumping back into the pile of duffel bags.

Chuck Dimer had not yet spotted the Nelsons as he circled the Northwest departure area. The clock on the big board registered 6:30 exactly; check-in for the San Francisco flight had just begun. There were three businessmen in suits standing in the first-class line and a growing number of other passengers arranging themselves in the coach-class queue. Chuck looked quickly around the large hall for Steve Nelson and his sons. Nothing. He sped over to a bench by the up escalator where they'd agreed to meet. Relieved, he saw Greg and Laura there.

"Laura, good to see you," Chuck said. "How's your little guy?"

"Hi, Chuck. The surgery went well, but he's still not conscious."

"Over there —" Greg interrupted. "That's Steve, coming in through the automatic door."

"I don't see the boys," Laura whispered.

"Let's wait here a sec," Greg said quietly, "see how this plays out."

"There they are!" Laura blurted as Kevin followed several paces behind Steve, carrying two duffel bags. Impulsively, Laura started to go to him.

"Wait," Chuck said, "not yet."

"Where's Mike?"

"Just wait. Steve's leaving Kevin with the bags and he's going back out."

"Mike must be outside."

Again, Steve hauled more duffel bags. This time he was followed by Mike, who was struggling with a long rectangular case. Steve seemed to be barking orders.

"Dear God," Laura gasped, "he's got Steve's rifle case."

They watched as Steve dropped the bags abruptly before taking his place in line, leaving the boys standing slumped along the wall.

"They don't look too thrilled," Chuck whispered. "I've got a car right outside. What do you think?"

CHAPTER THIRTY-THREE

Celeste watched anxiously as the Diamonds drove away. All of this was so strange. Why hadn't Greg told her he planned to use her condo? It wasn't like him to let strangers use it. He was always so considerate of her property and her independence. Only once before, about a year ago, he'd arranged for a client of his to use it, and he had made a big deal of checking with her, getting her approval. Maybe he just didn't care enough about her permission anymore. Or maybe he figured what was hers was theirs, and maybe that was okay now that she was so close to a real commitment that would merge her — her possessions, her needs, her very soul — with Greg.

Or maybe the reason that he didn't tell her was the possibility of real danger. Danger to the Palmer child. And Molly Palmer was still in there. Well, she'd check to make sure the family was okay, and pick up the design sample books she'd left there last time. Then she'd drive back to Tampa. She certainly couldn't stay here with the Palmers. It was just before six, and she wouldn't get home until midnight. Maybe she'd check into a motel off of I-95. If only she'd brought her travel kit and something decent to travel in, she could leave from the Jacksonville Airport. She'd left enough business clothes in Atlanta, but then her car would be stuck in Jacksonville. It had been really silly to come here.

As she drove up the long drive lined by tall red hibiscus, she gazed with approval at the lush manicured lawns and flower-studded gardens before wondering whether Greg had given the

Palmers her garage door opener. Rather than drive all the way down to the underground garage just to find their car in her assigned spot, she decided to park in the lobby lot out front. It was then that she saw that same car — that dark sedan. Yes, a dark blue Mercury with tinted windows, sitting in a parking spot directly in front of the building. A stab of fear cut through her. Her instinct had been right. Someone had followed Carrie.

She knew that she had to warn the Palmers. She quickly swung her silver BMW into the nearest space in the visitors' section. As she walked toward the lobby, she was tempted to peek into the other car, but she was too scared and too much in a hurry. Besides, with those dark windows, she probably wouldn't be able to see inside.

Instead of calling up from the lobby, Celeste used her key to access the elevator to her third floor suite. Once she exited the elevator, she'd be in a small foyer. Then she'd knock at the door, expecting the Palmers to let her in. What she met when the elevator door opened was the barrel of a gun aimed at her chest. She gasped at the weapon and the buff young man with the floppy blond hair and matching, bushy eyebrows who held it.

"Who are you and what are you doing here," he demanded, Gestapo-style.

"Please put that down," she said, once she'd caught her breath. "I'm Celeste Marin. I own this condo. What's —"

"Oh," the man said, the eyebrows shooting up in confusion. "You have identification?"

"Sure," said Celeste. "I'm just going to get it out of my bag. Okay?"

"Slowly," he stepped closer to monitor her careful movements.

"Listen, I can clear this up. I just spoke to Carrie Diamond, the lady who just left with her daughter. I know that you're here protecting a child. I know that Chuck Dimer hired you. He's working with my fiancé, Greg Klingman."

She must have sounded credible, because the man holstered his weapon as soon as he'd scrutinized her driver's license.

Celeste read the embroidered insignia on his cream-colored golf shirt: D. J. SECURITY SERVICES.

"Okay, ma'am, why don't you come in?" he said, opening the door between the foyer and living room. "Name's Regis Adamsky." Inside suitcases in various stages of packing were strewn about. "We were just getting ready to leave."

"Yes, I think you should leave, but —"

"Tried to get in touch with Mr. Dimer," the security guy interrupted. "Let him know about the couple that just came and took their little girl. I was supposed to protect them both, but I couldn't stop that mother. I hope I didn't fuck — oh, I'm real sorry, ma'am. Didn't mean for that to slip out."

"Hurry up, Dirk," Celeste heard a woman's voice call from the master bedroom.

"Let's think this though, Sally," a man's voice. Must be Mr. Palmer, Celeste figured. "Carrie Diamond didn't say anything specific, and I don't think Don even wanted to take Elizabeth. Nobody knows where we are. That was the deal. And with this Regis guy here —"

"I wish he wouldn't keep that gun in plain sight. It frightens me," the woman's voice said.

Celeste's eyes flew to the bulging holster on the security guy's hip and she cringed, wondering if he'd ever had to use it.

"Let me help you, missy," Adamsky said, stepping forward.

Celeste turned to see a little girl in pigtails hauling a canvas suitcase out of the guest bedroom.

The big blonde man rushed to help her, and the child rewarded him with a generous smile. The little girl then looked expectantly at Celeste. Remembering that she was deaf, Celeste waved to her and smiled encouragingly, not knowing what else to do or say.

Adamsky set the suitcase down by the elevator, before grabbing a blue blazer and slipping it on. "Why are you here, ma'am?"

"Mr. Adamsky, I'm glad you're leaving," Celeste said, still fretting about how to communicate with the child. "Listen, I think that Carrie Diamond was followed out here. You see, she came to my house. I live in the Carrollwood section of Tampa. There was a car outside my house — dark blue Mercury, heavily tinted windows. And that same car, I'm pretty sure, is out there." She pointed out the window toward the parking lot.

"Holy shit," Adamsky's face turned red. "Holy shit. Followed? All the way from Tampa? You sure?"

"Quite sure," Celeste said. "That's why I came here. To warn the Palmers."

"Man, I gotta get them outta here," Adamsky ran both hands through his already ruffled hair. "But how? To where? Shit, I gotta try Dimer again."

"Somebody followed Carrie? Is that what you said?" asked a middle-aged man, tanned with wavy brown hair, and startling blue eyes. He'd emerged from the master bedroom with a querulous expression and his hand thrust forward. "By the way, I'm Dirk Palmer. You are?"

"I'm Celeste Marin, and yes, I think so," Celeste said, reaching to shake his hand.

"Let's go then," he directed Regis, who was still on the phone, looking like he was on hold.

"Sally, you gotta get a move on," he shouted toward the master suite.

"Miss Marin owns this condo," Regis said as soon as he'd disconnected the call.

"What's going on?" demanded Palmer.

"I talked to Tracy Epstein at the Dimer Agency," Adamsky reported with authority. "She said to hold tight. She's trying to locate Mr. Dimer."

By now the pretty little girl had sidled up to her dad, her smile transformed to a worried frown.

"Miss Marin," he said, using his hands in sign language. "I want you to meet my daughter, Molly."

Celeste held out her hand toward Molly who smiled again.

"And Molly, this is Miss Marin. This is her condo."

Molly responded, enthusiastically communicating with both hands.

"She says she loves it. Wants to stay longer. Wants us to let her go swimming in the pool and in the ocean."

"Please tell her, when all this is over, I'd love for her to come and stay and do all that."

Dirk did, and the little girl grinned shyly.

"Who are you talking to, Dirk?" the same woman's voice.

"Come out here, Sally. Celeste Marin is here. She owns this condo. She —"

"In a minute, I'm almost done packing."

"I'm going to start hauling this stuff to the car." Dirk picked up a suitcase in each hand.

"Not yet," Adamsky put up his hand. "I'm waiting for instructions."

Palmer faced Adamsky, "You mean they told you to just wait here? After what this lady just told us? Somebody followed the Diamonds all the way from Tampa, and we're supposed to sit tight?"

From the backseat of his car, Manny watched as the dark-haired lady entered the lobby, nodding to the concierge with obvious familiarity. It was the lady from Carrollwood, the one Diamond went to see this morning. With his binoculars, he saw that she headed for the bank of elevators marked "8." Inserting her key, she pushed a button. "Third floor," he muttered. "Gettin' lotsa traffic up there. Gotta move fast."

He reached into a container and extracted a packet of oiled rags and his stash of miniexplosives, the type that went boom when detonated, but did very little physical damage. Having already pulled on a pizza delivery uniform, he strode toward the lobby, carrying a pizza warming box in which he'd carefully placed the inflammables.

A sole white-haired man decked in golf gear stood in the spacious lobby, soon disappearing into another elevator. It was now up to Manny to distract the concierge long enough so he could settle in without being seen. From the pay phone outside, he placed an anonymous call — a concerned guest reporting a toddler wandering alone out by the pool in the back, precariously close to the edge. It was five after six now, and Manny watched as the overweight, frizzy-haired concierge abruptly pushed back from her desk and waddled toward the door at the rear of the lobby.

Heavy brocade drapes in rich greens and yellows flanked the tall windows adjacent to the banks of elevators. Using them as cover, Manny easily maneuvered himself over by the stairwell near elevator "8." The drapery would make the perfect start for a smoldering fire, which he planned to light just as the concierge returned to her desk. This would attract her attention, and when she panicked, she'd start fumbling to find the right emergency number, which would give him time to get to the stairwell the Palmers would have to climb down during the building evacuation. Amid all the confusion and chaos, he'd simply take out the kid from his spot on the landing. Short range; silencer attached to the 9-mm Sig Sauer. The emerging residents would provide him the cover he'd need to escape through the lobby. The parents and that dark-haired lady would be distracted by the fallen kid long enough for him to sprint the few yards to his car. He'd be out of there before the firemen or cops even reached the scene.

Yeah, that was a plan.

As Manny struck a match to an oiled rag, the draperies by the window went up in smoking flames faster than he'd dared hope. He slid the pizza box beneath one of the lobby's many armchairs on the other side of the room. The fire spread fast engulfing a pair of overstuffed chairs. He was already under the staircase when the concierge sounded the building's main fire alarm. He knew the automatic sprinkler would soon quell the flames but with the mini-explosives he could detonate from a remote position, there'd be a full evacuation. All he had to do now was wait for the kid to come down these steps.

Within seconds, he heard anxious voices above, then footsteps in the stairwell. An old guy and lady came rushing down from a second floor unit. Manny moved fast and stood on the lower landing, still in his pizza man uniform, motioning them down.

"Bless you," the lady said, "but you better evacuate the building too."

As they fled, Manny pushed the button of the device strapped to his wrist. A loud, yet harmless, explosion filled the lobby. Silent and motionless, Manny waited under the stairwell as voices above him spoke in urgent tones. If only the kid would be the first down, but he knew they'd never let her take the lead. Didn't matter, he had a perfect ambush position, and an easy escape route.

The Carrollwood lady was first. He peered up and saw how she kept looking up above her. Who the hell was she anyway? What did she know?

"Just one more floor," she shouted over the deafening blare of the fire alarm.

Manny soon saw a man approaching about half a staircase behind the dark-haired lady, a big blonde guy in a blue blazer with some kind of a logo and tan slacks. The target's father? Then the big guy turned around and picked up the kid with the pigtails.

Manny snorted with frustration. The guy was fucking up his shot.

Another guy and lady then appeared, fully one stair landing behind, the guy now carrying the kid. Each was struggling with a large hard-shell suitcase. Was that the mother? But who was the extra guy? Manny crouched, cautiously training his weapon on the guy now moving faster since he'd picked up the kid. Focus on the shot, Manny reminded himself. Don't matter who that second guy is. Might have to get two shots off in a big hurry — one for the kid, one for the big bastard carryin' her.

"This way!" the Carrollwood lady called again as she reached the bottom step. Then out of the corner of his eye, Manny saw the woman turn around. Obviously she would see him, gun in hand, aiming up the stairs. There was no time. Keeping his Sig trained on the target's back, he lined up a clear shot through the lungs to the heart. At that instant, the blonde hunk abruptly shifted the kid from his shoulder and cradled her in his arms.

"He has a gun!" the lady from Carrollwood yelled. "Get down!"

"Molly!" the mother screamed as she dropped the heavy suitcase. It came toppling down the stairs, glancing off the top of the head of the hefty guy who now lay on top of Molly. Rushing headlong, the mother landed spread-eagle on top of the security agent. The other man, slighter and older than the one carrying the kid, still weighted down by luggage, slipped and landed on top of the mother. Molly now lay buried — protected — by the three adults.

"Get up," the hefty guy grunted as he squirmed to extract himself from the weight of the two Palmers.

"Don't leave," screamed the mother as the big man struggled out from under the pile. "Stay with Molly! You were hired to protect her!"

He stood up and pulled out a shiny silver gun.

Manny waited under the stairwell. So the big hunk was a bodyguard. Figured. Shoulda factored that in earlier. The lady who had seen him and screamed had disappeared beyond the lobby door and for a moment he considered his options. Go up and kill all four of them? Wait for them to come down and go for the kid? Or just get the fuck out of there? Then he heard steps again from above. Cautiously, he peered up to see the bodyguard descending, his arms outstretched, holding a forty-five like he knew how to use it.

Manny leapt up, deciding on the "get the hell out of there" option. As he pushed through the door to the lobby, he heard a shaky female voice.

"Stop there!"

Manny glanced around. The lobby seemed deserted, but it was difficult to be sure through all the smoke. The draperies by the windows still smoldered, and the foul odor of the stagnant water from the sprinkler system that had left the lobby drenched was nauseating. Smoke irritated his eyes, and he hesitated, still gripping the Sig in his right hand at waist level.

The woman repeated the warning. "Stop!"

Then the door from the stairwell flew open. There was a "crack" as the heavy door struck Manny's right hand hard, knocking his gun onto the lobby's wet marble floor.

The Sig skidded across the floor, and Manny launched himself sideways toward Celeste as she emerged. She'd hesitated too long, not pulling the trigger of the Beretta she held shakily in her hand.

Manny flung himself at Celeste and in one smooth action, spun her around, securely pinning her in front of him as he wrenched the Beretta away. With the barrel of her own small weapon pressed against Celeste's temple, Manny turned to face the big bodyguard who'd crashed through the lobby door.

"Drop it now," he rasped at the startled agent. Quickly, Manny calculated his options. Right now his only thought was to just get out. Every fraction of a second threatened his escape. Any minute now, firemen and cops would be all over. The fire alarms still screeched.

Forget the kid. He could use the lady as a shield. Maybe shoot her depending on what went down at the car. If not, take her out later. But he really did need to get to his Sig, concerned that it could be traced to previous hits. He loved that weapon, and superstitiously used it almost exclusively, against his professional judgment.

"Do it now," Manny said as the bodyguard let his forty-five drop slowly onto the marble floor.

Still holding Celeste securely in front of him with one arm and her Beretta in his other hand, Manny kicked the shiny forty-five to a corner of the lobby.

"Okay, lady," he shouted in Celeste's ear as he quickly prodded her to where his Sig lay, "pick it up!" He nudged the barrel of the Beretta against her head as he loosened his hold on her so she could bend down and put the weapon in his left hand. "Hand it to me real careful."

Celeste bent down and lifted the gun from the wet floor. As if in slow motion, the weapon sailed through the air in the direction of the hunk in the blue blazer.

The startled security guard caught the gun and fumbled with the silencer to adjust it in his hand.

Still holding Celeste in front of him, Manny cursed and swung Celeste's Beretta, aiming at the exposed chest of the guard. He pulled the trigger. An unimpressive click. The security guard then aimed the Sig at Manny who'd pulled Celeste even closer to shield his torso.

"Motherfucker!" Manny spat before firing once again with the same impotent result. Tightening his hold on Celeste, he turned sideways, placing her between him and the guard. "Let's go, bitch!" he shouted over the scream of the alarm system.

There was a muffled "pop" and Celeste sunk like a dead-weight through Manny's arms. He dropped her on the spot and sprinted out of the lobby to the exit, waving Celeste's pistol as he went through the door. Two unlucky misfires from the bitch's gun or an empty chamber? Manny struggled to think. Could he shoot his way outta here? Play innocent with an unloaded gun? Hell, he hadn't even fired. Too fucking late.

Sirens and flashing red lights were converging from every direction, cops crawlin' out of everywhere. On the ground, cuffed and surrounded by more cops than he could count, he heard the surly voice of authority read him his rights as the dark-haired lady lay motionless on the lobby's pinkish marble floor.

He cursed himself — and Frank Santiago.

CHAPTER THIRTY-FOUR

"You're right, Chuck," Laura jumped at Chuck's suggestion, "let's just go get them!"

"I don't think airport security will stop us as long as we have their mother here, Chuck," Greg offered. "Might be another story if it were just you and I. Good thing you came, Laura."

"Sshh," said Chuck. "Did you hear that?"

"Paging Mr. Greg Klingman." A woman's voice emanated from the public address system. "Paging Mr. Greg Klingman. Please go to the nearest airport phone."

"What the —?"

"Gotta be important if they tracked you here," said Chuck with a frown. "Hopefully it didn't register with Nelson."

Greg loped toward the nearest phone. Chuck's eyes roamed the vicinity, constantly returning to Steve as he surmised that he'd heard the page when he turned back for a prolonged, very deliberate look at his sons. With a distraught look on his face, he appeared to say something loud enough to attract the attention of the woman ahead of him in line, who turned in obvious agitation.

"Excuse me?"

"What the hell is going on? That guy with the ponytail's been up there for ten minutes," Steve growled. He'd been sweating non-stop since Lopez dropped him off at the airport entrance.

She nodded. "I know. I don't know why it's taking so long to check in."

There were still six people ahead of him. And what about that page? He listened for it again. Greg Klingman? Could that be the same Klingman from that damn Tampa law firm? At this point it didn't matter, he needed to get through the line pronto, stay clear of Santiago, and find an out-of-the-way place to wait with the boys until the flight boarded. How in the hell did that damn law firm find out he was here? He needed time to process what Lopez had told him. Could it be bullshit or did they have enough to charge him with Kim's murder? Could Lopez make it stick? What awful shame he'd suffer if the world found out he'd let Laura go down the way he had. Fuck, the whole world was caving in on him, and all he wanted now was a new life with Mike and Kevin. Steve's eyes darted around as he stood helplessly in line. He had to cut forward in line fast, but how?

And how had it happened, how had he shot Kim that night? She was so scared when he got there, asking him to show her how to use that thirty-eight. When he started to, the damn thing just went off. Kim went down. He'd wiped any prints off the gun with his shirt and fled out the back door. Then to his horror, the police found Laura there and blamed her. What could he do? There was no going back, not now, not ever. He had to get on that plane. Lopez was right — it was a mistake, an accident.

An accident.

It took a few minutes to find a phone. It was now 6:43 p.m. and Greg had to move fast. Anything could happen — this was Laura's window to get her boys back.

"Greg, it's Rob," said the excited voice as soon as Greg picked up the page. "You need to know what's happened. Is Chuck with you?"

"Bad timing, Rob. Things here are about to pop."

"Greg, it's about Celeste, and —"

"Celeste? I don't have time right now. I know she's upset, but —"

"She's just been shot, Greg. At the condo on Amelia Island. All

PATRICIA GUSSIN

hell's breaking loose. Some guy, a hired hitman looks like, apparently went after the Palmer girl."

"Celeste was shot? What are you talking about?"

"The girl's okay, but Celeste took a hit."

"Huh? How could this . . ." Greg stuttered. "Celeste at the condo? She didn't even know the Palmers were there."

"The details are just coming in, but Greg, your fiancée was a real hero up there. Saved the kid. You know she packs a Beretta?"

Greg was speechless.

"Listen, don't worry. She's on her way to the hospital in Jacksonville. And Greg, they say she's asking for you, so —"

"She wants to see me? Is it serious?"

"Touch and go, but they're taking her to the operating room."

"Operating room? What —"

"Apparently, Celeste went after this guy with her own piece. It misfired, or it wasn't loaded, or something, and the hitter grabbed her. Chuck's guy fired the shot that hit her, trying to stop the other guy."

"Good God, Celeste had her gun? She hates that thing so much she won't even let me show her how to load it. Listen, I'll be there, Rob. Tell her I'll be there."

"Will do. What's the situation there, anyway?"

"Situation?" Greg repeated dully. All he could see was his beautiful Celeste, imagine her bleeding, hurt, needing him.

"Has Nelson taken off with the boys?"

"Uh, no, not yet. Look, Rob, get word to Celeste that I'm on the first flight out of here. Tell her I love her. Tell her —"

It wasn't until Greg heard shouting that he looked over and saw that Laura and Chuck were not where he'd left them. Still holding the phone, he craned his neck in an attempt to find the source of the commotion developing at the ticket line. Steve Nelson seemed to be in the center of some angry people. Where were Chuck and Laura? Looking here and there, Greg finally saw Laura running over toward Mike and Kevin. Chuck was walking purposefully in the opposite direction, toward Steve.

* * *

Frank Santiago chose that moment. Dressed in nondescript khakis and a plain white tee shirt with a Detroit Tiger baseball cap pulled down over a longish blond wig and black sunglasses, he slowly approached the angry group just as a Northwest agent stepped in.

"You just can't cut the line," said a stocky woman in a loud, angry voice.

"We've been waiting longer than you," said her husband.

"Such a rude young man," said someone behind Steve.

"I have a sick child!" shouted Steve as he pushed away the hand of a burly man blocking him from reaching the ticket counter. "I've got to check in early so I can give him his medicine."

"Sir," said the pleasant young gate agent as he made his way to the center of the controversy. "What's the trouble here?"

Literally dripping with sweat, Steve lied, "I gotta get through. My kid —"

"Wait your turn, mister," said the stocky woman as she planted herself directly in front of Steve.

"Okay, okay." Steve put up his hands in surrender and the young agent nodded affably, walking back toward the check-in podium.

Feigning a look of curiosity, Frank Santiago nudged his way closer until he stood beside Steve. Quickly and carefully aiming his weapon to a spot just below Steve's left rib cage at an upward angle, he pulled the trigger. There was a loud "pop," like a champagne cork. Steve slumped and slid to the floor, falling against the husband of the loud, stocky woman. Everyone from the airline agent and clump of irate passengers to merely curious bystanders looked first at each other, then down at Steve. As the group's gaze focused on the bright red blood seeping through Steve's light blue polo shirt, all activity in the airport seemed strangely still before a few women began to scream.

In less than a minute, Frank was in the waiting car. The clock registered 6:46 p.m. Hat, glasses, wig, and gun had all been tossed into the trash can outside the exit doors. Mission accomplished. He'd be on I-94 before the cops figured what the hell was going down and in Chicago in time to catch the Delta flight back to Florida. Another identity, another change of clothes for the flight, and no one would even suspect that he'd been anywhere near Detroit.

As he swung the Fairlane around the corner, only feet away from the airport exit, he heard the sound of sirens. They were coming from everywhere. Then, to his horror, the huge steel apparatus next to the exit gate came crashing down. Airport security vans came at him from every direction. He was trapped. Without a fucking gun. Trapped.

Laura reached Mike and Kevin just before the scuffle by the ticket counter. Sitting on their luggage now, they were just staring apathetically ahead. Kevin saw her first and a huge smile broke out across his face. He nudged Mike. "Hey, it's Mom!" It sounded like a cheer.

"Shut up," Mike groaned. "I'm not in the mood for your jokes."

But Kevin had already jumped up and ran to a beaming Laura, who grabbed him in her arms.

"Mom, Mike said you'd find us!"

Mike was suddenly standing as Laura reached out and embraced him, Kevin still clutching her waist.

"I can't believe you came!"

"That's right, and I'm taking you and Kevin home with me." She glanced around, looking for Greg and Chuck. She just wanted to leave with the boys. She'd deal with any consequences later. But where were they? Steve was up there somewhere by the ticket counter, thankfully not even paying attention, but a crowd was gathering —

"But Mom, Dad's up there. He's —"

"I know what he wants, honey," Laura said as she held her eldest son tightly. "I'm so relieved that you got through to Mrs. Whitman. Otherwise, I wouldn't even have known —"

"We told him we didn't want to go to Alaska, didn't we, Mike," Kevin piped.

"Yeah, but can we just leave now?" Mike gestured to their luggage. "What about all our stuff?"

"We'll leave it. But we've got to find Mr. Dimer first, he's got the car. And before Dad sees me here."

"Look at all those people." Kevin pointed toward the growing cluster where Steve was.

Laura followed his gaze. She saw Chuck shout something into the ear of a dark-suited man with slick black hair — someone she recognized with a flash of terror. Detective Lopez? He was already talking into a walkie-talkie. What was he doing here? Was he here to arrest her?

Chuck had bolted away from the growing crowd and ran right past her and the boys, charging out through the exit. What was going on? He should be with her now, not running off. This was her chance to get the boys out! She saw Greg run over toward the growing crowd. Lopez was nowhere in sight. Why all this confusion? Greg eventually glanced back at her with a strange, haunted look.

"Where's Dad? Something happened," Mike said. Before Laura could stop him, he ran over and elbowed his way into the group. Near the ticket counter, everyone was looking down at the floor, down at the crumpled form that lay on the gray industrial carpet that was quickly staining red — with Steve Nelson's blood.

Laura heard screams. After momentarily holding him back, she suddenly grabbed Kevin by the hand and followed Mike. A sense of catastrophe, more acute than even the litany of disasters that had overtaken her life in these past weeks, filled her. Threading her way through the onlookers and clutching Kevin's hand, she finally saw Mike, looking down and standing very still — too still. She pushed through to him, still clinging to Kevin's hand. Greg grabbed her shoulder from behind and forcefully spun her around to face him.

"Give me Kevin," he said simply. The distress on his face

telegraphed something terrible. "Go," he instructed, "I'll take Kevin. You go to Mike. We'll wait by the exit."

"But Greg —"

"Now, Laura," he commanded, taking Kevin's hand and turning away.

Her heart hammered as she entered the throng of people. Then she saw him. Steve, crumpled on the ground, his face and hair wet with sweat. And the blood, everywhere, seeping out from under him. So much blood.

She reached out for Mike, trying to pull him back, to shield him, but he wouldn't budge. "Mom," he shouted, "do something! Dad's bleeding!"

Laura sank to the carpet. "What happened?" she demanded from the crowd who had moved away just enough to give her some space when Mike announced in a loud voice that she was a doctor.

"There was a pop. We heard a "pop," a man close by reported in a quivering voice. "Was that a gun?"

"I thought he fainted or had a seizure or something," said the woman who'd challenged him in the line. "He said his kid was sick, not him. Do you really think he was shot?" she asked her husband.

Laura tore at Steve's bloody shirt. What else could it be? This massive, this quickly. There was a collective gasp as she exposed the gaping hole in Steve's chest. She knew then that the bullet had destroyed the left ventricle of the heart. Carefully, deliberately, she placed her bare hand in the bloody wound, feeling for familiar structures. Laura herself gasped as she palpated the huge hole with its tattered edges. Irreparable. Covering it rapidly with her sweater, she leaned forward to check the carotid pulse that she knew would not be there. None. Respiration? No, how could there be?

"They're coming with an ambulance," a voice called.

"Here, here," another voice rang out as the crowd silently parted. "Over here."

Emergency attendants rapidly moved Steve's lifeless body onto the stretcher as Laura went through the useless motions of mouth-to-mouth resuscitation. She had to, her sons would expect it of her. Because it was a chest wound, her specialty, they'd assume she could fix this. They'd never understand the futility, the nearly instant mortality as the bullet ripped apart the big muscle of the heart.

Frantic, Laura looked around for Mike, praying that he hadn't seen her reach into the hole in Steve's chest. Finally she saw him, silent and stricken by the exit, standing beside Greg and Kevin.

"We'll meet you at the hospital," Greg called to her when their eyes met.

Her pink top was stained with the darkening red of Steve's blood as was the front of her white pants, but Laura continued to lead the rescue team through the motions of resuscitation as they expertly loaded the ambulance and took off, sirens screaming.

But none of it mattered. Steve was dead.

CHAPTER THIRTY-FIVE

Steve Nelson was pronounced dead by the emergency room doctor on call at Henry Ford Hospital at 7:30 p.m. Any minute, Laura would have to go out into the waiting room and face her sons. How could she explain that there was nothing she could have done? Would they think she had not tried hard enough to save their dad? They had experienced the escalating animosity between her and Steve through the last several weeks. Would Mike and Kevin think that she just let him die? She closed her eyes for a few moments. Could this all just be a terrible nightmare?

Laura asked for a few moments alone with Steve. She kissed him on the forehead and then slowly, tenderly, caressed each cheek. Tears flowed as she remembered the tall, handsome young man she'd met in college and married. How much in love they'd been. How could everything have gone so horribly wrong? Steve wasn't a bad person, and neither was she. First they'd just drifted apart. They'd both made mistakes. But by the end, they'd become bitter enemies. What could she have done over the years to prevent it? She'd tried to talk to him, but he'd just never let her close enough, emotionally. And then there was Patrick. When Steve found out the truth, she knew he could never forgive her. She'd always known that. His manhood was affronted. How ridiculous of her to think she could hide it forever, that one night. Now she somehow had to face all five of her children. Tell them that their father was dead.

Dressed in a clean, green scrub suit with a knee-length white lab coat, she approached her sons with red-rimmed eyes. They sat with Chuck Dimer away from the ER's main waiting area, in a secluded room normally used for staff conferences.

"Here's your mom, guys," Chuck said as she walked in. To her, "I thought it'd be quieter in here."

"Thanks, Chuck. Mike, Kevin," she said gently.

"How's Dad?" asked Kevin.

"He's . . . he didn't make it," she said softly, more tears welling.

"He's gonna be okay, isn't he?" continued the boy.

"No," Mike practically shouted as he glared at Kevin. "He's not gonna be okay. Didn't you hear what Mom just said? Dad's dead!"

"That's not what she said," Kevin challenged his older brother. Then his eyes searched Laura's. "Is it, Mom?"

"Kevin, Mike, your father is dead," Laura said tenderly as she knelt between them, reaching for their hands.

"Oh, no, Dad," sobbed Kevin. Kevin had never faced death, Laura realized. None of her children had. To him, it was just something that happened on TV, some abstract fantasy. Something they talked about in religion class. Why you had to be a good person, so when you died, you went to heaven.

"What happened, Mom?" Mike asked matter-of-factly.

"A man made his way into the crowd and shot him," Laura answered simply. She knew she had to be totally honest with her eldest son.

"Why? Why would someone want to shoot Dad?" He looked at her through his own tears now.

"I don't know."

"Laura, boys, I think I know," offered Chuck. "The man that shot your father," he looked at each boy directly before going on, "was the same one, we think, that killed Kim Connor back in Tampa. Best guess is that he thought maybe your dad knew he did it."

"But why?" Mike blurted. "Dad really thought Mom did it.

Kev and I kept telling him that there's no way that she would do that, but he wouldn't listen."

"I know," Laura said slowly. "Chuck, do you really think it's him?"

He nodded. "I was suspicious when I saw someone walk directly toward Steve when tempers were flaring in the ticket line. Good disguise, phony hairpiece, but the same build. When he fled the scene, Detective Lopez called airport security to get those exit gates down. Well, you know the rest. And the Tampa cops finally got their killer."

Laura looked at him quizzically. "But how did Detective Lopez know that Santiago would be in Detroit?"

"Mom, why couldn't you save Dad?" Mike challenged in a shaky voice. "Even though you hated each other, you should have tried."

There it was: the dreaded question. Laura looked into his eyes. "Mike, we didn't hate each other. Listen, you have to believe me. As soon as the bullet hit, it tore open the large chamber of the heart. The man who did this knew just where to aim the bullet. You know when I knelt down to try to find out what happened? The hole I found was too big, much too big to ever repair. Your dad was dead the instant the bullet hit him."

"Then why did you do mouth-to-mouth? Why did you go with him in the ambulance?"

"Because I was working on reflex," Laura said shakily. "Maybe hoping for a miracle. Maybe just not wanting to believe it myself."

"Oh, Mom," Mike finally sobbed, "I know he did some mean things to you, but he was our dad."

Laura and her sons embraced.

"Laura," Chuck said softly, "I have a car outside. I'll take you to the airport to meet your flight back to Philly. I've got tickets for the boys too."

"Yes, we should go. Get back to Patrick." Laura finally broke down. "How will I tell him, and the twins?"

"Mom, it'll be okay," said Mike, holding Laura's hand. "I'll help you tell them."

"Come on, Mom," urged Kevin.

"Let's go," Chuck said softly. "I'll stay and take care of everything here. The police will want to question you, but with Patrick in the shape he's in, they'll wait. And, Laura," Chuck went on, "about Greg. It was urgent that he get back to Tampa tonight. I'll tell you what happened later on."

"Oh," was all Laura said. Then, "Oh, no, Chuck. Steve's father. Has anybody told him? Am I supposed to do that?"

"I don't know," Chuck answered. "But it's gotta be soon, before it's all over the news."

Laura nodded. "I should do it."

She asked Chuck to stay with the boys while she called Jim Nelson.

Steve's death had occurred too late to be announced on the six o'clock news, so Laura hoped she'd reach Jim before anyone else did. Jim Nelson may not have been the ideal father, but he had loved Steve in his own restrained, passive way. Laura wondered, as she had so often before, if the Nelsons had been a normal, happy family before Steve's twin, Philip, died so tragically. Maybe if Jim and Helen had been able to talk about it. Maybe if they'd taken Steve for therapy, things would have been different. Maybe the rift that had grown between her and Steve and Steve and the twins...

"Hullo?" Jim Nelson answered on the second ring.

"Jim, this is Laura," she could feel her voice falter. "I have something terrible to tell you. I hate to be —"

"What's the matter? Is it Patrick? Oh no, Laura, I'm so sorry —"

"No, Jim, it's Steve. He's dead."

"What?" Jim gasped. "Did you — no, of course not."

He thinks I did it, Laura realized with a start, and then she explained what happened as best she could though sobs emanating from both sides of the line.

"So many mistakes," he kept sobbing.

"I know, Jim," she said each time.

Then she heard a loud snort. Jim blowing his nose. "You know, Laura, whoever did this to Steve had nothing to do with you. Something to do with Kim Connor, apparently, but not you. You know, I still think that you and Steve would have eventually got your lives back together. You and Steve and all the children. Steve was just hurting and he can be stubborn. Know what he said just before he left? Said he had one big regret — that you two never make it out to Elvis's show in Las Vegas."

"Yes, we'd always promised ourselves we would, then Elvis went and died." She hesitated before vocalizing a factoid that flew into her mind. "Did you know that Elvis — Elvis Aron — was an identical twin? His twin brother died at birth, Jessie Garon. Oh, Jim, I'm sorry, I don't know what made me say that."

"No matter, but Steve said that he wanted to take you to Graceland some day."

"Thanks, Jim, for being so kind to me. I did love Steve, even through all the terrible times."

"What will you do?" Jim asked.

"Right now, I'm leaving for Philadelphia with Mike and Kevin. I need to tell the younger kids, but I just don't know how I can."

"I understand, and Laura, I need to apologize. Who am I to judge what goes on in a marriage? Can you forgive me?"

"I don't need to, Jim, but thank you. We do have to talk about Steve's funeral. Where to take his body —"

"I figure you're still his legal wife, so it's up to you. Of course, I would prefer Traverse City where Steve grew up, but —"

"I think that a funeral and burial in Traverse City would be best too. St. Patrick's, where he was baptized and made his First Communion. And," she added, "where Philip is buried. I think that Steve would like to be buried next to his twin brother. You know, he never forgave himself for what happened. Always blamed himself."

"Thank you, Laura," Jim Nelson said quietly.

"I'll make arrangements for his body, once you give me the name of the funeral home you want to use."

"Will you be here, Laura, for Steve's burial?"

"Yes, of course, and the four older kids. And Jim, will you make sure they sing "How Great Thou Art"? Steve's favorite gospel song. Did you know that Elvis got a Grammy for it?"

"I will. And please let me know how Patrick is doing."

"I'll call you tomorrow."

"Please."

"Okay then," Laura said simply, and hung up.

Laura and her two sons flew East at nine p.m. No one spoke much during the two-and-a-half-hour flight. Mike and Kevin each took a window seat and stared out at the deepening night, trying to stifle their snuffles, and Laura sat in the aisle seat next to Kevin, her arm around his shoulders, staring dully ahead trying to figure out just how to break such tragic news to the other children. Not until tomorrow, she decided. Let them sleep in peace for one night.

But how would they handle Steve's death? How would she manage on her own?

Within moments of arriving at the Sheraton suite across from the hospital in Philly, the phone in Laura's room rang. It was just past midnight.

"Yes?" She answered cautiously.

"Only Chuck, Laura."

"Oh Chuck, it's you." She had all but forgotten about him.

"I know it's late, but I wanted to make sure you got in okay. Also wanted to let you know what's going on in Tampa and why Greg had to get back. Turns out that a hitter was hired to find and kill the little Palmer child, the one who identified Frank Santiago at Steve's place the night Kim was killed. The guy's a professional, obviously hired by Santiago."

"Dear God, that's terrible. I had no idea."

"It's a long story, but we were keeping the child in Celeste Marin's condo on Amelia Island, over by Jacksonville."

"Celeste, Greg's fiancée? Yes?"

"The one and only. As it turns out, she got suspicious and showed up at the condo at the same time the hitter was setting up the hit. She tried to save the kid and got herself shot instead. That's why Greg left in such a hurry. He wanted to make sure you knew."

"Dear God. Celeste, will she be okay?"

"Looks like it. Bullet pierced her lung and lodged in her shoulder. It was a freaky thing, but she'll be fine."

"And the little girl?"

"Molly Palmer's fine too," Chuck reassured. "Now that we've got Santiago, she should be okay. The guy who tried to take her out's in the slammer too."

"I have to say, my head is spinning. I've been so absorbed by my own problems, I haven't realized what other people have been going through, because of me. I never even thought about the danger to her — to Carrie's daughter."

"That's understandable and yes, Elizabeth was staying with Molly Palmer. Both are fine."

Laura breathed a tired sigh. "Thank God. Tell Greg, and Carrie, I don't know how I'll thank them. And Chuck, one more thing. What was Detective Lopez doing at the Northwest terminal?"

"Right." Chuck paused. "Well, maybe that's what separates the police from us mere mortals. Apparently he got a tip that Frank Santiago might be on Steve's tail all the way to Michigan."

"I see," Laura said, not really understanding. "But why didn't Lopez apprehend Santiago before he got to Steve?"

"You saw Santiago's disguise," Chuck said with no further explanation.

"Steve must have known something about Santiago, maybe from Kim."

"We'll see what the scumbag says. So far, he's demanding a lawyer," Chuck said. "It's probably best not to speculate."

"You're right. I'm not sure I even want to know. But, Chuck, thanks for being there with me tonight. Thank you for everything."

He sighed. "We did our best, Laura, but it just wasn't good enough. So very sorry about Steve."

"Chuck, I just don't understand."

"Yeah, I hear you, but how's the little guy?"

"I'm on my way to check him out right now."

The next morning was bright and sunny and Laura felt a spark of hope when she awoke before remembering that there was still more to face: how to tell the twins and Patrick about Steve. Before trying to sleep last night she'd called her parents, asking that the kids not be told until she got there. The minute she opened her eyes around six, she checked in with the hospital about Patrick's condition — improving — giving her at least some small sense of relief.

After waking the boys at seven thirty, they all walked down the hotel corridor to her parents' suite. Mike said, "Mom, are you going to tell the twins about Dad right off?"

"I don't know, honey. What do you think?"

As soon as Carl Whelan opened the door to the hotel room, everyone hugged and cried and hugged even more. Eventually, Laura nodded to her parents and her sons.

"Nicole, Natalie, my darlings, we have to tell you something," Laura said. The room went deadly silent and the family arranged themselves on the two king-size beds. The twins flanked their mother on one, the boys on the other with their grandparents.

Nicole's eyes narrowed as she looked around at all the somber faces. "Is it Pat?" She turned to look at Peg. "Grandma, you said this morning that he was doing good!"

"It's not Pat, Nicole," said Kevin.

"Well, I don't want to know," said Nicole in a familiar stubborn tone.

"It's Dad," said Mike.

"Somebody shot Dad," Kevin cut in. "He got killed yesterday." His blue eyes brimmed with tears.

Laura and Mike's eyes met. So leave it to Kevin, they seemed to say.

Natalie's eyes searched her mother's. "Mom," she pleaded, "don't let Kevin say such awful things about Dad." To Kevin she said, "Kev, that's not funny."

"It's not a joke, Natalie," said Mike stoically.

"Yeah," Kevin went on, "Dad was gonna take us to Alaska. To get us away from Mom. And we were at the airport and Mom came and . . . and this guy came and just shot Dad. Right, Mom?"

Laura nodded.

"At the airport," Mike repeated.

Nicole stared at Mike. "I don't believe you."

"It's true," he said, glancing away.

As Nicole blinked in disbelief, Natalie just dissolved into tears. Holding both girls tightly, she murmured, "It'll be okay, babies, it's okay."

"No, it won't," Nicole said. "We won't have a dad."

The boys shrank back, trying hard not to cry. Laura held onto her daughters as she started to sob, rocking both girls gently.

After a while, the Whelans suggested that the kids have some breakfast.

Laura nodded and stood up. "Kids, I'm going over to see Patrick now. You'll stay and eat with Grandma and Grandpa, okay?"

Nobody answered. Laura looked at their distraught faces. "Patrick's still sleeping, but he's going to be okay. We're going to be okay now, I promise."

Laura walked across the street to CHOP slowly, trying now to focus on how her youngest child would react to Steve's death. She was awed by Nicole's reaction. Nicole had made no pretense of her dislike for her father and yet she seemed distraught at the news. Laura's limited experience in child psychiatry told her this did not bode well. Could the child somehow be blaming herself for what happened to Steve? Later, Laura told herself, worry about Nicole later. Right now she needed to concentrate on Patrick. At least, the little boy would be spared the abandonment that Steve had intended. There was no need for him to know — not ever — that Steve had rejected him, or even more importantly, that he was not Steve's biological child.

As Laura walked into the intensive care unit, her heart fell. Patrick's bed was empty. An aide was stripping off the bedding with practiced, efficient moves. Laura froze. Too often an empty bed signaled the death of a loved one. Just as a deep blackness surrounded her a strong hand on her shoulder drew her back to reality.

She spun around, expecting the worst.

"Laura." It was a familiar voice. "I'm so sorry about what happened to your husband."

"Oh, Tim!" Her frightened eyes bore into his. "Where's Patrick?"

"Upstairs. He's off the ventilator so he doesn't need the ICU bed. Come on, let's go up."

"Oh thank God. Tim, I thought — everything bad has been happening and I thought —"

Tim smiled broadly. "Wrong. Come on, let's go see. This you're gonna like. We're pretty pleased at our handiwork."

"Yes, of course. Let's go!"

Patrick lay alone in a semiprivate room, hooked up to a heart monitor and connected to an intravenous line and a urethral catheter. His eyes were closed as Laura tiptoed over to the bed and kissed his forehead. "Patrick?"

The child stirred and his eyes opened slightly.

"We've been using short-acting sedatives so that he'd wake up just as you arrived. Looks like we timed it just right," Tim beamed.

"Patrick," Laura repeated, again leaning over to kiss him on the forehead. "Honey, you awake?"

The child's eyes opened more widely and a smile crept over his face. "Mommy."

"You've had a nice long sleep, baby."

"I'm sleepy. Do I have to get up now?"

"Here, buddy, let me prop you up a bit." Tim pushed the button on the side of the bed.

"Wh . . . what's this?" Patrick's eyes left Laura to examine the tube in his nose and then the wires coming from all directions. His free hand touched the bulky protective dressing covering his entire chest.

"You had an operation, honey, remember? We're in the hospital. You're doing just great, but you have to stay in bed for a few more days. Okay?'

"Oh, yeah. Kinda —"

"But you're doing great," added Laura with a reassuring smile.

"Can they take all this stuff off me? My throat hurts," Patrick rasped.

"Soon," said Tim, "but I'll tell you what. If you're hurting we can give you some medicine. And, you can start eating once we get this one out." He pointed to the tube in his nose. "And that'll make your throat feel better."

"Okay," said Patrick weakly, "I'm tired." He looked up suddenly. "Where's Dad?"

"Oh, he's not here right now," she gulped. "Honey, try to go back to sleep, okay?"

The child was asleep before he could answer. Laura turned to Tim. "Dear God, how can I ever tell him?"

"You will, but not right now."

"Next time he wakes up? Should I? What will it do to him, to his heart?"

"Kids are tough, Laura. He'll be okay. He has you and the other kids."

Laura stayed with her youngest son for a few more minutes. Then she and Tim left quietly to join the others across at the hotel. Halfway down the hospital corridor she met her father, coming to sit with Patrick.

"Dad," she fell into his arms. "I didn't tell him, I just couldn't. He'll be devastated."

"I know, I know. You'll tell him soon. You go on now, I'll stay with the little man."

"Thanks, Dad. If it weren't for you and Mom, I just —"

Carl Whelan shook his head slowly. "You and the children are safe, that's what matters. The nightmares are over, and you can get back to your life now."

CHAPTER THIRTY-SIX

It was the day before Thanksgiving as Laura and Roxanne sat at the round table in the staff lounge sipping a cup of tea, a plate of homemade cookies on the counter. Both were exhausted after a long day of difficult surgical procedures and looking forward to the long holiday weekend.

Laura kicked off her sturdy, scuffed nurse shoes and fluffed her hair as it cascaded down from the surgical cap she'd worn all day. "So what's on the agenda for tomorrow?"

"Mom's doing the cooking, thank goodness. Louis, Will, and Louis, Jr., and of course my little Jose, are coming over. I really miss that little guy since they moved to one of those big old houses in Hyde Park. As soon as he's well enough, Louis plans to start the renovation."

"That's great, Roxie."

"And he's so grateful that you worked things out for him at the hospital. Getting them to cover the medical bills and the half million settlement means so much, I can't tell you. It's not only the house, but now they have a replacement car, a big station wagon. And, well, a life."

"Which you are a big part of, if I'm not mistaken." Laura grinned at her friend, relieved that she'd made the decision to stick by Roxanne during the resolution of the Ruiz malpractice case. As soon as she'd returned to Tampa from Philadelphia, Laura set up a meeting with Cliff Casey, Tampa City Hospital's CEO.

* * *

"Look," she'd told him that first week of September, "I don't want trouble for the Hospital, but what happened to Wendy Ruiz in the ER that night shouldn't have. You know that Sam Sanders has subpoenaed me in a malpractice case, and even though I'll be a so-called hostile witness, I'll have to tell the truth."

"Laura, you're a physician," Cliff replied. "You know how hectic things were that night. The whole Ruiz family coming in at once, swamping the ER. Two dead on arrival, and the child had a transecting spinal injury. She would have been a paraplegic."

"I know that, but it's no excuse for mismanagement of a chest wound and you know it, Cliff. I think you should settle the case. Mr. Ruiz will not make unreasonable demands if you offer to settle."

"Well, his lawyer isn't sounding so reasonable," Cliff pointed out. "Three million dollars and going for punitive. Triple damages, that'd be nine million."

"I think if you offer something fair, something equitable, Mr. Ruiz will overrule his lawyer. I don't think he wants to go to court, but he's desperate. Please give it a try."

Laura kept at Cliff until he finally directed his attorneys to negotiate something they could absorb. The hospital would be hurt if Laura testified against it, hostile witness for the plaintiff notwithstanding.

"I'll make you a deal," Cliff had said. "I know that you've just gotten back with the kids, and you'll have to get them settled in for the new school year, and get settled in your own life. But what I'd like you to do is take on the additional role here as director of the emergency room. We need someone with your strict standards and intimate knowledge of trauma care. Since you trained at City Hospital in Detroit under the pioneer of modern trauma management —"

"Yes," Laura said softly. Even her face softened, her eyes suddenly bright.

"Yes, you remember Dr. David Monroe, or yes, you'll do it?"

"Both."

Cliff nodded. "Good. We can work out the compensation later. It won't restrict your private surgical practice, so you should come out pretty good financially."

"I'll manage. I would like to do this," she said with finality. "I think I can make a difference."

"Then it's settled. We'll clear up the Ruiz case, and Laura, on a most positive note, your former patient, Mr. Harvey Weintraub, has offered to donate another huge sum — five million — to the hospital for use at your discretion."

"That's terrific. I'd like to use some to modernize the ER — oh, do I have ideas," Laura said with a smile. "And, Cliff, there's one more commitment I need from you. It's Roxanne Musing. The hospital's been giving her a hard time over her involvement in the Ruiz case. Can you stop harassing her and permanently assign her to my surgical cases? She's an excellent surgical nurse."

After Cliff agreed, Laura headed upstairs to her next meeting in the hospital cafeteria — with Greg Klingman. They sat at a far table with cups of coffee.

"I've got news to tell you." A grin covered his face. "Celeste and I are getting married. In two weeks. Small family wedding in Maine, where she's from."

"Oh, Greg, that's wonderful! She's a fortunate woman. I'll never forget how wonderful you were to me when my whole life was coming apart. And in the midst of it, your fiancée was shot trying to save that little girl! You two are really lucky you have each other."

"I know. We're each planning to slow down our professional lives. She quit the interior design firm that kept her out of town so much, and I just promoted both Rob and Carrie to senior partner. We want to have a family right away, and, well, things couldn't be better."

"What about Celeste's physical condition? I mean, from the gunshot wound?"

"Well, as you know, the bullet went through a section of her lung, which made the lung collapse. When they removed a portion of it, they said there shouldn't be any long-term problems, and so far, she's been feeling great. Does that sound right?"

After a moment, Laura said, "Yes, but if you don't mind, I'd like to see Celeste myself — just to make sure."

"Absolutely. Thank you. The bullet eventually lodged in the shoulder. Almost nicked the axillary artery, but missed by a hair. She has a scar from the surgery. I hope it never goes away. It'll always remind me of how lucky I am."

Smiling, Laura reached over and squeezed his hand.

"And what about you," he asked, "will you be okay?"

"Now that I'm back in the OR I'll be fine. And it looks like I'll be taking on additional responsibility in the ER."

"That's terrific. And how're the kids doing?"

"Everyone's back in school. Including Patrick, who's doing fine. They'll be stopping his medication soon. Mike and Kev are glad to be home with their friends and spending every free moment playing baseball."

"Bet they were pretty annoyed that the Yankees beat the Dodgers in the World Series."

"'Annoyed' is too nice a word."

Greg smiled, then paused. "It's going to be hard to raise three boys without a father. Hard on the girls too."

Laura nodded. "I can only imagine. I even had to take Nicole to a child psychologist. She's become even more difficult, and moody, depressed, maybe."

"They say kids should work through these things, right?"

"That's the idea. Natalie's always been shy, but we talk a lot, and she seems fine. I think Nicole's carrying the guilt of Steve's death. She always resented how much time he spent with the boys and was pretty vocal about it. I hope going back to school will help."

"I don't see how she can blame herself. Steve's death has nothing to do with her."

"We know that, but it's hard to tell what goes on in a kid's mind. Anyway, it's awful to say, but I'm glad that Santiago's dead. At least there won't be a trial."

"Right. It didn't take the 'organization' long to snuff him out. Bullet through the head in the transport van from Michigan to Florida. How classic is that? Just wish the same would happen to that bastard Gonzolas. Imagine killing a child for money. But once he skipped bail, I doubt he'll ever get caught."

Laura winced. "You know, I still don't know what made Detective Lopez show up in Detroit that day."

"It was Chuck. He didn't tell you? He'd gotten a tip from that old friend of Kim Connor's, that Carmen woman? I remember specifically because I spoke with her on the phone that very day."

"What day?"

"That day in Detroit, when Steve was killed."

Laura winced again. "Oh, that's something I didn't know."

"Apparently, she'd seen Santiago and overheard him talking about what he was planning to do."

"I see. So Chuck contacted the detective and he showed up in Detroit? It's amazing how fast it all happened, isn't it?"

Greg nodded. "I agree. Turns out that Lopez had a personal vendetta against Santiago — he'd killed the detective's former partner."

"Oh, that's terrible. What an evil man he was. I just can't imagine, choosing to kill another human being."

"You and me both."

"I wonder how many other people Santiago killed or had killed or executed?"

"Too many, I'd guess, but his death was a big loss for Jake Cooperman, he wanted to try that case so bad. But Lopez got a promotion for bringing him in. You know, turned out he was a pretty good guy, even Chuck got to liking him."

"Not me, after what he put me through," Laura breathed. "I wonder why Chuck didn't tell me about Carmen?"

"Keeping a confidence?"

"I see. Well, as for Santiago, at least we won't have to rehash all that speculation about Kim Connor and Steve. I'm not sure how the kids could've handled that."

"Well, now they won't have to."

"In large part that's thanks to you, Greg. Celeste is getting a wonderful guy."

Now it was the day before Thanksgiving and Greg and Celeste were already expecting their first child, while Roxanne and Louis had begun building a new life together with his three sons.

"Laura, tell me the truth. Do you think I'm too old for him?"

"Louis? Rox, you're only thirty-eight."

"Right, only. And he's only thirty-two."

"But he does come with a built-in family."

Roxanne laughed. "That's one way to look at it. And what about your family? Janet? Ted?"

"Ted's doing well — after a bout with malaria right on the heels of that cholera epidemic. But he'll be home for Christmas. And Janet, we just found out, she'll be home too. With that beautiful Vietnamese baby they just adopted. She's ecstatic, and my kids will finally have a cousin."

"That'll be so good for your mom and dad. Having everyone together after all you've been through."

"Tell me about it." Laura walked to the counter and reached for one of Roxanne's mother's oatmeal raisin cookies.

"Careful now, you'll gain back all that weight you lost," Roxanne teased. "So, who's cooking tomorrow, you or Marcy?"

Laura laughed. "Marcy, fortunately. But, Roxie, I have to confess, we're having a visitor."

"Ohhh? I'm listening."

"His name is Tim Robinson. He's a pediatric heart surgeon in Philadelphia. He's the one who made all the arrangements for Patrick. He's — well, I knew him when I was in med school in Detroit. He's just a friend, really."

"Laura, you've been holding out on me!"

Their conversation was interrupted by an urgent page. "Dr. Nelson, Dr. Laura Nelson, call the emergency room STAT."

Laura picked up the phone. "When? How many? I can be ready in ten minutes. Operating room eight."

"I-75," Laura said. "Three kids joyriding in a convertible hit an abutment at an overpass. One's coming in DOA, one will go to orthopedics, the third — ours — is unconscious with head injuries and a punctured lung. Give me a minute to call home. Can you scrub and get the OR set up? They'll be coming through the door in about fifteen minutes. Let's see how well the new trauma team performs tonight."

"On my way," Roxanne pushed back her chair, "but you'd better change into those cute new glasses so your contacts don't attack you in the middle of the case. It's going to be another late night."

After Roxanne rushed out, Laura dialed home. "Marcy," she said, "you know how I said I'd be home early? Well, there's been an accident on I-75."

"Don't worry," Marcy replied. "I'll take care of everything, except you didn't tell me he was so handsome."

"What?" Laura blushed. "Is Tim right there? Let me talk to him."

"Tim, hey, you got there already. Sorry I'm not home yet. You know how it is. The kids have all kinds of plans for you this weekend, especially Patrick. I'm sure he's already nailed you with this year's Super Bowl predictions. Listen, gotta go scrub. Lung trauma. See you tonight!"